RED DOG

WILLEM ANKER

Translated from the Afrikaans
by Michiel Heyns

Pushkin Press

Pushkin Press
71–75 Shelton Street
London WC2H 9JQ

Published by agreement with NB Publishers
a division of Media24 Boeke (pty) Ltd

Red Dog was first published as *Buys* in 2014 by Kwela Books,
an imprint of NB Publishers, in Cape Town, South Africa

First published in English by Kwela Books in 2018
First published by Pushkin Press in 2019

1 3 5 7 9 8 6 4 2

ISBN 13: 978-1-78227-422-3

Photograph of map by Anton Jordaan. This map appears in the book
Reizen in het zuidelijk gedeelte van Afrika, in die jaren 1803, 1804, 1805 en 1806
by Hinrich Lichtenstein (1813 – 1815, Dordrecht: Blusse),
and is reproduced with the kind permission of the
JS Gericke Library's Africana collection.

Offset by Tetragon, London
Printed and bound by CPI Group (UK) Ltd, Croydon, CRO 4YY

www.pushkinpress.com

For Christine

Wat sou hulle makeer het, daardie brakke?
om weg te dros uit gawe buurte
– Peter Blum

What could have possessed them, those curs?
to stray from charming neighbourhoods

1761 – 1798

~

1

Come and see! The lizard on the rock, white ant in its beak. Its jaws start churning. It surveys its surroundings, all along the kloof. Its chomping subsides, its eyeballs roll. The colour of its head and forepaws proclaims its readiness to mate. It displays its red-brown back and ruff. It looks up, swivels its neck to the right. The blue skin of its neck strains and stretches.

See, behind the crag lizard I arise from the rock. I dust my hat, light my pipe. Behold me: I am the legend Coenraad de Buys. Come, let me contaminate you, my reader of tainted stock. If you read this, you see what I see. And I see everything. I am of all time, I am immortal. Do not call me soul. I have a multitude of names. Call me rather Coenraad, or Coen if you are my mother or sister. Pen me down as De Buijs, De Buys, Buys or Buis, just as you see fit. Call me King of the Bastards, Khula, Kadisha, Moro, Diphafa or Kgowe. I am all of them. I am omnipresent. I am Omni-Buys. You will find me in many embodiments. You will come across me as itinerant farmer and anthropologist, rebel and historian. I am a vagabond, a book-bibber, a smuggler, lover and naturalist. I manifest as hunter, bigamist, orator, pillager, patriot, stone-shagger. I am a warrior and a liar; I am a scoundrel and a teller of my own tale. I am going to blind you and bewilder you with my incarnations, with my omnipotent gaze. I am a bird of passage, I am the wind beneath your wings. Stroke the small of my back and you will know I am no angel. I know you well. I know you can't look away.

May I bewhisper you further? The little hairs in your ear vibrate as my breath comes closer. Migrate with me through human memory, over the unmarked dusty wastes as far as the primal footprint, the first built fire, the troop of ape-like creatures heaving erect in the grasslands. Hear the feet stamping in the caves. See the half-human animals scratching and painting on rock faces, how they trace the trajectories from animal to human, voyages between hand and paw, snout and nose, transitions to the other side.

How far are you prepared to follow in my footsteps? Have you taken fright already? Behold the scars of my passage, the marks of my skin on mother earth. Note well: My hide is this dust and sand. Hear me in every footfall, every hoof-fall. See me reflected in every eye gazing into a fire: I am both mark and mirror. I am of this land, bred from stone.

See, the crag lizard swallows the termite, minutely adjusts its foot, scarcely skims the soil. Listen, history is starting to quake, the dust of forgotten battles and unrecorded deaths is shaken up, quivering under the seething surface.

Rush headlong with me in the frantic flight of time to where the hunters and diggers of roots are shouldered aside by herdsmen and tillers of the land. Onward, through eras of wandering and settlement. Hurry past seafarers planting crosses in their wake. Skim past shipwrecks named for saints, smashed to smithereens on the rude rock of Good Hope. Come wade with me through the rivers of blood: pulsing from noses during dances, spurting from bodies, pouring down hafts and blades of wood and iron, later from bullet wounds, primordially from the wombs of mothers, from hymens and umbilical cords; all the blood always slurped back into the soil.

As through the spiral in the barrel of a gun, more rapidly with every rotation: Streak over hills and dales and Company's Gardens, over the land, this dumping ground for northern brigands and heretics. Skim along over the cries and sighs of animals and humans. Fly over the importation of slaves and then the importation of horses, over the bones of the Strandloper and the remains of Van Riebeeck's midday meal, over forts called castles here, over the first Dutch Reformed sermons, the first sugar, the first brandy, over the blood, over riot and revolution, over drawn-and-quartered rebels and black holes of incarceration. Flash over wars and Christians and Hottentots and Caffres and Huguenots and Dutch courage and chicanery and pox and Groot Constantia and the Great Fish, over rivers that erode and borders that overgrow. What are you looking for here? Do you know why you're looking for me? What are you going to do when you find me? Go on, go kneel by any carcase and see the flies cluster like a cosmos opening into bloom; see! This here ground obliterates and digests. It slurps up history and boils it down to nothing.

Listen, the songs of the land resound over it all. Hear the songs of men, the songs of the veldt, the skirling and screaming. Just listen to the beat on metal and sticks and stones and oxhide, on bellies and hoofs, on stoneware from the earth. All over this wretched earth the roaring and bellowing, the yowling and yelping. The claps and the cracks. So loud, so quiet. So delicately the salamander places its foot, I could swear it can smell the blood in the soil.

Perhaps you feel safer in the back rooms of museums? I am the feeler of the fish moth in every archive. I have access to every page. I feed as I read. So let us riffle through the names on maps of new rivers and new mountains and lines of longitude and lines of latitude and missionaries and old gods and a new nailed-down god and churches and caves and the cradle of mankind. Speed-read through murder and mayhem and scouts and pioneers and rebels and vagabonds and clashes and punitive expeditions and slave rebellions and cattle rustlers and colonisers and corpses, all the corpses. Verily, even at this distance the echoing blows and gunshots, yes, even from the pages of blushing historians. I have seen it all, read every word. I forget nothing and forgive mighty little.

Come and see! calls my voice in this semi-wilderness. Come see the land break open its seals for you. Here where the shepherds shall have no way to flee, nor the principal of the flock to escape. Here where the Milky Way is spread out like the spine of a half-dead dun horse deliriously holding up the heavens over De Lange Cloof. Plains with flakes of rock and sand sometimes as red as old blood and sometimes as white as bone. In the north and the south serried mountains lie like petrified elephants heaving themselves out of the earth and then slumping back halfway and over centuries are once again buried under bush and stone. You can still see the wrinkles of their shoulders, the old necks and flaccid trunks, stretched out, spent, for miles across the landscape, but when you think you can hear them sigh, it's only the wind. The mountain slopes are lush, the kloofs wet and overgrown with ferns. The rock ridges gash open out of the green hide of the hills. The people build their houses near the rivers and name their farms after the rivers. The farms lie in a row, cattle territory at the far end of the kloof, a world of sitting and contemplation. If you get up and look around you, you can see your whole farm and from afar you can espy your damn neighbour approaching.

If you look carefully, you'll see the little house of stacked stone and bulrushes. If you listen carefully, you'll hear the people in the house bustling around the dying body of a father. The lizard you will not see again. It was rapt at sunset by the hawk.

See, I'm standing in the doorway. I am eight years old. I look like my mother. My father is lying on the narrow cot. His back arches like a Bushman bow, then he sinks back again. Maybe some creature bit him in the veldt. Perhaps he chewed the wrong leaf. A few days ago he came home and complained and nobody took any notice. My mother scolded him for a laggard and lazybones. He went and lay down and never again spoke a straight sentence and never again got up. In the kloofs jackals and hungry dogs are calling. Shreds of candlelight bob up and down in the washbasin. My sister sits down next to me, her fingers form shadow figures against the wall. My father's hands scrabble at his stomach. A bellowing, then the drawing up of the legs.

Oh God! My Lord God.

My mother Christina rebukes her husband; he falls silent, mutters something inaudible. Mother instructs us to carry him out of the bedroom cot and all and place him by the hearth. She oversees our doing, walks out. I go and stand by her side; she pays me no heed. My eldest brother comes into the house with a headless chicken, slits open the belly and presses the spread-eagled fowl onto his stepfather's chest to draw out the fever. Father once again calls to our God born in deserts and wars and thrusts the fowl from him. Mother commands another flayed-open hen. This time the bleeding warmth is tolerated for longer. I sit in the corner and peep from under a heap of hides how through the night chicken after chicken is pressed to the cropped-up chest. With the first glimmering of dawn I help Mother to plaster his chest with cow dung. I spread the steaming dung, feel the tremors under the skin.

Don't touch me! Father bellows.

I step back.

Stop your nonsense, says Mother.

Father is silent.

They slaughter a goat and drape the guts over the body. My sister brings water. Mother goes to stand in the yard. My brothers and I rinse the blood from the dung floor, massacre chickens and stoke the fire in the hearth. Father's convulsions drive our little lot like a troop of sleepwalkers until with a sudden starting up and last spasm as if the limbs wanted to tear themselves free of his innards, he sighs and dies. I hunker by the fire and regard my father: Jan de Buys, Jean du

13

Buis the Third, grandson of a Huguenot, son of a rich Boland farmer. His death, like his life, small and meek.

Come, let us dig up my parents' remains from the archives: At age twenty-two father marries Christina Scheepers, twice-widowed, eight years older than he. Grandfather de Buys, the old scoundrel, sends Father packing with a wagon and a few over-the-hill oxen. The couple – and Mother's five children by her previous husbands – hit the road. They drive their little cluster of cattle until they pitch their tent on a deserted piece of land next to a random stream. Husband and wife and children and Hottentots build a house of reeds and grass and clay, and live there while Christina bears two daughters who hardly show their little wet heads between her legs before dying and are buried without names in holes that are covered up and not marked and leave absolutely no scar on the face of the earth. Father and Mother do not know the territory and the cattle die of the poisonous grass and bulbs and a drought claims the rest of the herd. They wander through De Lange Cloof and by Mother's account I am born in the year 1761 on Wagenboomsrivier, the farm of one Scheepers. We roam further afield. Thorn trees and ferns grow in the kloofs and leopards dwell on the slopes and we squat with family and acquaintances. A year later Father signs for the quitrent farm Ezeljacht in the Upper Lange Cloof, where the pasturage is more abundant. Father and the older sons and the Hottentots build a house. A reed partition divides the interior into two rooms. The bulrush roof trails on the ground. Christina bears more children of whom two sons and two daughters survive.

When the rest of the house is stunned to sleep by shock, I stay sitting and looking at my father while the fire in the hearth slowly fades. That morning I am eight and overwhelmed; every now and again I get up and feel him getting colder. Today, in my all-seeing, I look back. I see my beloved father lying there in his house like the houses of other migrant farmers. Habitations of which purse-lipped English travellers will one day write that they look more like the lairs of animals than the homes of human beings. At the time of his death he's long since been totally routed by the woman and her ten children. A poor man, his estate barely seven hundred rix-dollars. A lifelong, very gradual and inexorable surrender. A fatal politeness and compliancy that would have rendered even the feeblest resistance to the poison from the veldt too self-assertive for him.

~

By late morning Mother is assigning tasks like every blessed day. The bustling runs its course around the body, displayed on the cot. On the floor lies a little posy of heather that somebody placed on the body and that fell down and that nobody picked up again.

I try playing with my brothers and sisters. My brother with the long arms carries me around on his shoulders. My sisters want to hold me and cry. The younger brothers and sisters seek comfort from me. I don't know how to comfort. I slap my youngest brother when he starts crying and then he bawls more loudly. I go and hide against the house, underneath the window. Mother is standing by the body with her arms folded. She sees me, walks to the window and looks straight through me and pushes the wooden shutter back into the window opening. I walk around the house and enter by the door. Mother is standing next to the body again. I press my head into the dark and soft pleats of her dress. She places a hand on my shoulder. The hand moves over my back and rubs up and down and presses me close and then drops to her side. I look up at her and she says something that I forget instantly and I walk to the river and strip shreds of bark from the trees and watch them floating away on the water and throw stones in their wake. By afternoon two of my sisters come looking for me and press me to them and start wailing again. The sun shifts; I wander around the yard. My brothers are all busy and grumpy and nobody has a job for me and nobody wants to play. I inspan my knucklebone oxen on the dung floor.

Get out from under my feet, she says.

I'll be good, Mother.

Go and play outside. You can't be a nuisance in the veldt.

I'll sit still, Mother.

Outside! There's nothing there for you to break.

The sun sets. The moon rises. I lie between my brothers and sisters in the front room and listen to our mother snoring in the bedroom. I hold the sister closest to me as tight as I can. Until she wakes up and knees me away and turns over.

At the funeral I watch them weeping. Something barks me awake in the night. I get up from the heap of over-familiar bodies slumped on top of one another like a litter of backyard kittens. I walk away, I stand still. The house is a dull smudge against the stars. I turn away, walk on, turn around and look at the house again to see if anybody is coming to look for me. If anybody should rush out of the house now, I'll run away, but not as fast as I can. One of my older brothers will catch up with me and plough me into the dust and drag me home and flay me.

I walk to the house of my half-sister Geertruy, my godmother Geertruy and her new husband, David Senekal, at the far end of the farm, and I don't look back again. The moon is hanging too heavily; the treetops can barely hold it up. The farm is big, more than three thousand morgen, and on this night much bigger. It is cold.

I stand still, look around me. Geertruy is not far away. If I go and knock there in the middle of the night, she'll carry on about it. Mother is not far. If I go back there, my sisters will wake up and comfort me.

I sit down against a red rock that looms up from the scrub like a gravid hippopotamus. I dig next to the rock. The soil soon becomes friable; I dig further. I curl up in my hole against the rock lying hard behind me and of which I cannot imagine the nether end. I scrabble soil all over me. I press it hard against me like the back of my sister. Everywhere herds and flocks and swarms are calling to one another; they warn and threaten and lure. Once I see steam rising out of a pair of nostrils against the pale moon and then the eyes glittering in the bush and then nothing except wings breaking branches. The moon glides past and reflects against the rock above me and spills out onto the ground in front of me. The little I can see in the meagre reflection of the distant light tells me I am safe, and beyond that, I tell myself, everything I hear is only the wind in the brushwood.

I wait by the side of the yard until the people start stirring. I knock at the door. Geertruy opens and takes me inside and spreads a straw mat in front of the fire in the living room.

A few months later Mother marries Jacob Senekal, the young gallows-bait brother of Geertruy's David. Mother is forty-eight and Jacob twenty-eight, but Mother is a pretty woman with a good many teeth for her age. By candlelight she looks younger than Geertruy. Two years later our grieving mother buries Li'l Jacob as well. The clods have hardly covered the coffin when a next Jacob arises, one Helbeck, who comes to share her bed and brood at Ezeljacht.

∾

I've not been away from home for long. I have trouble sleeping in the strange house. I cuddle up to the kaross, think back to the bodies of my brothers and sisters who kept me snug on such nights. I steal into the other room where the family sleeps and crawl in next to Geertruy and David and their child. Dumb-dick David chases me out of the house. The next morning after we've consumed our daily eggs and griddlecake in silence, Geertruy takes me aside and explains the sleeping arrangements here. She presses me to her and holds me like that and I don't let go and then she takes my arms from her. She goes into the house and gives the baby breast and when that dog-dick David catches me peeping, he gives me a thrashing and the next day the piece of putrid pig's pizzle wallops me once more.

∾

Geertruy is sitting with me under the tree, so old and gnarled nobody knows any more what kind of a tree it is. It is so tall, I've never managed to climb more than halfway up it. On Tuesday mornings she teaches me to write in Dutch. It is hot, but I draw the kaross closer around me. Last night I dreamt. I was against the red rock again, I covered myself with soil again. Then I sank away, the soil covered my face, poured into my nose and mouth. In the dream I suffocated. I woke up cold and wet and hurt. I opened the door, coaxed one of the yard dogs inside. The dog settled on my kaross; I snuggled up against him.

The dog is called Ore, for his large flapping ears. He is sitting next to me under the tree. I am still cold. Geertruy is teaching me about *zijn* and *hebben*, being and having.

Ik ben, zij is, het is, jullie zijn, she says, I am, she is, it is, you are. *Wij zijn. Zij zijn.* We are. They are.

She waits for me to recite the list. I look at the white sunlight beyond the shade of the tree. The soil is quaking with heat.

Ik heb, u heeft, jij hebt, zij heeft, hij heeft, het heeft, jullie hebben, she says, I have, you have, thou hast, she has, he has. *Wij hebben, zij hebben.* We have, they have.

I repeat after her, make a few mistakes so that the lesson can carry on as long as possible. Only she and I. We have each other and are of each other. *Hebben* and *zijn*, to have and to be. The house and the other people are over there. I shuffle closer to her, try wriggling myself in under her armpit.

When do I *zijn*, when do I *hebben*? I ask.

You use *zijn* if you are talking of something that is on its way, to somewhere else, but a particular somewhere else. From here to there. In a direction. Verbs that speak of something that is moving, changing.

Oh, I say, and understand not a whit of it.

Coming, beginning, dying, shrinking, seeming, preventing, staying, looking, appearing, touching. And becoming, she says.

Becoming?

Yes, everything that becomes.

What does not become? I ask.

She is silent, looks up into the body of the tree, the branches above us as thick as crocodiles.

> *Zijn* for departing, she says. *Zijn* for jumping in, for walking past, climbing up.

My teeth are chattering. I fiddle with the kaross, put my arm around the dog.

> Coen, she says, note well. We say verbs are words of working, because words can work hard if you yoke them properly like willing oxen. Words are tools. You must learn to use them like a saw or a hammer. Come, think of more words that take a *zijn*.

Falling? I ask. Sinking?

Yes, she says. Always *zijn*.

She presses me against her, strokes the kaross.

> Remember, Coen, what you are must be more than what you have. Most verbs need a *hebben*, but don't forget the *zijn*. *Zijn* is how you grow from the inside. One day when you are old, you'll see how your *zijn*, your being, has grown, big and strong like this tree. As long as you've given it enough water. *Hebben* is what you can count, everything you've accumulated.

What do you mean, Geertruy?

She pretends to be hearing something near the house.

> I hear the baby crying, she says.

Wij hebben elkaar; wij zijn van elkaar. We have each other; we are of each other.

~

Damnation David flattens me with a blow one evening when I correct the head of the household's pronunciation of the Dutch God's High Dutch Word, and he thrashes me half to death when I drive the cattle into the kraal too late, and he beats the shit out of me when I sit too still in the house and look at him and smile.

~

I don't want to bore you. A year after I ran off, I walk over to Mother's homestead. Ore follows me at a trot. Mother is still pretty and the first Jacob is still alive behind his milky gaze. Mother is yelling at the Hottentots. She kicks a suckling pig that's forever under her feet. She sees me coming, goes into the house and comes out with her hair under a bonnet. She awaits me at the door.

And to what do we owe this honour?

Good day, Mother.

Yes, good day. You're thin. Don't they feed you?

We stand and talk at the door and she doesn't ask me why I ran away and I don't ask her if she misses my father. While we talk, she directs the affairs of the farm with hand gestures and biting commands. I start to say good bye; she tells me to wait. She goes indoors and returns with the clothes that I left there and that are now too small. She says if they don't fit me any more, I can pass them on to Geertruy's offspring.

It's a girl-child, Mother.

What is that to me.

I walk back to David Dunderhead's house. On the way I chuck the clothes into the rhinoceros bush. A cloud of thistle seeds puffs up. I watch the sun setting. See the mountains grimacing with golden teeth. The kloof turns into a flared-open snout. If you live here, you wait for the clamping shut of these jaws you call home, you wait for the gnashing to commence.

Not far from the homestead Ore comes to a standstill. He listens to the distant barking of other dogs somewhere in the veldt behind us. The barking sounds different to that of the yard dogs. His tail creeps up between his legs. He comes to stand against me, he sniffs the air. Yowls and growls stick in his throat. The barking dies away. Ore trots on ahead, anxious to reach his own yard.

~

Sometimes I go back and talk to Mother. Sometimes she rubs my shoulders and says I'm going to grow tall, tall as my father, one day perhaps taller. Sometimes I touch her cheek and then I feel a little muscle contract when she clenches her jaw. She and Helbeck will move away shortly after my fourteenth birthday and I'll never see her again.

~

With my father's inheritance I buy two cows and a dozen sheep. David Dimwit lets them graze on his part of the farm and they multiply. At eleven I am taller than my brother-in-law; at thirteen I'll be more than six feet tall. During the day I herd cattle with Saterdag, a Bushman child, perhaps a year or so older than I, but younger of body, named, for no particular reason, for the sixth day of the week.

David Donkey-dick caught Saterdag's mother before his birth. Fortified with brandy and the singing of a few hymns, Demon David and the surrounding farmers ventured into the veldt that day to hunt Bushmen. Saterdag's mother told him about that day's hunt: the Hottentots lure the Bushmen out into the open and the Christians await them with flintlock muskets. The farmers' lead runs out and they pour stones into the barrels and carry on shooting. They round up the surviving men and cut their throats, since they've run out of ammunition. The creatures don't know this. The empty rifles pointed at them make them submit completely. They stand awaiting death with their eyes already fixed on some other destination. The women with babies and children younger than six are divided up between the farmers and taken to the farm and made to live among the Hottentots. The women are given to Hottentot men and the children to Hottentot women to raise, so that their savagery can be tamed. When another Bushman tribe is noticed in the district, Saterdag's mother disappears one night, leaving him on the farm, her child who no longer was her child, but from an early age had taken after the farm hands among whom she was held captive.

21

I play with the Hottentot and Bushman children, we throw claystick and stones, we fish and steal eggs and fight. I play with the children but I don't befriend them. It's only Saterdag who keeps following me around. The Christianised children call us David and Goliath. When they pelt us with stones, David hides behind Goliath, the biggest and smallest whippersnappers on the farm. No stone is going to make this Goliath fall upon his kisser. I'm not the goddam farmer's godforsaken son. I'm more at home among the huts than near the homestead. The children don't treat me like a Christian. I don't anger easily and I put up with the teasing, but sometimes something cracks and then for weeks only Saterdag dares come close to me. My clothes are forever either too small or too big. When in one year I outgrow three pairs of shoes, Geertruy gives up trying to shoe me. At the homestead I am on my own. Saterdag doesn't venture into the yard. He remembers what his mother told him about the Christians and their guns and how a horse shod with iron can trample a Bushman to shreds.

One fine day in my twelfth year David Deathshead wallops me a last time. I hit back. He picks up his tooth from the ground and the next day he breaks a Hottentot's collarbone with his fist.

That afternoon I spy on him to see how one skins a leopard. Geertruy comes walking up. My swine-syphilis godfather's arms are dripping blood and fat up to the elbows.

I can't chase him away, David.

You must do what you have to do. I'll pay him a wage, but that savage is no child of mine.

He is a child.

Did you see how he hit me? Have you seen how he looks at me? How he laughs at me.

He's not laughing at you.

He laughs.

One of the farm workers knocks me awake where like every night I am still lying under a kaross in the living room. Ore grumbles in his sleep. There were wild animals in the sheep kraal, says the herdsman. Three ewes have been bitten to death. I'm the man of the house. The braggart-boss of this poxy farm is on his way to the Cape with a wagonload of butter and hides. I run to the kraal, Ore enjoying the game, snapping at my heels. The toothmarks are all over the bodies, the innards have been lugged out and have caked dry, the blood a crust on the dry grass. I am twelve years old and have been herding cattle for years and know that their lives are my life. My mouth gushes gob and I retch. Ore licks up the vomit. I go to fetch gun and ammunition from the house. I clamber up a chair, grab the muzzle-loader lying above the door over the plastered-in kudu horns and for the whole goddam day I follow the tracks. The yard dog sniffs at every bush we walk past. The further we walk, the more uneasy he becomes. By late afternoon I find two abandoned Hottentot huts next to a third that was burnt down years ago.

The ground around the huts was once cleared, the stones of the fireplace are still arranged in a circle, but today everything is overgrown. Grasses tendril in between smashed earthenware bowls. The bones of the erstwhile inhabitants lie scattered and half-sunk into the ground. I pick up a long thighbone and examine the toothmarks. I step on a half-buried skull. Ore yelps, leaves a puddle and skedaddles into the bushes. I call after him, but he's gone. In the biggest hut I find two little skulls. I pick up one. A lead pellet rattles in the echoing cupula.

I look around me: they are everywhere.

A pack of dogs surrounds me. Ruddy-brown hair in ridges on the back, like jackals with longer legs, the younger ones born after the skulls had long been empty, the whole lot of them gone feral years ago. One of the oldest gasping in between the growling. The ancient dog's fur is mostly scuffed bare, a thong with a few beads still around the neck. Did the gnawn thighbone lying over there belong to the person who plaited the thong? They encircle me on nimble paws. I'm twelve and

I'm pissing my pants. The young dogs are strong and lithe and beautiful. Just when I think I can track their circles, one ricochets hither and thither on some freakish impulse in defiance of all pattern. The foremost dog's muzzle swivels close to the ground, a hairy fin across his back. He is redder than the others, larger. His teeth are bared, his eyes are alert and his growl is soft, so soft. It's the bitch behind him, the one I can't see, that lunges for my throat. I throw her off me. She hits the ground. I stamp with my foot until the ribs break. A male with a gash across his snout is on top of me already and the butt of the gun slams into its head just in time. I pull the trigger, the next dog's lower jaw disappears in a spray of blood and bone. The thunderous crack, the dogs berserk, snap at each other, retreat into the bushes foaming at the mouth, strong streams of piss. I am out of breath, I have been shouting without being aware of it. I have time to reload before they approach once again from the bushes. After every shot they retreat, then attack again. I shoot three dogs, one after the other, before the red dog stands his ground and the others fall back. The dog leaps the gun out of my hand. We are on the ground and at each other's throat. He bites me in the arm, the blood spurts out instantly and blinds him. I grab hold of him and kick him to one side and pick up the impossibly heavy gun. The red devil is on top of me again, the even redder butt connects him in a soft spot. I get to my feet, the other dogs are on top of me. There are bite wounds all over my body and the blood is flowing freely. I ram the barrel down the gullet of the nearest dog and pull the trigger and the creature explodes from the inside out, all over the others. The gang disappears into the thickets. I sink back into the sand, crawl into the nearest hut. In front of me stands the red dog; in the dusk he growls contentedly. The gun is not loaded. The only bullet is rattling somewhere inside the skull of a child. The teeth are bared, slaver drips onto the ground, dust puffs up from the trampling paws. I am on all fours in the entrance. The dog is standing under the hole in the centre of the roof, as if trapped in a pillar of sunlight. I am on my knees, grab hold of the branches around the entrance and drag them down to the ground. One side of the hut collapses. There is no way out any more. I crawl towards the dog. He growls and barks and snaps at the air. He is young but fully grown. On my hands and knees we are of a height. I carry on crawling. I can feel his breath on my cheeks. The beast starts backing off. It snaps. The jaws smack in the air, echoing under the domed roof. I creep forward. The dog retreats until it stands cornered against the grass wall. I glower at him, the dark eyes in which I am reflected. For a moment we are deathly silent. Then I bark. I bark as loudly as I can, till my throat is raw. Just listen to the yells and barks and everything in me exploding out of my belly and lungs, out through my teeth. Somewhere amidst the racket the dog is upon me and I bite and tear and bark till my voice and teeth and jaws give in. I open my eyes. The dog is lying against me, on its back, tail folded up over its pizzle in a pool of foaming piss that drains away into the soil. See: Coenraad de Buys gets to his feet and spits out the ear of the dog.

The dog is motionless, except for the waves of breath rippling through its body. I am dizzy, my shirt and trousers heavy with blood. I walk backwards, lift the reeds, and carry on walking backwards into the full sunlight. Only when I reach the bushes do I turn my back on the hut and the dog inside. I walk back to the farm, my legs and arms covered in bruises and bite marks. The blood prickles and pumps in every lesion, separately and simultaneously. The sun grows cold and small behind the mountains, but I am still far away from the home-stead. I make a fire in the clearing before the moonless dark prevails. I scrabble the soil loose so that I can lie softer, scatter sand over myself. The sand scratches my wounds, but it is warm. I hear a rustling outside the firmament of firelight. I see the glowing eyes of a dog in the bushes. Ore? I murmur. I want to get up but can't. The red dog comes closer, sits down just outside the circle of fire. I lie back and then I see nothing more behind the thousand eyes of the flames.

By milking time I'm back in the yard and collapse and the maid rinsing bowls by the house screams and a Hottentot runs out of the kraal and carries me into the house and I hear Geertruy exclaiming and I only wake up the next day. For days on end my godmother follows me around, watching for signs of rabies. I see her looking. I don't tell a soul about me and the dog in the hut. I am not rabid, but note well, I now move differently. The stronger I grow, the lighter my step. Do you see how I sniff the morning air, my noise raised like a snout? How I perk up before anybody else hears anything? At night I no longer open the door to that yard dog. The wounds do not fester, but blood is blood and blood has mingled. Listen to Geertruy talking to the house maid:

> The child's been bitten badly. He's caught something from the animals, but *what*, Mientjie, that I couldn't say.

Two weeks later I'm in the veldt again with the cattle. The cattle look around uneasily; then I notice the red dog with one ear. He doesn't come any closer, but makes sure that he is seen. This time the rest of the pack are with him, in the underbrush behind the red one. The one-eared male ventures out of the trees on his own and stands in the long grass and gazes at me before once again slinking into the dusk.

∼

I grow bigger and stronger. The house also grows. The more the Senekals realise they're not going anywhere, the more cramped the little house feels with its four-foot walls and its reed roof. Pasturage is not bad here, they say, water not scarce. A new, bigger baking oven is in due course added to the house. A room is built on and yet another later on.

At the age of fourteen I move out of the Senekal homestead. I build a hut on the edge of the yard. I steal a few planks from Duffer David. Reeds and clay from the river. Rocks that I go and hew out when I feel the urge to beat up somebody. Geertruy is starting to show again with a second child. Klein Christina, named for her grandmother the runaway bitch, has turned six and is all over the house, already with the Buys bloody-mindedness. My hut is full of bulges and eruptions like the pimples on my face. The rocks and planks form straight lines;

intersected by the arches of reed and tumid clay. A house it is not. Geertruy says I haven't grown into my long fingers yet. Dim David says I'm a carpenter's arse. He's right: I can shoot and climb mountains, but hammers and nails are dumb and dangerous in my paws. I am ill at ease in the homestead; ill at ease in my body. On horseback I have a good seat, but even in my own hut I am antsy. As soon as I'm inside, I want out, and as soon as I'm out, I miss my den. Every few weeks I demolish part of the hut, build a new section and another bit collapses. I can never decide where the window should go. Every day or two I bash another window hole into the reed-and-branch wall facing onto the rocky hills. After three months I break out the whole wall and plant a thick wagon-tree trunk to take over the load-bearing function of the wall. Now I can see what I want to see. In the hut is a low table of leftover planks at which I can sit cross-legged on the ground. I dig a hollow in one corner in which I cover myself with hides at night.

I'm forever fiddling with the framework of the hut. The roof sinks ever lower. A cracking sound at night, a few thin branches snap. An almighty crash, the whole lot shudders, and a portion of roof settles on the ground. Geertruy replaces the hide blinds in front of the homestead windows with wooden shutters – unglazed, but more in keeping with the standards of the neighbours. Before the onset of winter I plaster the outside of the hut with clay to keep the heat inside and the rain outside. At the homestead the door opening makes way for the chimney shaft of stone. The door moves to the side of the house. Inside the hut I'm forever digging away at the hollows to make them deeper. Dipshit David builds his walls higher, plasters them, whitewashes them. I visit the homestead less often; it turns into more of a permanent residence by the day. Officials journey past and they inspect and record and approve.

The Senekals' house arises in the course of months, inconspicuously and prudently the thing burgeons and bulges like a whitewashed anthill. The walls whiter by the day, until one morning you could swear

27

that there were two suns rising, one on each side of me; my hut sinks ever deeper to the level of a jackal lair.

I crawl into my hut, curl myself up and look at the stars. Orion looms overhead. I grow fast and go to sleep quickly. When I'm not too tired I measure my shaft. One of these days an ell! Believe me, I can squirt up to six feet already. The Hottentots give me dagga. At times I miss company, but as soon as I find it, I want to get away as fast as possible. I take long walks till far into the night. On my way back I usually loiter past the extinguished dung-and-bush fires next to the Hottentot huts. The grass is showing yellow already one early morning when I crawl in among Saterdag and his people where they're all lying in a heap snoring and fighting for the few hides on the floor. The next morning they go their way as usual, as if I'd always been sleeping there. Three weeks later it just seems simpler to go and lie among them again when my jackal hole feels too big.

When I'm not hunting, I'm in the veldt with the cattle, and often there is no light in my hut for nights on end. Geertruy asks me now and again where I sleep, but gets no reply out of me. In the morning before daybreak I sometimes walk down to the stream and drill a hole in the river clay and take off my clothes and poke my prick into the hole and stretch myself out flat on the earth with arms and legs spread and when I shoot my load, I push my face into the soil. So there, you wanted to know it all, didn't you. I wash myself in the river. After a particularly energetic clay-bashing there is a strange rash that leaves me feeling feverish and I pray all night for forgiveness and healing and the next day I'm even more feverish and I'm shitting water and I go back to the river and I bash my bride with conviction till I see visions and fall asleep on the clay body of the riverbank and when I wake up I can remember the dream and my fever is broken.

I'm sitting in the sun against the stone wall of Geertruy's kitchen, oiling my rifle. Nowadays Geertruy has to invite me formally to a meal. I seldom turn down these invitations, but I never just turn up out of the blue. When I'm invited, I always arrive at the homestead early. Then I settle down outside and find something to occupy my hands while I watch the Senekal children playing with their minder. Maria, with the Malay eyes and the Hottentot hair. She's younger than me, but her body is ripe and ready. I chiselled out the star of Diana on the butt of the rifle myself and set a copper star into it. As soon as I touch a gun, my hands get clever, smaller, slimmer. I oil the wood of the baboon-butt. I follow the grain of the stock, my nose pressed to the wood. I coat the barrel with a different oil and a different cloth. The trick is not to manhandle the barrel. Take your time. For a while just see how slowly you can do it. The cloth mustn't press on the metal, it should just touch. And then again a vigorous polishing till the metal grows burning hot. I never speak to her. I clean the rifle or cure a hide or smoke. Especially when David Devil-cramp is in the offing, I smoke furiously and wait for him to say something. At table he will then slap at an invisible flea or make some comment about my clothes smelling like a Hotnot's.

There are fleas all over, David, Geertruy will then say.

But at least we try to smoke the creatures out. Once in a while. We try . . . *He* doesn't try.

I want to brag to Maria. I want to tell her that I'm one of the best-known hunters in the area. I'm one of the big shots. For weeks on end I'm away with the men of the district who come to fetch me for the hunt. They always bring me a horse. There's only one here at the Senekals' and I'm not allowed near him. Sometimes they invite his excellency Sad-sack Senekal along, but mainly not. The two of us don't ride in the same commando. As soon as Geertruy loses sight of us behind the first ridge, we're at each other's throats. When it's a punitive expedition, we both of us have to go along, but for hunting they choose one of us at a time. And I'm the one who never misses a shot. I smoke my pipe and make showy smoke rings within smoke rings, but find no word to say to Maria.

While we're eating, Maria sits cross-legged in the corner with the children. She teases Stienie and waggles a ragdoll in front of her face till the little one starts crowing and rolls face down on the kaross. Maria's dress strains over her buttocks, oh her buttocks, and shifts up to where an inch of thigh shows above the knee.

At age fifteen I shoot my first elephant. Because I'm not of age I'm dependent on the big-dicks to dispose of the hides and tusks. I get a fraction of the payment for my own pocket. The other hunters soon cotton on to the fact that I don't have much truck with money. I'll swop tusks and hides with them for a better gun. Sometimes I keep some of the hides for my hut. The hunt itself is enough for me. Mostly I go hunting on my own. After I've spent a few days in the veldt on my own, horseless and shoeless, everyone says I'm easier to get along with. Geertruy tries to get me to give up blundering into the bushes on my own, but without much conviction. She knows it's better for everybody's peace of mind. If they keep me in the yard for too long hauling butter barrels or thatching roofs, then everyone gets to know about it. Even Saterdag is given it good and hard if he nags at me on such days. Back from a hunting trip, I'm usually invited to supper straightaway, because apparently I'm then well behaved at table. Of course on such days there is also for a change enough meat to share. My first lion? A mangy male, an aged loner, kicked out of the pride. Was almost as if the beast *wanted* to be shot.

Geertruy dishes some more meat for David the Dreck and asks if I've had my fill. No, Sister, on the contrary.

On the hunt on my own my circles around the yard become ever wider. If my duties on the farm permit, I nowadays stay away for a week or more. In the hunting ground my ears prick up at every branch that snaps. Every drop on a blade of grass is perilously suspended. My sweat and the sweat of the quarry. The twittering in the trees. The piss against the trunks and all the thresholds of demarcated territories

in which loud-mouthed males rule. I criss-cross it all with my gun.
I know the rules of the veldt. The better I get to understand the rules,
the freer I become. In the veldt I can mark, bark, fight and piss out
the limits of my own life among the other creatures. In a Christian
home you are coddled while you are small and stupid, but you gradually
become ever less free the better you get to learn what is expected of
you. In a whitewashed house every little copper jug must be polished
and every little carpet must be beaten every morning, but all around
you as far as the eye can see and further it's just dust and stone and
bush. In the veldt nothing is dirty. A grey stone does not need polishing.
A thorn tree does not need dusting.

I excuse myself from the table, go and sit on the kaross with the
children and the minder with the skin smelling of fat and herbs.
I unpack the wooden blocks on the dung floor. Geertruy and her
Appointed Master pretend not to see me at their feet. They talk more
loudly and chew with more conviction. The conversation stumbles
and bumbles, they struggle to stuff my springbok meat down their
gullets. I pick up the little one, who starts bawling. Geertruy sends
out the children and their minder to the back room. I take my seat
at table again. My godparents eat in silence. The thighbone in the
dish still has quite a bit of meat on it. I start carving off the meat;
then I take the bone and push my chair back. I put my crossed legs
on the table, my clodhoppers under my godfather's nose. I tear a bit
of meat off the bone, smile. The father of the house jumps up, slams
the door behind him. Geertruy shakes her head, follows her husband
out of the room. My springbok is delicious.

Saterdag and I are sitting and smoking near the herd of cattle in a
stretch of gnawn-bare pasturage. It's too hot to talk. We're sitting under
a large protea bush, our eyes swollen from the previous night that
turned into morning and the sun that rose more blindingly than ever.

At night we steal karrie, the honey beer of the Hottentots. We make

31

a fire and nobody misses us. We squat on our haunches and sometimes the one-eared dog comes to sit with us before the hordes of eyes like stars in the undergrowth recall the dog to the pack and they fade into the brushwood. There are evenings when we lose fist fights and start them, evenings when the beer emboldens us to walk across to gaggles of giggling Hottentot girls.

I scratch at my first growth of beard. Clumsily and showily I clean my pipe with a long thorn. The headache throbs behind my eyes. Snot-slime Senekal's shepherd dog, goddam good-for-nothing Ore, is lying in the grass. The only sign of life the tail that flicks at a fly now and again.

Among the leaves of the protea above us a spider is spinning in a bee. The legs of the red-bellied spider move fast and featously. It spins threads around the bee's wings, avoiding the sting. The bee's abdomen aims its useless poison dart at the spider. Every movement enmeshes it further. The eight-footed attack is launched simultaneously from all quarters and on all fronts. The wings vibrate faster and faster the more restricted their space becomes. The humming of the bee becomes ever more frantic, ever more furious, until the quarry's last counter-attack comes to nothing and the bee subsides. The sting is no longer trying to sting. The wings go still. It can't move any more. It's not that the bee gives up. The bee never gives up. It fights and weakens until there is nothing left of it. Saterdag leans forward, puts out a hand to release the bee from life. I push a hand to his chest.

Let be.

Saterdag looks at me, then looks away, straight in front of him. Intently I watch the slow and purposeful cruelty until the spider is satisfied that the bee will never escape and, after a last caress over the cocoon of the quiet quarry, hoists itself up a thread of its own creation. I start loading the rifle, pour in the gunpowder and, instead of a lead pellet, a stone. I get up, stretch myself and look down at Saterdag.

Run.

What?

Run.

Saterdag jumps up, runs. I fire a shot into the air. The sheep scatter in all directions, the herd all of a sudden hundreds of individual sheep. Saterdag does not look around, runs faster. I carefully put down the gun, race after him. Saterdag swerves left and right through the undergrowth. I storm straight through the slangbos and cat thorn, my leather pants soon full of snags. Sodomite Senekal's Ore charges along, an imbecile frenzy over the sudden excitement. Just before the tree line I plough the Bushman into the ground. I catch up with him at a run and without slowing down I run into him from behind and end up on top of him. Saterdag starts struggling free. I push his hands against the ground until our breaths stop racing. The farm dog comes closer inquisitively to make sure the game is over. The tail is wagging and the tongue is hanging out. The slavering fool tripples around us. I sit up straight and smack the brute across the snout so that it retreats yowling.

    Let the dog be, Buys. What's he done to you?

    It's no dog.

    He's the best sheepdog we have.

    That's because it's more sheep than dog.

    Ore is a good dog.

    A dog with a name is no goddam dog any more.

Saterdag shakes his head and walks behind me. We start herding the sheep.

    What's eating you?

    We can't sit around on our butts all day.

~

Like every year, the Senekals attend the cattle auctions. Apart from Communion it's the biggest agglomeration of the year: three days of chitter-chatter with everybody from all over, three days of grubbing and boozing and swopping and cheating and here and there a smidgeon of adultery. I'm foreman and have to go along to see to the cattle. David Dumbwit and I steer clear of each other, speak only when necessary.

His blatherskite buddies are there; I have my affairs to see to. It's good to get out among other people, people you don't feel you want to murder.

At the auction grounds there's a fellow in the saddle fresh from France who does things with a horse I've never seen before. Look, it seems as if the horse isn't even conscious of the rider, so liquid its movements and so subtle the rider's commands. Man and horse merge into one new and strange animal. The hoofs are lifted high, are put down firmly, as if the horse wanted to expend all its power and passion in the lightest footfall, as if its whole being depended on each step, as if all movement were display and all movement were totally subjected to an invisible force that brooked no blemish. The rider is without past or future. He is sheer arms and legs, stirrups and saddle and reins, everything attuned to the tiniest tremor in the horse's body.

Just see how cockily he stands there, the young Buys, the stuff-strutter with the feather in his hat and his hand in his side. Just see them standing there talking to each other, the horseman in French and broken High Dutch and Buys in the ever-mutating Dutch of the Cape Christians. See how hand gestures take over when words fall short. How young Buys interrogates him until the man manages, after a few unsuccessful attempts, to excuse himself.

The first morning back on the farm I saddle Sweat-stain Senekal's horse. One of the farm women goes and tells the boss, who bears down upon me all shouting and swearing. Who the devil do I think I am to mount his horse? I bring the horse to a standstill, then take it through a few of the dance steps that the Frenchman showed me. David Dogshit falls silent. He stands for a while watching me. Before walking away, he mutters that I may borrow his horse once I've completed my day's tasks.

Every late afternoon I'm in the saddle and the moon is high before I walk the horse to cool it down. I'm informed that Soup-socks Senekal tells the whole world except me how surprised he is that he and this strange pipsqueak share an interest in horses. I can see how it pisses him off when the horse is more responsive to this uncouth hooligan than to him. I make sure that he's present when with great fanfare I rechristen the horse as Horse. I make sure that he sees I'm watching when the beast no longer responds when he calls it by its old name. After a few weeks he's inclined to forbid me once again to get near to Horse, but Geertruy says his word is his bond. I've practised and perfected a smile that I keep at hand just for moments like these, a smile specially crafted for my beloved godfather.

~

During that year and the following you can come and look for me among the huts of the farm folk. On such a summer's evening I'm sixteen and loitering among the fires. Children hang about me and I lift them up on my shoulders. They crow with pleasure and their parents call them in. I walk past the hut where I know she lives, a few times, and ask nobody about her and she doesn't appear. I go and sit with a group of young Hottentots and we talk about the cow and her udder that started festering that afternoon. One of the Hottentots has a birthmark on his face and vomits on the fire and the others laugh and I see her nowhere.

On a later, cooler evening you can find me next to a fire drinking beer with two old cattle-herds who talk of drought. Now and again they peek at me. I sit and drink what they have and promise to give them back the next morning what I've drunk and they laugh because they must and say I'm welcome and I don't ask them about her and much later I get up and walk to another fire.

In winter the wood is wet and the fires smoke and the old men are older and when they see me they slip into the nearest hut with their calabashes. I fight when I'm drunk and sometimes I pretend to be drunk so that I can lash out more savagely and on none of these evenings does she appear and on every one of these evenings I look up too quickly when her name is mentioned. Piccanins who should be in bed by now taunt me with her name when they see me approach. The young

Hottentots laugh but not out loud. Early one morning the karrie makes me vomit and I take a young half-caste girl to my hut. I lie with a woman for the first time. I remember what she smelt like and how bony she was and that she didn't want it and how quickly it was done. In the following weeks I jump two more and sit around with Saterdag who never talks about her.

Towards the end of winter the fires are small and the people keep indoors. I still now and again sneak up to where I can see the shadows of her and her family moving around in their hut, but I don't come out of the bushes. One night the sky is open and the stars shower down all around me when I get up from the fire where a few souls have elected to brave the cold. It's freezing out here, but my jackal hole is too stuffy. The men around the fire all have their reasons not to be with their wives in their huts. They sit still, the only dance being the shadows in the smoky flames. I walk into the veldt with a calabash. There's someone walking behind me. I stop a few times, listen. The footsteps are light, but not accustomed to prowling in the dark. The figure stands still as soon as I sit down. The dark outline stands watching me for a while and then walks back in the direction of the fire. I drain the calabash. Snivel-snot Senekal's brandy scorches my throat. I go home. As I walk I look behind me to see whether I don't recognise one of the shadows. In front of my hut she's waiting for me.

My father is scared of you.
Whatever for?
He sees you walking up and down in front of our hut. He says you're wearing a trench with your feet between your place and ours.
I walk in many places.
So I hear, yes. But nowadays you only walk in one path.
Father says he's going to beat me to death if he catches me with you. He says you can't look after a woman. He says you can't look after yourself.
I look after myself. I built this house.

My father says this thing is no house, he says ostriches build
better nests.
So let your father come and build me a house.
If you tell him to, he'll have to do it.
What are you doing here?
Why don't you talk to me at the Master's house?
I talk.
You never talk.
What do you want to talk about?

We sit out the night in my ostrich nest and she tells me about her
life and her parents and her little sister who died the previous year
and her father who paces muttering up and down in the hut and hits
them if the pacing doesn't help and the children of Geertruy whom
she looks after and knows better than I do and I tell her nothing but
I listen to everything she says and I don't forget any of it. It is morning
by the time she starts talking more slowly. The most important things
that had to be said have been said. She allows me to touch her. The
dress she starts taking off was my mother's and was Geertruy's. We kiss
until she has to go and skim the milk for goddam David's goddam butter.
My prick isn't having any. When she's gone, I work up a hard-on by
hand and harrow a plot of ground where I'm lying and wipe myself on
the kaross. I walk past the dairy and see her there, fishing out the
spoon that has fallen into the vat. Her arms are dripping cream. I turn
away, walk in the direction of the veldt, stand still and turn around
again and check behind me again. See, she's coming towards me.

She's barely four feet tall. I lie on top of her, it's as if she disappears
into the ground under me. When she bends over me, I'm a child
between her breasts. She is soft as no other body is soft and she smells
of animal fat and buchu and the stuff she uses to starch Geertruy's
bonnets. The following few months we search each other out in the
veldt and behind the homestead and there are toothmarks on our
bodies and our crotches are raw and sore.

～

Regard us well, spy on us if you can, because after two centuries I can still not capture our lovemaking in words. Words like passion and all-consuming create no pictures of her nipples. Geertruy taught me to read and write properly; I know what it's worth. Rather unbutton the front of your pants or slip a hand in under your dress and see her back straining.

~

See, I look much older than twenty that day when I walk far into the veldt. The thunderclouds are massing low and full. The black clouds make the plain seem brighter, the greens and yellows sharper. I pick tracks at random. I home in on an oribi spoor, then foot by foot I follow the tracks of a mountain tortoise. I follow a footfall as long as the pace pleases me, until an alluring track crosses the previous one. I follow a klipspringer in the direction of the river; I trot and run along the bank with the speed of a rhebok. The stream winds its shallow course through the poort. Then the spoor that piques my notice is above me in the air: the whistlings of swifts flashing over and past one another, as if knotting and unknotting invisible loops. On their way northwards. I wonder how far Ezeljacht is from France and my ancestors. Dancing and chirking they stretch their sable wings, the wings wapping like hands clapping all around me. They break their circles and fly high into the sky. One of the swallows skims down low over my head and disappears into the ridge across the river. For a moment it seems as if the bird flies into the rocks without breaking its speed. Then another one sweeps down, a wide curve, and it, too, flies into the rocky ridge. Two crows hover in the sky, cawing, high above the swallows. The birds funnel down, one after the other they fly themselves to smithereens against the rocks and then shoot out again reborn.

When I get closer, I see the cave on the other side of the stream. An overhanging rock in the ridge into which the swallows disappear. The place into which the swallows evanesce is more than an overhang but not yet quite a cave. In sunlight you'll carry on past it without glancing up; in a thunderstorm it will be like a mountain stronghold to you, a palace hewn out of the earth. It's not much of a hiding place, but it is a womb or fort for somebody searching for one or the other and not finding anything else in the vicinity.

In the middle of the stream I step into a hole, am suddenly up to my waist under water. Then I reach the reeds and a few paces up take me to the cave. I struggle through the umbrella thorn. I walk in under the overhang where the birds flew straight into the earth or should be lying smashed in front of the rock. I find them chattering in the cracks, hidden in mud nests under the overhang. The rocky roof is soot-blackened. The walls are covered in paintings.

Great vague figures in charcoal extend across the rock walls, to the left many pictures in ochre. The soil is tramped solid; generations of feet have danced here. A long, narrow gash extends a foot or so above the surface. It is dark in there and smells of dassie shit and nobody will ever know how far back it goes. Among the painted beasts are figures that are human and no longer human: dancers with the forked tails of fishes or water maidens or swifts.

I turn around to the chattering behind me. The swallows fly to and fro past the overhang. They are scarcely a few arms' lengths away, but however close they are, they still look like far-off falcons. Believe me, the sun reflects in their right eye, the moon in their left.

The sky is emptied of their noise, my eyes on the rock face again. Neither-fish-nor-fowl people in a ring. Rust-brown figures with swallow-tails bent forward, leaning on walking sticks. This drawing is small, all the figures fit easily under my hand. I jerk away my hand, wipe my damp palm on my trousers. A few figures in the centre of the scene, more prominent, with delicate fingers clenched around dancing sticks, convulsed with the power boiling inside them, and under it, next to a line tracing an upside-down arch and disappearing into the rock to the left, a school of winged creatures that, arms stretched back, swim-fly along the line, until they melt into the rock.

39

It seems as if the figures enter and leave the outcrops and cracks in the rock. At times the figures seem to start up from smears of paint. I can see that the drawings have been spread out against the wall since whenever, but it's not the sheer age of it that keeps me here. Age is nothing to be proud of. I can't get my mind round the pictures, but I keep gazing. All that I'm sure of is that the guy who painted this stuff was not confused. I walk home. The lighter clouds have been burnt away before the sun. The overhang and its swallows and picture put behind me. The moon like a faded stain of last night's shining, still in the sky.

~

Months later Geertruy is making soap. She asks the children in the yard to fetch her some ganna bush for the lye. The children tell tales of a leopard lurking in the kloofs of late. She asks me to go with them to keep an eye. I drag Saterdag along for company. We find a leopard track and walk up the kloof with the children's voices echoing behind us. At the far end of the kloof we come upon more pictures. Nothing as delicate and clear as the swallow people: faded eland and elephants against a rock without overhang where the sun and rain efface the traces of human beings.

Saterdag goes quiet and runs his hand over the drawings. I tell him about the swallow people in the poort. Saterdag remembers what he was told as a child. Stories about his mother and the old folk who once hunted in the mountains before they were brought down to sit and fatten the Senekal cattle. He tells me about the rock that is the veil between this world and another. He tells how worlds melt into one another in the caves where magicians ape nature and where people turn into birds to fly to the other side and how the drawings keep these voyages in motion. He tells it all to me as he remembers the old folk told it to him and in this way he mimics and parrots them without ever having danced like that.

I don't pay him much attention. Saterdag drones on. Now and again the children come and listen to a fragment of story before scrambling into the ganna bush again.

> Those swallows, Coenraad, they know when to move on, they know when the bad weather with its lightning comes. Nobody can catch those swallows. They fly so fast because they're little more than wind. Those wind birds. Windvogelen.
>
> We make ourselves small, Windvogel, I say. Like a light breeze. Then, one day, from out of the blue sky we let loose a goddam storm on them.
>
> Windvogel, says Windvogel, deep in thought. Windbird. Yes, he says, Windvogel gets me together more than Saterdag.

∽

I come of age and I sue Scrotum Senekal because he's not paying me my share of the butter profits. He promised to pay me for my labour on the farm. Every blessed time we walk past the four butter-churners, it's the same story. Swears high and low that half the proceeds of the butter will be mine as soon as I turn twenty-one. But for the last few years the wet blood-fart has been too much of a spineless slacker for the month-long journey to the Cape markets. One evening I ask him again about the butter. He grumbles in his greyer-by-the-day beard about the low prices. How the butter has started stinking by the time they get to the Cape. He whinges about the Bushmen and the foot-and-mouth and the ravening creatures lying in wait next to the road for an ox wagon. I sit back and listen with my smile. Geertruy jumps up and starts mewling and snarls something at me. She says my heart has gone cold. I say it's because I no longer lie by their hearth like their damn dog. The case is turned down and I appeal and the magistrate rules that Snail-trail Senekal must inspan his oxen and get his hind-quarters to the Cape and give me the money. So there, thank God for the powers that be. Hardly two years later the magistrate gets to hear about us again when I batter Snake-slime Senekal half to death.

∽

41

With the money that I at last get out of David Doddle-dick, I sign a leasehold on a piece of fallow land near the Kammanassie Mountains, to the north and inland through the poort. It's not quite far enough from my family, but I don't expect very many visits. My brother Johannes abandoned the land recently when he packed up for the eastern frontier. I called there from time to time and liked the black soil, the grey underbrush, the sudden spaces opening out from the ever-stifling Cloof. I don't tell anybody; why should I? Of my being a father I don't say much either. What can one say? It makes Maria happy. The baby's hair is red like my beard.

I wake Maria one morning and tell her to start packing. I fetch Windvogel and we go and herd my cattle and sheep.

Go fetch your bundle, I say. Tie it up good and fast.

The rain is on its way. I saw it the previous evening by the meagre light of the crescent moon and by morning the mist from the sea is pouring over the southern mountains, all along the Cloof like milk boiling over. Surging cold churns over the mountain until the grey mountainside disappears. The shimmering mist settles behind the trees at the foot of the mountain like a second mountain, a solid spectre. The buttermilk clouds join heaven and earth and undo both.

I fetch my saddle in the house and cart the thing on my back over the fields to David Deathwatch. I tell him that Windvogel is coming along. Bumcrack-boil Senekal is not impressed. The Bushman who grew up among his Hotnots and guzzled his food and nowadays calls himself Windvogel Whatever can't just bugger off at will, he says. The sooner I clear out from under his feet, the better, is his decision. But if I trek, I trek alone. I smile. I have my own land. Scurvy Senekal is no longer my boss. He prattles on about how he raised me and how he fed me and that he deserves better than being dragged in front of the magistrate for a few barrels of butter. I look down at my godfather, then up and into the distance.

Windvogel wants to come along.

He can want what he wants, he's my Hotnot or Bushman or

Godknowswhat and I decide where he puts his flat feet, I don't care what the creature calls himself nowadays.

I smile.

So what's so bloody funny now?

I'm just thinking what you're going to look like soon.

I was like a father to you.

I was your tame Hotnot, I was never your child.

David Damnation loses his temper and then two of his teeth when my fist meets his face. He staggers, stoops to pick up his hat, then comes upright again. On his head here below my chin I see the sunburnt bald patch.

I'm done with you. Take your stuff. Hotnot-humper.

I'm not done with *you*, I say.

The smile again. Then the fists again until he's lying flat and doesn't get up again. I chuck his saddle off Horse's back and cinch my own. Li'l Senekal mumbles something on the ground.

I ride to the homestead and take my leave of Geertruy.

Did you say good bye to David?

After our fashion.

Go well, Little Brother.

Go well, Sis.

She doesn't press me to her and doesn't cry and watches me riding away on her husband's horse in my makeshift wagon with my common-law wife and my bastard child and my Bushman friend till she can no longer see me and then, I know, she stays watching the wagon trail. I ride on and look back.

What was to follow in my wake on that yard is all too predictable: The maid who screams as Shit-shanks Senekal walks into the kitchen. Geertruy whose eyes narrow when she hears the screams. My sister who turns around in the gravel, back to her husband's house, to face the wrath awaiting her there.

A red dog with one ear and the hair bristling on its back comes walking out of the brush into the wagon trail, sniffs the air and watches

43

us moving past. It puts out its tongue to taste the first few drops. It trots behind the wagon. Something rustles in the bushes on the road ahead. Maria points at two more dogs trotting along in the grass. The rain sets in. Further along in the bushes another ten or so of them, spread out in front of and next to and behind the wagon in the veldt; a whole pack.

∾

The farm has a name already, and I don't mess with it. De Brakkerivier, The Brackish River, lies over the first ridge behind Ezeljacht, but here the soil is already of a different kind, harder, barer. It's a part of the world that changes its nature like day and night every half-hour's ride on horseback. The coastal forests are not far behind me; beyond the Kammanassie Mountains in front of me a semi-desert lies far and wide. Look: slangbos, thorn trees low to the ground, slate and a few ostriches pecking at the stones. We outspan and instantly form part of the background.

The wattle-and-daub hut that we devise with frames of lathing covered with clay merges with the ridge. It's a stronger and bigger construction than the nest in which Maria and I have been living for the past few years. Windvogel and Maria help and scold and eventually take over the building when I start nesting again instead of building. I stand watching them, how nimbly their hands work, how they can plait reeds and plaster clay. I rub my hands, scratch at the calluses, but the fingers remain blunt and stupid.

A month or so later a few runaway Hottentots arrive who beg for work and they also build huts for themselves and herd my cattle and slaughter a sheep as needed. I sit and smoke and contemplate the limits of my world and do absolutely nothing.

In summer I'm thirsty all the time. I wander into the veldt and return with a skin pouch full of honeycomb, some larvae still in the comb, and a body swollen and red from bee stings. I chuck the lot into a dish and go and sweet-talk Maria to make karrie. She puts water on the fire, pours lukewarm water on the honey. She comes to sit outside with me against our reed house like an upside-down basket. She takes the clay pipe from my hand and smokes. I try to smile with my swollen face. She takes a strong puff before returning the pipe.

You must build us some walls, she says.

What for, come winter we'll be gone again.

For what do we have to trek along with the sheep? Can't we just send the shepherds? Settle down here good and proper?

You come and sit here. I can't stare at those accursed kopjes year after year.

I press her to me and we kiss and I let her go and I scratch at the bee stings on my cheek. Her skin is tight over her belly again. I stroke the oiled stomach. Look how those forearms squeeze out the honey into the bowl. Look how the point of her tongue sticks out while she's straining the karrie must through a gauze cloth into a flask.

Do you want to go for a walk? My feet need to get out.

I scratch at the blisters.

I'm waiting for the karrie.

The stuff has to ferment for days, Buys.

I'll wait.

She walks into the veldt and disappears over the ridge, buttocks tight with umbrage. The naked child comes out of the hut. My daughter is two years old and has her mother's mouth and her mother's rare slave name: Elizabeth. She never cries, hasn't really started talking yet. I try to pick her up, but she struggles free. She sits down in the dust and looks at me. Later she moves closer into the shadow of the house. Now and again she looks round and smiles; as soon as I get up and come closer, she runs into the house.

When the karrie is ready at the end of the week, Windvogel and I start drinking in the morning and by the afternoon we are racing around on two wild ostriches until Maria comes to harangue us.

But good God, Buys! Get down from there! You look like you're sitting on a chicken! You're going to break the bird's back!

I jump down and chase her around a bit, then I launch an attack on the child. I fall down in the dust. She comes to stand over me and laughs with a little hand over her little mouth. I pick her up and she wriggles free. Then I'm after her again with a roar. She makes for her mother, cackling. I throw Maria over my shoulder and drop her on our bed of hides. After a while we become aware of Elizabeth peering at the two tussling, groaning bodies. Then she sees a gecko by the door.

By dusk I'm coming to my senses on the bench in front of the door. Against the waves of golden fire on the horizon the silhouette appears of an ox wagon without a canvas hood. Five withered mangy oxen trudge on, the front one without a yoke, hitched up with leather thongs like a draught horse. Two Hottentots, one in front of the oxen, the other on the wagon chest. A raggle-taggle preacher in what remains of a top hat and tails is standing on the back of the wagon loudly lamenting his depraved soul. He plucks off the last of his buttons to show me his breast, roasted red. The vagabond missionary clings to the flaps of the dilapidated wagon and shouts imprecations in German and High Dutch about rivers that will run with blood and dark men in dark nights with long knives and the spattering spit seems to dry instantly to the raw blisters on the God-crazed fool's mouth. The Hottentots gesture feebly in my direction with flaccid arms while lashing the oxen listlessly and driving them along the road. The man scratches at his breast and becomes quite spirited when Maria appears from the reed door. The wagon is still halfway down the road when the stinker starts performing elaborate curtseys. He wishes me a prosperous harvest. He introduces himself under some or other Germanic surname. He enquires after the way to Swellendam, while the oxen plod on to Couga, further and further away from Swellendam. I smile at the man and proclaim that they are following the strait and narrow road, that it's long and hard and overgrown with thistles, but that it is indeed the right way. The man, already bereft of his senses and now also of his destination, gesticulates grandly in my direction. He bows again before starting to curse the Hottentots for their laxity and warning them that the laggard will never attain the Joyous Jerusalem. The wagon creaks to a halt. The emaciated emissary of God jumps downs; his knees buckle under him. The flies feast undisturbed on the blisters of the babbling salvager of souls, nor are they swatted away from the cheeks of the Hottentots. He gathers a fistful of sand, kisses it and proclaims his love of this prospect and the quality of the soil and asks in a highly convoluted manner if he can help me with the harvest in exchange for a blanket and a sweet potato twice a day.

Does it look as if I plant anything?

He looks around him and sees the arid bushes and the aloes and low kopjes and the cattle way over there and the few Hottentot huts hardly distinguishable from the veldt or from my hovel. I splutter at his confusion.

You can harvest just what you like, my dear fellow.

The preacher starts orating about how the Lord nourishes each one of his creatures and how for weeks he's been preparing meals from the Garden of God. I have an elephant rifle in my hand and I march towards the man. He grabs the whip from a Hottentot and lashes out clumsily at the oxen.

I am going, good Sir! I am on my way, the narrow way, as indicated by you! he shouts at me.

I take aim and riddle the back of the wagon with the gravel with which I've loaded the gun. The oxen trudge on. While reloading, I bethink myself, put the gun down, run after the wagon, jump on. In a great voice I start preaching at the dumbfounded missionary and his Hottentots. I proclaim long stretches of fever dreams from Revelations that Geertruy taught me to recite. I shout:

And when he had opened the fourth seal, I heard the voice of the fourth beast! And it said, Come and see! And I looked! and behold! A pale horse! And his name that sat on him was Death! And Hell followed with him! And power was given unto them over the fourth part of the earth! To kill with sword! And with hunger! And with death! And with the beasts of the earth!

I carry on harrowing the little congregation hearkening to me gobsmacked. I caution them against the forest paths leading off the strait and narrow, the black women lurking in pools in this country ready to leap upon you and the cannibals and the extirpation of the Christian by the Heathen and monsters and the beasts straight from the clefts of Hell. I castigate them in advance about the dagga and the liquor that will rot their souls and the buttocks of the women and the breasts upon which they will perish. The leader of the bedraggled little team forgets about the oxen and the ramshackle outfit limps to a halt in the middle of the road where my voice starts resounding among the kopjes. I spread my arms and square my chest and once again resort to High Dutch:

> And the kings of the earth! And the great men! And the rich men! And the chief captains! And the mighty men! And every bondsman and every free man! Hid themselves in the dens and in the rocks of the mountains! And said to the mountains and rocks: Fall on us! And hide us from the face of him that sitteth on the throne, and from the wrath of the Lamb!

I fall silent. Only the cicadas and the last sentence respond in the kopjes. Then the last blast of the trump:

> For the great day of his wrath is come! And who shall be able to stand?

The four men look at one another. The wagon groans into motion. I sit down flat on my arse in the wagon and laugh. The Hottentots look at me. The top hat and tails realises the peroration is over and starts mumbling to himself about blasphemy and the dissolution of the soul. I remain sitting, snorting, drunk all over again, on my way along with them in the wrong direction deeper into the wilderness, until they've rounded the bend at the drift. Then I jump down and go and pick up the gun and fire a last shot low over their heads and trot home. Geertruy was right: The right words and a loud voice are stronger than a whole team of oxen and pack more of a punch than an elephant gun. Maria comes walking towards me. I can barely hear what she's shouting, but I can guess that she's not happy with my way of receiving the men of God. I rush at her, push my head between her legs, lift her backwards over my shoulders and run straight to the conjugal bed.

~

If your name appears on the official list for commando service, you have to attend the annual military manoeuvres at the nearest landdrost's offices. The business drags on for a whole week. For someone from De Lange Cloof like myself that means being away from home for more than a fortnight; to Swellendam and back is more than a week on horseback. If you have a decent horse. You have to ride your own horse half to death on the way there and take your own gun and go and blast away your own lead at a bunch of targets and consort companionably with the burghers of the district and try not to beat anybody up. Only illness or incapacity serves as an excuse – sad souls like Jacob Senekal whose poor old eyes could never see all the way to the targets.

I'm very happy sitting on De Brakkerivier. Nobody bothers me, I bother nobody and around me everything perishes and flourishes. Days dawdle like seasons. I don't wander far from the house. Every thorn tree looks like the next one. I do, though, find it impossible to pass an anthill without churning it up with a stick.

I have no desire to ride to Swellendam to establish who's got the prize pizzle or who can shoot straightest. Brandy is scarce and I prefer to have mine on my own. I have no desire to horsewhip old Horse, unshod and cantankerous, all the way to Swellendam. Maria's hardly washed the blood from the new baby and I have to be on my way again. The gun I leave with Maria; if they want me to shoot, they can lend me a Company musket and melt the candlesticks on their groaning drostdy tables to provide me with bullets. I slip a dagger into my belt in case somebody decides to stalk me at night. Horse is old and crotchety but he can outrun any creature, Bushman or lion. The Buys men turn up regularly for these manoeuvres, perhaps I'll bump into one or more of my brothers there. But I'm not going to go looking for them.

When I ride into the straggle of buildings they call Swellendam, there's a brawl in front of the taphouse. The two farmers have both had their fill of fighting, both of them are on their knees in the street. They trade blows with long and heavy arms. Not a single blow misses its target, they're both too tired to duck. A few churls of the civilian militia loiter around till both of them are flat on their backs and then drag them off to the cells. I go and report for the manoeuvres. The clerk charged with filling in forms realises I have no weapons with me apart from the rusty dagger. I'm fined twelve rix-dollars and this far and no further will they push me. I get onto my elderly horse and ride out of the miserable little whitewashed outpost. Only after my mortal demise and my rebirth as Omni-Buys will I read in the moth-eaten minutes what I missed. For instance that Petrus Ferreira of De Lange Cloof that year at the manoeuvres won a brand-new tobacco casket as second prize in target shooting. May the plague rot his bones.

Back among the grey bushes of De Brakkerivier I tell Maria to bundle up and tie together our domestic effects once more. I go to fetch Windvogel from under a willing and able young woman and tell him to inspan our oxen. The Hottentots see that I'm preparing to clear out. They also start gathering their few belongings. Most of them will wander further to neighbouring farms for work, but a few young ones without ties of women or children opt to take their chances with us. I fling a torch on the roof and watch the reed house go up in flames. Elizabeth dances around the house and is transfigured to a shimmer in the flames. Maria settles the baby securely in the wagon. She takes up position on the wagon chest and cracks the whip. In the year 1785 I leave behind everything I know and trek to the eastern frontier.

2

We trek through the interior, track the well-worn routes of earlier
migrations to the far ends of the Colony. Sometimes the grooves of
wagon tracks are clearly visible, sometimes they disappear for days
on end and we simply drift from one fountain, spruit or watering hole
to the next. We stop as seldom as possible, only when the wagon breaks
down or I spot an eland and gallop into the drifting mist on Horse and
don't return without a carcase. Most days drag by monotonously, others
begin on a barney and end in bedlam. The baby, still nameless, bobs
along on the voyage, wrapped in a kaross, lulled by the creaking and
groaning of the wagon never to recall any of it, and laughs and sleeps
and cries and for the rest lies there gazing at the wagon tilt that is the
limit of her world.

Maria sits on the wagon chest, cracks the whip over the bone-weary
beasts and curses them by name as soon as they flag. The Hottentots
drive the little herd of cattle, Windvogel for the most part on the back
of the ox he got from me as payment the previous year. I sit with
Elizabeth in front of me on the horse. She doesn't sit in the saddle,
she finds it too close to another human body. Her little naked body
is draped around Horse's neck. If I touch her to make sure she's seated
securely, that the sun isn't scorching her, she screams or growls. It's
just she and the horse, but if I tell her the names of animals and plants
and stones as we go, she repeats the names in a whisper from within
the tangled depths of the horse's mane. It's only when she's on the
verge of sleep that she sits by me tugging at my beard, the red furze
a forest for her fingers to forage in. Her complexion is not as fair as
her father's, but lighter than Maria's. The sallow skin and red hair
render her an object of open interest to the few passers-by. As soon
as they register her grey eyes, they cease their greeting and their
blathering and look away and then lift their hats to me and my own
grey peepers. At night we sleep in the wagon. On cold evenings the
baby lies curled up against the mother-belly as if hankering back to it.

When the jackals call in the hills and the hyenas laugh next to the wagon, the red-haired child sits up straight, arms around the knees, watching over us.

From the saddle I survey the bushes and the grasses and the thorn trees and the anthills like towers of Babel. Sometimes I pull up next to a rock formation or a plant that claims my attention, but while there is still sun, the wagon stops for nothing and nobody. I follow the wagon on horseback, my thoughts already straying to other rocks or leaves or wandering off into the distance. I'm not here on a voyage of discovery. I'm on my way to the border. The few people who call this region home have no use for me here: the Christians hunt the likes of them, and they in turn rob and murder the Christians in that old cycle of devastation without beginning or end. Here you keep a low profile and you don't stay in one place for too long. The Bushmen must never think you want to settle in.

Sometimes we cross the paths of other wagons, sometimes people on foot or on horseback, but nobody makes a lasting impression on anybody else. We don't outspan at other farmhouses like most people. The customs and the conversations in there are what I'm getting away from. When supplies run low, we sometimes stop over at a kraal. The Hottentots readily barter sheep and edible bulbs and honey, and treat Maria well, this diminutive queen with her gigantic white husband and her Hottentot underlings.

In one kraal of an evening the Hottentots are dancing. When Elizabeth comes to sit by me near the fire, in no time at all there are several figures squatting around her in wonderment. They can see she shies away from human contact. They approach slowly, careful not to startle her. One presses a finger gently against her shoulder. She looks at the finger. He presses an ochre-tipped finger to her nose. She giggles, presses her own finger to the Hottentot's nose. After a while she allows the enchanted Hottentot to stroke her hair. She climbs onto my lap, but allows them to mark her little body all over with ochre hands like the hands they press against the walls of caves. Eventually the little crowd win her over; she scrambles down from my lap. They lift her onto their shoulders and dance around the fire. She looks like the afterthought of a flame, red and lambent but less so, as if fire had a shadow that could dance with humans without consuming them.

Sometimes I do call at homesteads to angle for news. As the trek wends its way eastward, you need to look ever more closely to identify a hut as Christian turf. Heathens live in round huts; Christian wattle-and-daub huts are rectangular. The news is never good. The Christians I talk to are mainly refugees who abandoned their farms on the eastern frontier and crawled back deep into the embrace of the Colony, only to be robbed and slaughtered here as well. The accounts of these fearful god-fearing folk are as void of meaning as the cairns on graves.

One afternoon one of these gormless Christians crawls out of his mud hut to greet me. A broad-brimmed hat on his head and the tatters of what were once military shoes are the sum total of his apparel. His whole body is peeling with sunburn. He babbles on about Caffres and locusts and his failed crops and this is what he knows and this is his life. How could he know what Omni-Buys knows and what would it be to him that Louis the Sixteenth in this year of our Lord 1785 signs a proclamation declaring that henceforth handkerchiefs must be square?

When the wind blows through the grass or the shadows of clouds tumble over the slopes and kopjes, the whole moribund landscape seems to come to life and race past underfoot. The eye plays games in this endless place where days of trekking feel like standing still, and an hour or so of seeking shelter from a thunderstorm feels like growing old. By day the veldt is dead as dust. We trek past lions lounging under thorn trees, not bothering to bestir themselves for a whole herd of cattle. At the times of transition from night to day and from day to night the veldt is a deafening discord of life calling and cawing and rustling and racing as if aspiring to destinations beyond the multitudinous cycles intersecting here in the softly luminescent spaciousness.

By day I'm never alone with Maria. Our conversations are instructions to each other, schemes to keep the wagon in motion and the children in good health. At night when the offspring are asleep, we can love each other cautiously. If one of the children wakes up from the rocking of the wagon, we lie down giggling between the wheels or steal off into the veldt.

By day it's just me and the flatness. Usually I ride off away from the team and the wagon, where I can feel the openness and be afraid. On the plain there is nowhere to hide. My chest tightens and the soil binds my feet and pours lead into my veins. I race out over the plain with the thunder rolling and crashing and furious in the black clouds. The lightning bolts set fire to the horizon. There is no hiding place when the heavy drops and the hail start pelting down. It is *there* that I want to be. That is what scares me. Then I have passed under it and my breast fills with air and my feet become light; then everything is open, in front of and around and in me.

After such a storm the open spaces stir up something in me. I grab Maria from the wagon chest and throw Windvogel the whip, shout a few commands and race into the veldt with my darling wife who is trying to find her seat on the saddle until the wagon shrinks to a spot in the distance. As if the whole world is watching me, I make a great show of every movement. She just happens to be the woman with me; I am strutting my stuff to the veldt. Afterwards I lie against her and drink from her while she strokes my head.

Close your eyes, I tell her. Close them, nobody may see. I shut my eyes tight and we lie in the darkness and her milk spills into my beard. The team is trundling along slowly, we need not hurry to catch up with it. Back at the wagon the children are crying and Windvogel mocks us until I clout him.

≈

The sun is a lidless eye on the day that the big book with the drawings is found lying on the wagon trail. I read in it: ink sketches of giraffes, the long necks implausibly long, asses, leopards, then horses with rhinoceros horns, water maidens. The further I page, the more freakish the drawings. The lines blur into blotches. On every few pages there are maps in the finest detail and shading repeated over and over again in the book and sometimes scratched out. Every map stranger than the one before. I stuff the book into my saddlebag. I fill my pipe and smoke in the saddle. Before the fill is done, a white wig is lying in the road. Minutes later a black tricorn hat on a walking stick with an ivory knob, planted in the ground. Further along two worn black shoes with shiny buckles, neatly arranged next to each other. Around the next bend a jacket draped over a thorn tree and then some distance along the white shirtsleeves fluttering from a branch. The black velvet culottes we find spread out over a desiccated bush and then a naked man sitting under a waboom next to the road, legs spread, with his head on his chest. The sun-scorched fellow doesn't look up when he's hailed and doesn't stir when I place a skin pouch of water next to him. He pretends to be asleep. I shake him. He snores louder, rolls over and curls up with his hands under his head. I shake again; he draws his head in between his shoulders. I nudge him with a boot. He wriggles his body as if I'm a fly bothering him and snores furiously. The devil take him. I pick up the water pouch and we travel on.

And always, at a distance, the dogs. At night their lamentations and by day they are nowhere to be seen, except the one-eared male who takes up position next to Horse when I lose track of the wagon trail and cut into the veldt. Life and her perils, the miracles and death itself are not to be found on the wagon trail. I don't go far, I keep my people in sight. Old One-ear pants next to me, his legs less limber than a few years ago. I stand in the stirrups, survey the surrounds. You set yourself up as a target if you don't check behind the nearest bushes next to the road. Away from the wagon tracks you find signs of life. Other tracks and traces, warm ash in holes where last night small fires were made. A broken rifle, the butt end full of black blood.

A man wandering feverishly with vacant eyes, bent under the guilt from which he fled, dying for the water he drank too quickly.

We come across wandering Hottentot families looking for work, who no longer know how to live off the veldt, young people who no longer know the songs of the old. One of the families stops and talks and pleads and the following day I notice them a mile or so behind us. A week later another family following us with little bundles. Everything they have managed to gather on this earth wrapped in hides, cherished close to their meagre bodies. People who are not deterred by shots and curses and threats and eventually trudge along behind the ramshackle ox wagon. Tracks of lion and kudu and dry river beds. Deserted yards with carcases in the dust and skeletons swinging from trees in nooses, the clothes and meat long since redistributed. Burnt-down wattle-and-daub huts, occupied wattle-and-daub houses and huts and shelters that we pass by without entering, especially those where the invitations are too cordial and the eyes have too faraway a gaze and the words wash up against us in feverish stutterings. The solitude of the veldt becomes quite tolerable when you consider the potential danger in any encounter. This land is an open prospect where people burrow into crevices and hollows when they see somebody approaching.

We never see a shadow or a spoor of a Bushman, but at all times we are aware of the little yellow eyes on us and the little fires in the middle of nowhere that burn low every night and the next night a little nearer until one night a few of the creatures come and create havoc among the cattle and we shoot at them. Windvogel wounds one and leaps up from his station and starts crowing about his first Bushman and an arrow lodges itself right next to him in a branch and he pisses himself and starts crying.

We trek past more trees festooned with people like decorations, the rotting flesh, bits of copper on the swinging skeletons reflecting in the sunshine. We trek past lovely mirages. As we trek, the cattle drop dead one after the other, heaven knows why and who's going to halt to find out, and we trek past trees next to the road of which the bark has been stripped for food or in vengeance or in bloodthirsty delirium and then we've crossed the sorry couple of pools the people around here call the Bushman's River.

So that's how we end up in the Zuurveld, this expansive battlefield. Zoom up into the heavens with Omni-Buys and survey the Great Fish from above. See how the stream on its way to the sea takes a sharp turn to the east so that for a while it runs along the coast, before it swerves again and debouches into the sea. This right-angled swerve and concurrence with the sea creates a rectangular arena in which various groups of people all at the same time seek to graze their cattle and where between the ocean and the Fish and Bushman's Rivers they will be clamped and crushed as in a vice measuring fifty by eighty miles. Welcome to the Zuurveld, the land of sour grazing.

The banks of the rivers traversing the Zuurveld are overgrown with trees and thorny shrubs, dense and impenetrable to the uninitiated. As soon as you climb out of the gorges, you find some of the loveliest pastures on God's earth. This verdant grass is deadly. In summer it offers excellent grazing, but in winter the cattle start dying. The Zuurveld Caffres and the frontier farmers know that in winter you have to move your cattle to the sweet veldt in the gorges that are perennially verdant but cannot support heavy grazing. In summer the cattle move to the sour veldt again. Look, the deckswabs-made-flesh in the Cape draw boundaries on maps in offices. Any cattle farmer could tell them it's insane, these god-cursed borders that disturb and destroy grazing patterns. The farmers and the Caffres get het up. And by the time I end up here the whole lot is thoroughly pissed off. As soon as my cracked heels step onto my quitrent farm, Brandwacht, my thumbs start pricking like the whole sky crackles before a thunderstorm.

We build a shelter and I go to greet my big brother Johannes. A few weeks later Maria is standing waving me good bye with the baby at her breast. Elizabeth is standing next to her mother and does not wave

at me. Accompanied by the few Hottentots who can shoot I venture
into the bush. I'm like a child on Horse's back; I can't sit still and I
babble uncontrollably and order the little troop to go and peer behind
every kopje and in every thicket. At night I keep my trap shut next to
the fire or I get drunker and louder than anybody else. A week later
I return with a herd of Caffre cattle that look a good deal fatter than
the few half-dead beasts I drove all the way from De Lange Cloof.
I immediately put out of my mind the young Caffre and how he looked
at me when I shot him where he was guarding his cattle in the open
veldt, that first person I murdered. Later we build a hut and later a
proper house. And always, in the distance, the dogs. When we fine-
comb the veldt for Caffre cattle, red-brown smudges flash in the
corners of our eyes. At night their eyes gleam in the bushes around
the house. My Hottentots try hard not to see them. Nobody mentions
them, nobody chases them away, nobody takes aim at them; God help
the scumbag who dares.

~

A year later I walk into the wattle-and-daub house. The swallow darts
in at the door before me and up to its clay nest under the rafters. We'd
hardly moved in or the swallow pair followed and devised their own
clay-and-wattle home against the roof. I wanted to clear them out, but
Maria insisted that they brought good fortune to any marriage. The
little creatures mate for life. I said it's not as if we were married and
Maria said they come and go with the seasons and the rain. Any farmer
would thank his lucky stars for a pair of swallows that foretell the
weather. The bird-brains twitter all day in their nest but I let them be.
They're not that much worse than the chickens and the suckling pig
and the cats and the kids. It's Maria's house, I'm not here very often.
If she wants to build an ark, it's her story. The veldt is mine.

The veldt is mine, as it belongs also to my cattle and the Hottentots
who look after my cattle and the Caffres who bring their cattle to graze
and don't clear out again. What kind of a Colony is this, where you

can't move your arse at the furthest reaches, as if those who are inside want out and those who are outside want in? And there on the border-line, on the riverbank where the whole lot come face to face, no tribe wants to back down before any other; there's a chronic butting of heads and a preening like young cocks.

I regularly do my rounds on the other side of the border. No Cape-bred fellow with silk stockings and scented powder in his wig is going to tell me which river I'm not permitted to cross. If the river wants to stop me, the river can stop me, but that is between me and the waters. And the Great Fish is a bugger when it's in flood. Then that border is a bloody *border* and you can talk all you like, you're not going to get across it. But sometimes the Great Fish is no more than a waterhole in a barren riverbank where hippopotami yawn with gruesome teeth. Sometimes it's narrow and deep, sometimes broad and vague and shallow. Sometimes you can cross by foot. But it is always brown with soil, as if the very sand wanted to get out of the Zuurveld and march down to the sea, the great and eternal boundary where everything flows into everything else and drowns itself and from which all Christians and pen-pushers emanate. In no place and on no day does the eastern border look the same. Nobody steps into the same Fish River twice.

Barely an hour's trek from where we struck camp this morning, the yellow grass of the plain feels like a long day's journey away, as if time itself got snagged here in the long thorns that claw and clutch. The water, thick and strong as Maria's coffee, winds through the kloofs where the thorns grow lush and kudus appear and disappear in tracks that only they can see. In these thickets you could disappear very quickly, for ever if that was what you wanted. To cajole the cattle through this lot is a bloody manoeuvre, even where the water is shallow. There are hiding places aplenty; here everything happens mysteriously. I don't hear the shell of the tortoise crack under the wagon wheels in the drift, only see the river floating the shards of shell and limbs down-stream. This primordial creature that for thousands and thousands of years has been scrabbling unchanged under the indifferent sun. How do I know this? you ask. When I wonder about the soul, I read about vertebrae and magma.

The stream is powerful. It takes what it will. It doesn't ask before it takes. You have to heed it, even though you don't heed laws. I frequent the river. I know the river almost as well as the Caffres know it. See, the two groups are standing on opposite banks of the Fish. They don't look at each other. They are standing on opposite sides of the border watching the border between them coming down in flood and swallowing a sweet thorn and swirling it along and calving a chunk of clay soil into the water. The bartering of cattle and tobacco and copper proceeds without violence. The Christians and the Caffres are wary of each other and joke coarsely among themselves to cover up the tension, but the Hottentots riding with the Christians are taciturn and watch both groups with narrowed eyes.

I pick up words readily as they drop around me. A year or so after my arrival on the border I'm fluent enough to laugh with the Caffres about the Christians who have foreskins and nothing else. If you want to survive here, you buddy up with folks. Farmers of the area who know with whom and how cattle can be bartered. If they turn up on your farm to hear if you want to go and barter cattle with the Caffres, you saddle up and trot along. You must first learn the rules of the game before you can play on your own. Before you can rewrite the rules. Eight or ten armed horsemen are better than one Christian and his gang of Hottentots. This doesn't mean that you have to strike up bosom friendships. It doesn't mean that you can't laugh with the Caffres about the lot on your side of the river. The Christians laugh too, because they see me laughing. I wink at my white pals and I nod at the Caffres.

When both groups have taken from the other what they can and both groups are satisfied that they've screwed over the other, they return in opposite directions to their respective wives and children and their just about identical homes of reed and clay.

∼

At home we all sleep next to one another on a pile of hides. The baby is swaddled separately in a hide against the wall. Maria lies in the middle, Elizabeth and I on either side of her, each with the head on one of her breasts. Somewhere in the night Elizabeth crawls over Maria and comes to lie between her parents. The hides don't cover us properly. I lie awake, uncomfortable with the child half across me. The little body is thin, I feel the skeleton under her skin. I think of how easily the little bones can break. I can't settle. If I change position, Elizabeth will wake up. Then Maria will wake up. Then all repose will be shattered. I lie dead still and stare at the rush ceiling above me. I listen to the wind buffeting the house, how the rafters gnash and the reed door hammers at the thong tying it down. The wind inhales through every crack and then exhales again in a great sigh as if we're lying inside an organ of a larger animal of wood and reed and stone. I take one little arm in my hand, lift it up, feel it, the fine frangible bones, the soft flesh, the little hand seeking my hand and clamping a finger. The child huddles up against me, the little head pressed into my stomach, a soft sigh, then a gurgle. Elizabeth has caught a cold. Tomorrow she'll be ill. The child is weighing down my arm, but I don't change position. If I were to move now, she'd wake up and start crying and turn around, away from me. She's never before lain against me like that. Even if to her I'm just a warm object she snuggles up against and even if she doesn't know what she's doing, it's something that must last as long as possible. I don't move. I listen to the child and watch the little body slowly inhaling and exhaling and now and again twitching in a dream. We lie like that till the sun rises. I get up stiff and sore, and the day begins.

∼

They pay me almost a year's rent to supply wood for the new extensions in Graaffe Rijnet. In 1787 I borrow a few wagons and load them with yellowwood planks – more than a thousand-five hundred feet of wood – and five Hottentots and two Caffres and trek to the settlement that the Cape periwig-pansies transmogrified a few months ago from farm to town. Word is that they offered one Dirk Coetzee a shit-sack of money for his woebegone farm in a horseshoe bend of the Sundays River and baptised the place Graaffe Rijnet, for the bibulous governor and his wife who between them pour and cram the contents of the Company's coffers down their gullets.

As we travel, the mountains multiply slowly, one calf at a time, like elephants. The dogs turn up the day after I leave Brandwacht. The red dog takes up position by my side and trots next to my horse. The rest of the pack spread out around the wagons, at a distance from the wagon trail, glimpsed only here and there and now and then. The dogs make the Hottentots uneasy. They are used to the phantom dogs that always hover somewhere around me in the veldt, but normally the dogs keep their distance. This trip is different. We are far from home and from any habitation. By the time we outspan, the dogs are around the camp, usually eight or ten of them, sometimes as many as fifteen. They lie around the camp in groups of two or three. A few venture as far as the fire, where the one-ear is lying by my feet. I don't touch the dog. He doesn't snool for attention like tame dogs. The dogs gobble up the bones that are thrown in their direction, but for the rest keep their distance. It is as if the dogs are traversing the same territory as us, but in a different sphere. As if they're moving across the same veldt, but in a different time, and would canter straight through you like ghosts if you didn't get out of their way in time. A day before we reach Graaffe Rijnet, the dogs disappear: I wake with the first light, tightly wrapped in my kaross. The red dog is lying gazing at me. He trots along next to Horse till late in the morning and then suddenly swerves east and is gone among the low shrubs.

We cross the shallow river, the wagons creaking and screeching over the rock shelves. The trampled strip of soil would seem to be the street; the huts and clay hovels sporadically on either side then presumably the town. Horses stand tethered in front of the houses, here and there smoke drifts out of a chimney, more often out of doors and windows.

The geese in the street heave and hiss at the oxen. Some curs trot up to the wagons and try to piss on the turning wheels. One of the thatched roofs is on fire. A few bystanders in the street are watching the inhabitants carrying out their possessions and dousing the roof with buckets of water. I ride past a wagon smith, a carpenter, advertising their trades and skills on the street. After the journey across plains that extend as far as the earth's warping like rotting wood, it seems as if the town is huddled up against the mountainous mass emerging from the soil like a wall. As if you would sleep more soundly with a mountain at your back. Overripe quinces lie on the ground in front of a scanty hedge. Goats gnaw at everything they see. I ride past what I'm told was once Coetzee's stable and shed, apparently now the jail and church and school. My wagons have to pull up when a Hottentot drives a herd of oxen along the street, heading out of town. A falcon sits on a roof tearing at a thing with a tail that is still quivering.

I park my wagons next to the drostdy, the converted homestead of the Coetzee family. Part of the thatched roof collapsed with the conversion. Two Hottentots are thatching the roof with reeds. From what I can make out the poor dumb sot Woeke was sent to come and lord it over the wilderness and keep the peace from here to Swellendam. I start undoing the thongs securing the wood. A man walks past in the street. He looks me straight in the eye. He bothers me. His face is long, his beard is trimmed and his hair cut short. He is big, almost as tall as I, but slimmer. His bearing is that of a rich man, even though his clothes are old. Where the material has been scuffed through, it's been neatly patched. Tears have been darned with a meticulous hand. His shoes are worn but clean. He stops, gazes at the clouds massing around the mountain. His nostrils dilate and contract as he sniffs the air. He nods at me, lifts his hat. I don't return his nod. He walks on. His footfall is light. Only in antelopes have I seen such ease in a body. He doesn't look around again. Who does this upstart think he is?

Somebody comes running from the drostdy, a puny little fellow in a too-large uniform, ironed and clean as far as the knees, muddied all

the way further down as far as the just about invisible shoes. I regard
the fellow. We're both about twenty-five, but to me the man looks like
a child. To the pipsqueak I must, I suppose, look as all the border
farmers look to the Cape-coddled powder puffs: bloody-minded,
brutish and feral, garbed in leather and hides with the regulation
long beard and longer hair. Do you think he wonders where the hair
ends and the pelt starts? I square my shoulders and tower over him.
I introduce myself.

I ask the soldier who the man is who walked past a moment ago.
He says it's Markus Goossens, the new schoolmaster.

> That smug little snob and his little attitude won't last long on
> the border, I say.

The soldier looks at the retreating schoolmaster. I ask him where I
should dump the wood. The soldier directs me to the back of the
buildings where construction is already under way. My workers start
unloading the wood. I stoop at a fire, rake out an ember and light my
pipe. A tallish man, prematurely bald, with a body soft as a woman's,
comes to stand next to me. He puts his pipe in his mouth and glares
at the fire at his feet. He stoops to the flames and staggers. I rake out
an ember from the flames for him. The man is neatly dressed, his
waistcoat embroidered in more colours than I've ever seen on a single
piece of cloth.

> You're not from here, I say.

The man tries to talk while clenching his pipe between his teeth.
A drooling of slobber dribbles down his chin.

> Stellenbosch. I've been in the Cape and Stellenbosch all
> my life.
>
> What does it look like there?
>
> Greener. Mountains. People don't eat with their hands.

The man laughs. He takes a metal flask from his inside pocket and
offers it to me. I swallow the genever. It's too sweet, but I don't say no
when it's proffered again. The soldier from earlier fusses around us
again. He whispers something in the man's ear. The man says he's

busy, he can't be disturbed now. The man taps me on the arm, starts saying something. When the soldier interrupts him again, he turns around too fast. He has to clutch the young man's shoulder for a moment to keep his balance. In my ear he slurs something about the singular qualities of a Caffre cunt. The whippersnapper clears his throat, embarrassed on behalf of his boss. I accompany both gents into the drostdy. Behold: Landdrost Moritz Hermann Otto Woeke with his arm around the neck of Coenraad de Buys, cackling. I sit the landdrost down in his chair behind his oaken desk and the little soldier ushers me out as quickly and politely as possible, with an extra rix-dollar in my pocket for my loyalty to the Company and their seventeen lousy lordships and my sealed lips.

~

We pitch camp outside the town. There are plenty of dry thorn trees around to lug together into a makeshift kraal for the oxen. Towards evening fires are lit and my Heathens hunker down, each lost in his own dream. I saddle Horse and ride into town. I ride down the main street and peer into lighted windows and sometimes a hand waves at me. Horse carries me past dark vegetable patches with trailing shadows. When I pull up I hear water dripping from the leaking canal into the parched soil. I've heard many stories of the carousing in the Cape, but in this Colonial backwater only the treetops dance in the breeze. I stop a passer-by and ask him if there are women to be found anywhere in this town and the man says Nothing to rent, here you have to marry or buy, Mijnheer, and he laughs and I ride on as far as the last building and turn around and ride down the road again to the other end from which I came. The moon droops low and depleted.

I've just galloped past the last house when I see a small group of men walking into the veldt. In the distance I see fires. I follow the men, join them. They don't talk much among themselves. They walk fast. They say they're going to watch the fight. Somewhere in the darkness I hear something that could be singing. Who in God's name would

stand serenading the veldt at this hour of the night? We walk in silence
until the singing subsides. Then the conversations start up again.

A while later a rider trots past, back to town. By his hat I recognise
the damn schoolmaster. I ask the men if our master is coming from
the fight. They laugh and say No, Master Markus wouldn't let himself
be caught there. I ask them why the piece of misbegotten misery is
so uppity. They look at me askance. They say he's quite a good sort;
he simply keeps to himself. I ask them whether it was he who was
caterwauling like that in the darkness. They say they don't know and
what business is it of mine.

Arriving at the kraal, we find a few men waiting next to a wagon
with animal cages covered with hessian bags. Fires are burning in the
corners of the kraal. Twenty or thirty men are dawdling around,
laughing and telling jokes, most of them are drunk. Three men are
standing to one side where the fire doesn't reach. Two bull-baiting
terriers, seasoned and raddled fighters, and a massive German mastiff.
They are standing well apart from each other. As soon as the dogs
come within range, they leap and snap at each other. A man with
bandy legs and long arms summons two Caffres. They lift one of the
cages from the wagon, haul it over the kraal wall and place it in the
middle of the kraal next to an iron pole hammered into the ground.
The bandy-legged man drags a chain from the depths of the cage and
locks the chain to the pole. One Caffre stays behind in the shallow pit
of scuffed mud and straw and sawdust. There's a shout and suddenly
everybody presses up to the kraal wall. The men jostle each other to
have a better view. The Caffre rattles the bars of the cage and something
grunts and bumps in there. The faces around the kraal seem bizarrely
distorted and inhuman in the shadows of the flames. I see the smith
and the owner of the inn in his absurd velvet suit and farmers and
builders and everybody laughs and drinks and gobs. Somebody tosses
the Caffre a spade. He picks up the spade and scrambles onto the
cage and knocks out the peg locking the cage and jumps from the cage
and swears in his language and runs to the wall. The men jeer at him

and nothing happens. Then a big baboon comes walking out of the cage with a chain around its neck. He runs as far as the chain permits, the chain tightens, jerks at his neck and pulls him off his feet. He falls on his arse and the men guffaw and gob. A man with new shoes climbs onto the wall and walks all around it waving his arms and his hat and asking for bets. As soon as his hat is full, he climbs down. As if this were a signal, the men with the dogs climb over the wall. They release the three dogs. The dogs charge the baboon. Creatures human and animal go berserk and blood flows. From the direction of the wagon other shrieks from the throats of what could be baboon and leopard and hyena and jackal and other animals that no human has contemplated for long enough to name.

The baboon utters a hoarse bark, fights furiously until it sees the dogs are drawing strength from its fury. It goes onto its hind legs, extends its arms to the younger of the terriers and screams. The dog charges at the baboon, leaps aside and feints and leaps again. The dog's fur is marked with the scars of previous bouts. He won each encounter because see, he's alive. The dogs shiver and yelp, but keep a wary eye on the length of the chain, stay out of reach of the baboon. See the dogs dancing around the baboon. One goes straight for the baboon, then jumps back from the fangs. If they can't get hold of the baboon, they snarl and snap at each other.

The baboon has been fighting in the veldt from infancy, because see, he too is still alive. When a dog comes close, he jumps up in the air, but the curs are clever enough not to be trapped under him. Sometimes a sudden cuff with the arms, or a more surprising grab with the back legs. The ape tightens its circle, the chain slack enough for a leap. The dogs know these monkey tricks. See, they're tiring him out.

In the kraal there are no orderly formations; the fatal circle becomes a universe where soil and skin and straw and teeth and hair and blood blend into new terrifying creatures that suck everything around them into a sinkhole. Surprise attacks, then moments that expand into ghastly silences before the teeth find one another once more. The baboon rips open the mastiff's throat, chucks it aside with a human hand, the graceful animal instantly a limp heap of skin and meat.

The terriers charge when the baboon tries to climb up the pole. The biggest dog gets hold of the ape's hind quarters and rips him open from below. The baboon's hands let go and the other dog is on top of him and digs into the innards and tugs at the guts. The ape is hanging between the throttling chain and the dogs that each has hold of a length of gut. The gaze and the screams of the baboon, like those of somebody on a rack, floundering between forces tearing him apart from three directions, are unbearably human.

A man vomits and his friends laugh and gob. Somebody bumps into me and I look around into the beggar's face and he looks away.

The baboon grabs the nearest dog and brings the animal's face up to its own. Do they know how much they look like each other? With the ravishing jaws that decorate many a farmhouse, it tears off the face of the fighting dog, who until recently resembled the proto-wolf from which all dogs are descended.

I rub my thumbs and index fingers together until I can feel a static crackling. The remaining dog keeps tugging at the guts. The baboon curls up against the carcase next to him and there is a tremor in one hand and something like a yawn and I see something in his eyes and then he is dead.

Money is exchanged; the panting young terrier's tongue is hanging out. He tries to shake off the blood. He stamps his paws. His ears are drawn back. His eyes dart to those of his owner and then to the baboon. His owner puts on the chain and takes him home. The two Caffres throw the dead animals over the wall and bury them. I stand watching until the kraal is deserted. Young men my own age try offering me spirits, try telling me about the most accommodating girl in Graaffe Rijnet, try talking about anything else.

$\sim$

I ride back to our camp and find Windvogel and Gert Coetzee the half-caste Hottentot by the last embers of the campfire. They don't talk, each thinking his own things.

A star shoots across the length of the Milky Way. I see the wonderment of the two men.

> God has chucked out his old milk again, I say. It's beneath him to drink clabbered milk. He only scoffs sacrificial lamb.
> Master mustn't blaspheme like that, says Gert.

Some or other preacher put all sorts of things into the Hottentot's head. Gert has never been able to tell me who the man was, one of the wandering prophets criss-crossing De Lange Cloof in donkey carts hoping to come across lost souls. According to Gert the man's name is Master and when I ask Master who, then the reply is Master *Master*, Master.

> That's the backbone of the night, up there, says Windvogel. It keeps the sky up in the sky.
> That's no bone, it's the Lord bringing light to our dark land.
> Oh, bugger off, Gert!
> You don't know the Lord, Vogel. I shall smite thee by God! I shall devour thee by God!
> How do *you* know the Lord, Gert? I ask.
> Master told me about him. We were all in the garden together, don't you know, and then we had to get out and then everything got buggered up.
> And when were you in that garden, Gert?
> No, Master, don't you know, it was before Jan Rietbok came to plant vegetables here.
> And then you had to get out of Eden?
> Yes, Master. And then the flood came, don't you know. And everybody drowns and we sail that ark.

Gert is silent for a minute, lost in thought.

> I still remember that pigeon.

I start spluttering. Windvogel erupts in a fit of laughter implausibly violent in a body as thin as his.

What's Master laughing for, and you, you good-for-nothing
Bushman?

It's quite a story, Gert. Master Master taught you well, I
placate him.

Master thinks it's all just stories. What does Master believe?

The Caffres say that smear of stars is the hair bristling on the
back of a fierce dog, I say.

Does Master believe it?

That as well, yes. Come on, you must get some sleep, we're
moving on tomorrow.

The two men walk off, jostling each other, to where they made their
bed under the wagon. I remain sitting. Later I add more wood to the
fire and watch the dry wood surrendering to the reborn flames.

The next morning the men start loading the wagons. I walk off into
the veldt. In the distance I see a dog-like creature darting from a bush.
It could be a wild dog, or a jackal caught short by the sun. The animal
is far away, all I can see is the red-brown stain skimming over the level
ground. The creature is on its way somewhere, or simply gone. I watch
the animal becoming a piece of running grassland, how it disappears
into the grass and then leaps out from the brushwood again. As if it's
playing. As if there's enough velocity to allow for play as well. As if
velocity is itself a game not needing anything else.

I walk on, the wagons get smaller and disappear.

I clamber on top of a large anthill. I look around me. It is grassland
as far as I can see, in front of me as far as the Graaffe Rijnet mountains;
behind and next to me the flatness stretches as far as the eye seeks
a point to focus on and finds nothing. The horizon is not a point, it's
where everything perishes. I look around me:

Red dog!

Then as loudly as I can:

Red dog!

I look all around me.

Later I climb down and walk back to the camp. Windvogel sees me and comes running to meet me.

Buys, where have you been? he shouts.

He comes to stand in front of me, out of breath, hands on the knees.

We've done packing. The men are waiting just for you.

You must stop calling me Buys when the others can hear. They think you're trying for white.

Yes, Master, he says mock-deferentially.

Bugger off, man. Tell that lot to have done and start moving on. I'll catch up with you tomorrow.

As you say, Master.

I'll thrash the hell out of you, you cheeky Bushman, I shout and take off and chase my only friend on earth through the scrub back to the wagons.

In the camp I think my thoughts and the lot leave me alone. I saddle Horse, roll up a hide blanket behind the saddle, fill my powder horn, throw a few lead pellets into my jacket pocket and take my rifle. I also take one of the Hottentots' rifles and a Caffre's short assegai. I push the extra rifle and assegai into the rolled-up kaross. Windvogel fusses around me again.

Do you need a hand?

You stay with them, see that the lot keep to the road.

What are you going to do?

Make trouble.

I ride back to Graaffe Rijnet. The people out and about talk about the Bushmen who are attacking families at Bruyntjeshoogte and the commandos that are useless and aren't shooting enough of the creatures. People talk about the rain that no longer listens to prayers. People tell how a crow pecked out the eyes of a baby the previous week. The veldt is empty and dry and soft flesh is scarce.

When the moon is drifting discarded in the sky like a dented tin plate, I lie in wait at the kraal for the men and their dogs and the doomed zoo on the wagon. It is weekend, there are more people here tonight. The wagon with the cages comes trundling along. Tonight's dogs are standing in wait already. The young bull terrier is back, its wounds not yet healed. Its comrades for the evening a greyhound and a mongrel, a solid chunky animal without a tail and the eyes of a true believer. There are four cages on the wagon. They lift one of the cages down and open it for a large hyena with an outsized muzzle over its snout. The hyena is calm, used to people. It's also been here before.

The men howl at the moon like ruttish backyard curs. The wind is keen and bleak; the only cloud in the sky is covering the moon's shame. The two Caffres drag the hyena on its chain over the low stone wall, the hind legs dig in on this side until the neck can take no more and the animal stumbles over into the pit. The Caffre removing the muzzle gets nipped and the men roar with laughter.

Outside the kraal the dogs are barking more loudly. The hyena shrinks back into itself and tugs at the chain. A drunk stumbles over the wall and staggers and kicks at the hyena and turns around to the onlookers with his hands in the air and laughs. Behind him the animal leaps forward until it's checked by the chain, just short of the drunken sot's mug. The man gets a fright and his friends laugh at him and gob. I walk up to the wagon. With the short assegai I aim lightning-fast jabs at the soft pelts in the three cages until all sound ceases. I drop the wet assegai and walk in among the crowd with the two rifles over my shoulders and nobody looks at me and to everybody I'm just another face with something in the eyes and a clenched mouth that has something to bite back.

The hyena trots along the circle circumscribed by the length of the chain, then hunkers down next to the iron pipe. It looks at the people, then at the dogs and then at the fires. It lies down. It gets up when the dogs scramble over the wall after their handlers. The chains are slipped off; they make for the hyena. The hyena barks and howls from the depth of its throat. They snap and bark and embrace each other on their hind legs with the front paws around each other's necks. The open mouths seek each other out like those of hungry lovers. The greyhound grabs hold of the hyena by the snout. The hyena shrugs itself free and bites the dog across the back with the mongrel also already upon him from behind. He shakes the mongrel off and bites. The bull terrier is keeping to the sidelines, still sated with last night's blood. The hyena pins the greyhound to the ground and bites at the throat and misses and bites again and adjusts its grip and bites deeper.

Somebody asks me about the hyena in the middle.

It's not my hyena.

The man looks confused, asks me how much I've got on the hyena. I say I did not bet anything.

On whose side are you? the man asks.

A windbag with a sack for a shirt scolds and hisses and apes the fight in a farcical mime. When the hyena pounces he and a henchman grab each other in the same grip as that in which the hyena and the dogs are tearing at each other. His mouth gapes open when the hyena barks, his teeth gnash when the dogs growl, as if he's the puppet and the dogs the ventriloquists.

The hyena retreats, its mouth stretched open, a sharp yelping. The dogs circle. The hyena leaps, first at one dog, then the other. The greyhound lies bleeding. The bull terrier has an open gash across the back, the mongrel's snout is in shreds. The hyena is red all over except for the white sinew dangling from its paw. The animals fight without surrender, as if they've fought and died a thousand times in other bodies in other arenas.

The men around the kraal are now talking more to each other, bored with the bloodbath. They're staying for the bets, but the fervour has dissipated.

The firelight finds the hyena's eyes. I once again see the same thing I saw in the baboon. A pure thing, something that I have only seen this close up in animals in traps.

I make my way through the wall of shoulders, firmly push aside those who don't give way. The mongrel is in tatters and has no chance any more but does not stop charging. Its owner climbs over the wall, tries to get the chain on his dog again. The dog bites him and the man curses and his friends echo his curse raucously. I look at the men on the other side of the kraal, some of them with spatters of the fight on their faces. They shout and bark and gob and wipe the blood from their eyes and how can they not see it? I step back, suddenly afraid that the hyena's chain will snap, and then I hope the chain will snap and I smile and then I've already swung the one flintlock from my shoulder and aimed it at the hyena and pulled the trigger. The powder ignites and while I have to keep the rifle aimed at the target for an eternity while the powder burns and launches the bullet out of the barrel, the men around me all of a sudden stand struck sober and stupid. The hyena crashes down. I already have the second rifle in the foul face of the drunken lout next to me and I open up a passage through the crowd and have to smack one pipsqueak with the butt of the rifle and then I'm on my horse and gone.

Some distance along I hear somebody calling after me. A rider follows me and shouts about the value of the hides and how much I owe him and you can't just shoot another man's animals. I gallop on and the man carries on shouting after me, but never tries to catch up with me. A few hundred yards along he adjusts his pace to mine. He hollers until his voice is raw and the words are mere sounds and the shouting just a shouting and he gives up and turns back to his pals.

At daybreak I wait for the men to wake up while I boil water. We travel back to Brandwacht. I sit silent in my saddle and wonder why wagon trails always wind even though everything is flat and straight in front of you and nobody asks me any questions but they talk among themselves.

On the second day out of Graaffe Rijnet we notice the dogs in the underbrush again. A red one trots out in front of Horse. It's not the one-eared dog that I wrestled. This one has a fresh mark across the snout; both ears are erect. He is broader and darker and younger than old One-ear, his eyes wilder. The pack leader is dead, long live the pack. What happened to old One-ear? Tick bite? Old age? Did he have to defend his position with his teeth and was he too old? Was he bitten to death or did he wander into the wilderness, a defeated loner? Life surges on, the pack lives for ever. The dogs have a new captain and I have a new shadow.

At home I bustle to and fro around the place and at night I lie awake. Maria manages after a few days to drag the story out of me.

And so they let you go just like that?

They wouldn't shoot a man for a hyena and a few apes.

You know they shoot for far less.

How must I know why they didn't shoot me.

You were angling for it.

I went back for the animals on that wagon. I knew I was going to blast the daylights out of whatever was let loose in that kraal.

Oh come on, Buys, I know you. You also wanted to see what they would do to you. The Graaffe Rijnet boys.

I'm silent.

You didn't shoot the dogs?

What for? They'd been tamed already.

~

In winter when the river can hardly flush away your piss, my comrades and I and our Hottentots trek through the bushes and kloofs and river to Caffreland and return with cattle from the Mbalu kraals. A few nights later Langa's people trek through the bushes and kloofs and river and get away with cattle from my kraal. A few days later I trek through the bush-grown kloofs and the dry river and return with Langa's cattle, and a few days later Langa treks through the overgrown kloofs and the Great Fish River and returns with my cattle. Langa is eighty and he's always fought and he'll always carry on fighting.

When I come home on a strange horse with a herd of strange cattle

and a wagonload of ivory, buck hanging from the wagon tilt, and
guns – chests full of smuggled guns – Maria comes running out of
the house and she takes up position a few paces in front of me and
I walk up to her and she steps back and stops when I stop and looks
down and closes her hands tightly over her thumbs and presses her
hands to her sides and looks up quickly:

Your child is dead, she says.

∼

The baby was buried behind the house against a hill, a heap of stones
piled on top of her little carcase. Maria takes me to the heap of stones.
I have still not said a word.

You couldn't have waited? I say.

How was I to know when you'd be coming home? You're forever
drifting about.

I am silent. I sit down and pick up one of the stones. I stroke it, knock
it against another stone.

I should have waited with the burial, she says. But I didn't think
you'd mind. You were gone. It was starting to stink.

That's all right, I say. It wouldn't have been of any use.

I wait for the afternoon to heat up properly. I go and chop wood and
ride a distance on my new horse that does not yet recognise my body's
signals. The following morning I'm awake before sunrise. I walk up to
the hill with a pickaxe. I hew rocks from the incline that one day when
we've all copped it will become a mountain. I take out the rocks and
split them further until I can pick them up. When my people come
and ask whether they can help me I chase them away. I carry the rocks
to the heap and pile them on my daughter's body.

After a week the pile is higher than the house and wider. Maria
comes to stand before me with her arms akimbo.

You never even gave her a name. You never touched her. She
was nothing to you.

Now she's become something.

She wasn't a heap of stones.

I can touch the stones.

In the course of the next few days I spend less and less time with the stones. The new horse is clever. The person from whom the Caffres took him, whoever he was, had taught the animal things that other horses don't know. The horse is big and dappled, and when he runs, the speckles blend into a snowy nightmare bearing down on you. My flame-haired Elizabeth can't keep her eyes off the massive animal that runs so fast. It looks as if his hoofs don't touch the ground, as if he's going to slide into the air and rend it apart. She draws a picture of the horse in the sand and shows it to me. The horse has eight legs. She names him Glider and I call him, for her sake and despite my aversion to animal names, Glider. I teach my daughter to ride the horse. I teach the horse subtle signals that others won't notice. I teach the horse to pick up its hooves all the way under its chin and put them down thunderously as the Frenchman's horse did, but with more fury.

In these days it comes to pass that a couple of cattle disappear every now and then. When the herdsmen come to complain, I tell them to shoot when they see Caffres wandering around where they have no business to be. I hand out guns. When the number of missing cattle on my farm increases to about twenty, Coenraad Bezuidenhout turns up on my turf. I've heard stories about this farmer, one of the most notorious in the district. I offer him a bowl of coffee. He says, Pleased to meet you, we must join forces against the Caffres. He's heard I can shoot like no Christian in these parts and that my horse can outrun an assegai. He says talents like that should not be hidden under a bushel. Bezuidenhout and I and a few armed Hottentots set out for the Caffre kraals and return a week or so later with more cattle than were missing.

Elizabeth talks to me about the horse. I'm allowed to lift her onto the horse. In the evenings I go to add more rocks to the pile until one evening I start chucking them down. I climb onto the pile and look around me and then I start breaking down the pile. When all the

rocks are lying about around me, I call two Hottentots and order
them to cart off the rocks so that nobody will ever see that there used
to be a pile here. I leave only the few stones of Maria's little heap.
I walk into the house that evening. Maria is a few weeks pregnant and
is salting biltong.

     May I ask? she asks.

     What for?

That night the little woman holds me tight and strokes my head and
slowly rubs me hard. I mount her and she touches me gently and
tenderly and that infuriates me. She becomes aware that I'm trying to
hurt her; she goes quiet. Later we lie together, careful not to touch
each other, like two wounded animals.

∾

It's in that year or the next that Gert-who-remembers-the-pigeon
absconds. Just check in the Colony's documentation how the
baptised bastard-Hotnot Gerrit Coetzee starts tattling. Read there
how the scoundrel in 1793 declares on oath that I, on pretence of
hunting elephants, cross the Fish River to the Caffres and rob them
of their cattle, as many as I see fit. According to the declaration,
I drive the cattle to my farm and if the Caffres object I make them
lie on the ground and then I flog them with whips or sticks or whatever. The bastard of a convert declares further that in the course of
one such incident I allegedly instructed the Hottentots Platje and
Piqeur to fire on the Caffres. The first-named killed five and the last-
named four. To this the reborn Hotnot then adds a declaration from
Platje that testifies to my so-called mistreatment of my goddam farm
labourers.

    Look me in the eye and ask me straight out and I won't deny any
of this. Why should I? I listen to these accusations and I nod. I don't
know and don't care a damn where he digs up these stories, but
don't tell me that that god-cursed lump of typhoid-turd called Gert
ever went along on these raids. That Hotnot couldn't have hit his own

misbegotten foot at close range. I would never have taken him along. He was there about as much as he ever played with Noah's pigeon.

∾

On 21 March 1788 I receive a letter from my uncle:

My heartily commended nephew Coenraad de Buys

I have to inform you that Langa has let you know he demands payment from your good self for beating his Caffre, otherwise he will immediately attack afresh. He considers it a challenge to himself and the Christians must not think that he is scared of waging war.

With greetings from us all.

I remain your uncle,

Petrus de Buys.

I don't receive many letters and I save the letter and read it again and again. While I'm reading it, my fingertips tingle.

3

And it comes to pass in these days that there is strife in the royal houses of the Caffres like unto the strife in the royal houses of Europe. While the French start honing guillotines for royal gullets, the Caffres also wipe out one another for new kings and new orders of things, and the horizon in Africa, like that in Europe, is full of smoke and empty of everything else.

If I'd known the saga of the eastern border before moving there, I'd never have set foot there. If you want to relocate to the eastern frontier, be sure to bring more munitions than books. You can survive in the here and now if you can shoot straight, but history is going to snap your spine and kick you while you're down.

I understand that you want to get to the story; the murk of history surrounding me makes things hazy. But I was part of that bedlam, the bushes and the blood and the young Caffre girls, but also the dates. So let's keep it short and sweet: Paramount Chief Phalo rejoins his ancestors in 1775. For his sons Rharhabe and Gcaleka, too, life is a thing full of sound and fury that has to rage itself out so that they can depart from it. Gcaleka follows his father three years later. Rharhabe, like so many fathers then and still now, has to see his son and heir, Mlawu, choke on his own blood and die rucking with a spear in his chest. He arises from the corpse of his son and fights on against the Tambookies until he also dies on the same plot of ground and the year is 1782.

Mlawu's son is Ngqika and he still sometimes rides piggyback on his mother and plays in the dust and runs around with scuffed knees and cannot yet rule. Mlawu's younger brother, the great general Ndlambe, assumes a seat on the adorned ox skull before the Great Hut and keeps it warm for the little prince. Ndlambe is a warrior and his people love him for it. He is big and strong and not four years old. He understands war and carries on waging war. He immediately resumes his father's campaign against the Mbalu and the Gqunukhwebe, because sons wage war for their fathers. His discourse is muscular and supple like his limbs and drenched in ideas about the never-ending struggle for self-preservation and suchlike crud that in all times has fouled the lips of men who have to rule, but know only how to fight.

The Caffres have no central authority with whom the Company can negotiate. When the Company in a state of mild confusion declares a river a border and a farmhouse a drostdy and sends a retired Stellenboscher and a handful of mounted constables to guard this border, the Caffres only see a river where the border is supposed to be and they stream across it. On the eastern bank of the Fish River a drought decimates the cattle and the game, and a regent decimates the Mbalu and the Gqunukhwebe. The Mbalu and Gqunukhwebe and their cattle move in among the Christians and their cattle on the near side of the river. They roam across quitrent farms in quest of pasturage and game and survival, trapped between the belligerent farmers and the battle-ready Rharhabe warriors. The Christians and the Caffres both farm with cattle and both regard their cattle as their wealth. Both dwell in reed-and-wattle huts, have dominion over their wives and pray to their gods who demand similar sacrifices of flesh and fire. The Caffres have the numbers and the Christians have the fancy script of loan contracts and Bible verses. The numbers produce no algebra and the script no pretty poems, nothing but blood. The Christian tribe of Europe gets annoyed and the Mbalu tribe of Langa gets annoyed and the Gqunukhwebe tribe of Chaka melts away into the impenetrable maws of the kloofs.

Chief Langa is the brother of Gcaleka and Rharhabe and like them also a man with a temper. As tradition dictates, he leaves the stormy environs of the home of his father, the House of Phalo, as a young man and establishes his own captaincy. Langa is a hunter of elephant and rhinoceros. The House of Mbalu, renowned for its bellicosity and bravery, this most warlike tribe on the border, is named after Langa's favourite ox and in this year of our Lord 1788 Langa at eighty-three still has all his teeth.

Farmers no longer dare leave their farms. When Cornelis van Rooijen sends his labourers to drag up thorn branches for his cattle kraal not half a mile from his house, a horde of Caffres come rampaging out of the bushes with shields and assegai and chase the wretched Hottentots back to the homestead. He says the farm is no longer his. He says they set fires, they come and ask for food with weapons in hand, they pilfer, they overgraze the veldt, they murder the tame Hottentots and they trample the wheat.

When Ndlambe and Langa combine to take up arms against the Gqunukhwebe, Chaka's followers suffer huge losses of man and beast. They trek westward into the Colony and settle down. Langa takes almost all Chaka's cattle; his Caffres are impoverished, therefore they hire themselves out to the farmers for food and cattle. In the late eighties of the eighteenth century there are thousands of defeated hungry people swarming into the Colony and starting to steal the farmers' cattle. A godawful mess. Here endeth the history lesson.

∼

At twenty-six I'm in my prime of life and all the world knows my name. My Hottentot shoots one of Langa's warriors and the old goat dictates the letter to me that Uncle Petrus refers to. Later in 1788 I am summonsed for three schellings' overdue tax.

The pen-pusher, with his clothes that don't take kindly to dust, brings me the summons and stares unabashedly at the brazen Hottentot woman and the bare-bummed little bastard bustling about my knees.

Mijnheer, there is also the matter of Chief Langa who charges you with assaulting one of his Caffres? he says.

I went to retrieve my cattle. The Caffre with the cattle resisted, yes. So I chastised him. Mijnheer.

Mijnheer Buys, it is the exclusive privilege of the authorities to administer punishment.

I smile:

You have no authority over the Caffres.

I ignore the summons. It comes to nothing. Shortly after this I forge the signatures on a petition against the Company.

∼

The surrounding farmers get to hear of my shooting skills and my lightning-fast horse. They are told that I can read and write better than any of them. They hear me talking and some of them grumble that I swear something dreadful, but they can see everybody listening to me. They come and drink Maria's coffee and they blarney and blandish me until I agree to attend their meetings. At one such meeting of aggrieved farmers I say just enough to allow them to think that they were the ones who decided that I should draft a petition to the authorities. I record the farmers' complaints about the Caffres and ask the authorities to investigate the matter. Five people sign their names to this: yours truly, Lowies Steyn, Johannes Hendrikus Oosthuyse, Pieter Viljee and Hendrikus Vredrikus Wilkus.

Then I write a second letter. I correct one or two spelling errors and slip in a sentence that wasn't there before. The farmers are fed up to their back teeth, pissed off, says the sentence. If the authorities are going to do nothing we'll go and claim back our cattle and drive the Caffres back over the Fish River ourselves. I must confess, below this second petition (dated 11 August 1788) I myself sign the names of nine people: the original signatories, excluding my name, and then also the names of Pieter de Buys, Gerhert Scholtz, Cornelis van Rooijen, Vredrik Jacobus Stresoo and Andries van Tondere. I create a distinctive signature for each of them and, even though mine is missing, every signature is sullied with the flourishes and curlicues of my own name.

Go and look by all means, the tracks have been covered up. These petitions, original or otherwise, went missing even at the time in the self-perpetuating and proliferating labyrinth of colonial red tape. The letters may have got lost, but the all-seeing VOC finds out that they are forged and they vomit accusations and judgements all over me and my good name. Any orator will tell you that the truth is the best sparring

83

partner. At the next meeting I get to my feet and smile my smile and address the Christian soldiers.

I stand before the men, solitary amongst the accusing eyes in the front room of a crushed farmer. They look up at me, even the ones standing. I'm the tallest, the biggest man here. I open my trap and believe me, neither my wife nor my friend nor my child, neither my labourer nor my horse, has ever heard me talk like that. My voice is a honeyed bass, not the normal growl. I am voluble and fluent. My voice adapts its pace to the secret rhythms that inflame and enchant people, that persuade them that what they are hearing are lucid and logical arguments, especially where the head and the tail are wrenched as far as possible apart in my serpentine sentences, so that they convince themselves that somewhere some sense must be lurking and that in my euphonious outpouring I'm connecting up things that they have never before considered in conjunction, possibly because I end each sentence on a platitude, but one hailing from a totally different sphere to the rest of the sentence, a tail to the sentence like that of a scorpion with a sudden sharp sting at the end, the right words in the right places when they most want to hear them and then a sudden about-turn that leaves them gaping and that then inspires me all the more to new heights and clichés and makes me rampage on at ever-increasing volume while my eyes never release theirs, eyes that gullibly and hazily plead for more, eyes that cannot let me go but don't see me at all, an audience at my feet gobbling up their own shit – which I merely dish up to them in appetising form – for sweetmeats, and never for a moment wonder about the smile that at times, during pauses in the ever-waxing sentences, fleetingly and involuntarily plays around the corners of my mouth and vanishes, and I can see that not one amongst them considers that one can smile and smile, and be a goddam villain.

I persuade the burghers that I, before the only and most supreme God, was assured that what I wrote was the truth that indeed has already taken root in the heart of everyone there present. I signed their names in the firm conviction that, had time permitted, and had I had

84

the privilege of their presence, they would have dipped the quill and would have inked in their names themselves under my words, which if the truth be known were also their words.

The burghers gape at me. I feel bigger than my seven feet, I am kindled by my own voice. My words trickle over them like gum from a thorn tree and render the world viscous and glossy until they're persuaded that the forgery was a forgery in form but not in spirit. Later I am informed that my audience told the pen-lickers that even though their names were forged they wholeheartedly agree with the contents and that they would at any time upon request come and furnish their names under any such document. I excuse myself as soon as I can and go and pull my pizzle under a tree.

The VOC is a company on the verge of bankruptcy with a kicked-open anthill for headquarters, and the charge of forgery, as well as the complaints contained in the offending document, leads, as in the case of my overdue rental and tax, absolutely nowhere.

～

In September 1789, without cancelling the lease on Brandwacht, I register in my name also the quitrent farm De Driefonteinen on the Bushman's River, and six months later also Boschfontein, near the Sundays River Mouth.

Brandwacht has for a long time been trampled by Caffres who come here to hunt and to graze their fat cattle. In 1790 I get a licence to hunt elephants and I pack my stuff to leave. I'll take my family to Boschfontein, where the grazing is still good and the Caffres are not so much of a nuisance. Then I'll venture into the bundu on the track of elephants. We are busy throwing the last of the furniture onto the wagon when a cocky little man in a preposterous hat and a ruffled shirt comes riding up. With him are a few Hottentots clutching their flintlocks and their reins. This little whippersnapper introduces himself as Captain Ruiter.

I've heard of this gentleman. The half-Hottentot-half-Bushman deserter servant who went and squatted on the Fish River with a gang of thugs from both the races boiling in his blood. Ruiter's gang of freebooters plundered the Caffres, until the yellow-arsed gang deserted and left him there to make peace. Not too long or he's Chaka's pet poodle. Now Ruiter and his Gonna Hottentots have also, like the Caffres, come and wormed themselves in among the Christians.

Captain Ruiter with a great show of formality requests permission to stay on on my property. I've had it with this botheration.

> You stay here, what's it to me, I say. I'm clearing out in any
> case, this land has been trampled to dust.

Later I will hear what a terrible nuisance the Gonnas were, how the Caffres and the commandos both apparently came to look for Ruiter on my land, and then I will laugh.

I walk into the empty house; outside, the pregnant Maria cracks the whip and the wagon jolts into life. I stand in the centre of the front room, look up at the rafters, the swallow's nest empty and crumbling, tap my foot on the anthill floor. I built this house and lived here for almost five years and it was home and now it's an empty shell of reeds and stone and brittle and cracked clay. I kick a chunk of slate until it gives way and a section of the wall caves in. I tap the floor again lightly, then walk out fast. I think of the earth under the house, the immeasurably heavy weight just under the thin layer of loose anthill soil. I feel something pre-human and stupendous. I ride after the wagon.

On Boschfontein there is a homestead already, a largish house that doesn't need much work. The previous farmer left not long ago. Probably back to De Lange Cloof because the Heathens were beginning to graze too close by. Windvogel and I fix the roof and stamp the floor solid and at night I dream of dark waters under the house, stagnant black water without ripples, the smooth surface that is not disturbed, the measureless depth without end.

Houses on the frontier plain are not rooted in cellars or foundations, these huts of Christian and Heathen alike barely graze the dust, do not penetrate the earth. The hut is deposited on the soil like a nest in the veldt.

I don't stay on Boschfontein for long. I see to it that my people are settled, and then I go to see what the sea looks like. I've never seen the sea. In De Lange Cloof people sometimes ventured over the treacherous rock faces of Duivelskop to go and fish, but the Buyses and the soft-bellied Senekals never developed a taste for shell snails or fish scales. For my people it was always the bush that beckoned. I stand on a dune and gaze over the water. Thought the sea would be bigger. The water is saltier than I thought. The Hottentots are minding the cattle, Maria is minding the house, I gaze into the distance.

Maria says she's tired of forever cleaning up after everybody. She scolds me vigorously when one morning I wrap all the food in the house in a cloth and throw it onto the wagon and try to kiss her and walk away to where my human herd is waiting for me. She looks them up and down: my shadow Windvogel, Coenraad Bezuidenhout, his windbag brother Hannes and Van Rooijen who's forever whingeing.

We venture into the kloofs to go and goad elephants. If an elephant is angry enough, you feel pins and needles all over your body and the hair on your neck stands up straight and your whole skin comes alive. Then you shoot. At home you stare into corners. Curl yourself up like an animal in its hole.

~

News from Europe is slow coming to the Cape. The fashions at the Castle are apparently almost a decade out of date, but the seditious ideas from France make landfall here faster than any new dress patterns. The words liberté, égalité and fraternité are insubstantial and vague enough to fly over here at speed. In Paris the citizens storm the Bastille in the name of liberty and on the eastern frontier there's nothing left but liberty. Indeed, as is always the case with messages that have to travel too far, the French slogans have a totally different look when they arrive scurvy ridden and scuffed in Graaffe Rijnet.

After 1789 the farmers no longer even pretend to heed the Company's death rattles or the drunken musings emanating from the drostdy. The Caffres, the Bushmen, the Christians – every last one of them more frantic and more violent by the day. Farming families flee to Graaffe Rijnet to devour the last supplies. Landdrost Woeke shilly-shallies and swills. Secretary Wagenaar resigns and the Company appoints Honoratus Christiaan Maynier in his place. Let them all muck up together!

Alliances are struck and severed; now Ndamble wants to take up arms against the Mbalu and the Gqunukhwebe with the Christians, then he combines with Langa to hunt down Chaka and Chungwa. The Gqunukhwebe disappear ever deeper into the bush of the river valleys, all along the coast as far as the Gamtoos. See, the Gqunu-khwebe and Mbalu are crushed like mealies in a stamping block, like so many other people in so many other places where overripe and overblown powers press up against one another.

The Caffres soon get the message that a horse and a gun don't make a Christian immortal. Before long they also notice that the scraps of copper and iron and the strings of beads that the Christians offer for their cattle are a swindle. The destitute leave their kraals and come to work on the farms. If the farmer neglects to pay such a Caffre, or thrashes him too often or straps him to a wagon wheel and takes a few turns with him and then horsewhips him, the Caffre goes to complain to his chief and the farmer is plundered and his house burnt to the ground. At this time many Hottentots in their turn abscond from the farms and go to stay with the Caffres because the farmers mistreat them. When the farmers come to look for their stray Hotnots in the Caffre kraals, sometimes on their own farms, the Caffres chase them away. In 1789 more than sixteen thousand Caffre cattle and a few thousand Caffres are tallied on one quitrent farm. The Christians are spoiling for a fight, but the Caffres cluster together in hordes, not one by one like the Christians who can't tolerate their neighbours. They no longer beg for food; they now take it.

I oil my gun. I apply the wood oil liberally. Then I start polishing it slowly. Only two fingers, till both fingers are numb. Elizabeth plays around my feet in the front room. Maria is outside, jabbering with Windvogel. The window is narrow, a strip of sunlight shatters in shards over the rough-hewn table.

A bureaucracy understands maps, not land. A Company does not understand war, it flourishes in meetings. If you have the patience, come and rummage with me in the archives of the bureaucratic Colony: Woeke, ever leaner and drunker, is told to negotiate with the Caffres. The plan is to buy out all Heathen claims to land to the west of the Fish River. Negotiation follows upon meeting follows upon deliberation. Chaka and Chungwa go nowhere. They allegedly bought the land between the Fish and Kowie Rivers from one Captain Ruiter for fifty head of cattle. Nobody knows from whom Ruiter bought the land. Oh, bugger off! The other Caffre captains say they'll clear off out of the Zuurveld – if everybody clears off, Heathen as well as Christian. Woeke trots home and writes more letters to the Political Council and the Council says Let the Caffres be for the time being, just keep the Christians within our jurisdiction. The Council whispers: We have no paperwork for the other side of the Fish. The Company does what it does best and appoints a commission, consisting of Woeke, the retired secretary Wagenaar and new secretary Maynier, to go and talk to the Heathens. The commission does not succeed in persuading the Caffres of the principle of private property of land. We find your culture charming, says the commission. We'd love to be friends, but please just stay on your side of the river. Once again gifts are exchanged and the pen-lickers sit with slavering mouths and tongues lolling from wet lips and make notes about the physique of the Heathens and the condition of their teeth and the size of the bulges under their loincloths. The retired and reappointed Wagenaar is left on the border on his own, without a single soldier, to maintain the dignity of the authorities and to intimidate all of the Caffre Kingdom with his wig and his stockings.

Caffres wade through the river and come to collect my cattle; they're hardly back in their kraals when I go and collect my cattle and a few more. Few places on earth are as busy as the banks of the Fish. Every hunting expedition becomes longer, every elephant scarcer and older and more enraged, every punitive commando more brutal. Around us families congregate in laagers. The authorities don't send the munitions they promised. I'm quite happy staying where I am. Maria no longer misses me when I'm not at home.

I lie with my wife and she rubs my head. I look up through the roof beams. I miss the swallow's nest in the rafters at Brandwacht. My sons Philip and Coenraad are born to me. Just spit and clay, I think. I turn on my side and look at Maria. She's carrying low, the next one is going to be a son again. There is a new hair growing out of the mole on her ear.

Graaffe Rijnet at last acquires its first minister, Jan-Hendrik Manger. On Sundays he preaches twice in High Dutch in the school that used to be a stable. When Woeke fails to turn up for a meeting in the Cape, the Company sends Captain Bernard Cornelius van Baalen as acting landdrost. He writes a wordy report about the disorder and corruption, which nobody, with the exception of course of yours truly, Omni-Buys, ever reads. Most people who don't have to stay in Graaffe Rijnet, he writes, have long since cleared out.

I and Christoffel Botha with the rotten teeth, and the Bezuidenhout clan and a few Prinsloos smell blood and riches.

Smell! I tell them.

What do we smell, oh great Buys? they ask.

They call me their friend; I call them whatever I have to call them to keep them trotting along in my dust. We persuade all that is a veld-wagtmeester to launch a punitive commando. I tell Officer Barend Lindeque and Veldwagtmeester Thomas Dreyer that it's all the fair weather that causes deserts and that drought can be broken only by storms. I tell them how I caught a thief red-handed. The Caffre was slaughtering one of Botha's cattle, but when I dragged him to the chief by the scruff of his scrawny neck, the Caffres sent me packing and the pestilence stood there laughing at me. Our cattle are now disappearing every day, but if you go on commando with me, you always return with more cattle than were stolen. They say that on punitive expeditions my gang and I shoot a bit too freely among the Heathens. And apparently we shoot the Caffres who hunt on our farms. But we are big men and strong and what we aim at we hit. We are indispensable on every commando.

If you mess with us, we mess with you: Langa, whose kraal is now situated on burgher Scheepers' farm, goes hunting with his warriors. When they get to Campher's homestead, he locks Langa up in his house. They say the old warrior hasn't slept for years on account of the pain in his back. Campher takes Langa's shield and assegais and knife and knobkerrie from him and holds him hostage until the old chicken thief has to buy his liberty with cattle. Hannes Bezuidenhout keeps the sons of two Caffre captains captive on his farm until the captains pay him a ransom of four oxen. Then there's Hannes' brother, the scoundrel Coenraad. His brothers I call by their first names, but he is plain Bezuidenhout – he's the one responsible for the stories about the Barbarous Bezuidenhouts. If you know him as I know him, you know he's *the* Bezuidenhout; he is the legend. And besides, there's only one Coenraad around here. The very Bezuidenhout who farms a different farm every month. He who, when the mood takes him, threatens that he'll thrash to death every goddam wretch next to the Swartkops River; he who that year locks up Chungwa in his mill and hitches him up like a mule and teaches him with a horsewhip how one makes the thing go around.

~

The sky is pressing down when in 1792 after an exchange of cattle I ride home with the cattle and the woman I took from Langa. I am thirty-one and have three farms, a wife and four children, a whole bunch of Hottentots working for me, a multitude of cattle and now also a Caffre princess, barely sixteen with a skin stretched tight and glossy like stinkwood. She says her name is Nombini. She sits up proudly on the wagon as if she's laced and corseted. Her two offspring can't let go of the big nipples. The pack of ridged dogs run up and down next to the wagon. They chase one another, snap at each other in play, and drive the oxen mad. In the clouds the first thunder is crackling. When we crest the ridge and see my farm on the plain, the Sundays River shines like a Milky Way and my house with the candlelight in the window and the fires of the Hottentots working on my farm and the fires of the Caffres who graze their cattle on my farm are scattered like smouldering stars in the dark grass. When we get closer and ride in among the fires, the constellation disintegrates into mere points of disconnected light.

~

There's no end to the rain. The thatched roof at first keeps out the water and then no longer. Whoever used to live in the house before knew how to build a decent chimney. Maria is sitting with the new-born Johannes at her breast, Elizabeth with little Philip and Coenraad Wilhelm on her lap in her usual place next to the fire. Coenraad Wilhelm is sucking at her thumb. Then also Nombini and her children.

I chase the chickens up into the rafters and scrabble a place open for myself between the cat and the other cat and the pig that nobody can keep out of the house any more. Maria and Elizabeth are scared of the thunder. Elizabeth is sobbing. Maria busies herself placing the few basins under the leaks, so that her hands shouldn't tremble. Nombini and her brood are dead quiet, look around them at the mealies and the biltong and tobacco and pots and pans hanging from the purlins. The animals make only the most essential movements, so as not to lose warmth. Nombini gets up and looks at me and Maria and picks up a porcelain bowl from the table and sits down again and holds the bowl in both hands and rotates it slowly between her finger-tips. Maria lets go of the basin and grabs the bowl from Nombini's hands and puts it back on the table. Nombini comes to sit with me where I'm trying to file down an ingrown toenail with a wood file. The children look at one another and look at the adults and are quiet and then they all start howling in unison. Maria trips over the cat. The cat yowls and the children get a fright and break the rhythm of their crying and then carry on howling.

Goddammit, Buys, there isn't room for everybody here.

I press Nombini to me and say something in her ear and she goes to sit with her children. Maria cooks meat, throws sweet potatoes into the pot. The few tin plates I haven't yet melted down to harden my bullets are set out on the table. My wife and children and I seat ourselves. My new wife and her children go to sit in the corner. I tell them to come and take a seat. We eat. Nombini licks her fingers clean and her mouth is anointed with fat. Maria watches me watching this stranger wrapped in her kaross, the long legs. I speak to her in Xhosa and she doesn't say much. I speak to my children in Dutch and now and again I peep at Maria.

I take the Bible from the shelf.

Come let us worship.

I undo the copper clasp and open the great book, dust puffs up into the air. Some pages are missing. Things get left behind if you carry on moving. I read solemnly. I watch Maria closely, knowing how with each holy word I try to soothe and placate her, and seeing how the damn words don't achieve a thing.

Then again Abraham took a wife, and her name was Keturah,
I read out.

Nombini's fingers once again grope for the cold porcelain. She takes a red bead from the folds in her kaross, drops it into the bowl and watches the bead spinning around on the base. Is she wondering who is rubbing the hurt out of Langa's back tonight? She turns the bowl round and round, looks at the fine blue patterns in the porcelain without beginning or end. I understand only too well, with the coming of evening people feel sorry for themselves, but she's got to stop this bullshit. I see that little lower lip tremble. Should I feel sorry for her? The Caffre woman has never in her life seen a plate of food such as the one she's just devoured. Poor thing, does she see in her Heathenish mind's eye the Christians cantering into her kraal on their great horses, the hooves kicking dust into the calabashes of water that she and the other young women fetched from the river?

> And she bare him Zimran, and Jokshan, and Medan, and Midian, and Ishbak, and Shuah.

The girl is strong, her lip is no longer trembling. Still, while I read, I wonder about my new wife's faraway eyes. Whose little bead is she rattling like that in the bowl? I know what you're thinking: She's scared, she's a child and she's far from home. Rubbish! You haven't spent days on end with her on a wagon. You don't know what's swirling around in that pretty little head. I read, but all I see is how she rubs old Langa's shoulders, how his back relaxes under her hands, how she lies listening to him snore. All the nights she spends lying against that skin that death has already started picking from the bones. Does she see stars when he spurts in her? Was she proud of her husband when he came forth from his hut and stood up straight and took off his kaross and pushed out his old chest and walked towards us, the Christians?

> And Jokshan begat Sheba, and Dedan. And the sons of Dedan were Asshurim, and Letushim, and Leummim.

The little red bead keeps spinning in the empty bowl, deafeningly, I can't hear myself read.

> And the sons of Midian; Ephah, and Epher, and Hanoch, and Abidah, and Eldaah. All these were the children of Keturah.

Maria shifts around on her chair and sighs exaggeratedly.

Was Nombini worried when the Christians and Langa and his captains congregated in a close circle, the talking growing softer, more urgent? Did she see how I towered over them all, my beard, my mane? I remember she screamed when one of the Caffres staggered back. He was big, that Caffre, one of Langa's strongest captains. Had he

talked to her and gone for long walks with her before Langa took her
to wife? Do you think she did things with him as well? How far can a
little Caffre girl go with a man if she still wants to marry intact? Was
his rod in her mouth? Did she allow him access to her hindquarters?
His brow was bleeding. Had she seen what happened, heard the blow?
I know she saw when I strode towards him, stood astride him, pulled
him up and threw him to the ground. The other Caffres stood still.
I let the Caffre go, spat on him and entered the circle again. I'm not
proud of it, but what does she know of bartering cattle and taking
back stolen cattle? You have to make yourself felt in the first minutes.
What does she know? I said something to Langa and shoved him.
Where was she then? Did she see and what does she see in the little
red bead that is rotating ever more furiously in the bowl?

And Abraham gave all that he had unto Isaac.

Could the little girl see how her Caffres fought back, how blows
from fists fell and whips cracked and the blade of an assegai flashed?
How we Christians, dammit, also took blows and lost blood, until
somebody cocked a rifle? Does the little creature here at my table
know that they were *our* cattle, Christian cattle, that we drove out of
the kraal? Well, most of them. Quite a few of them seemed familiar.
In any case, I went to talk to her husband again and then the old
bugger wasn't laughing any more. Did he, there with me, seem older
to her than that morning in bed?

But unto the sons of the concubines, which Abraham had,
Abraham gave gifts, and sent them away from Isaac his son,
while he yet lived, eastward, unto the east country.

I pointed at her. She looked down. I see once more how I and two
Hottentots walk towards her. She looks prettier the closer I get to her.
A few of her husband's young men follow us, hands clenched around
assegais. One of the Caffres runs ahead and takes up position between
her and me, I the evil blond giant. The Hottentot to the left of me
shoots the Caffre in the chest and he stays down and his blood pumps
out of him. For a moment it looks as if there's going to be a massacre.

One warrior hurls an assegai, but it lands between two farmers.
A Hottentot fires but misses. A Christian lashes a warrior with a
sjambok. Langa shouts at his warriors to stand back.

They weren't the only ones who were scared. We weren't looking
for bloodshed, dammit. Could the girl see, there where she was
standing, how this big Christian's hands were trembling by his sides?

*And these are the days of the years of Abraham's life which he
lived, a hundred threescore and fifteen years.*

The farmers and their tame Hottentots looked around in confusion.
I took off, my hands now fists, made for the nearest Caffre between
her and me. The wretch was hardly fully grown, probably as old as
she. I start thrashing him. He is down on the ground and is holding
his frizzy head. I don't stop. Somewhere somebody shouts something
and then there are hands trying to drag me off him. I let go of the
Caffre and hit out at the Hottentots trying to hold me back. All three
of the creatures. Did she join in the laughter? I heard them laughing,
the Caffres roaring with laughter at the crazy white man laying into
his own Hottentots. Did she look away then? You're also going to want
to look away. Go ahead and try. Try to turn your head when I get up
with blood around my mouth. Try to look away when the Hottentot
staggers to his feet, pulling his hands from his face as if they're stuck
to it. She *did* see. Just look at the way she regards me. The poor Caffre
girl beheld it all and understood nothing. I am not ashamed. For what?
She knows nothing. The Hottentot looking up with the white bone
where his cheek used to be.

*Then Abraham gave up the ghost, and died in a good old age, an
old man, and full of years; and was gathered to his people.*

I wiped my hands on my trousers. Walked up to her. She looked at
me and didn't move. She mustn't come and act the victim here. Didn't
she, when I bent over her, lick that little hand, the one that's now
making such a fuss about the damned little bead? And didn't she wipe
clean my bloody beard and lips with that same little hand? Yes, girl,
what are you looking at? You know that right there in the dust, among

your Caffres, with that gentle, slow wipe across my mouth, you gave yourself to me. You wanted to be the wife of the wildest among the wild. You were scared, but you couldn't keep those little kudu eyes off me. Now you're still looking. But with a different look.

> *And his sons Isaac and Ishmael buried him in the cave of*
> *Machpelah in the field of Ephron the son of Zohar the Hittite,*
> *which is before Mamre.*

Maria pushes her chair back and I stop reading. She doesn't get up. Nombini's little bead is lying still in the bowl. She puts the dish down on the table. The Lord alone knows what a woman thinks when she looks at you like that. Does she remember how I hoisted her onto my horse? How her old husband spat on the ground and did nothing more? How her people glared at her? How we loaded two more girls on the horses of the Hottentots? How the other two put up much more of a fight and scratched Van Tondere's face? How we rounded up the cattle? How one of the young Caffres stood in our way and was taken apart with our rifle butts and sjamboks? How we rode off and nobody followed us? I'm sure the girl remembers it all. Now I am sorry that I covered her eyes when I looked back and saw Langa's Caffres descending upon the cheekless Hottentot who had fallen off his horse and killing him with stones and assegais.

> *The field which Abraham purchased of the sons of Heth . . .*

I see how Maria is looking at me; I lose my place.

That night I went to lie with her and made her mine. I told her my name is Coenraad. But why would the girl think of that now, if there is so much she can reproach this Christian man with? Does she remember how gentle I was with her? Oh no, if she thinks at all of our first lying together, she'll think I was like a goddam pipsqueak when I touched her, uncertain and hesitant without her assent. That she had to reassure and encourage me before I could mount her properly. That I looked mighty proud of every gasp I could squeeze from her. Why would the girl think that it was a long day for me too? Why would she remember how I lay behind her all night long? Would you believe it, the next morning the girl tells me that I muttered and sobbed in my sleep. Just what a man wants to hear on his honeymoon. Should have left her right there in the veldt for the hyenas. As it happened, we chased the other two girls into the veldt with sjamboks that morning. But my little princess remained seated next to me. She could have run off with them if she'd wanted to. Why would I want to stop her, haven't I got a wife? But she remained sitting and now she's sitting here and glares at me and doesn't want to let go of the little bead. I seize her hand and force it open and grab the thing off her palm and put it into my mouth and chew it fine and swallow. She remains sitting. I find my place in the verse:

> There was Abraham buried and Sarah, his wife. Here endeth
> the Lesson tonight.

Maria gets up, takes the porcelain dish from Nombini's hand again, this time more politely, and puts it on the pile of plates.

> Is the whore going to help me wash up, or am I Hotnot to
> both of you now?

Maria, don't be jealous. You're my wife.

> I wish I was, Buys.

You are, that I promise, my beloved dear Sarah. Weren't you listening to what I was reading?

She walks away, sighs, then turns around:

> Jealous, Buys. I wish I was jealous.

The lightning flashes and outside the whole world scintillates. In the bright glare of the lightning nothing remains hidden and we lot at the table see each other as we are and the surface of everyone's countenance is illuminated for an instant and reveals no depth and is wholly unknowable and then it is dark again and the shadows drape soft comforting masks over our faces.

~

On this night the house is steamed up with the breaths of human and animal. It is as if the air itself turns to smooth and damp walls. The rain has stopped but the dripping carries on. The house is full, even the pig has to sleep outside and the pig never sleeps outside. The house feels empty. The house feels big and endlessly known, endlessly repetitive. As if there are passages and halls into all eternity, as if every drop dripping into the bowl has to resound. But nothing sounds in this house.

I lie next to Nombini in the front room and listen to the faraway thunder and Maria's snoring even further away.

The next morning the clouds have gone and the air is translucent. I yell at the Hottentots. The jackals have been at the sheep. I take Nombini to the labourers' huts and tell them they have to build her a hut as the Caffres build their huts and she'll stay among them and they will listen to her because she is my wife. The Hottentots talk among one another and look at the young woman who remains standing there when I walk back to my house. The young girl who doesn't look back – as I look back – to see where her man is going. She remains standing, alone and with two children on her arms, and looks at them.

At dusk two days later I ride to her. I twist Glider's reins around a branch and sling the roll of hides over my right shoulder and the two guns over my left and I don't stoop low enough to enter the hut. I curse and she laughs from her beautiful belly. That evening she and I sit by a fire in front of the hut and the labourers coming from the fields greet us cordially and walk on. Towards the end of the week I saddle my horse and go hunting elephants and don't find a single one and come back home.

~

It is still autumn, but see, I'm hibernating. I sleep till afternoon, then walk up and down in the house wrapped in hides, go and lie down again. If I go far enough, all the way to the end of sleep's labyrinth, I find silence. The house is bigger than any I've ever stayed in before, but the longer this winter sleep lasts, the more the house shrinks around me. As if the reeds on the roof and the clay on the walls are compacted around me like a nest and then, weeks later, as if the walls turn sticky and soft and enfold me like the membrane of a chrysalis.

My people soon learn to leave me alone. For the most part I don't hear them and if they do make me aware of them, I roar at them before spinning myself into my chrysalis again. I curl myself up in my karosses and bedspread that I've thrown down in the corner of the room. Maria sleeps on the bed. She says my groaning keeps her awake. She says I am welcome to go and lie with my Caffre girl. I remain lying in the corner.

I concentrate on keeping as still as possible, every movement is considered before it's executed. I know the soul of every muscle. Late in the afternoon of a day of which I do not know the name I lie staring at a snail trailing across the floor. I look at the fury with which the snail crawls out of its shell. Just see the horns slowly unfurling.

The children are buzzing around Maria like blowflies and ask after their father.

He's lying in wait, I hear her say.

For what? they ask.

She sends them out. She is a mother, she knows about withdrawing into shells, the preparation of a passage out. Her mouth twists when the child kicks inside her. Do you think that when she's standing like that looking at her Coenraad lying on the ground under his hides, do you think she sees me and thinks of snakes in their holes? Or do you think she remembers how her father in their hut at the Senekals paced up and down every night?

In the late afternoons I disappear. Then I go to the sea. On the plain the wind blows without cease. You can't hear the sea from the house, but it's not far. I hold the shell and turn it over and touch it, careful not to break it. I lick at it. While I'm looking at it and holding it, the shell's shape makes absolute sense to me, and as soon as I think of it again under the heap of hides, it becomes wholly incomprehensible. How could I have known that twilit afternoon that the shellfish excretes its own house? Who could possibly have told me that the building material seeps through the creature, how it distils its miraculous covering according to its need? I press the shell to my eye and see darkness; I press the shell to my ear and hear the sea. I could not then put it into words, can still not do so, but what I saw was something of an eternal shaping and reshaping without cease.

Back at the farm I do put two things into words to two people. The first is Windvogel, to whom I say: Count your blessings, friend. You live alone. The second is Nombini to whom, when I am sure she's asleep, I whisper: In a shell you don't need a door or a gate, everybody is too scared to enter.

~

I owe six years and five months' worth of quitrent on Brandwacht, one year and eleven months on De Driefonteinen and one year and five months on Boschfontein: a total of two hundred and twenty-four rix-dollars. The Caffres stream over the border and murder Christians. The Christians blame me because I look for trouble with the Caffres and have dealings with their women and then on top of that smuggle them weapons. Why smuggle guns to the Heathens who rob me and whom I rob? To strike up alliances on both sides of the border? Not to chuck all my eggs into one Christian basket? Simply to make the game more interesting? Indeed. Inter alia.

Farmers start abandoning their frontier farms and moving west, back to civilisation. Nobody believes me when I lay charges against the Caffres who steal my cattle, because who would trust such a totally depraved creature? No Christian's wife opens the door to me, no Christian calls at my farm. My own family no longer knows me. The landdrost and his lackeys don't bother me with my debts, as long as I stay out of their way and keep my trap shut and eke out my miserable existence on my godforsaken stretch of sand that through all the ages has been washed into the sea by the Sundays River.

The drought returns, and the locusts and the migratory buck

devour and trample everything that remains, and the Christians who haven't yet trekked west now trek west.

On 21 January 1793 the French chop off the head of their king and on 13 July Marat is murdered in his bathtub by a woman with a kitchen knife and later in that year Langa, whose wife is now living with me, takes all my cattle and burns down my farms and my house and everything in it and leaves me adrift in poverty.

4

Note well, the silent and lurking Coenraad on his farm is not the terror-inducing De Buys on the frontier. I am both of them and neither. Nombini says my eyes change as violently and suddenly and unobtrusively as the seasons. But Maria always mutters the same refrain:

You're just like all the other men I know.

~

Officer Barend Lindeque is taciturn and compact and tough. His arms are tanned sinews and his eyes blink too fast, as if the sun is always too bright. He has a wife and children, but he's that kind of man who feels the Lord is spying on him when he's with a woman. When the wanting takes hold of him, he has to go on commando or go hunting or commit violence against his neighbour because the Lord is all-seeing. Barend Lindeque covets his neighbour's house and his neighbour's manservant and his ox and his ass, but above all he covets his neighbour's wife and maidservant. At the meetings about the Caffres he sits in the corner with folded arms and listens and utters no word. One day he says to me:

Nobody is going to do anything until somebody does something. Early in 1793, while I was still a man with a house on a farm, he sees a little Hottentot girl bathing in the river and the water shimmers like stars on her skin and he leaps onto his horse and charges to my remote homestead and says to me:

Get your guns. We're going to hunt Caffres.

Maynier is a prick and he prattles and prattles and it's not going to scare any Caffre off our cattle. Ndlambe also has his knife in for the Caffre rebels who loll around this side of the river and don't bow to his authority. I regularly go and barter cattle and guns with the chief and we understand each other and he receives me in his hut. Lindeque and I and a whole faction of farmers gather some fat cattle and travel across the Fish to the milk and honey and unfamiliar thighs of Ndlambe's Great Place. We ride into the kraal. The Caffres are cautious and Lindeque and the other farmers have to wait with the armed warriors. I ride on to the big hut. Ndlambe's greased belly gleams in the sunlight and the leopard skins and beads judder with every movement. He welcomes me, this rare Christian who brings him guns for cattle. Ndlambe seats himself on the ox skull in the clearing before his hut and I seat myself on the rock under the lion skin. We talk and we laugh as the Hottentot interpreter translates the universal humour of dirty jokes. The chief's advisers do not laugh at our jokes and keep a wary eye on the farmers at the entrance to the kraal. I switch to Xhosa and the chief dismisses the interpreter. We devise war plans. We get up and shake each other by the hand as the Heathens do it and then as the Christians do it. Ndlambe presses me to his breast and offers me and my comrades all the creature comforts of the kraal. I take two young girls and the other farmers select young girls and we stuff ourselves with the meat and porridge and whey around the big fires and watch the dances and go into their huts and do unto the young women as men do with subject women. Everybody, except Lindeque who all through this night is assuredly wide awake and blinking and pacing up and down in an empty hut.

Only late the next morning on our way back to the Fish River do I inform my comrades that we are now allies of the amaNdlambe and that Christian and Heathen are now as blood brothers together going to wipe out Langa and Chaka. Lindeque blink-blinks and starts having second thoughts. He asks whether it's too late to abandon the plan, and I laugh:

Indeed, Brother; hopelessly too late.

Oh Lord, deliver us from what we actually want, says Lindeque and I yawn.

You're lying to yourself and Maynier is lying to himself, I say: War is the only honesty remaining in this waste land.

∾

I'm sitting at the back of the hall, gazing out of the window at Graaffe Rijnet's dust. Across the road a man is sitting in front of his house chewing tobacco and a riderless horse walks past and somewhere I hear crows. I put my head out of the window for fresh air. I see the slave curing on the gallows.

The meeting creeps through the agenda and I don't know the date is 6 May 1793 and I think of Nombini and Maria. I haven't been home for a long time. I think of the Caffre girls in Ndlambe's kraal and I smile. When Van Baalen announces that Secretary Maynier will be the next landdrost, all the men around me jump to their feet, but I have to stay seated because my breeches are straining across my crotch.

Master Markus the goddam nightingale is also sitting in the back row. He listens attentively, but does not utter a word. When the men start squabbling heatedly, flinging abuse at each other and the Company, I look in his direction again. He is no longer there. Must have walked out at some point when I wasn't looking. I can't understand why that man doesn't get buggered up each and every day.

Captain Adriaan van Jaarsveld, the man with the pomaded hair and the trimmed beard, gets up in the midst of the mayhem. As usual the men fall silent when Van Jaarsveld clears his throat. Everybody knows the story of how in the course of a punitive expedition he came across some Heathens. His men throw out handfuls of tobacco before the Caffres. The Caffres scrabble around among the Christian horses, the assegais forgotten, their hands full of tobacco. Van Jaarsveld gives the order to shoot. He and his men mow down most of the scrambling Heathens. Since then both Caffre and Christian have called him the Redcaptain. He delivers a long address and concludes with He who loves me, follow me! and marches out of the door. The men look at each other; most have sat down again. Then a few heemraden get up and follow their Redcaptain. Every Christian has his own notion of what to do with the Caffres and every one splits off with his own gang. All that they have in common is the conviction that the Caffres must clear off from their farms and that the Company must clear off altogether. I sit back enjoying myself.

~

Ndlambe sends two thousand warriors to guard the crossings in the Fish River. Lindeque's commando attacks the Zuurveld Caffres on 18 May 1793 without the permission or knowledge of Landdrost Maynier and drives them back to the river where Ndlambe is lying in wait and that is the start of the Second Caffre War. The skirmishes are brief and only three or four or five Caffres are killed in the campaign and the rest disappear up the kloofs. Many fugitives leave their herds behind in their haste and we loot eight hundred cattle and give Ndlambe four hundred.

Ndlambe is impressed with the Christians and even more so with the cattle. He once again offers me young women, once again I don't say no, once again we rebel farmers make merry with the Caffres up to the first glimmering of dawn. We have overstepped not only the Fish River border but also the Colony's law. You make a different kind of merriment when it could be your last.

The next day Lindeque and I talk to Ndlambe. With bloodshot eyes and aching heads and loins we plan a bloodbath. Lindeque, indeed the only one without any notable tenderness of loin, leaves us others wide-eyed at the proposals pouring from his bloodthirsty mouth. The farmers and the amaNdlambe will combine to attack the remaining Zuurveld Caffres and wipe them out utterly. When he sees before his eyes the massacre taking place, Lindeque does not blink even once.

~

The parched soil is white with frost when our Christian commando sets out that morning to meet up with Ndlambe's army. The Christians are jovial and curse and boast about how they showed their wives who ruled the roost before they left and how they also showed the Hotnot bitches, whose lips up there and down there are the reddest

106

and smell the strongest. A drunken farmer fires shots in the air. I ride on ahead with Lindeque. We don't talk. Lindeque is blinking so fast it looks as if his eyes are hurting. Look, he sees the world as a series of flashes with a rosy tint, like blood in a river. I see my dogs running on the perimeter of this node of horses and ruttishness and lead.

Near to the mustering place I hear something like the flapping of thousands of wings and a light thrumming as if the earth is short of breath. A Christian next to me curses and Lindeque swears and bridles his horse and the animal staggers. See, here on the plain where the thorn bushes open up before us like velvet curtains, a sea of warriors are sitting in formation on their shields. They are young and strong and lusting after violence and excited by death as only young men can be and naked and daubed with red clay and some of them sport blue crane feathers on their heads and there are thousands of them and they stamp their feet and seethe like a tempest and chant in anticipation of the blood that must flow and will flow and my fellow Christians see this horde that is as one and they fall silent and then they turn around and more than one pisses himself and they flee and I flee with them and their panic spreads like a pestilence through the Zuurveld and distant farms become deserted farms and farmers fling what they can onto wagons and clear out and the Caffres see the wagons trekking away and the blind terror in the eyes that cannot afford to look back and they know that those guns in trembling hands are not almighty and the Mbalu and the Gqunukhwebe and all that is Caffre comes down on the Christian homes and herds and Hottentot servants and slaves and burns down the houses and drives off the herds and kills the labourers and slaves and the names of these people are recalled by no one, and go and look, they're not recorded anywhere and they are just dead and gone and of these raids only statistics remain, like the 4 farms out of 120 that were not plundered and the 40 Hottentots that were killed and the 20 homesteads that were burnt down and the at least 50 000 cattle and the 11 000 sheep and the 200 horses that were stolen and the 25 families fleeing the

Zuurveld and the rest that form laagers in groups with 50 heavy wagons in a circle and the thorn bushes in the openings beneath and between the wagons and then Chaka and Langa attack Ndlambe and the corpulent king who cannot understand why his allies deserted him must crawl back across the Fish and in these plunderings four Christians are killed, Johannes Grobbelaar, Juriaan Potgieter, Stephanus Cloete and Pieter Vivier, and the Caffres catch a Christian boy of sixteen, one Stroebel, and nobody ever hears anything about him again and I'm hardly back home when the day breaks that Langa, whose wife is now my wife, takes all my cattle, burns down my farms and house and everything in it and leaves me adrift in poverty.

I send my wives and children to my henchman Jan One-hand Botha until I can get another house built. Jan stands with his pipe in his hand and waves me good bye with his stump. While I'm seeking to avenge myself in the course of the next punitive expedition, while I'm wildly hitting out and shooting and chasing after Caffres into the bushes and only returning to the Christian fires late at night, my brother Frederik – who played with me when I was small but now hardly knows me – is severely wounded and my uncle Petrus gets hit in the chest with an assegai. I sit through the night holding my uncle's hand. I ask him about my father. He says my father was a brave man to stay at home and see that the yard was kept cleared. My father was brave to teach his sons to shoot and ride and not to go hunting too far and to sleep with the same woman, that Christina, he says, every night. By dawn it seems as if Uncle Petrus is going to make it, but then he dies while I'm fetching him water.

～

I ride into Graaffe Rijnet. There are wagons and tents everywhere between the houses. Children and women are wandering around in the streets. Bezuidenhout scratches at his red beard that reaches almost to his belt and looks at the woman walking past him and looks at the little girl she has by the hand. He tells me that the women are streaming into town because the Caffres leave them alone. They only burn down the farm and take the cattle and torture and murder the men. But the women and the children they leave alone.

We also torture and murder, I say.

But we know better than to leave the young girls alone, Bezuidenhout laughs.

We ride on to the drostdy where Maynier's commando is to muster. Neither I nor any of my comrades have any time for the new landdrost, but when there's a commando that wants to drive out the Caffres and take their cattle, we're ready and willing. In front of the jail one of the militia is tying a Christian to a pole and then he starts whipping him; the man howls like a baboon.

Maynier is highly learned and fluent in Dutch, French and English, but doesn't understand warfare. The Political Council orders him to avoid violence and to negotiate peaceably with the Caffres. As an immortal I, Omni-Buys, have many an idle hour for my little obsession: the history of which I was part, but of which at the time I couldn't see anything beyond my own broken nose. I laugh from my immaterial belly when I read in a battered book that for these negotiations Maynier requisitioned the following trinkets from the commissioner, as gifts for the Heathen:

300 pounds of beads,
200 knives,
300 pounds of copper plates,
150 pounds of wire for bracelets,
300 pounds of tobacco,
150 tinderboxes and flintstones,
400 pounds of bar iron and
150 mirrors.

Oh, the wondrous abysm of lists!

The Caffres take the gifts, but want no truck with peace. That is when Maynier receives instructions to drive them from the Colony. He assembles a commando of eighty Christians and thirty-seven

Hottentots. Ferreira's Lange Cloof commando joins us. I read Ferreira's letter to the commissioner in which before his departure he begs for a few items for the advancement of bloodletting:

1 000 pounds of lead,

2 000 pieces of flintstone,

hand grenades and

any available field guns.

Believe me, no hand grenades or field guns came our way.

When Bezuidenhout and I arrive at the drostdy, a bunch of men are already standing around in front of the buildings smoking and muttering. Maynier comes walking out onto the stoep. His face and neck are red and full of freckles. He has no chin. His clothes are all show. The shirt with the frills, the breeches, the stockings of silk. The suit was tailored for him in the Cape and belongs in the Cape and won't last a day on horseback by the banks of the Fish.

There's no place for a prick in those pants, says Bezuidenhout.

Why should there be?

A man in front of us looks around and clears his throat at our comments on the local authority. Bezuidenhout slaps the pestilential prattler on the back of the head when he turns back. Maynier greets us and reads administrative arrangements from a piece of paper. He asks Redcaptain van Jaarsveld to lead the commando as commandant. Van Jaarsveld tousles his greasy hair and the hair stands up straight and stays like that. He thanks Maynier for the honour and lists his excuses for having to decline:

His horses are not up to the journey and

his wife is ill and

he has too few labourers to keep his farm going.

The men around me snigger at the stylish Van Jaarsveld's discomfiture. Maynier minces hither and thither and his dandified collar darkens with sweat. He asks Captain Burgers with the ears to lead the commando and Burgers too declines:

He doesn't have any horses and

he is scared the Bushmen may plunder his farm when he turns his back.

Maynier shakes his head and giggles in disbelief. He offers the command of the commando to all the officers who turned up. Every single one declines this dubious honour. Where Maynier's chin should have been his face starts trembling. He castigates the officers for their dereliction of duty and all of them persist in their respective lists of excuses. Maynier proposes that he himself should lead the commando. All the burghers agree unanimously. Later in the inn we laugh at the silly pantywaist who wants to muck in among the bushes and the Caffres in his embroidered waistcoat. We'll all ride along, just to see what the little bantam cock does the first time a wild Caffre or a lion charges him.

I send a Hottentot to One-hand Botha with a letter to Maria telling her they needn't keep food hot for me. While taking apart my gun, I consider what I'll do to One-hand if Maria or Nombini doesn't say no to him loudly and clearly and firmly enough. Because believe me, he's going to try it on with them, I know it, because I would have. I oil each part separately and when I remember the Bushman we met on our way here, I cut another notch in the butt with the older notches keeping tally.

On Glider I'd easily be able to travel from Graaffe Rijnet to the heart of the Zuurveld in three or four days. Maynier's commando with the wagons full of provisions and munitions travels mighty slowly. Besides, we have to stop every now and again to fend off Heathens. We don't encounter many of them. Chaka and Langa – damned Langa – left only a scattering of their men and a few head of cattle on this side of the Fish. This little lot keep track of the commandos and then send their Hottentots through the river to go and report to the chiefs.

Maynier does not ride out in front of the commando as is usual for leaders, but gets the farmers who know the veldt and the bush to lead the way. He trots in the middle, shielded by the big men around him, on a huge bay that he can't mount unaided. Every morning a Hottentot has to help him onto the horse. We jest among ourselves – but loudly enough for him to hear – that he should rather saddle one of his coiffured dogs. The nights are cold. Maynier wants to keep the fires small, as if all of the Zuurveld and Caffreland didn't already know of us. At night I lie wrapped in two karosses and listen to the night. All that I hear are the hyenas and jackals and owls and the farmers around me who have been away from home too long and are too cold and then lie too close to each other and then the grunting. One night late Bezuidenhout slides in behind me and mumbles things I cannot hear. His beard is warm in my neck. He moves closer and in under my karosses and I let him have his way. He growls as he rams himself into me. Then it's my turn and then I'm no longer so cold. I drift off for a while before we're in the saddle again with the break of day and make raucous jokes about all that is tit and arse and cunt.

In the course of the next few days we don't shoot many Caffres, but we do manage to plunder over two thousand cattle. Maynier looks both satisfied and terrified. He hasn't fired a shot, has hardly issued an order and mostly just looked on in confusion while the Christians were doing what they've been doing since childhood. Then, one morning after shaving and putting on his outfit, which is already showing signs of wear and tear, he orders the commando to cross the Fish. Ferreira and other burghers whose callused palms mirror the landscape try to dissuade him. Maynier squirms uncomfortably on his horse. His foot slips from the stirrup but he keeps to his resolve. He wants to cross the drift at Trompetterskraal. Ferreira says the Caffres will see us trekking across and then simply drive their cattle over the river. With the whole commando in Caffreland, the Zuurveld will be undefended and the Caffres will be free to invade and lay waste the Colony once again. Maynier asks him if he's clairvoyant and nobody laughs.

I know this land, is all that Ferreira replies.

Maynier pretends not to hear him and talks to the officer next to him. He flicks his horse too hard, the animal takes off in the direction of the drift, almost leaving him behind. Ferreira, small and squat and with a surprisingly loud voice, shouts after Maynier in God's name to leave part of the commando on this side of the Fish to defend the goddam Colony. Maynier manages to rein in his horse, halts and returns to Ferreira. The two men glare at each other. Maynier grinds his teeth audibly, a muscle twitches in his cheek. I burst out laughing. Then some of the others also laugh. Maynier's horse retreats from Ferreira and takes up position in front of the commando. He gives the order for Ferreira and me to be dealt lashes. Nobody moves.

We trek through the drift, over the border into Caffreland. In the bush I spot the red dogs once, but they stay out of the way of the raucous Christians. And behold, as soon as our last horse sets foot on the far bank, the Caffres drive their cattle across the river and over the border into the undefended Zuurveld and go and hide out with their cattle in the undergrowth along the Bushman's River and Sundays River and murder and thieve as far as the other side of the Swartkops River and the remaining farmers in the area are once again in terror of their lives and flee.

∾

The commando spans out. A few burghers set off to shoot game for the griddles. I sit to one side with Botha, Martiens Prinsloo, the two Bezuidenhouts, Campher and Van Rooijen and talk about hunting and women. I tell them the stories I have heard of baboons lazing about fat and contented on the farms where food is easy to plunder and the lions and leopards have long since been shot out. The young males no longer have to fight for survival and don't have far to forage for food. They get bored and pursue antelopes and jump on them and rape them howling on the run and shriek like the four horsemen in the last book of the Bible.

A Gonna Hottentot named Hans turns up in the camp along with a group of peaceable Caffres. He convinces Maynier that they are of Ndlambe's tribe and also want to bugger up the rebels Chaka and Langa. Maynier is overjoyed at the greater numbers and Hans and his Caffres join the ranks of the commando. The farmers smell a rat. Stoffel Botha says he recognises some of the faces; he says *those* mugs he's seen with Chaka and *those* with Langa. He's not happy with the Caffres that appear out of the blue and increase in number every morning and are welcomed into the commando. He tells his Hottentot to watch them at night. The Hottentot comes to report, out of breath and scored by thorns, that these Caffres leave the camp in the evenings and set fire to anthills and dry grass and other fires appear on the horizon and then disappear. He says that Hans' Caffres are never from Ndlambe, they are warning Langa and Chaka. Botha tells us and we tell the commando leaders. Maynier says we need the trackers and they know the territory as we farmers don't know it. He says Hans' Caffres must stay and Hans' Caffres stay. The glares of the farmers leave them in no doubt as to who invited them. Sometimes there's a fight but not much and what's the use. Hans' Caffres trek with the commando until the commando is disbanded.

Three weeks long we yomp around in Caffreland. Up and down and to and fro, the trackers notwithstanding. Maynier spends eight days looking for a drift over the Keiskamma River, but there is nowhere that an ox wagon can cross. We decide to leave the wagons on the west bank of the river. The horsemen wade across the river mouth, deeper into the wilderness. I ride at the back and keep my trap shut and look around me and listen to all the nothing being spouted around me. I stroke Glider's belly under me. How soft animals' bodies are, hardly more than bags of blood, only just held up by hollow bones. See, the man next to me sits blond and upright on his horse and he doesn't even notice that the mosquito is sucking the blood from his neck.

September is already unfurling its blossoms. The pen-pusher has now had enough of an outing and God knows it can't carry on like this. I talk to the commando and once again my oration is mesmerising and persuasive. This time I use short sentences. Exclamations. Slogans and a joke or two. That's all that's necessary. By sunset there are more or less two hundred men standing in front of Maynier's tent. I lift the flap and discover the chinless man inside, busy unlacing something like a corset. His little pallid belly, like something blind and unborn, wobbles over his belt. I say we want to speak to him. Maynier makes his appearance. The audience that he braves is furious and rebellious. A pace or two ahead of the rest I tower up above him insubordinately and grinningly and demand that he surrender command to Laurens de Jager of Swellendam. Maynier refuses and goes back into his tent and closes the flap. Oh, my mind's eye bores through that tent: I can see him sitting on his cot, all night long, how he stares at the flap, how he expects every single moment that it will blow open and that I will stand there with something sharp and deadly.

~

And in the course of the next weeks there are a few skirmishes and a number of stolen cattle are claimed back and I mark my gun till the butt is a criss-cross of notches. Then I sand the butt clean and oil it properly and polish the copper star of the hunting goddess on the cheek side and don't make any more marks on it. Believe me, when you've shot enough people the day comes when you have to stop counting. The commando calls at Ndlambe's kraal. The fat regent promises to round up the rest of the stolen cattle and return them to us. This comes to naught and we trek deeper into Caffreland. In mid-October we attack the Caffres from two sides and shoot a horde of them and catch a few and loot more than seven thousand cattle.

~

Back on the Colony side of the Fish Maynier attempts to cleanse the Zuurveld anew of Caffres. Those who flee across the Fish run up

115

against Ndlambe and he also slaughters among them. He murders Chaka and he captures Langa. Ndlambe offers Langa to Maynier as prisoner. The corseted clerk is disgusted at the suggestion that he accept a human being as a gift and reddens and declines the gesture emphatically. Ndlambe shrugs and Langa, the revered old chief with the sore back who still dreams every night of the soft belly of Nombini which he'll never touch again, soon dies ignominiously in a cage.

~

The commando can by no means drive all of the Caffres out of the Zuurveld. The burghers have horses and guns, but the Caffres have the undergrowth and the kloofs. In November Maynier disbands the commando and negotiates peace with the Heathen captains. The Christians are unhappy with the conditions of peace, but our complaints fall on the Cape wigs that keep ears warm and deaf. Before the Swellendam farmers are back on their farms, the Caffres are fleeing before Ndlambe and the farmers are back again on this side of the border plundering and pillaging and they have less food than ever and there is now no place on this earth that they can call home or hearth. We few farmers staying behind in the Zuurveld shoot at them all over again with the few lead pellets the authorities grudgingly grant us, angrier than ever because we've still not been compensated for our stolen cattle and burnt-out farms. Chungwa succeeds his father Chaka as chief of the Gqunukhwebe and Ngqeno succeeds his father Langa as chief of the Mbalu and both carry on fighting for survival. My band and I carry on whingeing that the Company must dispatch more commandos to go and claim back Christian cattle. As is our wont we threaten to take the law into our own hands, but Maynier is the supplier of lead and powder. And without the ammunition to back them up our threats are as hollow as our gun barrels.

In February 1794 Maynier packs his trunks of newfangled outfits and absconds for the Cape.

5

My dear Maria and Nombini

My dear Nombini and Maria

My dear Maria & Nombini

Geertruy taught me to write. She said the & – what's the thing called? – is another way of writing 'and'. When I see your two names next to each other like that, the 'and' drives the two of you further apart & places you behind each other. The & equalises the one to the left of it and the one to the right of it. The impossible gap between the two & the tying-up of the one to the other.

Sometimes at night I look at the maps in the book that we picked up next to the road. Do you remember our first trek, Maria? The dotted lines of the madman's routes run like the trails of snails, like those gnarled roots of ginger – twisting & knotting they wind their way from fast to slow over mountain & through valley & everywhere is road. Last night my finger tracked a dotted line & lo: a perfect &.

Today I'm puzzling about the difference between the and-and-and of how we move & the is-is-is that everybody wants of us. Everywhere I go they ask my name, they ask: Who are you? You two are an &, & I too am an &. It's a picture of how we live. Where does life lead you except to this place & this place & this place, this brush of the pen, the movement turning upon itself?

I don't know what I want to say. I want to be there with you & I want to be here. This letter is going nowhere.

Tell Windvogel I

I miss you both & the children.

I am your husband & father.

Coenraad de Buys

& looking at it now, even my signed name looks like an &.

I put down the quill, smudge the wet ink with my hand, crumple up the letter and walk out into the searing dryness of the Graaffe Rijnet night.

∼

Note well: The Colony is in hock to a bankrupt and completely corrupt company. The dissolute Company is skulking between the dykes of a country that has long since lost its supremacy at sea and has been waging war against France with Britain since 1793. Or so we hear; all news is half a year old here. It is uncertain who is ruling us. Believe me, in this year 1795 prophets of doom and men of business and deserters are standing on the Cape shore peering at the horizon. They can only guess whose flag will be fluttering from the ship's mast that will be the next to appear above the sea line.

∼

After a year and a half's absence I ride back to my wives and children where they are still living with Jan One-hand's people. One-hand Botha lives on Rautenbach's frontier farm and my Maria and Nombini and their children live with Botha. Squatting with squatters. I ride up to the yard, then I rein in the horse and Glider lifts his hooves all the way up to his chin, the neck arched. In front of the stoep I yank the horse up onto his hind legs, the front hooves frozen in mid-air. A light flick on the flank and Glider neighs majestically, descends to all four feet and tripples up and down in front of the house as if the earth were made of glass. Elizabeth comes running out. She has grown tall, must be about ten by now. Her hair redder than ever, loose about her shoulders. She looks me in the eye, stops, turns on her heel, walks into the house and closes the door. I unsaddle. Nobody comes out. I walk Glider to cool him down. Nobody comes out. I tether the horse to a bray pole next to the house. Jan One-hand comes out.

I sit and talk to One-hand and he gesticulates wildly at the distance with his stump and splutters when he talks. We exchange news and drink brandy. Nombini comes out onto the stoep with coffee and plonks the mugs down and doesn't look at me and goes in again. Inside by the hearth I can hear Maria gabbling with One-hand's wife, Martie. They vie to outdo each other in haranguing Nombini. Windvogel comes to greet me with his head on his chest and his foot scuffling the soil. He mumbles a few commonplaces and saunters off.

One-hand sounds off all sputtering and stuttering about the revolution of the French. He recites what he's heard from the thin man with the heavy accent, one Jan Pieter Woyer, the new doctor in the district, and his shadow, the school teacher Campagne, who's been peddling this new religion for months. One-hand attends all that is a meeting where Woyer or Campagne preach Equality and Fraternity, the Temple of Reason and suchlike dreck. I leave the coffee, sip at the jug full of spirits and gaze over the farm. Coenraad Wilhelm is four and Johannes is two and the brothers are playing in the sand in front of the stoep. I look and look and see nothing of myself in them. One-hand is blathering on about Jacobins and kings and guillotines and wonders whether he can build one himself for Maynier's mis-begotten head. I get to my feet when I hear Maynier's name. In a few days I have to be in Graaffe Rijnet again. The much-esteemed landdrost has summonsed me on the allegation of a Hotnot that I supposedly hit him. Now the mongrel mutt is apparently living in the same house with the losel of a landdrost and scoffs his food and must probably service his wife as well because the Lord knows Maynier couldn't do it. And I, Coenraad de Buys himself, must one of these days brave wind and weather to go and lend ear to the fatted Hotnot's grievances. I smile at One-hand:

> Well there you go. You build your guillotine so long, I'm going to fire up the fellows in town a bit and see what happens. Perhaps we can also chop off a few heads. The devil take equality and fraternity. But liberty sounds like a good idea.

~

Later that afternoon I go and track down Windvogel. We talk and yet
don't talk. What can I tell my friend about what I've been up to, and
what can Windvogel tell me that will keep my attention? In due course
we grease the silence with his brewed beer. We go and round up two
wild asses and see who can race furthest on the creatures before
coming a cropper. Soon we're both lying in the grass and laughing like
a lifetime ago. When the beer evaporates, Windvogel goes all surly
again and disappears from the yard.

The house falls quiet and the crickets take over. Maria wants to
know what I'm doing here.

> I missed you. I'm coming to see how my most beloved wife is
> and my most beloved children.
> And the Caffre woman? Is she your second most beloved
> wife? Or your other most beloved wife?

She does not wait for me to reply.

> And now you want to take off again.
> It's not that I don't want to stay, Maria. The landdrost is
> summonsing me because I chastise my labourers.
> Now why would you call here only now if you know you must
> push off again tomorrow? Where have you been?
> I suppose I can stay another day or two.
> Where have you been, Buys? Your children are growing up
> and they think One-hand is their father.
> You leave that man alone.
> Jissis, Buys, I swear . . .

Nombini comes to stand in the door. She has grown older. Only now
do I see how her dress strains across her stomach.

> Are you pregnant? I ask.

She nods. I leap at her and hit her and she cries. Maria jumps on my
back and hits me and screams. I throw her off and calm down.

> Buys! Shut your women up! One-hand shouts from the
> bedroom.
> Where were you, Buys? Maria asks as she leaves.

I lie on the little cot in the front room until everyone is asleep. Then I go and crawl into bed with Maria where she's lying next to Nombini in the back room. She lets me have my way, lies with her arms close to her body. Nombini is awake and turns to face the wall and doesn't even pretend to be asleep. I spurt into Maria and get up and go and lie in the front room again. I lie on my back and by my sides my fingers clench and curl. Before sunrise I quietly go and wake Elizabeth. I want to lift her onto Glider, but she takes my hands off her and jumps onto the horse herself. We ride a while and go and sit on an anthill and watch the sun rising. I'm not allowed to hold her, but she tells me how Martie is teaching her to read. She tells me what she's learning from the Hottentot children. She doesn't tell me stories, she names the things she's learnt. She counts aloud as far as she can. Four hundred and eighty-two. I say That's far enough. When I drop her at the house, One-hand has left for the veldt and the women are bustling about in the yard outside. I hurriedly eat the leftovers from a bowl by the hearth. Elizabeth asks if she should call her mother to come and say good bye. I ask her how she knows I'm on my way. She goes out by the door and outside the sun catches her hair and for a moment I want to take her with me and never return. She walks up to Maria at the far end of the yard. Maria holds her close. They look in my direction, but I can't hear what they're saying. I tie my belongings to the back of the saddle and snitch a few bullets. Nombini comes strolling into the house and when she catches sight of me she instantly turns on her heel and struts out. I leave One-hand a pile of money on the table and ride to Graaffe Rijnet. Hardly passed the farm's beacon stone when the barking besets me.

Just outside Graaffe Rijnet, across the river, fifty-odd farmers gather who want to get back their land and their cattle and want to get rid of Maynier. Somebody asks if we shouldn't fetch Master Goossens. Hear what he has to say. Why? I ask. What's a damned schoolteacher got to teach us about politics and revolutions and warfare?

Mister Markus doesn't get as worked up about the authorities as we do. He sometimes says things we don't think of, says the windbag.

Prinsloo snorts and says:

The fellow thinks he's better than us. He thinks he's too high and mighty to get angry.

He gets to his feet to make space for the outrage coursing through his whole body:

Last time when we granted him a turn to speak, what did the little cock of the walk say? Don't you remember? He said – and here Prinsloo pitches his voice high like a woman's: We must be sick, brothers, and yet joyful, in need and yet blessed, dying and yet contented, in exile and yet at home, cast down in disgrace and yet cheerful of spirit.

Prinsloo's voice descends to its normal pitch:

I say that miserable moper must bugger off!

I wonder what that pious pedant-prick would have come to preach at us today. But I'm glad he's not here. I don't know the fellow from Adam, but the mere fact that he's in the offing makes me jittery. People who keep their calm in the midst of this godalmighty jiggery-pokery and injustice, they wind me up even further than I am anyway.

On 4 February we sign an accord, the *Te Samenstemming*, a memorandum of the rebels' grievances against Maynier. I utter the right words in the right ears and for the rest I remain silent and smile. My eyes swivel and my fingers tingle against one another. The Triegard brothers and Van Jaarsveld, whose hair is sprouting more luxuriantly and glossily than ever, bear the document to the drostdy. They say they are speaking on behalf of *De Volkstem*, the voice of the nation, and demand a meeting with every single soul who's employed in the service of the authorities. For two days we wait for a reply. The doors and windows of the drostdy remain sealed. It seems to me that everybody here, including the landdrost himself, has lost sight of the fact that quite a few of us are actually here to be arraigned for our methods of disciplining our staff. I'm not going to refresh their memories. The heat is pressing, the people sighing, the cattle dying. Everybody stinks. Martiens Prinsloo and I and a few other farmers with ants in our pants ride up and down along the hills outside the town. To and fro, two days in a row, swearing and cursing all the way. When at last at the appointed time we gather in front of the drostdy, the doors remain shut. Forty or so of us, with our forty horses and our forty guns. A few rebels take up position on the stoep and read out the *Te Samenstemming* as if it were a proclamation by a new landdrost. Maynier comes charging out and asks them what they think they're doing. Immediately he is surrounded by a group of men in a strangulating circle. When the circle opens up, he walks out, pale but flushed, and takes refuge from them on the edge of the stoep and mutters something like And with that I resign. He goes inside again. Hannes Bezuidenhout charges after him and drags him out by his fancy collar. Hannes manhandles Maynier over to the men stationed on the stoep. A few Christians wander around the drostdy to the slave quarters behind the building. Believe me, in no time all hell is let loose: Nowadays, apparently, the Hottentots who wanted to testify against us live in those selfsame slave quarters. Maynier remains standing in a daze looking at the men in front of him. We shout and scream at him and Hannes chivvies the landdrost out in front of him as if dishing him up for the ravenous rebels. Nobody hears the cloth of his jacket and shirt tearing. The men return from the slave quarters with a dozen Hottentots at gunpoint. Hannes lets go of Maynier when he recognises one of the Hottentots.

> You! I know your filthy mug! Now watch what happens to a
> runaway Hotnot!

He grabs the Hottentot and hits him. He turns to Maynier, who is still standing stock-still gazing at this lot.

> And what are you looking at, you prickless scumbag? This is
> not your house any longer. Scat!

He charges onto the stoep and flings the landdrost from his last platform. The dishevelled dandy gets up slowly and dusts himself and makes his way between us with lowered head. It's dead quiet, all you hear is the flapping of his torn silk jacket. As soon as he's passed through the throng, the farmers erupt and clap hands and guffaw and gob and bellow.

I'm one of a small group of Christians staying behind after the show is over. In front of us stand the Hottentots who came to complain of us to Maynier for maltreatment. We take the Hottentots behind the buildings and belabour them with fists and whips and sticks until we've had enough. Meanwhile Hannes is standing to one side regarding the Hottentot who used to work for him. After the rest of us have had our revenge on our labourers, he speaks softly to me and his brother Coenraad. The three of us tie the Hottentot down and fling him over a donkey and ride out of town with him. In the hills, from where you can see the town basking in apparent tranquillity, and see the inhabitants tracing their usual routes like ants as if the Company's rule hadn't just been overthrown, we kick the Hottentot to death and dig a shallow grave and cover him up and level the soil.

The next day the whole town knows that Maynier and his family have left for the Cape from fear for their lives and that he departed with his wagon and his convictions and nothing else. We also kick out the officials who supported Maynier's peace negotiations with the Caffres. I'm one of those who kick hardest. Reports reach the town that a member of the Political Council, one De Wet, a true man of The Law if his name is to be believed, has been sent to visit Graaffe Rijnet and report back to the government. My pals and I sit in front of the drostdy and watch the wagons creaking by. After a few days there are not very many people left in the town. The few who stay, stay indoors. Now and again you see a curtain or a screen briefly lifting and the white of an eye peeping through.

The men occupying the town and dubbing themselves Patriots, we farmers who are now squatting in the drostdy or camping in the town, rouse one another to a raging carousal. The freedom so suddenly dropping into our hands and the terror at what may follow, that of which no man dare speak, drive us to a mighty swilling. For more than a week my friends and I hit and howl and drink and laugh and frequently pass out. Van Jaarsveld and the youngest of the Triegard brothers punch each other to a pulp in the street until neither one can stand up straight any more. With a last blow from Van Jaarsveld Triegard stays down. The Redcaptain squats down astride him and brushes his lovely hair from his face and starts punching afresh until a few Patriots drag him off. Triegard's jaw is broken and he's bitten off the tip of his tongue. He looks for it and picks it up and then collapses again.

When the Patriots sober up, most of them realise that they've signed nothing and have no inkling as to what is actually written in the *Te Samenstemming*. The men drink a little water and lots of coffee and when the headaches have subsided the Patriots collect two hundred and seventy-six signatures on a petition charging Maynier as a tyrant and his wife as a wanton. Believe me, *I*, Coenraad de Buys, and my fellow Caffre-copulating Patriots, accuse the officials of indecencies with Heathens. Etcetera the rebellion.

I stay in and around Graaffe Rijnet, sometimes sleep on the floor of the drostdy, sometimes in the veldt. Now and again I stay over on the farms of friends. The ground is hard. In the mornings it's more of an effort to get up than when I was minding Smut-face Senekal's cattle. I don't go home. I no longer have a home. I have too much of a home. After two months De Wet comes riding into Graaffe Rijnet. His retinue – an officer, a secretary and a penman – pitch their tents in front of the drostdy. Olof Godlieb de Wet looks older than his fifty-six years. He questions the burghers politely and is shocked at the crudity of the bush and veldt and farmers. Rumours abound that there's a government commando on its way to come and murder all the white farmers. I take up position in the street and raise my voice and proclaim:

France stands by all nations that overthrow their rulers! Here on the frontier you can holler what you like. Stories and rumours wipe one another out. The only facts are the bushes and anthills and bullets and blades.

In June word reaches us of another rebellion; in Swellendam there are apparently also Patriots. Then the news of nine British men-of-war that have anchored in the Cape. A month later word reaches us that Swellendam has already surrendered again.

De Wet quarrels with a farmer about his way of dealing with his Hottentot; on the 16th of June we kick him out of town as well. I stop the Patriots who want to tackle old De Wet. But when they get stuck into his retinue, I participate. My knuckles bleed, skulls crack. Everything blurs, it's just me, here, now, and the body in front of me.

On the 6th of July Willem Prinsloo and six other farmers proclaim a Citizen's Government and hoist the revolutionary flag of France. The white and blue remain and the orange turns red and the rebel leaders elect the *Representaten des Volks*, the representatives of the people, on behalf of *De Volkstem*, the voice of the people. They refuse to pay taxes to the Company, and to the devil with its laws! They call their government the National Convention. The Patriots, in a spirit of civic goodwill, suggest that Van der Poel, the new landdrost appointed by De Wet, should also, like Maynier, pack his bags and relocate to the Cape. They appoint Jan Booysen in his stead, and in August a local man, David Gerotz, takes over. He is the landdrost and he is the Head of the National Convention and the people are starting to refer to the Republic of Graaffe Rijnet, even though there is no authority whatsoever in charge. Everybody wants to rule and nobody wants to follow and the whole lot has been bankrupted by the Caffres and the drought. They request that the Reverend Manger should stay on to marry people. He tarries a while; then, one fine day, our Lord's spokesman also vanishes without a trace.

126

On 16 September 1795 the English officially assume command from the goddam VOC and Viscount Macartney becomes the first British governor at the Cape.

~

Exactly a year after the uprising our latest landdrost – who's keeping tally? – turns up at the drostdy: Frans Reinhardt Bresler. The Reverend Manger greets us gawkily. The Cape has smacked him on the wrist and summarily sent him back with Bresler. Despite our threats, seventeen burghers, so help me God, welcome the new landdrost. Gerotz checks the street up and down to see whether my gang is anywhere to be seen, then hastily escorts the landdrost into the drostdy. During the monthly meeting of the National Convention – verily, revolutions end up making bureaucrats of the most hardened rebels! – we summons Bresler to come and explain his presence to us. Bresler sends word that he will speak to us at two o'clock. By that time he's already hoisted the British flag and rung the drostdy bell. He tries to persuade us to take the oath of allegiance to the British. Not a soul stirs. Through the window I see a young man scrambling up the flagpole. His two friends are egging him on from below. He yanks down the flag and they run away with it. Bresler stops talking when the whole crowd jump to their feet and come to stand at the window and laugh and cheer on the young bucks running down the street with the flag. I get up and walk out and nobody stops me.

~

The Graaffe Rijnet summers are long and a man gets thirsty and bored. I and a few familiar faces carry a table and chairs out into the street. We load the tables with the last flagons of brandy and genever and glasses and jugs from the drostdy and start whiling away the long hot afternoon. When Bezuidenhout starts target practising on the house across the street, the owner of the house comes running out and lambasting us. My mates first look him up and down and then apologise for our conduct. We ask him what he has that would be in order for us to shoot at. The man instantly makes for his house, but before he can shut the door, we've crossed the threshold. We rummage in the house, but don't find that many targets. Then we hear the bantams crowing in the back yard.

Half an hour later a row of fowls are dotted across the street, buried up to their necks. We take turns to blast off the little heads with their red combs. The man and his sons stand ready next to the street and as soon as one of the little heads explodes, one of them runs up and reclaims their chicken from the ground to go and cook it so that the loss won't be total.

I take aim. Before I can pull the trigger, a shot cracks over my head. See, the chicken-neck fountain. I turn around and Bresler approaches with a smile and a gun. He is thirty, his wig just as powdered as that of any other pen-pusher, but his eyes have more of a spark.

What does Mijnheer prefer, a thigh or a breast? I ask.

What is one without the other? Bresler asks.

I'm the only one who laughs, the others look at one another, uncertain what the landdrost wants.

I don't want to interrupt your feast, says Bresler.

It's not a feast, it's just what we do. You must visit more often, Bezuidenhout ventures into the conversation and comes to stand next to me.

While he was sleeping off his hangover, someone plaited his beard like a girl's hair with a ribbon at the far end. He left it just like that and has been using it all day as a stalking horse for increasingly dirty jokes.

And what is a pirate doing so far from the sea? Bresler asks. The men gape at him, uncertain whether they're being mocked, praised or swindled. He puts a hand on my shoulder.

Buys, we haven't spoken yet.

Can I pour you something?

Please. This heat . . .

He rubs his red neck. We go and sit at the table while the pirates carry on beheading the chickens.

How can I help?

I'm just coming to shake your hand. Seems to me nobody can administer the law here without your blessing.

I look down at him. He looks up at me, but in a way that doesn't feel like looking up. My height bothers him not at all. I take a swig from the flagon, Bresler swigs as well. I fill two bowls. I drain mine, Bresler his. Bowl for bowl is drained and Bresler doesn't twitch a muscle as the liquor swills down his throat swig after swig.

The goddam law is ruining this country, I say.

I thought you were the law . . . you, the Patriots?

Am I imagining things, or do I see a smile?

The Company was a joke, I say. I could have taken this town on my own. But the English, I hear they're worse than the Bushmen and the Caffres combined. The Company didn't govern any goddam thing, they just kept the books. I hear the English guns in Algoa Bay can blow a man off a flagpole in Graaffe Rijnet.

The fucking English yes. They don't talk, they shoot. That's why I want to come and talk to you.

The what kind of English?

Fucking. Fuck. The only useful word in the English language. It's like a good knife. You can use it for everything.

What does it mean?

It refers to something which you fornicate or mess up.

Is it the English for a *fokkery*? To *fok* animals, to breed them?

The same word yes, but the English take it out of the stable into the house. Into the bedroom, says the landdrost.

The focking English.

Just so, says Bresler.

He takes the bottle and pours us both a shot. He looks up at the yells of the men. Another bantam has bitten the dust.

Buys, he says, while filling two more bowls: I'm told the

Portuguese girls in Mozambique are as pretty as ever and getting prettier all the time.

I look at Bresler and Bresler looks at me.

Aren't you growing stale hanging around here, Buys? Perhaps a year so on the East Coast won't be such a bad thing.

I smile at him. We look at each other. Another two bowls of brandy go down. I load my rifle.

Buys, can I talk straight?

Never thought I'd hear such words from the mouth of a landdrost.

The government wants you gone from the Colony.

Are they telling me or are they asking me?

I'm asking you. *They're* telling.

I take aim and blast the head off the last chicken.

Goddammit, Buys! Van Rooijen bellows.

Bresler doesn't look up from his brandy.

And as soon as the English have got their act together, I'm going to have to *make* you move.

What does it feel like, to sell your soul to the English? The focking English.

It feels as if times have changed.

Times maybe. Not me.

Bresler gets up, drains the bowl and slams it down on the table.

Stay, I say, the bottle is hardly half.

I don't drink, says the landdrost and walks to his office.

❦

Why are you fidgeting so uncomfortably? Of course it never happened. The truth is never like anybody's gaudy fantasies, it's always greyer: Bresler confronted me in the street and said I'd better get out or he was going to have to lock me up – something along those lines. I kept on walking and immediately put the conversation out of my mind.

❦

Doctor Woyer wanders around town in the afternoons and jumps on every soap box in sight and proclaims that a fleet of Dutch and French ships is on its way to the Cape. At the next meeting, on 22 March, the Patriots tell Bresler that we'll negotiate, but on our terms. Bresler sits listening to the conditions and then he starts cleaning his nails. He pours himself some of the genever on the table. While one Patriot is elucidating his insights into the future of Graaffe Rijnet – phantasms distilled from Woyer's revolutionary babblings, drunken ramblings with his friends and his hatred of Caffres – Bresler gets up and walks out. Three days later Bresler and the minister are on their way back to the Cape.

Gert Rautenbach and I and a bunch of obstreperous Patriots think it's nonsense that the Swellendammers caved in so easily before focking Britain. We decide to go and liberate Swellendam on behalf of us and ourselves and nothing comes of this except stirring speeches, an evening's piss-up and a few bruises.

On 14 June I address a meeting of militia officers, heemraden and Landdrost Gerotz. I say that I have travelled to the kraals of the Caffres and appeased the Caffres as far as possible. The meeting thanks me for my trouble and requests me please to continue these negotiations and nobody seems very interested in my methods. They are without munitions and nobody among them would venture in like that among the turbulent Caffres. Around the end of that year a Hottentot turns up at the drostdy who fled from me because I supposedly beat him. The Hottentot reports that I'm not appeasing the Caffres on the Colony side of the Fish, am rather inciting them against the Christians. I was with the Caffres to barter. All I know is that their beer and women were to my taste. How am I supposed to remember everything that I spouted there?

Shortly after Bresler cleared out, the rebels also leave Graaffe Rijnet. The ridged dogs see the settlement is emptying out and start trespassing across the town limits at nightfall in search of carrion and pet lambs. Campagne gets arrested and deported. Woyer in the meantime has gone to Batavia and apparently persuaded the governor-general there that the burghers in Graaffe Rijnet are in need of munitions. He travels back to the Cape with a shipload of supplies. In Delagoa Bay the focking English are lying in wait for his ship. No aid is forthcoming from overseas. The government embargos all supplies and munitions to Graaffe Rijnet. A small military force under Major King prepares to come and subjugate the district. Forty burghers, under whom Van Jaarsveld, no longer feel up to sustaining their own republic without supplies and without outside support. They write a letter to Macartney and request the return of Bresler and the Reverend Manger. The letter reaches the Cape shortly before King's scheduled departure. Around me every last burgher subjects himself to the focking English. Amnesty is granted to all burghers except Woyer. Even old Martiens Prinsloo tells me that day:

It's no use any more resisting like that.

It's no use, no.

I hold my peace, look around me, my fingers snapping faster and faster.

So what are we to do now? I ask him.

Go home, Buys.

You go home.

We laugh. Somewhere a dog barks.

∽

After two years of absence and silence I ride back to my wives and children where they are still staying with Jan One-hand. The saddle chafes through my ragged breeches. When I see the homestead, I dismount in the veldt. I look in the saddlebag for my rusty needle and I darn the breeches for what it's worth. Maria says Elizabeth became a woman last month. I missed that as well. My son Coenraad Wilhelm is darker than Maria and six and almost as big as she. Johannes must be almost five and has ants in his pants. Maria doesn't say much but shows me our new daughter, Maria Magdalena de Buys, fat and brown and yowling and born in my absence. Nombini has moved in with Windvogel. I see the one or the other peeking out of the hut, but neither of them risks coming out. I've been pondering it for two years. I've rehearsed it over and over. The story always ended in the same way. I roam around the farm for two days, then I can no longer put it off. I go and sit in the hut and wait for them to come home. Both of them swear in their own language when they see me. I invite them into their hut. They sit down.

>Good day, Windvogel.

>Master.

>Stop your nonsense.

>Coenraad.

>A man gets lonely, I say. I know. And she's a pretty bitch. I know.

Windvogel looks up. He almost ventures a smile, then looks down again.

>We are friends, Windvogel.

>We are, Coenraad. I'm sorry, Coenraad.

>I also took her from another man. Where's the child?

>Must be playing.

Nombini doesn't stir.

>Bring the little mite. Let me see.

Nombini gets up and Windvogel and I sit gazing out in front of us and after a while she returns with the little half-Caffre.

>Come here, little one.

>We call him Windvogel, says Windvogel. Windvogel the younger.

I hold out my arms. The little boy comes to stand next to me. I touch his arms, feel his legs.

>A strong little guy.

>He's going to be big, Coenraad. Big.

I slap the child playfully on the bum and he runs out and falls and runs on. Windvogel watches his child go. I look at my friend. He is proud. He smiles. Windvogel turns to me and something he sees wipes the smile off his face.

What's the matter, Coenraad?

Run.

Windvogel's eyes instantly brighten again.

You've got fat, old Coenraad, you're not going to catch me again.

Run.

Windvogel nods conspiratorially and grins and jumps up and sprints out of the hut. Nombini watches him go, confused. I get up and stoop out of the hut and load my gun and watch my friend running over the plain. Windvogel turns round in running and laughs and checks whether I'm on his heels yet like so many years ago. Then he sees: This time I'm not running. His laugh is gone. He runs and he cries and he shouts No, no, Master, oh Lord Master, please Master! Swift as the wind, he lives up to his name, the name I gave him, the name he gave his son. Soon he is only a speck in the distance. I take aim and believe me I don't want to shoot. Every muscle in my body screams at me not to shoot. I shoot. The speck drops.

The moon is shining in through the window. I'm lying on top of Nombini. While I'm ramping furiously over her, she utters little whimpers that convince no one. I've forgotten what she smells like. When I thought of her on the lonely nights of commandos and rebellions, I used to think that I remembered her smell, so different to that of any other woman. But now, here with my snout in her neck, my rod rammed into her, she smells like every other little Caffre girl I've lain with in the last few years. She doesn't close her eyes and she doesn't look away. Nobody has ever looked at me like that. I am absolutely alone.

~

Bresler is back in Graaffe Rijnet accompanied by John Barrow, secretary to Governor Macartney. Barrow is a man who burns the midnight oil penning observations on the country and its people in little notebooks that he's never caught without. Yes, I, Omni-Buys, devour even the scribblings of this misbegotten misery. See what the blackguard writes about the English deserter who escaped from the Graaffe Rijnet prison: According to report climbed through the cell's thatched roof. Was locked up for the dirty jokes he told in public. Well, then, you don't say. Barrow proposes that a world power should take better care over the maintenance of its prison roofs.

In March 1797 Bresler summonses me to appear in the drostdy in a few weeks' time. There are complaints that I kill Caffres, abduct their women and assault and detain Hottentots on my farm. I don't show up. Together with one Delport and a counterfeiter I am declared an outlaw. A reward of one hundred rix-dollars is offered for me, living or otherwise.

While we're sitting and smoking on One-hand's stoep one afternoon, he says that Van Rensburg, who hates me with a hatred he normally reserves for Caffres, told Bresler – and Bresler told Macartney – that Chungwa is holding me prisoner. That I am passionately anticipating my hour of liberation in the cage in which I'm held. We have a good laugh. And when Jan then tells me of the rumours that I'm staying among the Caffres and am inciting them against Bresler and Barrow, that I'm going to come and invade Graaffe Rijnet with a horde of Heathens, we laugh once more. But watch closely, this time I'm laughing slightly too loudly. And my eyes are not laughing at all.

～

Note well: If you stand back far enough, or look closely enough, you'll see how the magma erupts bubbling through the crust and suppurates into the open. Fragments of the crust subside to fill in the absence of the molten centre. Thus the inside is transformed into the outside and the outside into the inside and the planet renews itself and destroys it all and everything has to start all over again in all eternity. There is life on the surface during the interstices between ice and fire.

～

According to report Ngqika's men visit Bresler in October 1798. I am told the landdrost asked after me. Apparently said he wouldn't rest until the Colony was rid of that scum Buys. They say the Caffres were suddenly silent and stony-faced. They talked among one another. All that Bresler could make out from the conversation was the name Khula.

Another fine story that makes me laugh up my leather sleeve: In April of that year there is apparently an Irishman who hangs around Graaffe Rijnet like a blue-arse fly. A drunken Irishman who tells all who are prepared to lend an ear that he's a prince and definitely not, as they are later to discover, a deserter. An Irishman who is too loud and can't hold his liquor. Who late at night tells his drinking pals he is on his way across the Fish, to Coenraad de Buys, king of the Caffres.

There are many places to cross the border with a wagon or two and your wives and children, your cattle and your comrades who have also been declared outlaws. See, at one of these crossings there are tracks in the mud: deep tracks of wagons and oxen and horses following one another in parallel lines, and then, barely visible, over these deeply rutted tracks, a swarm of light, shallow dog tracks that proliferate and coagulate and intricate and disperse.

1799 – 1801

1

How much grey matter have I not seen? How many sheep's brains have I not devoured? How many human brains have not lain at my feet in my time? A squelchy heap of fleshy mush with deep ravines that slurps and spatters under my sole and is instantly forgotten. It taught me nothing.

Come and look by all means, peering into my eyes gets you nowhere. They are not the windows to anything. Behind them only the moist darkness undulates. My skull is fully occupied with two grey fists. Come in, sneak past the eyes, enter by the ears, or panga your way through the boscage of the nostrils. Dart through any of the tiny cranial apertures into the interior. Chart and annotate to your heart's content, but don't feel too secure. Here be dragons. Shoot like a seizure through the multitudinous cells. Each more unfathomable than a beehive. On each of them an inscrutable map of my inbred destiny. Name each flickering and fold. Trace each capillary on your map. You have the words, you have your atlas, but you will recover nothing of me here. There are as many pulsating sparks in my brain as stars in the Milky Way. Words can forget about it and mathematics eternally lags behind. As it is in heaven, so it is in here. This anthill swells and swarms so prodigiously that the whole conglomeration starts reflecting upon itself. The Milky Way starts dreaming herself.

My thoughts wander along elephant trails, trodden generation after generation by forebears with longer arms and teeth and pizzles. Your compass chases its own tail. The paths do not lead anywhere, they merely start up and sprout offshoots and turn-offs. You and I get lost in here. We hear the pumping of the artery that will one day rupture.

Carry on tunnelling, through the lobes, burrow through the land-scapes where my tongue finds its words and where my fingers discover their purposes; deeper. It's dark in here. Cast away your map; grope your way along the slippery chilly walls and beware of precipices. Keep going through the raw offal, until you strike the first vertebra. Like the business end of a knobkerrie, the vertebral stem terminates in a sturdy burl. In this knob, things have been stirring since the beginning of time. Regard it well and you'll swear you can see a lithe reptile slithering over the cold grey hills of the forebrain. While you're still staring, the silver sliver slips into the slimy slit. This sly so-and-so hears nothing of what the rest of the brain mutters and grumbles. The lizard knows no metaphysics. A crag lizard has such a knobkerrie in its head, and so do I. So do the dogs who are never far away.

This reptile brain is what drives me. I am at the mercy of the juices in my body and the short circuits in my head. For years a constant sputtering combustion and then smothered in mud. The saps and shocks urge me to mark my territory and defend it. I am what I am. I piss on boundary beacons. I ruffle my fur and curl my lips, baring my teeth. I go courting, clothed in all the colours of the veldt. The prancing parade transports me to violence. Here dwells the germ of cunt-quest and buck-death. Evenings of endlessly squatting by the fire. You'll say that life on the frontier wounds us, that every mortal creature here staggers through life, struck deaf and dumb and always plundering, with the waters of destruction in his wake. I wouldn't know. I am what I am. I don't look back. The slitherer in me learns nothing; it does not utter fine language; it does not adapt. It feeds on the iron in my blood. The devil take table manners – its only need is to yowl and roar. My brain and vertebrae are silted up with the residual ooze of primordial wildernesses.

If you want to see me, you must get out of here. Mount the nearest impulse and ride it out of the brain across the spider's web of nerves. Let go of the fine threads bearing pain and pleasure. Slam yourself into the flesh clinging to the scaffolding of bone clawing at bone. Tear through the network of sinewy muscle. Drift a while with the blood and listen to the soughing organs and the phlegmy smoke-ruckle. Forge to the outside, to the pelt with its cicatrised lacerations. In the books of the Cape they call me white and of French stock, but here on the surface, between the hair and the pores, only the scars stay white. Get off my skin and begone.

$\sim$

You have to stand well clear to see me speeding. Just see how loosely my moleskin trousers fit over the flanks of the bay. I got thin among the Tambookies, miles and miles east of Ngqika and the border and Graaffe Rijnet. It is September 1799. My family I left with the Tambookies; now I'm galloping back to Ngqika. In these last few months Glider has had to carry me great distances.

$\sim$

I don't want to bore you. I'd hardly settled in with Ngqika and his mother, or I got mail. Just before Christmas 1798 a run-to-rags Hottentot hands me a letter where I'm outspanning over the border, in the lee of the frowning Amathole Mountains, at the end of the charted world, on the edge of the Milky Way. The letter says they're going to lock up Adriaan van Jaarsveld and in Graaffe Rijnet the revolution is still smouldering under the red soil. It's Martiens Prinsloo who's writing. He asks me if I'm in the mood to fock up the English good and proper. While Maria is still gabbling with the Hottentot,

I'm already in the saddle.

~

Just see me racing, back to the kraal of my sort-of-son Ngqika, my shoulders churning, old Glider's hooves floating as if the earth had relinquished them. My dogs, my extended shadow, as always behind and next to and in front of me. The new leader's ridge rises high and his ears lie back and he is pure speed and his bark is as nothing to his bite.

~

At the end of last year I raced just like this, that time *away* from the kraal, back to the Colony. Believe me, Caffraria was oozing milk and honey and I had just contracted marriage with Ngqika's mother. Yese, my gigantic bestial wife, Yese with an appetite that obliged me on those mornings after I'd been with her to mount my horse wearily and all too warily. Maria and Nombini were not charmed with my marriage. When I'm at home, the two are at each other's throats, except if they're both clambering on my neck. With Yese my yard is manhandled as no Christian's has ever been. Not that I'm complaining, but the Lord knows there's not much to do among the Caffres. Beer and meat are brought out all day long and a man needn't hunt any more than he's inclined to. Except if you feel the urge to hunt, because hunting is hunting. I must sit in front of my house smoking my pipe and looking impressive because the king's mother is now my wife and she milks me morning and night. They say she's a witch and her darling son dare not piss before she's nodded her double chin in consent. Then Martiens' letter arrived. So how does a creature like me refuse the opportunity to go and light a firebrand once again under the communal fundament of Graaffe Rijnet?

~

Now you have to get out of the way. My horse and I are hardly a speck on the horizon. At times you should be able to make out the colour of my eyes – light grey – but this is not a good time. I'm in a hurry.

~

With all of January's sweat in my shirt, I join the rebels on Prinsloo's farm. Everybody is jabbering at the same time. In between the bragging and the foreign French revolutionary slogans I get a grip on what's happening. Martiens is hoping to assemble a big commando to claim back cattle from the Caffres this side of the Fish. Same old story. He wants to sort them out once and for all and for that he needs a whole stash of guns and a bevy of belligerent farmers. He knew that Adriaan van Jaarsveld was in trouble with the Cape because of some forgery story or other and that nothing could make a horde of farmers hang together like when the English make out one of their number for a rotten swindler. Six farmers recruit twenty others who want to cause shit and this gang bullies and blusters a whole lot of others into joining up.

So then they tell me how Van Jaarsveld was arrested and manacled and was on his way to the Cape with Secretary Oertel and a few soldiers for the trial, when four days later Prinsloo and a few of the men present here today overpowered the soldiers along the way and gave them a good hiding and freed Attie. So now the heroes of the revolution are lazing around picking their noses and calling it having a meeting. As per usual I am the one who has to come up with the plans. I tell the band of mute mules what we need to do with this gang of focking English in the Cape and Graaffe Rijnet. Prinsloo and I write a few letters requesting the burghers in a firm yet friendly fashion to get their backsides to the drostdy on 12 February. We assemble two days before the event at Jan Bosch's place to ascertain exactly how many 'we' are. The meeting soon falls into disarray and fists are flying. I might just have overplayed my hand slightly when I proposed that, given that I was the Caffre king's new stepfather, we burghers should combine with the Caffres to take Graaffe Rijnet and drive the English back into the sea. That anybody barring our way should be summarily shot to smithereens and their cattle be divided among the Caffres in recognition of their trouble. Well, yes, the brothers in arms were not exactly taken with this proposal.

∿

I'm not far from Ngqika now. Over there, in front of me, lies the Keiskamma. When I pull up to give Glider a breather, you may just think it's an opportune time to sidle closer. Don't. As soon as you can smell my breath – meat and charcoal, tobacco, perhaps sweet potatoes – you must know you're too close. I'll saddle my horse and rush away and you'll end up under the stallion's hooves. In any case. In the end that revolution of Attie and Martiens' was no more than a goddam letter-writing exercise.

∿

The farmers of the Sneeuberg were grumbling that they had enough problems with the wild Bushmen, and that the English and the Caffres were none of their concern. So a few shitwits like Hendrik van Rensburg and Thomas Dreyer started thinking that we were getting too rough and tried to calm the lot down. I swear it was one of them who went tattling to Landdrost Bresler.

We postpone the whole business to 17 February, by which time we hoped that the Zwagershoek farmers would have joined us. As if things had not got too heavy to handle, I went and wrote a letter to the Zwagershoekers telling them they'd better turn up or otherwise they'd be traitors to land and nation and whatever else and I sign the thing as *De Volkstem*. I even got my hands on a letter from Bresler to Van Rensburg insinuating – if you were to read it out to the burghers in a certain way leaving out a sentence here and there – that the landdrost was supplying the Caffres with gunpowder and lead. Then the men started guarding the roads so that Bresler was not accorded any help from outside.

On the 17th we're on Barend Burger's failing farm near the drostdy. Probably about a hundred and eighty steamed-up farmers. I try to persuade the rabble to sign an accord I drew up. Some or other battle plan with a few words like fraternity and equality and suchlike crud kneaded in between the lines. Doesn't matter any more: during the ensuing struggle the thing was torn up anyway. The wretched Reverend Ballot turns up and tries, all nervously and stutteringly, to placate us. We give the fellow a bit of a runaround and then we trap him in the house. I make him write a letter to the landdrost asking that His Worship Bresler should please speak to the governor so that my status as a so-called fugitive and outlaw should be revoked, since our minister can find no evil in me and that in his opinion one day I would make an exemplary burgher of their focking little kingdom. The letter ends up Godknowswhere – probably in the postal Hotnot's little fire on a cold night – and I remain as free as the birds in the Lord's heaven to be shot to pieces by all and sundry.

We get word that soldiers are on their way. We go and round up His Honour Bresler and make him, with a gun to his mug, also write a letter. This one to General Dundas. Bresler writes that order has been restored, that no reinforcements are necessary and that Van Jaarsveld should be pardoned. Then also the following addendum regarding yours truly:

> The Burgher Coenraad de Buys has also appeared in the Village and requested that it may please Your Excellency to repeal the order given by the Earl Macartney to the Landdrost by an Instruction bearing date 14th February, 1798, by which he has been declared an Outlaw, we therefore beg leave to join our request to his that it may please Your Excellency to reinstate him in his former Burgher Freedom, he promising to Conduct himself as becomes a good Burgher and to answer this favour, and we being able to assure Your Excellency that the behaviour of the said Buys has in every respect appeared to us to be more than worthy of this exoneration.

These winged words, too, failed to have any effect whatsoever. Since any beggar with an ounce of lead on his person could at any time blast me to kingdom come and be rewarded for it and this revolution was nothing more than a protracted dictation session with intervals for roast meat, I found my way back to Caffraria.

≈

I notice that you persist in peeking. Be wary of wanting to read too much into the beard's first grizzling, the new wrinkles, or the numbed left thumb and index finger rheumatically feeling each other up. I push Glider till the saltpetre shows yellow in his flanks. See me shooting through the valley that lies simmering green and balmy among the mountains. Waterfalls cascade around me from the Mount of Calves. Here I ride my horse hell for leather to where the Tyume spills into the Keiskamma. See, there lie the huts of the Rharhabe Caffres, over whom my immense bride and I have dominion.

≈

So at Bruyntjeshoogte the rabble run up against the focking government's guns and Prinsloo and a hundred and fifty dust-farters all too readily lay down their arms before Vandeleur's shiny booties. When they are questioned, the scumbags jabber and gabble and spill their wettest dreams about Coenraad Buys who is raising a Caffre army against the English. Must have been affrighted of the general; he was reputed to have dealt one of his own soldiers eight hundred lashes for a bit of light plunder. Caffre armies were at the time the last thing on my mind. I merely wanted to get away from these farmers who sit all day chewing the cud and having endless meetings and then after all the grazing and guzzling don't manage to squeeze out a single seditious turd. They deserve the focking English. Needless to say, the whole lot of losels surrendered or took to their heels without firing a single shot. A few of them, the best of the worst, ended up here in Caffraria by the skin of their backsides.

146

So we learn later that Vandeleur was too shit-scared to come and look for us. He sends the so-called Commandant Hendrik van Rensburg to come and blast us full of holes – that would be me, Bezuidenhout, One-hand Botha, Christoffel Botha, Jan Knoetze, Gert Oosthuizen, Piet Steenberg and Frans Krieger. On top of that the focking government places a thousand rix-dollars on each of our unoffending heads. The bumcrack-boil of a Van Rensburg was according to report looking for a few men stone-stupid enough to come and turf me out here when the Third Caffre War broke out. My rebellious chums and I were clean forgotten, because behold: The border is on fire all over again, some say as far as De Lange Cloof. But at Ngqika's the grass was lush and the fleshpots overflowing.

What does truly itch my arse is what I read some two centuries later in my incarnation as Omni-Buys. About how the whole cursed war was supposedly *also* my doing. Goddammit, at the time I and my brood and Stoffel Botha's crowd were on our way to go and look for the Portuguese on the East Coast and that too was a bugger-up that forced us to outspan for quite a few months with the Tambookies, way off in the bundu, where not even letters or lies about the war reached us. It was among these very Tambookie Caffres with the prettiest daughters – I earmarked one for myself there – and the fattest cattle – I earmarked quite a few for myself – where I had to abandon my wives and children when my high-born stepson let me know that I had to stir my stumps, because there was crap in the land of the Caffres.

∾

And so it is back to Ngqika's Great Place that Glider and I now gallop at breakneck speed. Oh, it's a beautiful place through which we bolt. From fleshy grey elephant grass the blood-red flowers of Caffre trees spike at intervals, and the pale prickles of the lushest thorn trees. The veldt gets greener with every step, a lighter land with brim-full streams flowing from the thickly wooded mountains. I curse my horse past the blesbok and blue duiker and this morning a leopard disembowelling a monkey.

147

The Great Place extends over a green hill with a long slope gradually descending to a stream. Clusters of huts and cattle kraals and in between the fine web of footpaths. Between the homes there are no trees, the soil is trodden solid. In the centre a reed hut larger than the others, the king's hut, and on either side of that the huts of his wives, in deferential rows to left and right. In front of the larger hut is an open plot of ground where the king and his advisers meet and where he holds court. And it is here, a stone's throw from the kraal, where I rein Glider in and from where my stallion slowly trots through the people with hooves gracefully lifted and firmly and dignifiedly set down. I leap from the horse and ignore the crowd and walk straight to where I can see Ngqika sitting with two sunburnt palefaces in comical Sunday suits. The king of the Caffres gets up from the anthill and approaches with a flash of white teeth.

If you'd lost sight of me for a while, this must be where you catch up with me. Here, on the 20th of September 1799, with the rolling hills like the haunches of hogs for ever and beyond. As in all times, everywhere the droning of parrots and tree dassies and loeries and baboons. It is here where you now see me embracing the king, this son of mine, almost as tall as I. You'll try to read my face, but remember: What you take for emotion is just the contraction of muscles.

∾

Ngqika is young and strong and comely. He wears a long garment of leopard skin. On his head is a diadem of copper and another of bead-work. His cheeks and lips are painted with red clay and in his hand is an iron knobkerrie. The king takes his seat again on the anthill, the knobkerrie across his knees. I stand next to him and his captains come and sit around us. Behind us the king's wives, further back a hundred or so of his people.

Whatever was happening here before my arrival has upset everybody. The Sunday suits gawk at the Heathens surrounding them and then they gawk at me. One of them is tall and thin and tattered with an almighty forehead and the other is short and sweaty with fat fingers. Ngqika whispers that they are here because a god spoke to them. He wanted me here before he spoke his mind to these sorcerers. I praise him for his circumspection. The king puts out his hand and shakes the hands of the Sunday suits as I taught him. He asks the missionaries, through my mouth, for whom the tobacco box full of buttons is intended. The older missionary, evidently of the two the senior emissary of the Lord, replies that it's the king's own tobacco box. They are returning it to him in token of the fact that they are indeed the men to whom he sent it when they requested permission to step onto his land. They did not want to return it empty. He speaks in dour pure High Dutch. Ngqika thanks the men in Xhosa and I thank them in the expanding and contracting Dutch of these parts. The king says he is overjoyed to note that the government realises that he's the greatest leader beyond the Fish, since they're sending their sorcerers exclusively to him. Furthermore he'd like to know what their intentions are and what they want from him. I translate the second half of his speech. The missionary replies that it is their intention to instruct the king and his people in matters that will render them blessed in this life and also after death; that they are merely asking his permission to settle in his land, and expecting his friendship and protection, as well as the liberty to return to their own land when they should want to do so. As who would not. I convey the essentials to Ngqika.

While the missionary is talking, I scrutinise the fellow. A scrawny old man, probably in his sixties, solidly built, with a slight stoop, a delicate skin scorched red, the enormous forehead peeling, no hat or socks in sight. Balding, with long brown hair in his neck, a dusty black suit, the shirt and shoes in tatters. His face is long and finely honed, sharp nose with a network of bloody capillaries, small eyes, set wide apart under high dense eyebrows. A delicate sensitivity, as of somebody from a liberal-minded world, a world that can exist only as a corollary of war and imperium. A mildness that can flourish only in a sheltered life. Above the dark rings his eyes are watery. In them I read an instant and instinctive trust, something that you rarely see in those who carve out an existence threshing and thrashing on this soil. But the way this wretch carries his body testifies only to a struggle, something that claws and bites, that gnaws at him if he doesn't feed it. The missionary bows deep and extends his long-fingered hand.

> Doctor Johannes Theodorus van der Kemp. The title was gained in the study of medicine, but I am here to gain souls, he laughs.

I don't laugh. He gradually unbends himself from his ludicrous obeisance:

> I assume you are Mijnheer Buys and I hope you understand that the Lord has sent me to proclaim the gospel to these people, as soon as I have mastered their language.

I speak to Ngqika and Ngqika talks to me and I tell this Van der Kemp that the gospel must indeed be proclaimed to each and every one of God's creatures, but that they have arrived at a sorely inconvenient time. That the whole country is on fire, but that Ngqika, the true king of all the Xhosas, who desires nothing but peace and calm, is not in any way embroiled in the hostilities between the British and some of the Caffres.

Ngqika says the missionaries can't settle with him. He says he can't protect them, just as he can't protect his own people against his enemies. Kemp says there are only two of them and under the aegis of no flag; they will look after themselves. He says that there is nothing to be done about the disasters of war, other than to endure them in patience. That they are not asking for any other protection than what the king provides the least of his subjects, like, the blighter adds, the protection enjoyed by Mijnheer de Buys himself.

The king grants permission for them to outspan and pitch their tent. Van der Kemp hands out the rest of the trinkets he brought along to the king, his mother – Yese, oh Yese, you lusty witch, my splendid bride with the big belly and the softest behind and besmeared all over with clay – and his uncle Ndlambe, who nowadays under coercion bows his head to Ngqika. Old Ndlambe is leaner, the muscles are showing again. The royal family inspect the presents minutely. Yese drops a length of dress fabric. She summons me, she talks urgently. I grab hold of her hand and drag her away before Christian blood gets spilt. Behind me I hear Kemp and Edmonds – the smaller, younger and quieter missionary – scurry to distribute more buttons and knives and other things left in the wagon, until Ngqika and his uncle vouchsafe a smile. When Yese, somewhat mollified, walks back to her hut, I shoulder my way back through the curious onlookers and speak in Ngqika's ear.

Kemp gives me a letter of introduction from the babbling Reverend Ballot. In the two crumpled pages the minister asks why I didn't reply to his letter, in which apparently he jubilantly proclaimed that he'd arranged a pardon for me. Which god-forgotten letter? My self-professed friend Ballot laments the fact that I had trumpeted my distrust of the authorities so loudly that even Dundas in the Cape had heard of it and had rescinded the reprieve. But not to fret, the preacher writes, he has procured a second pardon for me. The only condition is that I should deliver up the other fugitives. Here, too, the dear Ballot assumes that he knows what I think: Since I would surely not sell out these friends of mine – *friends*, he says – he is sure that all – *all* – that is necessary for their reprieve is that they should write in humility to Dundas and confess their guilt. Go forth, evildoer, miscreant and robber! He concludes his letter by singing the praises of the anointed bearers thereof and asking that I should provide them with all assistance within my power – '*since that I deduced from your converse at Graaffe Rijnet that you hold the service of God in high regard*'. Goddammit. This world is run by letter writers, and all their fancy calligraphy will in the end never suffice to clean up the heaps of ordure it causes. I grasp Kemp by the shoulder:

> Understand me well, churchman. I'm not Graaffe Rijnet's tame Hotnot who's going to interpret your preachings and empty your slops in the morning.

He frowns and steps back.

Late that night the old misbegot will write about me most diplo-matically in his report to the focking London Missionary Society:

> *He said, that he found himself obliged to declare that he could*
> *by no means meddle with our affairs, nor give us any assistance.*

The last peg of the tent, like some great white wild bird in the veldt, has hardly been hammered home or the brethren Kemp and Edmonds receive their first guests. The missionary had better learn Xhosa quickly; I'd rather be digging bulbs with the women than translate Ngqika's profundities day after day. My king stands with a warrior on each side in the small tent and fingers and fiddles with everything. The cots, the crates, the spectacles and tobacco and tin wares, the plumes and ink. The king notices a little mirror by Edmonds' bedside. He whispers in my ear.

> The king says that glass is bigger than the one you gave him, I
> say.

> That is Brother Edmonds' mirror, says Kemp.

> I advise you to forfeit the mirror, Brother Kemp.

Kemp signals to Edmonds, who hands the mirror to Ngqika. The king takes the mirror and hands it to a warrior. Kemp's forehead reddens.

> Tell him he must promise to deliver the smaller mirror to
> Brother Edmonds.

For a moment I stare at him.

> As you wish, I say.

I say something to Ngqika in Xhosa. The king mumbles something in reply, takes a plug of missionary tobacco from the bag on the table.

> The king promises, I say. But I wouldn't remind him if I
> were you.

Note well: This world doesn't grind to a halt when a missionary turns up. In the fields little groups of women labour, between the huts they stack wood for the cooking fires, children run around, and if you look well, you may catch sight of a few men sitting fast asleep in the shade against the walls of huts. The missionaries

unpack, you don't miss much here. Rather go and find a kopje with
a view and watch the sun travelling past. At dusk you'll see the
women returning from the fields, others carrying water from the
stream, children driving cattle to the kraals and fires being lit under
the cooking pots.

~

The next morning Ngqika and I are once again in the tent of the
missionaries. We have coffee with the Sunday suits. At my insistence
Ngqika tries their rusks and immediately demands a recipe. I myself
stuff two into my pocket.

Later that afternoon I'm sitting with a chunk of rusk in my cheek
curing a blesbok hide when Yese turns up at my house. With her is
the Bengali runaway slave who swivels his buttocks like a woman.
He was already installed here in the kraal when my comrades and
I arrived. How he ended up here, heaven only knows. Yese keeps the
slave around, because apart from yours truly he is the only soul here
who speaks Dutch. I don't like the way the greased prick ogles me.
I make him sit down under the tree. I take Yese by the hand and go
into the murky little house.

    Are your people still not back, Buys?
She alone among the Caffres calls me by my name. To her son and
his people I am Khula – The Big One. But not to her.

    I had to charge back to come and hold your son's hand while
    he's talking to the crows of God, I say. I left my people with
    the Tambookies.

    It's good that you are here, she says.
I press her to me and smell the sweat in the folds around her neck.
When I'd just arrived here among the Caffres, she'd dragged me into
her hut and felled me and I'd thought it was a gigantic fat bonanza.
The next evening there was a feast with a plenitude of dancing and
gorging and guzzling and bigger, ever bigger, fires. Believe me, the
crystals of her eyes mirrored the devastation of the flames, their

153

inspired labours and the paradise in the ash. When I woke up the next morning, I was informed that I was married. It remains a sporadic felling and little more.

We grab and grope and kiss and lick and bite and collapse onto the heap of hides that makes up my bed. She lifts me from her and flings me to the ground and says something like I'm not lying for you, in Xhosa. She sits down on me and pulls down my pants and puts me inside her and her fluids instantly plash over my legs. She stuffs a tit into my mouth and she rides me ever faster while I'm instructed to suck ever harder and then to bite and just before I shoot my load she climbs off and straddles me with her shiny thighs and flattens my yard against my stomach with her foot and I spill all over myself and in making her exit she says I must take the Bengali to Kemp, there are things she wants to know from the white sorcerer.

I find Kemp and Edmonds in the wagon carefully covering up the few crates that won't fit into that tent. The Bengali scratches at an insect bite on his stomach.

> Mijnheer van der Kemp, this . . . slave . . . brings you the good wishes of Yese, the mother of the king and my wife in marriage according to the law of the Caffres.

Kemp and Edmonds introduce themselves. The Bengali snot-monkey with the little sly eyes and the smooth skin immediately starts questioning the missionaries. I'm convinced the fellow has dealings with Yese when I'm not around. The whoreson has the nerve to ask whether Kemp was sent by the British. Kemp remains nice and calm and sits back on the riempie chair and runs his fingers through his hair and strokes his majestic brow and says no he was sent by the God of heaven and earth who instructed him to come and proclaim his name under the mighty amaGaika. The slave, with a skimpier beard than Yese, his fright fired up by Kemp's calm, becomes aggressive. He churns on again about the focking English until I pick him up by the scruff of his neck and show him in which direction he must scram. Kemp jumps up and runs into the tent and emerges with a handkerchief and shouts after the young prick. He hands him the handkerchief as a gift to Yese. I apologise for the whippersnapper's arrogance. I help Kemp and Edmonds to move the wagon so that it will deflect the worst of the wind from the tent and then I chop them some wood and whatever I do, all that I see is Yese sprawling and panting under the smooth-skinned bumble-ballsack bouncing on top of her.

I'm still faffing about the missionaries when a few Caffres turn up with a fat cow as a gift from Ngqika and also the smaller mirror, which Edmonds receives with bent head. The little junior missionary is a pleasant soul, but too finely strung for this place. Kemp is a cultivated fellow himself, but underneath all the manners and placidity there is something in him, I don't quite know what – obsession, ferality.

That evening I share their evening repast of sweet potatoes and dried fruit and biltong. As I get ready to leave, two young Caffre maidens turn up giggling at the tent. The younger of the two is Hobe, Ngqika's buxom sister with the perky buttocks. They are bringing the missionaries calabashes full of clabber and junket. The missionaries take the calabashes and blushing and babbling try to get rid of the nymphs as quickly as possible. The girls see it and enjoy it. Later, when it starts raining, they're outside again, keening. They plead with Kemp to let them in. The poor God-elected wretches have to ward them off at the tent flap. Hobe strokes Kemp's claw and complains that her hut is leaking. He gives her a cowhide and then they're gone, only the giggles remain suspended in the stuffy tent.

I ride home, behind me the tent that's being washed away in the rain. Then I change direction and take up position outside Yese's hut and try to figure out if she's alone and turn away. She calls me in and dries me. Her body spreads all over me, her mouth is everywhere. I'm scarcely inside her or I spurt. She churns me up again and I can't stop thinking of what other men have done to her and how they did it and if it hadn't been me outside her tent, would she have invited any passing dangler in and what she would have done differently with him that she doesn't do with me and this time I don't last much longer and she smells of paint and clay and the third time I'm more up to it but roaring in my head resounds the sound of her telling me about how when she was young and a friend of Ndlambe appeared in her hut one night when she woke up and that he tupped her and that she doesn't know why she didn't say no or couldn't say no even though she was of noble birth and her virginity inviolable and even though the merest word from her would have had the man's head on a pole and that she's so ashamed that he could simply take what he took and I ram into her and she looks at me and I close my eyes and all I can think of is how she felt all those years ago when she did not yet have this immense lap and had not borne children and was not yet mother of the goddam nation and free to have come and gone with me – gone so far away – and why it had been so easy for that dog's-dick and she seizes me by the shoulders and I wonder why the hell I had asked so many questions and all that I see is how the young Yese can't say no and doesn't want to say no to him who staggered drunkenly into her hut and just takes what he wants and this time I am sure she also spends her savings and Godknows why it matters to me, but I'm not asking.

In the course of the next few days I'm forever being dragged along to the missionaries. Ngqika just can't get his fill of the new sorcerers. His mood swings between an excited interest in this novelty and an icy regard that intimates that he's looking forward to seeing them skewered on an assegai. Yese is also more and more twitchy. If anybody is to talk to the rain and the spirits *she*'ll be the one. She doesn't trust these pink-roasted preachers. What kind of man keeps on saying no to all the woman-flesh that her son is offering them? she asks. Ngqika feels flattered by the attention of the Christian god and is particularly taken with the strange objects he scavenges from the missionaries'

tent. I, the translator of Caffre distrust and greed and Christian euphoria, must on top of this every now and again stop the other outlaws from blowing the missionaries' brains out. If there's one thing the ex-rebels can't stand it's a preachifying. Then on top of that it's the English, the focking English, who have sent these two pious prophets to convert this lot of Heathens. Their blood is boiling and clearly it's only *more* blood that will cool down theirs. If Kemp converts the Caffres, it niggles at their peace of mind, what then makes our little raggle-taggle of outcast Christians so different from the Heathens?

Ngqika is so chronically with the missionaries that he starts conducting his councils of war at Kemp's tent. The king and his subjects call Kemp Jank'hanna, a hybrid of Johannes and the Xhosa word nyengane – unbreakable rock. Rock-head Kemp who deprecates all earthly delights. Ngqika's captains and Ndlambe sit around discussing Kemp and Edmonds in Xhosa while the two missionaries have to scurry around serving biltong and rusks and the coffee that Ngqika drinks till he becomes as antsy as a naughty child. His captains argue heatedly whether the missionaries are spies and if they are here to bewitch the king with poisoned wine and murder him. Ngqika stands in the tent and teaches Jank'hanna a word or two of Xhosa. Back in the midst of the gathering he's greatly pleased with the missionary's musket and the bag of bullets in his arms.

I go to check that the poor man has another gun. He is affable, but I can see that he sees straight through my smile that hitherto has blinded everybody. He sees that I am the king of Graaffe Rijnet. Believe me, he sees the coldness and the relentlessness at the back of my eyes. I tell him he must resign himself, Ngqika won't decide whether they can stay until he's spoken properly with Ndlambe and Yese and his sister. His sister has been summoned, but she lives far away. I tell him that he should keep it as much of a secret as possible that he's working for the London Missionary Society. I tell him that it's possible that I've turned the Caffres against the English. When Ngqika spoke to an Englishman for the first time, he couldn't understand who these people were or what they wanted or where they'd come from. Later Khula explained it to him like this: Imagine the whole Colony is a farm. Then the Cape is the big kraal, the Great Place of their king. The English have taken over the kraal and are now ruling the whole farm. These focking English are not from around here, they are robbers and plunderers; they are the Bushmen of the sea. Kemp starts laughing and I don't have to apologise overmuch for having slightly complicated his arrival.

I sleep with Yese in her hut in the Great Place. Early the next morning I set out with the inquisitive to go and see Kemp preach. Kemp is overjoyed to see me there and I'm overjoyed to see the titties bounce while the preacher incites the Heathens to a song of praise of which they don't understand a single word. After the singing and praying have subsided, Kemp tells me how Hobe again last night came visiting and was very forward and brought them milk and then didn't want to clear out. He speaks judiciously, his voice precise, his sentences well constructed. He says that he sometimes wishes he could go into a swoon. He is sorry that he can't just vanish at will. I can see him choosing each word meticulously. He says that he would like to give in to his weakness, that he no longer wants to resist the wounds that the world inflicts on him. He speaks of a different affirmation, to assume towards and against everything a denial of courage, a denial of morality. His voice trembles. What am I to do with such an outpouring other than to tell him that I'm convinced that he was sent by God and that his place is here – between Hobe's thighs, I'm tempted to add. The next moment he's talking about his next sermon. I interrupt him and place a hand on his shoulder. My family is far away, I say, but when I have them with me again, I'll bring them along to his church under the tree. And as soon as I've fetched my family, I'll build him a house. Kemp weeps and clasps me to his bosom, and believe me, he washes less frequently than I.

2

Edmonds is puking. The poor fellow doesn't get off the slop bucket.
Top and bottom outlets, and sweating something horrible. Kemp says
that apart from the belly runs and vomiting the man's head is also out
of kilter. Believe me, in my time a Caffre kraal and a frontier farmer's
yard were not always the most hygienic places. A plot of ground can
take only so much piss and shit and bones and rotten meat and then
no more. Sensitive systems like that of Brother Edmonds don't endure
it for long. Even among the most uncouth Christians and the most
robust Caffres spurt-shitting was never a rarity. Besides, the wretched
Edmonds' distressed stomach and soul are hardly accustomed to
fermented milk, clotted Caffre porridge and half-raw meat, roasted
on the coals skin and all.

In between Edmonds' shitting and gnashing of teeth Kemp was
stuck with Ngqika and me the previous night. At some distance from
the tent, so as not to discomfit Edmonds with the smell of roasting
meat, Kemp makes a fire. He's a dab hand with his gridiron and in no
time Ngqika starts licking his lips and asks to be given the gridiron.
Jank'hanna the diplomat wipes the sweat from his brow with a dirty
sleeve and says it's the only roasting utensil he possesses, but the king
must do as the king sees fit. Ngqika replies in equally formal parlance
that he has no desire to deprive Jank'hanna of this precious item.
The king and his retinue stuff themselves and thank their host and
withdraw to their noble huts. I sleep with Kemp and Edmonds and
nobody is surprised when a captain turns up before cock-crow to ask
Kemp for the gridiron.

~

I pour myself some of Kemp's hellishly strong coffee. I sit in front of
the tent and bask myself into a reverie until all of a sudden a shadow
falls upon me. My son the king of the Caffres and his mother the queen
of carnal delight and cruelty are blocking my sun. Yese does not seem

impressed, neither with the puking preacher nor with his barefoot-brother missionary and especially not with me. They are here to receive a few captains from some or other battlefield. Ngqika is losing his campaign, every few months some more of the smaller tribes don't want to recognise his authority. Perhaps he's thinking that he will impress his captains by granting them an audience here before the white sorcerers. The confabulations lose Jank'hanna a mirror and a knife to Siko, Ndlambe's brother, and he also has to weigh in with the roasting, without his gridiron. If all missionaries could serve a roast feast like Kemp, all of Africa would be Christianised by the end of the year. If Ngqika could learn to roast meat like that, he'd rule over a pacific kingdom. Just see Yese's lips shining with beef fat.

Ngqika is all charm and smiles. He teaches Jank'hanna another few Xhosa words. He mistranslates a few words and invents a few. His captains laugh at the missionary when he turns to the fire. I assist the man with the meat, but don't assist him with his newfound vocabulary. The king asks Jank'hanna whether it's God's will that he doesn't wear a hat. Jank'hanna nods and strokes the peeling brow. Yese utters not a word, eats more than any of the warriors. When she excuses herself, she mutters that this white man is no rainmaker. He's just delirious with sunstroke. The look she gives me says I wouldn't dare follow her.

When everybody starts getting drowsy under the trees, Jank'hanna seizes the opportunity to conduct a prayer meeting. The few Hottentots who trekked with him from the Cape sneak up and find seats with the Xhosa captains. He starts with a prayer. When he strikes up a psalm, it's only a few Hottentots who dare sing along under the glares of the Caffres. A cabal of giggles and screams interrupts the awkward lauda-tion. Hobe and her little friends have returned all singing with the calabashes of milk that Ngqika has requisitioned. The maidens dance through among us, their juddering buttocks and songs equally blas-phemous. Jank'hanna's head sinks lower, as if he's talking to something under the ground. He prays furiously. He prays louder when Hobe rubs her shiny little tummy against his even shinier forehead. The captains laugh; he carries on praying till the storm subsides. Ngqika orders Hobe and her friends to be off. Even he has sympathy with this nutcase Kemp; my Heathen king and son restores the weird decorum of Christian praise. Do you see Jank'hanna wiping Hobe's sweat from his forehead? Do you see a crooked finger hovering under his nose before he wipes the hand on his back pocket?

~

That night Kemp confesses his past. He tells me about a carousing career that would shame even the Bezuidenhouts. He tells about brothels and liquors with strange names. He says he was born in 1747, which would make him barely fifty, not the sixty that he looks. The grandson of a minister, son of a professor of theology and from an early age in the shade of a brother sixteen years his senior, also a theologian. Raised in what he calls the aristocratic bourgeoisie, in the princely republic of the Netherlands. In his youth was even a friend of that noble knob of Orange. Studied philosophy at Leiden, but also anatomy, geometry, chemistry, physics, surgery, obstetrics, botany, metaphysics and logic. He learnt sixteen languages, including Hebrew, Arabic and Sanskrit. In his student days he avoided the taverns, but had a string of relationships with girls and married women. Then something erupted in him. He ceased his studies at nineteen, joined the army as a cavalry officer. The women would not leave him alone. He was attractive in his uniform, he says. When he describes the uniform, his hollow chest expands.

> You should have seen me, he says. The sky-blue cloak with the red collar, the gold waistcoat, the first-rate riding boots, the epaulettes, the high fur cap with the magnificent plume.
> Yes, I say, so that all the world can see you approach and blast you to pieces from behind the bushes.
> That is not how a gentleman wages war, Mijnheer Buys.
> Perhaps not, Kemp. But that is how a gentleman cops it in the bush.

161

For a moment he seems lost in thought, then tells me how as a young soldier he almost drowned under a punt and again a few years later almost drowned in the Thames. He checks to make sure that I'm looking at him:

> And for the next sixteen years, Buys, I gorged myself on every blessed godlessness that this world can afford.

In the course of his regular visits to the poorhouse in Leiden the matron introduces him to needy women and he sees to some of their more pressing needs. In The Hague he nails the wife of a hangman. Under the name of Jans he tups one Annie Paardekop, fresh out of prison, and also her friend who'd been locked up in Zeeland as an infanticide. I ask him whether it was one at a time and he says Sometimes; sometimes not. I question him as to how something like that works, who must do what to whom and what must go where, but he turns dour and prefers to enumerate his other excesses. Kemp the rake gambles and boozes and brawls and whores and in those days is convinced that Jesus was just another Jew and Mary much less of a virgin than she would have her neighbours believe. After his mother's death he steals a perukier's wife and keeps her in his room in Leiden while he remains in the garrison at The Hague. His father also dies and leaves him a stack of money, on condition that he give up the woman. He refuses and opts instead to impregnate her. She presents them with what he calls an illegitimate miracle, Antje. He drops the woman and keeps Antje. He meets and marries Christina, a wool spinner.

> Christina?

> Christina, yes.

> That was my mother's name.

> Was? My sincere condolences, Mijnheer. Did she pass away recently?

> Hope springs eternal.

He hesitates, then drivels on. Christina was Styntje to him, and his and Styntje's life together was sober and sedate. His marriage to someone from the working classes disgraced him in the eyes of his family and the orange prince. An officer could paddle the lower classes in the dark, but not marry them. His military career was over. He went to Edinburgh to qualify as a medical doctor. He examined the bodies of drowned people to establish exactly how they met their end. At night he wrote a philosophical treatise with the title *Parmenides*, apparently based on the name and reflections of a dead Greek.

His book maintains that there is far greater difference between God and all his mortal creatures than one thinks. There is no being other than God that has anything in common with God.

> I don't know about that, I understand my God. Well, in the first lot of books I get the idea.
>
> Our Heavenly Father is inconceivable, Mijnheer Buys.
>
> I have in common with him an acquaintance with wildernesses, jealousy and especially, Kemp, wrath.

The missionary smiles patronisingly, as if he and the Lord find me entertaining.

> Mijnheer, let us leave this debate for the bright light of the morrow.

Edmonds starts coughing something dreadful in the tent and Kemp goes to succour his brother. A few minutes later he comes and sits down again and continues his narrative. Apparently the VOC wanted to appoint him as major and post him to the Cape to come and share his military prowess with the troops here. He refused the post because he always did and still does abhor the VOC's policies and methods. I pat his hunched-up back.

The missionary falls silent as Edmonds streaks past us to seek out a bush. Kemp never got ill from eating Caffre food. He did not turn tail when Ngqika gave him such a chilly reception. He seeks inspiration and disquiet, every drop of excitement is squeezed from life. Every blessed impulse is seized upon and driven to its extreme – that one can read in the glittering eyes, sunk deep in the haggard face. He seeks out the wilderness and clothes every frenzy in Biblical language.

Edmonds has had it with the Caffres; they are dirty, their food makes him puke, the land is too untamed. He loves nothing here, because everything here can and wants to vanquish him. Kemp the scarecrow is untouchable. For the most part he wears the jacket without a shirt, his feet and head are raw. The more this god-cursed place mucks him around, the more ecstatic it leaves him. He carries on about his shame about his past, but just listen to him holding forth about his days in the dark back alleys of Leiden and The Hague. Listen to the nostalgia driving the self-chastisement, the longing for every whorish cunt, every dram and every punch, every kiss that was a love everlasting while the tongues could carry on their combat. This land isn't going to get the better of him. His head is indeed like stone, every thorn in his flesh or in his sockless foot is self-inflicted. If the food makes him ill, it's a test of his mettle that he does not dare fail. Every young woman who brushes up against him is a penance that he has to endure. He can't get enough. It's a thirsty land with thirsty people and this Christian is the thirstiest of them all. He is fifty-two years old and older than most people on their dying day. Life is what ages you, not the years. Driven by a divine dementia, he seeks to drink Africa dry. Johannes Kemp is like his namesake the Baptist at home in the wilderness. He will eat locusts and clothe himself in hides as long as the world keeps him enraptured. He feels no pain. Even the godforsaken Bushmen wear sandals. Do you know how hot the rocks sizzle here in summer? Do you know the thorns of this land? I see the smirk on your face at the Christians and their bedtime stories. You're wondering how I, the savage Coenraad de Buys – the bigamist and murderer and thief and you name it – believe in our Lord and Father when there is only flesh and dust to be seen. And now I'm asking you: Do you know the divine delirium, the glorious frenzy that drives people like Kemp into the wilderness and will one day let him die drained and satiated and with a magnificent smile on his staved-in face?

Kemp falls silent again. I niggle a morsel of dirt out of my ear. He says his grief led him away from medicine and back to theology and cosmology and on to a rebirth and a calling to minister to Caffre souls. I ask him what grief. I can hardly hear him when tells how, on the afternoon of 27 June 1791, he and his Styntje and his Antje went out in a rowing boat on the Meuse close to their home. A sudden and violent wind capsized the boat and his wife and child drowned in front of his eyes. He says he was too scared to rescue them. He says his fingers would not let go of the boat. We do as men do and we keep our traps shut and hold fast to the moment and gaze into the fire.

~

At daybreak I leave the missionaries at their tent. Edmonds' stomach has calmed down. The little chap looks a bit lighter and more contented, as if he'd had to vomit out his last little bit of baby fat to adapt here. He's no longer sweating and is no longer delirious and is his old timid self. His tiny fingers are still fat. I leave the missionaries to their own devices in the hope that Kemp will nail Hobe and get it out of his system and I tell him this.

> My dear Buys, did you hear nothing of what I told you last
> night?

I smile my smile, the one that says I know things he doesn't know, and saddle my horse.

> Jank'hanna! I shout at him as I ride off. Indulge your guilt on
> top of that little thing! I wish you all the guilt you're capable of!

~

On the 3rd of October Ngqika marries for the third time. He can still not decide whether the godbodies may stay or must return to the sea whence they came. I've been trying for the last week to wring an answer out of him, but don't get a chance to talk to my son. I ask Siko to talk to our king. I hear nothing. I look in on Kemp on the wedding day; have they heard anything yet? Apparently Ngqika was there the day before, looked around again but took nothing, offered a milk cow for a few buttons and two old handkerchiefs. Kemp's faithful Hottentot Bruintjie wants to go back to Graaffe Rijnet; he says things are getting too heated hereabouts. This king has no use for them here; the people are looking at them askance. Edmonds also wants to push off, to Bengal.

>Mijnheer Buys, he says, this soil is not suited to the seed of the word of God.

I ride to the Great Place. Ngqika does not want to see me. I ride back to Kemp and make a fire. Ngqika can go and fart figs! He can get married till the cows shit copper coins, I'm going to celebrate with the missionaries. By dusk Kemp is once again bombarded with the whinges of his Hottentots and of Edmonds. They grumble and gripe to him about the leopards and the Bushmen and the sun. Kemp says the hand of the Lord has thus far protected them from the cunning wiles of Satan. Kemp says the doors that the Almighty unlocks with the key of David, no man dares bolt again. Edmonds moans about the savage Caffres. He says they'll never be at home here. Kemp says they followed him of their own free will.

>When I set foot on this shore, *this* I've told you before, Brother Edmonds, I knew that I was doing so with the death sentence already in me.

Edmonds with his trembling lower lip is on the verge of saying something when a captain appears at the tent opening with Hobe and another young girl. He offers the fillies to the missionaries and invites them to come and partake of the festivities. Edmonds explodes and abuses the Caffre and curses his name as the scheming spawn of vipers and seducers and chases them all away. The missionaries kneel immediately to conceal the bulges in their pants and start praying against the beguilements of the flesh. I wonder how Kemp would deal with such beguilements, on these sultry nights, if brother Edmonds were not sharing a tent with him. I bid them good bye; the two are so engaged with the Lord God that they don't hear me. On horseback I follow the captain with the young girls and accept the offer on behalf of Jank'hanna and load Hobe and her little friend on the saddle in front of me and go make them rejoice greatly by the riverside. I take them with me to the feast and I claim my place by the fire near my son the king. Yese does what she's supposed to do with a singing and a sprinkling of herbs and then disappears again. I go and seek her out in her hut. She says I can lie with her, but no touching. She says she's tired. She says I may hold her. A few years ago she would have joined in the dancing outside. She would have sneaked off into the bushes with me. We would have come back to the fire and laughed with the people and drained a calabash of beer and there would have been no end to us. She says she wonders about her son; she starts talking about her people and their future. I stroke her tummy and can't find the navel. I stroke lower till I come across a frizzle. She slaps my hand away. She snores.

The fires are still burning bright; Ngqika has gone to initiate his bride. I summon the soberest captain and tell him to go and tell the king that if he wants to treat me – his interpreter and adviser and husband of his mother – with so little of the respect due from a son to his father, then I'm getting out. Then I'm going back to the Tambookies and I'm taking his white sorcerer with me.

Beyond the flames the two young girls of earlier are dancing. In a haze of beer and meat I shepherd them out of the kraal. See me thrusting myself into the second one, even though everything I had to offer has already been spilt on Hobe's tummy where the little muscles dimple and flex. Did you see her roar with laughter when my seed spurted over her navel? I carry on ramming into the second one until she's weeping. I am the king here.

~

When the sun rises over the 5th of October I am with great display and blaring of trumpets inspanning my oxen so that every Caffre in Caffraria will know that Coenraad Buys, the great Khula, is not to be treated like a dog by any little whippersnapper. The next-to-last ox is still waiting for his yoke when Ngqika and his advisers are next to the wagon. The king demands to know what this inspanning is all about.

> You have said, oh king, that I am your father. But that is not
> how a son behaves. You have asked me for the hand of my
> daughter when she comes of age, and I have consented. I
> am your father and future father-in-law. I am nobody's
> goddam subject.

The chappie is all of a sudden ten years old again and inspects his feet and is full of apologies. I seize the opportunity and rip into him. Why does he distrust Jank'hanna? Why does he spit on the man's loving-kindness? The king mutters that the wedding occupied him. All the ceremonies, the arrangements, the preparations. I chase him back to Kemp. The advisers stay out of my way. On the way to the Christian tent one of the elders tries to warn me. Ngqika is cruel when he punishes, his people fear his temper and would rather eat his shit. They damnwell don't know the wrath of Coenraad de Buys. The king seats himself majestically before Kemp and delivers a long-winded address that I translate verbatim into my best Dutch. He gives the missionaries leave to choose a stretch of veldt on the other side of the Keiskamma and to occupy it. He swears that he will never insult or harm Jank'hanna. He takes copious leave and promises Jank'hanna three oxen.

The king and his retinue have hardly disappeared behind the nearest bushes when the missionaries start packing up. The next morning we find that five of Kemp's oxen are missing. Not all the Caffres are delighted with Jank'hanna's moving in. I go and look for the oxen, find them in a small kraal and go and lambast Ngqika about these transgressions. He orders the chancers to hand back the oxen. It rains and thunders without cease. I drive the oxen in Kemp's wake and catch up with them on the other side of the Keiskamma and the Debe. On 16 October, that accursed day, a few Caffres on horseback charge towards us and one jumps off and runs to me and tells me that my house and wagon with the Tambookies have been torched and that one of my Hottentots' horses was lying dead there and that my wives and children were missing and clears out before I can bash his skull in.

You cry to impress others. Every tear screams: Look what you've done to me. If you cry when you're on your own, then you cry to prove to yourself that your sorrow is not an illusion. With your tears you tell yourself a story of sorrow. With your crying you start to make yourself at home in your sorrow. I think of Maria and Nombini and immediately of Yese. I think of Elizabeth and how I will never give her to Ngqika. I see Maria in our hut on Brakkerivier. I wonder if Nombini lies as still under whoever now lays hands on her at night. I don't cry.

Two days later Stoffel Botha comes charging up on a dog-tired horse and shouts at us from a distance. He's raced from the Tambookies to come and tell me that Maria and Nombini and the offspring are alive. The Tambookie captain rescued them. I ask Kemp to pray with me. I howl so that the dogs start howling in response. I weep until Kemp, too, is moved to tears. When he consoles me, I believe myself.

The rain and thunder don't stop. Botha and I and the Hottentot Henry and Thomas Bentley the English deserter ride ahead to make sure that Kemp's ramshackle wagon follows the easiest and safest route in between the eleven smaller kraals, through the territory that slowly and relentlessly rises, this grassland bordered with forests. At five o'clock on the afternoon of 20 October the wagon draws up in front of my house. Kemp is quite taken with what he calls my oblong hut. He tells of the hyenas that at night sounded like the pleading of women and children and the laughter of men. He says one of the beasts two nights ago ripped apart one of the thongs on their wagon and ran off with a jukskei.

The next morning lightning strikes all around us. We stay inside with Kemp who leads devotions in my house. I give him to understand that it's a novelty – as long as he believes he's saving a soul, the old chap is happy. After a day or so the weather clears somewhat. Kemp and I reconnoitre the piece of land and he chooses a spot where he wants his house to be. By afternoon I find him turfing out grass to establish a vegetable garden. I go and look for something to shoot for supper and leave Kemp among the tussocks he's digging up, where every so often he leans on his spade and gazes out over the green fields and icy Mgqakhwebe River at the foot of the hill, the giant trees in the mighty mountains. I leave him where he's singing psalms about harts panting after water brooks and whatever. When I dismount from Glider to stalk a buck, my hands are clamped around the reins, frozen in cramp. My horse is still faithful, but in my body already the first betrayal.

~

The warm arum lily leaves tickle my hands. See, the once slender fingers are now claws criss-crossed with lesions.

When I woke up this morning under Yese, my front paws were crumpled up like dead spiders. She stroked them, picked them up and held them to her breast.

We are growing old, Buys.

I wanted to get away from the pity. She got up and left the hut. Perhaps she could see I'm not yet poor enough for alms. My beloved witch, if *you* start pitying me, it's all over.

I stretch out on the oxhide, try to open and close my hands, and drop off to sleep again. I wake up with my hands in a bowl of warm water. The bowl is full of arum lily leaves. She washes my hands carefully. She has never yet felt so soft. Here on her knees, with my hands in her lap, she's never been so submissive. See, there's nothing the matter with my loins. She smiles when she sees my yard tensing up in my pants, strokes over it. Yese folds the claws across my breast and drapes arum lily leaves over them.

Keep still, she says.

I don't move. She boils an arum lily's rootstock in the bowl, mashes the thing fine and pours honey over it.

Eat, she says.

The stuff is poisonous, I say.

The poison has been boiled out. Eat.

I eat.

Chew the root and spit it out when you no longer taste anything. Chew until your hands relax.

Where do you learn all these things?

I know old men.

People say that when Mlawu, Ngqika's father, went to fetch Yese from the Tambookies as a young woman, she appeared to him in a cloud of mist on a mountaintop. You know as well as I that she screwed the old dunderhead so silly that he couldn't see straight. People say that she paid lobola for her next husband and that they called him her wife.

I like arum lilies. When the water dries up, they die back to nothing and when the rains return, they erupt again from the rootstock. For months they can lie slumbering underground and then one day there they are once again. If you don't dig up the stubborn roots, you'll never get rid of them. People think themselves different from plants, because they don't look for long enough. Life is a series of eruptions. Like these flowers that get eaten by the pigs, I, too, come and go, I, too, lie in wait, I, too, erupt. Even here in the first heat of summer, in the late morning, lazy in the hut of my queen with my useless hands, my bud is un-nippable. She laughs at me where I'm lying with my pulsating frustration and my hands chastely on my chest under the pigfeed. She unlaces my breeches. My mouth crammed with leaves all chompingly adjusts to the rhythm of her hand's pumping. Soon it is as if I'm watching myself, the outsized farmer and the outsized Caffre queen.

I, Omni-Buys, have read all the writings concerning me. I know the world thinks Yese and I lusted after power and shared also the other lusts. We were reputedly as ruttish for each other as for the power that we shared here with Ngqika. You might not say it now, when you see me heave up my hips to bump against her hand, but it was something much less and much sadder that drew us to each other for that while.

On this morning in her hut we are both around forty, veterans of the flesh. My blond hair is going grey and straw-like, my hands are scrunching up. Her body expands as her power over the Rharhabe shrinks. When we're together, we do not age; here there are no young bodies to mock us with our own dying; here we don't have to promise anything.

~

It's barely light, the sky is open and bleak. The two Bothas and I and Faber and Steenberg and Krieger and of course Bezuidenhout ride out with a group of Caffre hunters. A bevy of Caffre women wave at us as we ride out of the Great Place. Ngqika wants me to show his warriors how Christians hunt. We do his bidding. We are more dependent by the day on the king's good graces. The crowd from Graaffe Rijnet are guests here and I, too, nowadays feel more like a guest than like the father of the king. After I left Yese, I sat for a long time last night with my musket, oiling it thoroughly, making sure that the gun didn't malfunction like my hands. Our horses and our guns are the only things that the Caffres value about us. I've told Ngqika on occasion that one armed horseman is worth at least one hundred warriors. If I want to stay here on my own terms, I can't afford to prove myself wrong today.

The veldt is dry, the sun filling the whole of the white sky. My dogs are nowhere to be seen. I shoot a kudu that slumps down more than a hundred paces away. The Caffres seem impressed. Glider remains calm after the shot and that surprises them even more. I ride out in front of the group, the horse's hooves lifted in a practised trot that few onlookers have witnessed. Tonight they're going to tell their wives about this. We stop for lunch under a few thorn trees, drink water and whey. The Christians gnaw at strips of biltong. When we first arrived here, we would all have eaten together, but with minds more troubled by the day, the two groups sit apart looking at each other, the jaws chomping.

When the sun shifts past the midday line, we move on over the plain. Botha and Faber each shoot a springbok and the Caffres pot three themselves. As soon as the hunt gets under way, the bunch get more at ease with one another. Every Christian on the frontier is fluent in Xhosa and the Caffres with Ngqika have also picked up a few Dutch words, especially the dirty ones. Do you see the camaraderie among the hunters? A bond beyond smooth talk that is found only among men in the open veldt sharing in the slaughter of animals. We are boys playing in the veldt and we are men caring for our wives and we are gods with the power of life and death over the fish of the sea, and over the fowl of the air, and over every living thing that moveth upon the earth.

In the course of the day we move in a lazy circle, a trajectory not one member of the hunting party has ever followed before. On the return, the sun low behind us, one of the scouts signals to us to stop. He runs back: Over the next ridge is a Bushman camp. The wretches will certainly have spotted us already. They're lying low hoping we'll move on, past them, contented with the carcasses we're carrying with us. Everybody glances around, suddenly tensed up; nobody spots anything in the ridges. Bushmen decide when they want to be seen. Sometimes they're human when they have to make haste, but for the most part they're nothing more than bushes with shallow roots.

The Caffre captain in charge of the hunt doesn't want to let slip such an opportunity. As soon as we get near their camp the Bushmen will show themselves to defend it and their arrows will be powerless against the tanned oxhide shields and the range of the rifles.

If you want to come closer to peer into the burning eyes of Bushmen hunters, you'll be trampled. The deserters and warriors who are now slowly encircling the creatures on this green plain are driven by primordial and complicated stirrings at the back of their heads, and they crave, with a dreadful craving, blood. Believe me, my semblable: Complication and extermination both become more palatable at a distance.

The plan is simple. The party immediately deploys in a long line, the horsemen distributed among the warriors. We surround the ridge behind which the cluster of screens shelters. Without any signal every-one charges at the same time. The first Bushman arrow finds its mark; a Caffre screams next to me. The man is still standing upright, looks down at where the arrow has barely grazed him and knows he is dead on his feet. Faber shoots the Bushman through the chest. Then we've crested the ridge, the shields judder with arrows and ahead of us the camp. The women and children try to escape into the undergrowth, but they are surrounded already. They run and crawl and retreat to the shelters and screens. The men's arrows shower down on us from behind and from the front, with little effect. We murder them one by one with lead bullets and assegais. The circle around the shelters contracts, the cloud of dust thickens. My eyes burn. A young Bushman bumps against me. I get a fright; he gets a fright. He wants to step back, I kick him in the chest. He falls, I step on him, bend down and slit open his throat.

Silence falls. I can see through the dust. The Bushman males are all lying dead around the huts. Those who ran away will keep running. I see something red in the bushes. Are my dogs waiting to scavenge? Among the corpses the hunting party walk looking for fresh sweat. A corpse does not sweat. Here and there an assegai or a hunting knife is pressed into a chest or a throat to make sure that what looks dead remains dead. I wipe my knife clean and replace it in its sheath. Apart from the warrior who was hit by the arrow earlier, nobody else of the hunting party has been injured. He stands staggering in the centre of the camp, his eyes already empty; everybody ignores him. A few women and children, here and there an older Bushman, peek out of the huts and then wish they hadn't.

Now the slaughter commences. Do you see how the women and the elderly are tortured and maimed and murdered? I told you to stand clear. Do you see now? How breasts are sliced off? How genitals are crushed? How sucklings are torn away from their mothers and thrown in a heap among the huts? How straw from the huts is thrown on top of the wriggling and wailing heap and how it's set alight and how the colour and smell of the smoke is like nothing that you or I have seen or smelt and how the slaughter carries on and how my comrades join in, in a trance of unbridled bloodlust? How Steenberg plucks off a child's arm, how a Caffre carries on wielding a knobkerrie at a heap of flesh that has long since ceased being human; how the butchers look around panting, their hands on their knees, and how the killing then is replaced by something far more calculating? Do you see?

The survivors are herded into a huddle, too tired and dazed for further resistance. One by one they are plucked out of the huddle, thrown down, pinned down and the soles of their feet sliced off. It takes longer than one might think; there is more scream left in these people than you can imagine. Then they are left there with the corpses and the burning heap of babies, not capable of walking any further, of hunting, capable only of sitting there and dying of hunger.

I suppose I should have warned you: If you want to see me, you must be prepared to see too much. I know what you want to read. I know what to whisper to you, what excites you, because that is what makes *my* breeches bulge. We're not that different. In fact, we become more and more alike. But beware, there'll come a point on this road we're so companionably walking together when it will be too late to turn around.

Not that I want to scare you off. Come, see, believe me, the worst is over. We travel back to our king. Some of the Caffres and Faber and Krieger and Bezuidenhout have strung ears and noses around their necks as mementoes. Behind us the first vultures descend on the Bushman camp. At the Great Place we are given a heroes' welcome and as if at a wedding buck are roasted and great fires are made and as always the young Caffre maidens dancing in the light. We old rebels sit huddled together and drink too fast and laugh too loudly.

∾

I inspan my oxen and saddle my horse and go to fetch my family. The Caffre dogs bark themselves into a frenzy when the pack of feral dogs take up position at the edge of the trees with lolling tongues, ready to follow me. I promise once again to build Kemp a house as soon as I'm back. Kemp immediately drops to those well-worn knees of his to thank God and his heavenly host for my help in guiding him through the perils of the land to this place of rest. He prays that one day there will be a church here that will blazon forth the Gospel to the far ends of Africa. He prays for altars and sacrifices and the light of civilisation and flames reaching up to heaven. He prays that God will have dominion over Africa. I want to tell him Just go and have a look around the corner, there is already a large enough altar of smouldering babies stinking to high heaven. I want to tell him My dogs and I, *we* have dominion here. But I keep my trap shut and go forth.

3

On 14 December 1799 I'm back with Ngqika. Maria drives the one wagon, I the other. Nombini rides on Glider. My children walk or sit on oxen. The wagons judder under the weight of the ivory and hides and the few sawn-off elephant's feet like tree trunks of skin and bone and ripe meat. I'm almost forty and to date I've lost three teeth, but my smile reveals no gaps.

And goddammit! I've hardly lifted my rump off the wagon, when I have to hear that none other than the motherfocking Maynier wants to see me at the Great Place. Go fock your fundament, shitstripper! I thrash the Caffre bringing me the news with my quirt and bellow at the bastard to get out of my sight. I shout that Maynier can lick my wagon-worn butt. The colonial cunt of a cur, nowadays Commissioner Maynier, is now apparently residing at the Great Place as the envoy of Dundas.

The house is still standing, but Maria and Nombini and the children take a while to feel at home again. While they were away with the Tambookies, I cleared away everything of theirs and piled it up in corners. They weren't here. They wander around the house and yard in a daze, searching for their stuff, fingering the furniture and walls, so that they can permeate the place again and make it their own. By evening the children are hard at play again and the women ganging up against me. Elizabeth has in the meantime started calling herself Bettie. Her hair has been cut short, it flares up on her head like a burning bush. She is prettier than ever. She is not meant for Ngqika; when she marries she'll be the one and only wife of the lucky chap who makes it past me.

On the sixteenth Bezuidenhout and Botha and their families come to greet us. We are sitting under the tree in front of my house when Edmonds and my friend Kemp come walking up. They have been to the Great Place to talk to Ngqika and the typhus-hound Maynier. I clasp Kemp to my chest. Bezuidenhout spits in his coffee and

empties the mug next to him. The Man of God tells me how he's
teaching Christian and Caffre kids to read and write, how he's
planting vegetables where his house will arise. He tells me about
Edmonds who wants to clear out; the man has been standing apart
all the time anxiously regarding all the yelling bare-bummed kids.
I can see Kemp wants to talk out of earshot of others. We go and
inspect his vegetable garden.

He's been busy in my absence. With the aid of four or five Caffres
he's dug up a plot of ground overlooking the mountains and the
seedlings are sprouting all over. He shows me the carrots and potatoes
and lettuce. He tells me about the letters Maynier has given him. How
Dundas wants him gone from here for his own safety's sake, that he
should rather go and preach in Graaffe Rijnet and to Chungwa's
Caffres. And see, over there the red and black berries, the gooseberries
and raspberries. He asks me to speak to the king regarding their
departure. Apparently Ngqika refused point blank and was not exactly
well mannered to Maynier. Here lie the calabashes, cucumbers and
pumpkins. When the king heard that Khula refused to see the
arsehole he apparently was all for wiping out the prick there and then.
Evidently Ndlambe and Yese had to sweet-talk to save Maynier's
worthless life. Kemp points the ragged nail of a big toe at where the
peach and apricot trees will flourish.

> Trees don't flourish overnight, Kemp, I say. It looks as if you're
> planning a long stay.
> I go where the Lord seeks me.
> Dundas is not the Lord.

He drops the subject, shows me where the seeds are planted that an
English captain brought from an island called Tahiti. He shows me
the oven he built. I say I'll speak to Ngqika. For Edmonds I don't care
a fig, but I'm not that taken with the fact that my only friend is planning
to leave me here among the Caffres and a few rockspider farmers who
can think no further than their foreskins. For a moment we stand still
looking at each other, then he takes off.

Come, Mijnheer Buys, I must show you! he shouts when he's just about made it to the thorn trees.

When I catch up with him, he's on his knees and scrabbling in the soil. He asks me for my knife and slices open the root that he's dug up. A turbid sap oozes into his hand. He holds up the hand for me to see. When he gets no reaction, he jumps up, stains my shirt with the black muck while shaking my shoulders:

Ink, Mijnheer! Ink!

You have to extend your garden, I say. The stuff can't grow all squashed up together like that.

~

Maria and I are having a barney when, a few days later, a tall thin fellow comes hammering at my door. He introduces himself as Tjaart van der Walt. I trust nobody who calls himself Tjaart. He says he's from Tarka where Dundas pitches his tent these days. He says he's come to take me back to the Colony. He's come with a full pardon. My outlaw days are over, I can move into civilised society once again.

I'm pleased at first and then filled with wrath. I shoulder him away from the door, grab hold of a loaded gun, and when our Tjaart finds the barrel under his nose, he turns tail and takes off across my yard.

What initially inflamed my wrath was my immediate thought that the arse-wipe wanted to lure me back to the Colony only to lock me up in the Castle along with the other rebels. But when later that afternoon I went out to take potshots at the congress of baboons making pests of themselves again, I started rethinking the whole business of my freedom: Here in Caffraria life is easy. And who's to say I'm not free here? Here it's only Maria and Nombini messing about with my freedom. Here I'm the leader of the other outlaws and deserters. Here I am father to the king, his counsellor, spouse to Yese, the most powerful woman since that Caffre queen from Sheba who screwed Solomon. For the time being. The noose is tightening all the time around this mode of survival, this migration between Christian world and Caffre world. These shifting alliances are getting ever more dangerous, ever more distrusted by both factions. But on this day at the end of the eighteenth century I can still survive in the interregnum. Here I can hunt and have all the powder and lead and coffee and brandy and what have you that my crooked heart desires, smuggled from the Colony for a bit of ivory and a few hides. Back in the Colony I'm just another failed farmer. A miserable cattle farmer without a friend on this earth, all because I'm not interested in puffy pasty white women. Women who can't wiggle their behinds under all those layers of dresses. The meek and mousy little women who are forever at prayer and yes-my-lord no-my-lord in front of the congregation, but behind the scenes stealthily and exceedingly slowly nag you into the grave because you can't and damnwell won't give them a vineyard in Stellenbosch. The bitches with their lips piously pursed and their legs chastely crossed that you have to skewer through a hole in the sheet.

The sun flares scarlet before it's extinguished. I walk home with the warm gun over my shoulder. A straggling of Caffres greet me and we share a joke that none of the dumb white shits around here would get – except of course Kemp, but you don't make jokes like that with him. I laugh with the warriors and walk up the grass slope to my home. It's too late to return to the Colony. I've got nothing left to lose on the Cape side of the border. But it's only when I look down upon the Great Place in the distance that I realise: The bunch of bureaucrats feel little for my earthly happiness and my troubles with whatever neighbours. The pest-plagued windbags are scared! Drop dead in ditches! Shit in your britches! Die! They want to destroy my connection with Ngqika. We are too dangerous; Khula is more dangerous than Coenraad.

~

There's no word from Ngqika. My son has not come to greet me since my return. Nor has Yese. I say to Kemp I hope they don't think we're abusing their hospitality. He is the king and she reigns. I am her husband, and yet I've now dragged my other wives here and I don't sleep with her any more.

Our queen is highly sensitive for such a thick-set person, I mutter to Kemp. A hippopotamus doesn't even feel a knife. Kemp suggests that she's not in fact a hippopotamus but a woman. I say So what?

Ngqika sends a few Caffres to fetch the elephant tusks that I brought with me. It seems they belong to him. I don't say a word and I walk to the wagon that's still groaning under my booty and return with one cracked tusk and fling it in the face of the nearest Caffre and kick the nates of the second nearest and chase them away.

On Christmas morning my son the king comes to visit with the broadest smile his dial can handle. He rattles off his apologies. He didn't give Jank'hanna and his crowd permission to clear out, because Maynier's presumption had irritated him. Furthermore, he didn't want to send them with Maynier. He could see, after all, that this man was just going to get into trouble with other captains and chiefs who are not as merciful as he. I ask him straight out whether he'd be prepared to let the missionaries go now. Then he turns all sullen again. He says he'll give his answer tomorrow. What is it about this forlorn fellow Kemp that everyone wants to keep him for themselves?

It's good to see Ngqika again. I ask him about the game in the area, but from the new rolls around his midriff I can see it's been a while since he's been hunting himself. In the course of the afternoon we stroll across to where Kemp is teaching the children. Ngqika doesn't even greet Jank'hanna when he sees the children. One moment the little ones are sitting still listening to the master, then the king is down on all fours among them, roaring all the while. He chases them around and flings them up in the air till they crow with delight. I have to laugh myself when the king follows Faber's little bastard up the tree and sits up there with the little brat taunting us with monkey gibber.

I watch them closely, my son and my friend. Ngqika is as much younger than I as I am younger than Kemp. Do you see the powerful

Ngqika scrambling up the tree? For how long can we carry on living like this? For me and Ngqika it's a world fading and vanishing, for Kemp with his alphabet and science and morality a world that can't change fast enough. See, the shiny-eyed Ngqika in the tree with the children, already a figment of the past. See there the old man Kemp, with his rod and his chalk and his stooped shoulders, the man of the future. And do you see me going to squat on a rock, between the two?

Jank'hanna doesn't seem too upset about his writing lessons ending in mayhem. When the children have gone home, we three sit under the tree. Ngqika asks the sorcerer how he's adjusting to life this side of the Keiskamma. He smiles when Jank'hanna tells him about the woman who mistook his flapping tent for an alien creature and took off head over heels and ended up in a pitfall for bush pigs. He laughs out loud when he hears of the Caffre who came upon Jank'hanna and his Hottentots kneeling in prayer with lowered heads. The man thought they were growling at him and were preparing to pounce on him. Ngqika says he himself at first wondered who Jank'hanna was talking to so earnestly under the ground.

> You are strange people, says the king. My people are sometimes scared of you and sometimes laugh at you. I'm sure it cuts both ways.
>
> Our people don't laugh as easily as you, says Kemp.

When the conversation takes a more serious turn, Ngqika asks Jank'hanna to pray to his white god for rain on the maize. Jank'hanna says God will send rain as he sees fit. That night a thunderstorm erupts; the lightning flashes all around us. The next morning Ngqika shakes the missionary to wake him up and find out how his god makes the lightning flashes. Jank'hanna explains to him and to me how electricity works. Neither of us wants to believe him.

I drag Ngqika away from my home where he's getting far too cosy with Bettie. With winged words I make him see what an important rainmaker Jank'hanna is. The king nods and it seems as if I won't be losing my friend the lightning conjurer to the Colony any time soon.

Then I play a different game. I tell Ngqika that Jank'hanna usually charges a few heads of cattle for such difficult prayers that save maize crops with such abundant rains. The king consents magnanimously. He asks me where he should send the cattle, since Jank'hanna doesn't have a kraal. I say bring the cattle to my kraal, I'll see to it that the rainmaker gets them.

Before setting off that evening on a splendid ox, the king declares that Edmonds can clear out any time he wishes, but that Jank'hanna is remaining right here. That if the governor wants to see his rainmaker, he can come and talk his talk here.

On 29 December Edmonds at long last finds himself on the wagon chest behind a team of oxen drawn up ready for the crack of the whip. With the combined and individual blessings of Ngqika and Kemp, he flails the long whip over the oxen, but the only sound is the tongue of the hindmost ox chewing the cud. The two missionaries confer for a long time and then their words dry up. Kemp whistles for the wagon leader. The boy takes hold of the bridle and starts walking. At long last the wagon is on the move. Edmonds' little plump hand keeps waving till he's far away, as if he's taking leave of old friends.

Somebody knocks at my door. The children have been snoring away for a while. Kemp is weepy; he tells me how he stood for more than half an hour on the kopje by his garden watching Edmonds' wagon disappearing slowly behind the mountains. If you go rummaging in his notes, you'll see what Kemp wrote that evening to his London superiors:

> Our separation is, however, not to be ascribed to a diminution of fraternal love, which I am persuaded is unaltered, but to an insurmountable aversion to this people, and a strong desire to live among the Bengalese. Oh that the blessing of Christ and his peace may follow him. Amen. Amen.

Believe me, only dear Kemp could have missed those pudgy hands – the little fellow who wanted to be a civilising influence in darkest Africa, but vomited all over himself when the light started dawning.

4

Summer is heating up by the time our little gang of Christians and
Hottentots start clearing the ground where the missionary's house is
to arise. Nobody was terribly excited about the job. I had to go and
kick Krieger and Bezuidenhout out of bed. Nobody sleeps as late as
white deserters. The grass is hacked out, rocks thrown on a heap.
Holes are dug for the poles on which the house will rest. Kemp is
off on his own chopping reeds for the roof. Every now and again you
hear a little yelp from the bushes when something slithers over his
bare feet.

At the hottest hour of the afternoon we are sitting under a tree,
smoking. Kemp comes walking along, one foot treading cautiously.
He stands inspecting us, not a shirt in sight. He touches his black
Sunday jacket with the white stains under the arms, takes it off and
hangs it from a branch. The lot around me try not to stare at the
emaciated white-and-red body. A few of them mutter a greeting as
he walks past them and sits down next to me.

How are you coming along? he asks.

It's easy here, the soil is not as hard as on the other side of the
river. There is plenty of water in the soil. A week, maybe two.

Thank you, Mijnheer Buys.

Christians have to look after each other here among the
Caffres.

But King Gaika says every day that he won't harm a hair on
our heads.

Ngqika likes talking, yes, but his people don't listen to
everything he says. I'm telling you now: The Caffres don't want
us here any longer.

But Mijnheer Buys, it's not only you and me here either. Surely
all your comrades and their Hottentots are here, all of them
with guns and horses.

I look at the men around me. Time is gnawing at their faces; convicts age more quickly than freemen. They're missing the Colony. They lost everything when they were reduced to seeking refuge here. For them it wasn't a choice as it was for me. It was survival.

> This bunch is building you a house because they're still wary of me, I say. But every single one of these miscreants would cut your gullet if he thought it could improve his lot.
> And not you?
> Not at the moment. I can talk to you.
> We don't really talk.
> I talk more to you than to any of these . . . these . . .

I gesture towards the blackguards around us and the empty kopjes over there in the distance when the appropriate abusive epithet doesn't present itself.

> In any case. Thank you. Coenraad. Where can I be of use?
> You just carry on chopping reeds, then I'll make you a roof that will stand up to the Flood.
> You're mocking me, Mijnheer Buys.
> And you notice it. As I say: I like chattering with you.

Kemp paces off the plan of the house with his long ostrich legs. It is late in January 1800 and the sun is stifling and the earth is sweating.

> It looks right to me, he says. About twenty-four or -five feet by nine or ten.
> Is that big enough for you?
> Mijnheer Buys, I'm not anticipating many guests.

Sounds familiar, I think. We pack stones on the outline of the house. We sit down in the prospective home, the stones the only markers that this is inside and that is outside.

~

A fortnight later the house has arisen. A house of branches and reeds like mine and those of the other fugitives. Twenty-four feet by nine. I spared no trouble. The reeds are packed neatly and tightly, the clay plastered smooth and the rocks that we rolled out of the way have been used for a chimney. I must confess, I was foreman, I helped haul things and hollered where I had to, but the actual construction wasn't mine. Building houses is a skill these hands would never acquire.

For the last few days I've kept Kemp away from the house. God's gardener is busy trying to harvest Caffre souls all day, but just in case he should have an idle hour or so, I devise a plan. I offer the Bengali who prays to the setting sun and Mohammed every evening – called Damin, I've since found out – a few plugs of tobacco to keep Kemp occupied. The next day Damin is sitting piously muttering during the prayer meeting. As soon as Thomas the deserter and the four Hottentots lift their hind ends under the tree and Kemp remains sitting on his own and gazing as if the branches were talking to him, the Bengali comes asking Kemp to teach him to read and write. Kemp asks if he wants to learn Dutch or the Caffre language. Damin says any language that will bring him closer to the word of the Lord. Kemp enrols him in the Dutch class. When Kemp is not occupied with prayer meetings and sermons and classes, I keep him away from the house under construction by telling him to sand down the door which I could at least hammer together myself.

Kemp sees his house for the first time on 3 February when towards dusk I come to drag him away from the jubilating flock. I help him pile his meagre possessions on the cart and strike the tent. We walk next to the oxen up the slope to his new terrestrial home. The place is standing, but I'm not happy.

I'm sorry, Kemp.

You built me a house, why should you be sorry?

You know a builder by his chimney. And that thing isn't going to draw. You're going to smoke yourself out of there.

As long as I have a roof over my head and a place to rest my weary body.

These thugs are more used to breaking down.

I feel a hand on my shoulder. Kemp laughs and says:

My dear Buys, the Lord sent you to me.
The house's wattle-and-daub roof appears over the ridge.

> We are none of us sent, I say. We come across each other,
> walk together for a while, then continue on our own and
> separate ways.

At the house the other Christian builders are awaiting us, with
the few prudently preserved calabashes of brandy. A pot is simmering
on the fire. One or two of them shake Kemp's hand. I propose a
long-winded toast to the house. Kemp is obliged to take a small sip of
brandy on himself and his house. The missionary thanks me by name
as well as the other outlaw farmers with an even more verbose speech
containing no fewer than four Latin quotations of which nobody understands a whit. We're boozing outside and the brandy disappears fast,
the pot soon forgotten. When I look for Kemp, he's nowhere to be
found. I find him in the back room measuring the doorjamb with a
leather thong.

> What are you doing, Jank'hanna? We're celebrating for you.
> It'll fit, he says absent-mindedly.

He looks around, as if he's searching for something.

> Will you help, Buys?
> Of course. With what?
> I want to move in tonight already. At least my bed and . . . there
> are a few things that I want to bring in out of the elements.
> We'll do that. I'll just get shot of the gang out there.

I go out and separate a few brawlers and tell them to go and raise hell
somewhere else. I grab half a calabash of brandy from Faber, who
staggers mutteringly into me in pursuit of his pals.

Kemp and I start unloading the wagon. We hear the hyenas laugh.

> There are more and more of the creatures hereabouts, he
> says. They're here every night, ever closer; in the last few
> weeks they've been pissing on the tent flaps.
> The scavengers are breeding furiously since the lions have all
> been wiped out, I say. This land is a torn-open cadaver.

We carry in the cot, the small wooden table, the even smaller desk, the two chairs, the trunk with clothes and books. In the back of the wagon is a large crate and three smaller crates, meticulously wrapped in thick cloths.

> Where do these go? I ask.
>
> In the back room.
>
> You must help me, it's damn heavy.

The large crate, taller than me and heavier than the two of us together, doesn't budge. I go and fetch three Hottentots. With some effort we manage to drag the crate into the back room.

> What kind of thing is in here?
>
> A printing press.
>
> So show us.
>
> It's late, Buys. Some other day.

The excitement has drained from his visage. He once again looks as if gravity is dragging him down to somewhere under the deepest depth.

> Then just a last sip?
>
> Just one, you hear.
>
> Just one. .

An hour later we are drunk. We are sitting in his house, on the ground by a small fire. Kemp tells me about a remarkable whore in Amsterdam who could do handstands. My eyes remain fixed on the door opening into the back room.

> She could, just like that, with her blonde hair brushing the
> floor, walk towards you where you're sitting on the bed and
> then embrace you with her legs around your neck. Oh, my
> dear Buys, where were you then?
>
> Show me that press.
>
> It's almost light. I'm preaching tomorrow.
>
> Their souls aren't going anywhere. Show.

I help him to his feet and drag him along behind me. I open the crate and start chucking beams and screws and bolts onto the floor.

> De Buys! That's a delicate machine!

It's just wood and iron, not the tender flesh of a headstand whore.

But Buys, it *could* be, you can tell anything with this thing. The whole Bible.

You don't say.

I'm befuddled. This is a task for another day.

Why so? Come. Seems to me this beam has to stand upright, and this lies across it.

Get away, let go. Let *me*.

You can make a whole Bible with this thing?

As many Bibles as you could want, Buys.

And stories of the flesh? I can read, Kemp, but I've never come across anything like that to read. Do people write such things?

There's a man in France, they locked him up on account of his stories; there were too many naked women being whipped in his books. Last I heard, he was in the Bastille.

And you can make any story you like on this thing?

Any story. But I must have the text to hand to pack the right letters into the press. I don't have that marquis' books. I can't think up his stories, and so help me God, I don't want to either. That life is over. These days I read only the Bible.

So let's make a Bible. I want a Bible for Maria. Then I can give it to her as a present tomorrow when she wakes up.

Tomorrow?

That's right. What's your problem?

You don't understand, Buys. Oh, dammee, let me show you. Pass that pole here.

Kemp trips over the empty floor in front of him.

I hold the upright poles so that Kemp can bolt together the structure. When the contraption looks like a gallows, Kemp slides a large screw into the top end and next to the flat plane a cast-iron lever with a wooden haft.

Are we making wine now or books?

189

> Exactly. They say the first printing press was nothing more than
> an abused wine press.

From one of the smaller crates Kemp takes out a metal plate that looks
like a frame.

> This is what we pack the letters in. One by one, but wrong way
> round, as in a mirror. The English call it the casket.
> Where are the letters?
> Over there, in the crate.

I upend the crate and blocks of wooden and lead letters spill all over
the floor.

> Dammee, Buys! Careful! As it is, I've got too few esses. You're
> going to break the things.
> Sorry, Bible-writer.

Kemp is on the floor gathering the letters and carefully packing them
back into the crate, kind by kind.

> Just let me be, he says. I'll pack the stuff.
> What must I do?
> Well, after this we have to ink the text.

He looks up:

> I don't have ink. I write with roots. We must get ink. Thick ink,
> not watery root juice.
> We'll make a plan, I say. You just pack your letters.

While Kemp starts setting down a verse of text letter by letter in the
casket I stand around touching and rubbing the frame. I tell him about
the book I picked up in the road, the maps and lists.

> Yes, Buys. Lists are the opposite of description. The less
> you can get your mind around something, the longer your list
> grows.

I strain at the screw. It resists. I tell him about the sketches of the
impossible animals in the book. I go to fetch oil. When I come back,
I see Kemp's bedroom: hardly more than ten by ten feet, reed ceiling,
clay, no floor, a cot, a desk with his papers neatly piled, a chair, a
trunk and, in the opposite corner next to the window aperture, the

three-by-five-foot printing press extending all the way to the roof and outside the night barking and yowling.

I press against the pole keeping the top level, making sure it's stable. Kemp carefully slides the text onto the frame and locks it in place. I regard the framed text. Most of the words are spelt out with individual letters, but some, such as *mouth,* have been cast as whole words on their own plates. The whole phrase *sweet as honey* has also been cast as one plate. I wiggle at the *sweet-as-honey.*

This honey is so sweet that the letters are sticking together.

It's a stereotype. The French talk of a cliché. Some words and phrases that are used regularly are cast as units. You don't have to set the whole thing every time. *Sweet as honey* occurs often in the Bible.

There must be many such blocks if you want to print the Bible, I say. The same things over and over. And God. I suppose there's a block for God as well.

Kemp starts laughing, where he's standing on unstable feet, hanging by an arm from the big scaffolding around the Biblical text.

Yes, Buys; God is a cliché.

He looks past me.

In Europe he's a cliché. But in this land . . . Here there aren't even loose letters for him, never mind a word. Here where they worship anything and everything, our Lord is an aberration.

You'll see yet, I say. The further you travel from the Colony, the more the words dry up. And the words for the things you can't touch are the first to go.

Kemp takes a deep breath and shouts:

Source! Way! Rock! Lion! Light bearer! Lamb! Door! Hope! Virtue! Word! Wisdom! Prophet! Sacrificial victim! Scion! Shepherd! Mountain! Dove! Flame! Giant! Bridegroom! Patience! Worm!

Kemp! What the devil are you doing?

Those are the words for God in the Bible, Buys. There are
more, so many more! Vine! Ram! Sun! Bread! Flame! Lover!
Dew! Saviour! Avenger!

Stop it, dammit! I shout and walk out.

Creator! Majesty! Love! Abyss!

Through the window I see Kemp hollering his last holler. Then he
goes to sit down on his cot and gazes out of the window into the
black night.

At the outdoor cooking fire I scrabble the thickest bones from the
untouched pot. By the little fire in the front room I churn loose the
marrow with my knife and suck it up and spit it out into a tin plate. I
shout at the missionary in the other room:

Come here Kemp! Here is the fat. We'll make you some ink.
Bushman ink.

As Windvogel taught me, I almost say, but I'm not *that* drunk. I hear
nothing, go to check where Kemp is. Find him on the bed, still
staring out of the window. When I touch his shoulder, I can feel he's
shivering.

Come and sit here by the fire in the next room, your machine
is taking over here.

Of course, Mijnheer Buys. I'm forgetting my manners.

Kemp gets up and sits down again immediately.

It's just a dizzy spell. They come and go.

You're just boozed up, man. Come.

Of course.

I rootle a few live coals out of the fire with my hands, throw them
into a bowl, place the bowl on the ground and crush the coals with
my shoe.

Black. For your ink.

I lift the bowl onto the table and open my breeches.

What are you doing?

I'm pissing. We need piss.

Why?

The charcoal must dissolve. I'm not going to walk to the river
for water.

I stand over the basin, swingle in hand. Kemp watches me. A thin
stream trickles into the bowl and dribbles and dries up. I have a
problem when people watch me.

I had a piss a while ago, there's nothing left, I say. Come and
do your bit here.

Kemp looks at me. Starts saying something, stops and opens his own
breeches and steps up. Now I'm watching *him*. He pisses till the
charcoal is covered.

That's enough, oh mighty one.

Kemp blushes, but doesn't stop.

Kemp! Stop it now.

He jerks his pizzle away from the bowl, piss splashes all over the
table. He doesn't stop, a pool foams up next to the table. My eyes are
shut with laughter and I scramble to get out of the way of the stream
under the table. Kemp shakes himself off excessively.

Shaking more than twice is nice.

He blushes even darker and closes his breeches. Then he laughs
as well.

I take a swig of brandy and slide the calabash towards Kemp. He
swallows. I cover the top of the basin with a flat hand and upend the
basin and make the warm piss run through my fingers until a black
mush remains. I pour it onto a plate and hold it over the fire so that
the porridge starts to dry. Kemp watches me, starts singing a German
hymn. I also hold the plate with the marrow fat over the flames. When
both plates are too hot to hold, I empty them into the bowl and start
mixing. I spit into the mixture until my tongue sticks to the sides of
my mouth.

Spit, friend, my mouth is barren.

Kemp giggles.

Why ever not?

He comes to stand next to me, still muttering away at the hymn.

He watches me, how I stand stooped over the bowl, summoning up slime from far down my gullet with choking sounds, until I'm empty. Only then does the man deign to contribute some preacher spit. I make him spit until it's enough. Then I make him spit some more. I carry on mixing the lot.

      Almost done. Now all we need is blood.

Kemp is clutching the table top with white knuckles, it looks as if his forehead is dragging him forward.

      I am in my cups, Mijnheer. It's been years since I've been drunk.

I hold out the brandy to Kemp.

      Quite, you're drunk already. What's the point of stopping now? For a few moments Kemp regards the calabash suspended in front of him and then accepts it.

      Have you ever before mixed this Bushman paint, Mijnheer Buys?

I pretend not to hear him.

      I would take it amiss if you made me spit and make water as a joke.

Goddammit, the missionary won't let up blathering.

      I once knew one of the savages. He told me stories of how his people used to paint before they were tamed. A Bushman is a pest, but he can draw an eland to life.

      And the blood?

I see the Bushman throat gape open under my knife.

      That apparently helps everything to blend together.

      What about eggs? In Holland the painters mix pigment with egg yolk.

      They say that if you're painting an eland, the eland's vitality must be in the paint. So the creatures mix eland blood with the paint. Otherwise you're painting a dead thing, they believe.

I see Windvogel running for his life. Kemp puts down the brandy and takes the bowl from my hands.

We're not painting an eland, Buys. The sun is starting to show.
I grab the bowl from him again, the stinking slush splashes onto
Kemp. I start mixing again. Kemp steps back a pace.

I only wanted to show you the press. We must get some sleep.
You get out, I say. Go to bed. You have to start saving souls
again soon. If I go home in this condition, I'll never hear the
end of it. Believe me, it's better that I hang around here a
while longer.

I stop mixing, look around me in the front room.

This concoction as true as hell needs blood. It flows, but it
doesn't really cling. They say the blood wakes up the paint.
Kemp comes closer once again, takes a long swig at the brandy. My
hand carries on mixing, my eyes searching for something that can be
bled. Next to me Kemp points his feet so that he gradually rises onto
his toes, slightly swaying. Then he swings both his arms, gracefully,
slowly, backwards. The arms shoot forward with all the speed and
strength in his sinews. He knocks me off the chair. The reed-and-rush
wall collapses.

But you little rapscallion . . .!

I leap up and stay down low and my shoulder finds Kemp's ribs and
we fall against the opposite wall and Kemp hits me full in the face
and I hit back. We wallop each other right through the wall. The wood
and reed and rushes give way. They fall into the house and out of the
house. We lie entangled across the boundary of the house and pummel
each other as hard as we can in the face. Neither of us fends off any
blows. Kemp seizes me with his tendril-like arms, long enough to make
eye contact for a moment.

Buys. Mijnheer Buys, he says softly.

I get up and dust the bits of clay from my breeches. I mumble
something, quite what I don't know myself. I walk into the house
through the newly bashed-in door. By some miracle the table is still
standing, the bowl of precious paint undisturbed. I pick up the chair,
sit down and carry on mixing. Kemp remains seated among the rushes,

just on the other side of the new threshold, and fingers his forehead, the open eyebrow ridge, the closed eye underneath. I don't look up. Kemp staggers to his feet and comes to stand behind me. He bends over me and presses both hands to the right eyebrow ridge so that blood splashes into the dish.

Blood, he says.

I can't help smiling.

You bastard.

I also bend over the bowl. A thick splatter of blood and a molar drop from my mouth into the printer's ink.

I watch over Kemp's shoulder while he slides the packed and framed letters into the press and clamps it in place.

Buys, it is your privilege to ink our text.

I press my hands into the brew, as thick as Maria's bean soup, and spread it methodically over the cold letters while I read:

And I took the little book out of the angel's hand, and ate it up; and it was in my mouth sweet as honey: and as soon as I had eaten it, my belly was bitter.

Kemp wheels the plate with the painted letters in under the screw. He places a sheet of paper into another frame in which a cloth is tentered. He places the second frame on top of the painted letters. He lowers the screw with a lever. He lifts it. He takes out the printed page. I grab the page from his hand and examine it. I touch a finger to the wet ink. I close my eyes and feel the weight of the letters pressed into the paper; the letters are impressed deep into the paper and on the reverse side they bulge out, as if wanting to break out. I let go of the sheet. The draught blows it in under the cot. I walk out to wash the Bushman paint from my hands. The printing press remains standing in the corner; the blood, piss and charcoal congeal on the letters.

5

The fat is in the fire. We're scarcely halfway through February 1800, when One-hand Botha's wife, Martie, is sitting with me, weeping. I pour her shots that she knocks back one after the other in between the sobs. She chokes when she starts talking.

On the twelfth Botha went to ask Ngqika for permission to move back to the Colony. The king is reluctant at first, but eventually consents, after Botha has given him forty oxen, four cows and a gun. Ngqika sends a Caffre with him to conduct him and his people safely through Caffraria. Botha's wagons had already been laden before he went to speak to Ngqika, and on the same day he sets off with Martie and their child, Hannes Knoetze and the wife and child of Frans Krieger – who was off somewhere hunting elephants.

By the next morning a few of Ndlambe's Caffres catch up with them and order them to return to Ngqika. They turn back meekly. When they reach one of Ngqika's former kraals, the Caffres tell them to outspan there among the abandoned huts for the night. A Caffre asks Botha to lend him his knife, and as soon as the creature has the knife in his hand, a bunch of Heathens charge out of the bushes and Botha finds an assegai in his side. He staggers into Martie's arms, where she supports him and pulls out the assegai. The Caffres are surrounding them. Another assegai is stuck into him. This one he pulls out himself with his single hand. Then they tear him off her and fling him down on the ground in front of her, from which he does not arise again.

Martie sits with me and relives every moment of that day. Do you see the bit of snot falling from her nose onto her breast? While talking, she rubs it from her dress. Do you see the left nipple perking up willy-nilly?

He looked like a big pincushion, she says. He looked at her and sighed and died, she says. They plundered and torched the wagon and drove the cattle back to Ngqika. According to report the king was upset when he received the cattle. He says he informed Ndlambe of Botha's departure and gave his uncle the choice of letting him go or bringing him back unharmed to the Great Place. Martie says Ngqika says none of this was according to his wishes. Apparently Knoetze had been warned in advance by the Caffres that they were going to slaughter someone and the two-arsed ratbag could sneak off in time.

Ngqika claims damages from Ndlambe and receives from his uncle two female slaves, a gun and two sick horses that give up the ghost two days later. He sends the slaves and gun to Martie and decrees that she and Krieger and Bezuidenhout will move in with me and Kemp. Whether this is in the interests of our safety or to have us all in a bundle so as to mow us down more conveniently, remains to be seen. Kemp offers his tent to the red-haired widow. My wives and children stayed with these people. How kind Martie was to them. I help Martie lift her belongings from her wagon. When I touch her shoulder a bit too compassionately, she says:

I'm not one of your Caffre women.

By the end of the month old Ndlambe flees across the Fish along with Siko and a horde of renegade Caffres. The Rharhabe kingdom has been torn in two. Ngqika has long been his own worst enemy. He punishes his people more cruelly than any king before him. Sometimes he claims the whole herd of the deceased, instead of the single head of cattle a king normally demands. Kings who enrich themselves at the cost of their people do not survive long. He threatens and kills his advisers and keeps them on a very short leash. Then there is Ndlambe, the old bull with the real power. Every day the people witness this mighty and proven leader and warrior. Every day they witness an alternative possibility: a king who has no need of Christians, who, if he does cooperate with them, does it from a high throne built of knobkerries and blades – do you remember how we took to our heels the first time we saw Ndlambe's army? The people say Ndlambe will chase the Christians back into the sea. Long sob story short: Ngqika is insecure and people smell insecurity on a king, as dogs smell fear. And then they bite.

Yese says a few Caffres tried to kill Ngqika and wounded him before they were battered to death. To hang on to any shred of power, Ngqika now has to petition the goodwill of the Hottentots in the surrounding areas, as protection against his own nation. Ngqika merely sends me word that his people are deserting him, that he fears for his life and is too scared to make the short journey to come and visit me. He can go shit straw!

I start looking to the north. Every branch that snaps in the night makes me rush out of the house gun in hand. With his nerves as raw as mine, Bezuidenhout the other evening takes aim at a wretched Caffre who after dark is all innocently driving his few cattle past the red-bearded barbarian's stand.

I try to bring it home to Kemp that things are getting dangerous here. I tell him that if an uprising were to flare up here, we'd have to help fight the rebels. Otherwise Ngqika would roast all us Christians over hot coals to feed his dogs. Kemp picks listlessly at an infected thorn in his foot.

> Beloved Buys, says the barefoot preacher, Jesus is the true
> king of the Heathens and they can do nothing to us against
> his will.

Well, there you have it.

By April our little band of Christians is so panicked that we start standing guard again as in the commando days. I start thinking that just perchance Kemp is the only Christian here who is truly safe. No Caffre would harm a hair on his huge head without bringing down the wrath of the king upon his gonads. At long last Ngqika comes crawling out of his hole. He says he's been avoiding his dear Khula because he'd been told that I wanted to shoot him. If the backstabbing squirt frustrates me any further with his little civil war that's rendering my beloved Caffraria just as unsafe as the Colony, I might just prove the tattlers right. Though I am pleased to see my son. We don't talk about his mother. Truth to tell, we don't talk much. We've both heard so many shit stories about each other that we no longer know where we're on or off with each other. He excuses himself with great formality and goes off in search of his beloved Jank'hanna. Ngqika wants Jank'hanna to instruct him in the Caffre alphabet that the white sorcerer apparently wrote up in his idle hours.

~

Poke around in his notes on the little table and you'll see how the missionary is battling to get a grip on the language of the Caffres. You'll see how time after time he starts with an outline and scratches it out and tears it up. He already understands the language sufficiently to save a Caffre heart, but the rules remain obscure. Somewhere between the sheets you'll find an alphabet of twenty-seven letters, eight of these vowels. Extensive notes point to the differences from the Dutch alphabet. In his report to the London Missionary Society he writes that Arabic script could perhaps be more suited to express the Caffre sounds. There's a short note on how European readers would struggle with the fancy swirls of the Arabic letters, but how, in their turn, the blessed Caffres also systematically need to get accustomed to the matrix of European script. He laments the fact that he does not have Arabic letters for his printing press. In the report to the focking British Colonisers of Souls you find these notes under the heading *Specimen of the Caffra Language*. Suchlike general observations are followed by the *Vocabulary of the Caffra Language*, a glossary as long as my arm.

The glossary is meticulously divided up into 21 classes and covers any subject you can name. As far as animals, excluding humans, are concerned, he lists 98 words and expressions that can be further divided up as follows:

Quadrupeds: 38 words, of which 9 refer to cattle;

Birds: 14 words;

Reptiles, insects and the like: 21 words, 8 referring to snakes;
Parts of animals: 25 words, apart from words like 'horn' or 'liver' and including among others 'honey', 'dung' and 'breath'.
Secondly you find 70 words under the vague heading *Of Mankind*, under which are found 4 different words for 'mother'.
Then, celestial bodies and phenomena: 25 words, including 'thokoloze';
Terrestrial objects: 18 words, including 'shadow';
Vegetables: 25 words, including most of the vegetation of the area;
Food and drink: 11 words;
House and utensils: 33 words, for instance 'assegai' and the word 'nadi', which according to our brother designates both 'mirror' and 'book';
Dress: 10 words.
Under 'diseases' you find only 5 Xhosa equivalents for pain, fever, the great itch, smallpox and flatulence. (Note that my lord Kemp pens down chronic farting in its original Latin: *crepitus ventris*.)
Hereafter the section on dignities, qualities, etc., starting with 'lord' and 'lady', followed by 'Christian' and 'magician'; further on you find the same word for a female servant and a Hottentot woman. The glossary concerning the nobility ends on equivalents for 'rogue', 'friend', 'enemy', 'thief', 'liar', 'lie' and, at last, 'hunger'.
In addition you find 32 adjectives,
77 verbs,
37 pronouns,
33 adverbs,
10 prepositions,
6 conjunctions,
5 interjections,
12 numerals,
4 diminutives,
9 comparatives and
84 phrases.

All in all he mentions 624 words and expressions of the Caffre nation, that on his sole authority, without any proofreading, was published in the *Transactions of the London Missionary Society*, Vol. 1 of 1804, to be distributed and plundered by plagiarists to the end of time.

~

Ngqika and Jank'hanna's summer of joyful language lessons is of short duration. On 27 April the whole gang of us clears out: I and my people, Kemp, the other Graaffe Rijnet outlaws, the German and English deserters who had joined us in dribs and drabs. Not even this lot of rebels and deserters want to linger in the midst of a civil war. We abandon our houses as they stand with no hope of ever seeing them again and two nights later we outspan on the banks of the Debe. Faber wounds a bontebok; the creature charges the wretched Kemp, but a second bullet floors the buck at his feet.

I walk in the veldt to cleanse my ears of all the whingeing. The pack comes to greet me while I'm taking aim at a kudu in thick undergrowth. There's something amiss here. The leader with the pointed ears is nowhere to be seen; now a hyena is leading the pack. Such a thing I've never heard of, but I understand. The hyena is no longer young, but bigger than the dogs. His scars say he knows all about fighting. He growls when he sees me. The wagging tails of the others make him calm down. Two of the bitches are pregnant. What kind of monsters will tear their way out of their loins? The hyena makes a wide circle around me and comes to stand before me, behind a rotten tree trunk. He is broad, even for a hyena. One of his fangs is broken. He turns around, the low back quarter speckled like a partridge. He lifts his leg, pisses against the trunk and disappears. Somewhere I hear a dog bark and then yowl. How long will the hyena remain the leader of the pack? The hyena is stronger than the dogs, but he's the only hyena. I shoot a fat peacock for the pot. My Bettie sticks the feathers in her hair and no Christian can keep his eyes to himself.

~

At the end of the month we trek across a mountain and pitch camp again. A week later I send a message to Ngqika where he's hiding from the rebellious Rharhabe in a Hottentot camp fourteen miles away. The king, my son, no longer trusts me and I him ever less by the day. From Yese I hear nothing, other than that she's placing curses on me and my wives and children.

Ngqika arrives with the dawn at our place. With him is the usual retinue of fifty men, each with a kaross over the shoulders and a single assegai or knobkerrie in hand. But all around the stand, I point out to Bezuidenhout, are lying some two hundred naked warriors, with all the shields and assegais that they could carry on them. Ngqika says the despicable Hottentots persuaded him that the Christians were conspiring against him, but our warm welcome was proof that he no longer need fear us. A captain leaps to his feet and takes his king to task: What kind of lying is this about his fear of us? What's happened to the plan to skin us alive? Our king looks about him all bewildered and laughs nervously. He demands Jank'hanna's horse and Kemp thank God does not argufy and gives the horse and Ngqika is on the horse and gone. One by one the warriors arise from the bushes and trot after their king.

≈

In May Krieger, Faber and I, with Bentley, the focking English deserter, saddle our horses and ride to the Colony to barter a few hides and tusks for munitions. I take part of Kemp's diary and a few letters along for him and entrust them to a kind farmer who is prepared to deliver them to Graaffe Rijnet, seeing that he's allowed to set foot in that dusty street without being shot to pieces. We return with sacks full of lead and powder, which emboldens the whole gang to move further afield. By June our camp is settled next to the Keiskamma. I mend my ox-cart's axle, and Kemp marvels at the hippopotami. He is truly chuffed with himself nowadays. At Ngqika's place he didn't manage to convert one single Caffre, but since we've been camping here Hottentots have streamed into the camp every day, devoured all there is to eat and walked off. Kemp lures the lot with food and then it's a prayering and a hymning to make up for the wasted time and souls. There are regularly rhinoceros tracks in the mud, but the wretched brutes now know better than to be seen.

My children fall ill one by one. Maria has to come up with cures and herbs. I am kept busy all day listening to and solving every plaint and problem of my fellow fugitives. Maria is fast asleep already by the time I crawl in behind her and press my snout into the back of her neck. In the morning she's up already by the time I wake up, but her smell clings to me till the afternoon's sweat washes her scent from me.

Not a hundred years later Ngqika puts in another appearance with one of his wives and thirty of his Caffres. It seems a terrible fever is raging at the Great Place. He's coming to seek refuge with us where Jank'hanna can keep the disease at bay with a mighty praying. In no time at all trees are cut down and the king builds a small kraal a stone's throw from our camping spot. I tell the men it's time we tested the Colony's borders. If we fire the first shots there are plenty of Christians who'll join in the shooting. I'm not going to spend my life sitting around in a goddam Sunday-school class.

~

We melt all that is lead or tin and with sacks of bullets that used to be mugs and plates, the other Christian men and I prepare by mid-June to take up arms against the Colony. Bentley remains behind to look after the old missionary and the women and children. Once again I have to cart along a whole mailbag of letters and diaries from Kemp. For somebody who sets himself up as a model of humility with his unshod paws and hatless forehead, it's a bit of a joke that he wants to jot down every bright idea and bowel movement and send it out into the world.

Before our departure I tell Ngqika of our plans with the focking English and our friends in the Castle. He seals his blessing on our campaign against the Bushmen-from-the-Sea by offering a few of his Caffres who can shoot. Everything goes swimmingly until we cross the Baviaans.

In the evenings when the other commando members are snoring away, I can't help peeking into Brother Kemp's jottings. The dear chap marvels at every plant and creature. He writes odes to the baboons in the kloofs and the parrots in the forests, waxes lyrical over the stink-wood and yellowwood; he measures the giant aloe and the enormous snails. His awe at ostrich eggs. His amazement at the honeybird that signals with its call that it has found honey and how you can then follow it to the sweetness. He describes sadly how his dogs tear a young steenbok to pieces. When I read these things, I start missing my old friend. And when he mentions that he conducts experiments on chameleons to try to ascertain how they change their colour, I think I must ask him about it as soon as I see him again and I know that I'll never again come across a man like him in this country.

Hardly have we set foot on the other bank of the Baviaans, than our little commando runs up against Chungwa's army. They give us a good drubbing. Most of the Caffre riflemen perish. Stoffel Botha is captured and Chungwa drags him to the drostdy. There the blackguard blurts out all our plans. How we wanted to drive the English from the Colony, how we would drag all the commissioners all the way to Caffraria and there do unto them what was done unto our comrades in the Castle and how, in the new Englishless republic, Krieger would be general and I would be king.

After our defeat against Chungwa we wipe our bloody noses. We're not too shamefaced: We were not even ten Christian guns and a hand-ful of Caffres against a whole horde. We ride back to our camp on the Keiskamma, back to the goddam hallelujahs.

~

If you as much as look askance at the grass, it catches fire. Our cattle are lean; food is scarce. I haven't even unsaddled, when Kemp comes

205

running up to me to jabber about Sara, Bezuidenhout's wife. The little converted Hottentot girl is inseparable from Kemp these days. Even now I can see her standing and spying on our talk. She, too, is the one who dares tell Kemp what no one else, myself included, feels up to telling him: how the Christians, every time he goes to piss or pray in the bush, slip into his tent and rob him – smaller stuff than what Ngqika is forever absconding with, but more chronically. Bezuidenhout's little wife is quite appealing, I can see why Kemp is so taken with her. She hovers about him like one of his flies, zooming incessantly and fluttering on about sin and hell and punishment and everything that tickles a preacher's prick.

I see the other Christians watching when I'm talking so earnestly with Kemp. The soul-scavenger tells me excitedly that in my absence Maria also decided that she was in need of salvation. Kemp just can't stay away from a married woman. To each his own, I suppose. But he'd better watch himself if he wants to meddle with Maria's soul. When I go and look up my family, Maria and Nombini say I should get out of the way, they're cooking lunch. The children don't seem to have noticed that I was gone.

On 11 August we trek on to a site lower down on the Keiskamma. That night the Christians sit around a fire squabbling about what to do with Kemp. They are still smarting from the defeat against Chungwa and another revolution gone to glory. The war is raging about us, they say. Why does the missionary lure all that is Hotnot and Caffre to us in order to convert them? He sows strange seeds in their wives' heads. Claims not to want to baptise Faber's child because he and his woman Leentjie carry on like Heathens. He must die, they say. It takes all my sweet-talking to have the old man's life spared. On the 16th we move four miles to the east, still further down the river, cross it twice and eventually camp on the lusher left bank. Late at night the whole of the camp to a man is wielding torches to scare off the plaguy hippopotami.

The mighty Keiskamma is little more than a trickle nowadays. The only moving things are the whirlwinds that toss about our tents every late afternoon. Deep into September even Yese is heard of. I don't think of her very much any more; all that I retain are faint twinges of jealousy and shame. Yese sends word that she doesn't get any rain made. There are malign sorcerers in the vicinity who stop up the hole from which the rain falls, she says. She says Jank'hanna must make rain, please. Later that week it's Ngqika's brother-in-law who comes to plead with Jank'hanna to dance for rain.

～

Bezuidenhout, Oosthuizen and Steenberg come upon four Caffres and a woman sitting next to the road roasting the hindquarter of a cow. They say they found the carcase in the veldt. Look, they say, here the Bushman arrows are still sticking out. We're just roasting it because we're hungry. We haven't stolen it. Steenberg shoots the spokesman in the head. The other two Christians are also obliged to shoot, so that the truth may be left lying here next to the road. They shoot the woman and two of the Caffres, but one escapes and comes tattling to Kemp; the woman, it seems, was his sister. Once again I have to sweet-talk and lie and connive or my friend the philanthropist will also get a ball of lead between the eyes.

～

I hear an unearthly screaming from Kemp's tent and go to investigate. He's bleeding an elderly Caffre. The man has rheumatism, he says. This bloodletting is reputed to help. I rub my fingers against one another, feel if they can still feel, praise his healing powers, and make my getaway.

～

A man can't walk two steps without bumping into a Hottentot tittle-tattling. The latest news is that three castaways emerged from the sea on a piece of plank and when they set foot on shore were immediately captured by a lot of Ngqika's Caffres. The men tried to escape but

207

were caught again and beaten to a pulp with knobkerries. One of them lay still pretending to be dead, but when he saw the Caffres slitting his comrades' throats to make sure they would lie still for good, he jumped to his feet and dived into the river and escaped. When we sound Ngqika out on this, he shrugs his ever-fatter shoulders and says they're like the hyenas of the veldt, they've got no business here. Bezuidenhout gets hold of the two bags of raw coffee beans on which the castaways survived and now we have coffee three times a day.

∼

When Kemp finds out that Bezuidenhout is planning to move to the sea, he gets anxious about Sara's soul. On 15 October he baptises the woman and her two daughters in the Keiskamma. Maria is so overjoyed at her friend's access to Eternal Life that, without asking me, she slaughters a sheep for the woman. On the 19th Kemp also baptises Sara's oldest daughter as Christina. As if there weren't enough damned Christinas in this world.

Ngqika gets to hear of Bezuidenhout's plans and with great ostentation makes sure that my pal and his household understand that this is Caffraria and that Ngqika will decide who lives where. Kemp is overjoyed that Sara will not be taken away from him. He knows all too well that his diary will be read by the whole of the London Missionary Society, and yet he betrays himself in his scribblings. Jank'hanna and Kemp increasingly diverge into two distinct people. Just listen to the musings of a ruttish preacher on the 23rd of October of the year of our Lord 1800:

> I now rejoiced in the prospect that I should again have an opportunity to feed her soul with the milk of the word of God.

∼

At the end of October we trek away from the Keiskamma and her hippopotami with the protruding ribs. The king of this parched land once again comes pleading for Jank'hanna to pray for rain; the witchdoctors are being threatened and executed. Ngqika promises him two milk cows and their calves. Jank'hanna says he'll pray and the king can keep his presents, but he should bear in mind that God's ways are mysterious and unfathomable and whatever else.

That evening we arrive at our old living space. All this trekking in pursuit of nothing, with Ngqika breathing up our bungholes all the time, and now once again back where we goddamwell started out from. Kemp says there's a Greek who maintained that Achilles would never catch up with a tortoise and that an arrow never really moved. I ask him whether he's ever shot with a bow. The Caffres who used to live here, the eleven kraals full of people and cattle, have all moved on in search of food and pasturage. They burned down the grass before clearing out and Kemp's branch-and-reed house, which I helped build with these two cramped hands and in the sweat of my brow, has perished in the process. My friend is in tears and on his knees.

Next to the chimney, which is all that is left towering over the veldt, stand the cows and calves that Ngqika promised. The rainmaker sends the herdsmen away with the gifted cattle and pitches his tent again, bolts together the printing press once again, makes his bed and sows the last of the vegetable seeds in the blackened grass.

I leave him there and run after the herdsmen. I tell him that Jank'hanna will definitely accept the king's gift, on condition that it's larger. The next morning the herdsmen come walking up the hill with another twenty cows. I take the cattle from them and say Of course I'll see to it that Jank'hanna receives the gift and send my love to my son and Jank'hanna's thanks to the king.

Jank'hanna prays fervently, his head banging the ground. He prays until the Lord's temper has been tried beyond endurance and in a fit of wrath he opens up his heavens and the whole of Caffraria is flooded. Ngqika and all his people flee before the deluge. The lightning flashes so fiercely that Ngqika sends to ask the white rainmaker: Tell your god that if he wants me to listen to him, he must stop deafening me with thunder. Day after day it pours down. People flee the low-lying areas.

The red barbarian Bezuidenhout seizes his opportunity in the midst of the mayhem, and at the beginning of November he and his people trek to the banks of the Kabusie. He takes Sara along, and Kemp starts cultivating some other woman's soul. Maria is with Kemp all day and every day, babbling on about her heart and soul. One night a tempest rips the missionary's tent to shreds. Maria wants him to move in with us. I say he can muck off, if the two of them want to blacken the good name of my house they can go and wash her as white as driven snow outside in the rain. Since the houseless Kemp contracts an acute case of belly-run, Maria's soul does after all remain in my house and out of heaven. Hardly has my own soul attained serenity, towards mid-November, or the Caffres start stealing my cattle. When Faber and his Leentjie also make for the Kabusie, even I, the father of Ngqika, start thinking it's time to clear out.

These days I'm avoiding both my friends. I don't have the stomach for squitter-shitting and puking. Kemp is permanently on his bucket and Ngqika is also out of sorts. He does not respond to my complaints about the cattle rustling. All that I hear are strange rumours making him out to be demented. Apparently Ngqika wanted to buy horses from two deserters. When the horses were in his kraal, he attacked the two men. It seems he pulled and pushed them around and cut the buttons off their jackets. When the poor fools asked him to return two buttons to button up their jackets against the cold, he pointed out the tree from which he was going to hang them. The two of them cleared out quickly. One of them arrives at my place badly dishevelled that evening, looking for Kemp. He says he lost his friend somewhere in the bush. The next morning the other one turns up on my doorstep and he looks even worse. Apparently six or so Caffres attacked him during the night. That same night a young shepherd is devoured by a pack of hyenas.

As December runs its course, we Christians keep to ourselves.

There are whisperings and suppressed curses and plans made and abandoned. All that becomes clear is that we are on our way, and quickly. We are informed that Ngqika has survived his fever and is lively as a cricket again, but even more unpredictable. We start slowly gathering our few possessions and stealthily packing. The plan is simple: Get out of Caffraria and fight our way through the eastern Bushmen. And after that? you ask. After that nobody knows.

It's a battle to persuade Kemp to come with us. Messengers from Maynier bring him a pile of letters and a bag full of clothes. They've hardly left or he distributes the clothes among the Caffres. One of the letters mentions that the Reverends Read and Van der Lingen have arrived at the Cape. They are looking forward to ministering to the Heathens with him, but for the time being they're remaining in the background until things calm down on the frontier. The evening before our departure I sit and talk to my friend for a long time. He agrees at long last to leave Caffraria when he is told that Sara and the other converted Hottentot women are leaving with us.

> My labours under the Caffres were not exactly a success, he
> says. I should rather throw in my lot with the few women for
> whom I do mean something.

He gazes for a while in the direction of the Great Place.

> I must be led in my life choices by my weakness, he says, not
> my strength. I must acknowledge my wounds, make my frailty
> my armour.

Why should I at this moment think of Geertruy and childhood writing lessons under the giant tree? Kemp drones on:

> Do you respect this, Buys, you who get stronger by the day? You
> who are led by your strength?
> Respect? In this wilderness you mustn't go looking for respect,
> Kemp. Here there is only meat and blood and cunt.

We let Ngqika know that we are going to shoot a few elephants and will bring back the finest tusks for him and on the last day of 1800 we clear out of Caffraria.

6

We trek to the Colony by one hell of a detour. What a cock-up this outing turned out to be. We had to travel in a wide north-western arc to avoid Caffraria and to forge our way through inhospitable and trackless landscapes. In the course of the next four months and some weeks we would travel in a half-moon, from the Kabusie down next to the west bank of the Kei as far as the Stormberg, then west to the Bamboesberg and at last south to Schapenkraal in the Tarka district.

Yes, Ngqika, we're going to hunt elephants. What do you mean, of course we're coming back. We're going to fetch Bezuidenhout and Faber from the Kabusie and then we're going to disport ourselves merrily in your kingdom with our guns. Yes, thank you for sending a whole gang of Caffres with us to help us with the hunting; thank you for not being over-friendly and mistrustful. Damn.

On New Year's Day 1801 we and our wagons cross the mountainous and invisible border between Caffre and Bushman. From the mountain we survey the whole of Caffraria, all the way to the sea. It's beautiful here, and wild. We sleep in the river sand of the Kabusie. The next morning I kick the lot awake, where they're snoring away, half buried in the sand like tortoise eggs. There are quite a few of us; every single Christian and deserter and outlaw has joined our trek. We must get going early if we want to do a day's journey in a day. Our flight needs to be swift, before Ngqika's mind changes again, like the fickle weather of his country. Into the saddle and through the river. Kemp leads his horse by the bridle. He falls, the horse gets a fright, stumbles and falls on top of him. The horse tramples him badly; I pull him out from under the floundering animal just before it's too late. The missionary is once again in tears. Nowadays if he's not puking he's bawling.

> I could see them under the flood, Buys. I saw my Antje and
> Styntje. Rest awaits me in the waters, Buys. *They* await me.
> Come on now, Kemp. We've got a lot of ground to cover
> today.

As we ride away, Kemp keeps looking back over his shoulder, back to the river.

By afternoon we have crossed the nek and reached the stands of Faber and Bezuidenhout. I'm almost glad to see the old bellwethers again.

The veldt here is teeming with lion and wildebeest, with us in the midst of this ancient confrontation. People who use their eyes to gaze heavenward sometimes see earthly things differently to those of us with our eyes to the ground. See what our missionary writes in his report: He says the wildebeest is so called in Dutch because it is indeed a *wilde beest*, a wild beast, a creature made up out of segments of different animals. It has the rump of an ox, the mane of a horse, the fringe of an eland, the horns of a buffalo, the tail of a quagga, the beard of a goat and the paws of a reindeer.

On the sixth we get rid of Ngqika's Caffres. Up to now they've trekked along with us with the few cattle they wanted to barter for tusks. We come across two Bushmen who are on their way to Caffraria to trade two tusks for a cow. We give them a cow and take the tusks. They are young tusks and freshly cut. There are more elephants around here and they're close. The Bushmen ask for another calf before they'll divulge where they found the elephant. We go and look for the troop and shoot two big bulls and pile the Caffres' arms high with tusks and hides and fat and feet. We give them an ox-cart and say Keep your cattle, these are gifts. I say we'll carry on hunting until our wagons are also full of tusks. I send them and their cattle back to their king with all good wishes and a prosperous New Year.

Without Ngqika's gawkers the group of wanderers is now composed as follows:
4 Dutch rascals – yours truly, Bezuidenhout, Faber and Krieger,
2 Dutch women,
2 Dutch children,
5 English deserters,
1 German deserter,

13 little bastards,

1 Caffre,

1 Caffre woman,

4 Hottentots,

6 Hottentot women,

15 or so Hottentot children,

2 little Caffre girls,

1 Tambookie boy,

1 slave and

1 missionary.

Only in these parts would such an assortment of oddities huddle together for the sake of survival. For the rest:

a flock of sheep,

a herd of goats,

300 cattle,

25 horses,

3 wagons,

1 ox-cart and would you believe it,

1 printing press.

~

The aloes grow high here and look different to those in Caffraria. The plants branch out luxuriantly, sometimes with fifty heads to as many branches of the same tree. The sap is richer, the leaves sparser, the leaf edges less curved and the teeth sharper. Cycads are everywhere in the veldt between grazing eland and wildebeest. On this day a herd of bontebok numbering more than four thousand moves past.

We cross a stream and spend another night on the bank, where Bushmen attack us before dawn. The Bushmen are driven back with a few shots. The only soul to get wounded is the Englishman Bentley, in the way as always. Kemp is immediately on duty with bandages and ointments that he conjures up from nowhere. The first arrow just glanced Bentley's head. The second remained lodged in his forearm – near the lower join of the radius and the ulna, if our doctor is to be believed. Kemp has been here with us in the bush for how long and he still believes that you can cure anything if you know the words for a man's component parts. The doctor manages to extract the shaft of the arrow, but the point has penetrated too far to be removed safely. He leaves the arrow point inside the Englishman and bandages him. I wait for the poison to start doing its job, but nothing. The deserter is evidently immune, or the Bushmen have run out of poison. The creatures also pot a dog and a cow.

When the sun sets, we don't make fires; the next morning the area between the tents and wagons is criss-crossed with the tracks of lions and hyenas and leopards. Rather these creatures than the Bushmen in whose hunting ground we're making ourselves at home.

With the sun full in our eyes we see a lion in the distance, so huge that the missionary believes the children when they tell him it's a hairy elephant.

~

Kemp looks more exhausted than ever, his eyes water and he walks stooped over with a hand clutching his breast. I ask him what's the matter. The missionary strokes the front of his shirt, tells me how he lay under the wagon the night before to get out of the rain. At some stage of the night the horses tied to the wagon balked at the sudden stink of lion on the wind. Kemp scrambled out from under the wagon to find rest for body and soul somewhere, then one of the horses kicked him squarely in the chest. He unbuttons his shirt and shows me the purple bruise.

You'll live, the horse wasn't kicking with intent.
Yes, Buys. It's nothing really, says the missionary, a trifle reluctant to admit that his wound is not life-threatening.
But Buys, he adds immediately and excitedly, not an eye could I shut for the rest of that night. The lions were circling me and roaring.
Then we can only thank the Lord that you are still with us,

215

Brother Kemp, I say, and hold back my smile until my back is
turned.

Kemp contemplates the bruise and keeps his shirt unbuttoned till
that evening.

~

On 10 January we draw up in front of steep mountains and we rest.
My hands are cramping. Maria rubs them with her dear rough fingers.
Krieger and Faber are sent to reconnoitre. The next day it's back across
the river, around a mountain as far as a great plain. In front of us lie
two rivers, the one winds from east to west, the other south to north.
The river closer to us is in flood, but I'm anxious about what Ngqika
will do when his Caffres turn up at the Great Place without his Khula
and Jank'hanna. We will have to cross here. We unload most of the
supplies from the wagons to make them lighter. We wade through the
stream with packs on our heads. Then back again through the river to
bring through the wagons and cattle. The stream claims a few cattle,
but for the rest we get to the other side unharmed. We stop before
the second river in a thorn forest.

Say what I like, the lot decide to stay here till they've had news from
the Colony. Nobody can decide on a final destination. Some want to
get to the other side of the Great River, others simply want to get back
to the Colony. For two weeks we camp right here in this fair and fertile
valley, with the Storms and Bamboes Rivers only a few days' trek away.
All too soon old routines reassert themselves. The women do what
women do, the men ride around or hunt or sit and gaze and ruminate
on the world. Kemp starts teaching again and Maria follows him
around all day and laments the fate of her soul. We see a few Bushmen,
but the scum run away. Before the end of the week we've built solid
laagers of branches around the campsite to keep out the Bushmen
and the worst of the beasts. Here and there some of our people even
build huts while waiting.

~

For days on end Kemp walks around wailing to anyone who'll listen about some scorpion bite that was more probably a mosquito. It is as if he's become more frail since our departure, as if he's used up the last of his resilience in surrendering his mission under the Caffres. Just when I think my fellow patriots have at last accepted him, he gets their blood boiling again by starting to pray and preach in focking English for the focking English deserters.

Faber catches two Bushmen driving twenty-six Caffre cattle across the veldt. He can see, of course, that it's stolen cattle, and he shoots and kills one Bushman from the saddle. The other one manages to stab or maim six of the cattle before Faber pots him too. Faber drives the cattle to the camp. The missionary is highly incensed when he is treated to the Christian's story. I have to take the old man aside and calm him down before Faber does him harm.

Kemp is seething, his whole body shivers like the reed that he is. I make him sit down and go and stand over him so that I become his shadow and say to him there is no life here without the spilling of blood. If he thinks that he, or the hosts of missionaries streaming into the Colony, are going to ennoble the people here in some way, that unity and accord are possible in this wilderness, then he's in trouble. Here we devour each other. Christians, Dutchmen, Germans, French, Caffres, Bengalis, Hottentots, Bushmen and whatever else. It's one great hunting ground. If he's going to carry on sorrowing about it, it's going to cost him his soul. His yearning for it to be different is going to consume him till there's nothing left of him. He can try to save a few errant souls. But mankind has long been beyond saving.

Upon waking up on 29 January, we discover that two Hottentots and the Caffre called something like Dakkam Jamma have absconded during the night with five of our horses and two saddles. Four of us ride out to search for them. Before the sun is shining from overhead, we notice three figures in a copse of thorn trees. The figures are stooped over, swaying. We dismount and walk closer when the deserters neither answer nor flee. The three men are being held upright by their guts that are twined around their arms and shoulders and tied to the branches. The bodies are perforated with arrow wounds. The throats of all three have been slit, the blood on their chests black with flies. The Caffre's prick is sticking out of his mouth as if he is taunting us from the realm of death with a new tongue. I'm busy cutting the bodies free when we hear a whistling. We are surrounded by a horde of Bushmen who are running around us in the undergrowth and poking out a head here and there to whistle or shout or laugh. The German fires a shot that only elicits more laughter. We leave the deserters to their swaying and jump on our horses that are pawing the ground with rolling eyes and charge away with the Bushmen shouting after us mockingly, some of them with their pizzles in their hands. A stone hits me in the back and I ride on.

Nobody sleeps that night and nobody makes a fire and nobody talks and the following morning we hitch up quickly and cross the next river and trek north to a next river that could be a tributary of the Kei and outspan on the bank and this night as well nobody sleeps and nobody makes a fire and nobody talks, except for the German who stands guard and now again thumps his chest with his fist and shouts searing defiance at the dark bush.

With the coming of the red dawn on the last day of the month we trek further across the plain. To the north, east and west the plain dead-ends in mountains. We linger past bush pigs, antelope, wildebeest, ostriches, buffaloes, lush grass and every conceivable edible root and bulb and fruit. We are surrounded with plenitude and peril.

Bezuidenhout recounts that when he was patrolling the surroundings last night, he encountered two lions and shot and killed one and the other one fled and he reloaded and pursued the lion and shot and killed her as well.

≈

A week later Maria arrives at the wagon all aflutter, fidgets here there and everywhere and wails away at one of Kemp's hymns. I sit with my back against the wheel chawing a plug of tobacco. In the wagon tilt above me she drops a saucepan and giggles to herself. I spit out the tobacco juice slowly. The bitter black syrup hangs suspended between my lower lip and the grass at my feet before it falls. I get up and peer into the wagon tilt.

What is it, woman?

I'm going to be baptised. I'm going to Jesus and my children are going to Jesus.

You're going nowhere.

He's going to baptise me in the river and the river is going to wash away my sins.

We'll see about that.

I walk to Kemp's tent where the old man is at his eternal scribbling.

You want to baptise my wife and this is the first I hear of it?

Mijnheer Buys, good to see you. I was just –

You don't do a thing with my wife and children without reckoning with me first.

But Buys, I assumed you'd be in favour of their souls being with you in the house of the Lord –

And then you want to go and wash them in the river. I'm the only one who washes my wife. If you want a woman, just say the word. But you leave Maria alone. As it is, you're talking to her more than is acceptable. You put all sorts of things into her head and then I'm stuck with it.

Kemp gets to his feet.

Buys, I have no designs on your or any other Christian's wife. Yes, I baptise by partial immersion. For me it designates being buried along with our Lord Christ in death and being resurrected along with him. I believe with all my heart that this accords with the Word. Was our Lord himself not baptised in a stream by the Baptist? If you have problems with my liturgy, you must say so.

I hold my peace. Kemp sits down again, starts writing and after a few seconds looks up again to see if I'm still there.

If you want to baptise my wife, then you do it as is proper, I say. Kemp smiles:

So let's hear it.

I sit down across from Kemp at the table. On the folding riempie stool on which I take a seat I'm just as high as Kemp on his wooden chair. I lean forward and grip the table on both sides. With every sentence I lift the table and on every full stop I put it down again hard.

Right. You sprinkle her, just a few drops as is proper. No drowning or burying or whatever.

The table slams down. Kemp sits back a whit, tries to hide his smirk.

If that is your wish, any time, Mijnheer Buys.

You baptise her on a Sunday.

Something in the table creaks.

I understand.

Right.

I let go of the table, sit up straight. Then grab the table again and lift it.

You baptise her after a church service.

The table hits the ground. A few papers float to the ground.

A good idea, Buys, then there will also be more witnesses before the Lord.

This time the table goes up and down before I speak.

And when you baptise, you say only the things that are said in the Dutch churches. No focking English church is going to take her soul.

Focking?

That's English.

Kemp looks away, but I can see he's laughing.

I am acquainted with the term.

The table slams down again.

Do you understand?

That is in order, Coenraad.

I lean further forward, another hand's breadth and we'll damnwell be kissing.

And apart from the little ones, you'll baptise Bettie as well.

Kemp moves his chair back.

Coenraad, Elizabeth knows by now what she wants and doesn't want. If she does not convert of her own accord, I cannot baptise her.

I want to lean back, remember too late that there's nothing behind me, opt to fold my arms instead. I smile.

Brother Kemp. If you want to baptise Maria, then you'll baptise Nombini's children as well. She does not care a fig or a fart for your God and my God and I have no problem with that. You should know by now, you can't convert a Caffre. Her children are not mine. You can see that for yourself. But I am their father and I will see them baptised.

Kemp jumps up and I follow suit. We stand facing each other, our heads brush against the tent roof.

What do you want of me, Buys? You know I can't do it. You know I can't baptise children of Heathen parents. If your concubine does not convert of her own accord, I can't baptise her children.

Is that how you feel?

I'm only doing my terrestrial duty, Buys. I cannot save those who are beyond salvation.

I put on my hat. Take that. I put out my hand.

Well, so be it, Kemp. Then we understand each other. You're not baptising a soul in my house. You can catechise till Maria can write better psalms than David. But you keep your sprinklings or your rivers or your goddam waterfalls for your self and your tame Hotnots.

Kemp tries to escape the hand that insists on shaking his. When I walk out:

221

And please do stop encouraging the poor woman to sing. If it gives me so much pain, just think what it must do to the great and pure ears of our Lord.

∽

Still no final destination has been resolved upon. The little band of refugees start irritating one another; something is coming apart at the seams. At the beginning of March the Bushmen's dogs roam the camp at night. In the mountains we see thirteen and sometimes fourteen fires burning. Life drags on. By the middle of the month the Christians are starting to squabble among themselves about where to next. Back to the Colony? Further eastward? North, over the Great River? Each has persuaded himself of his own scheme. I listen to my fellow outlaws talking. I see the English deserters watching us and wondering if they joined the right gang. I see the Hottentots starting to lift up their eyes unto the hills. From whence will cometh help for them, away from these errant Christians? Perhaps back to the wilderness from which they were tamed, perhaps back to the Bushmen and back to hunting and gathering and sleeping in caves. I see Bezuidenhout walking up and down in the camp as if there were fences and at night I hear the redbeard battering his wife.

On the 19th we come across a few runaway soldiers. The deserters share their wine from the Colony with us. The swilling ends in a boozing, blaspheming, blathering and buggering. The German flattens Bentley in the yellow grass and gets his breeches down before the Englishman can make his escape and seek refuge with the praying Kemp in his tent. In the early hours I fall into Nombini's tent and mount her but get nothing done and only wake up the following afternoon.

∽

Late one clear and warm evening at the end of March Faber and I are sitting around the fire mounting guard. I trawl in the pot for a bone that hasn't been picked clean.

What is your plan, Buys? Do you want to head back to the
Colony?

A man can use the Colony. They pay well for tusks and hides.
But to go and establish myself there again? I don't know.

I am told the border is open once again, he says. Most of the
people have moved away. The Caffres made it impossible for
them there. We could trek back over the Fish and vanish into
the bush there. The English wouldn't know where to look
for us.

I don't hide.

We can't bugger around in the wilderness for forty years like
the Israelites, Buys.

The focking English think we're trash. They don't want us back
in the Colony. The Caffres no longer want us in Caffraria. The
Bushmen don't want us in their hunting grounds. And the lot
here are going to start murdering one another by next week if
we don't find something for them to do.

What do you suggest, he asks.

What is every man looking for in this land? What is all this
fighting about?

Well, Buys, people do say that your head on a post would solve
most problems hereabouts.

Exactly, Faber. Because a land of robbers asks for the main
robber to be hanged, so that the other rascals can plunder in
peace.

Buys, you're stirring shit again.

No, listen. If in these parts you find a woman or a head of cattle,
then you know it used to be another man's. Everything is always
already stolen. Let's go and fetch ourselves some fresh cattle.

And women, Faber laughs.

And women, yes. We go and take ourselves fresh cattle and
women and make a herd so strong that we can buy cannon to
protect the kraals and velvet on which to nail our women.

Faber, grinning, scrabbles with a stick in the coals.

> And where are we going to find these treasures, Buys?

I answer the question I've been waiting for all evening:

> We bash our way through the Bushmen all the way to the
> Tambookies.

By the next morning the whole camp knows of my plan. Every
Christian and Englishman walks with a bounce to his step and winks
at me in passing. In the course of the next few days we start melting
kitchen utensils for bullets again. Kemp gets to hear of the plan and
starts trembling with dismay. His forehead blushes blood red when
he faces me foursquare.

> Buys, what are you doing with these people? You know you
> can't do it. You can't incite them to do evil.
> You play your games, Kemp. I play mine.
> Play? I don't play, Buys, I am in service of the kingdom of God.
> And I'm in service of the kingdom of take what you can before
> this place takes what you have.

~

A day or so before we were planning to start our campaign to the
Tambookies the horses start pegging it. On the Monday two keel over,
three on Tuesday and all the rest are ill. Some people think the disease
keeps to the plains. We drive the horses up against the Stormberg. By
Wednesday evening we are informed that three more have died. On
Thursday morning Kemp accompanies me up the mountain to where
the horses are kept. The missionary has recovered his health. Even
though he's much older, he keeps up all the way and doesn't say a
word when he stumbles or when branches scratch him. His jacket,
which he still constantly wears without a shirt, shows white under
the arms. He gabbles on incessantly about souls that he will save in
Graaffe Rijnet, about the land lying fallow before him to convert.
The Hottentot herders are glad to see us. They say they see Bushmen
in the night. The scoundrels keep their distance, but make sure

everybody knows they're there. I give the herdsmen the lead and powder I can spare.

Kemp takes off his jacket and cuts open one of the dead horses. He messes around up to his elbows in the animal's innards. With bloody forearms he shows where the guts are inflamed. Especially the colon and volvulus, he says. The good tidings, he says, is that there is no gangrene. He tugs at a gut, then he's back into the horse with only his shoulders sticking out.

> There's colic here, brethren, he calls out from inside the carcase. Did the horse cough?
> They cough, yes, master, says Ngei, Faber's Hottentot.
> Ah, of course. The midriff is irritated by the inflamed colon.
> The thing has copped it, Kemp, let it be now. I don't want to have to snuggle up to you in the mountains tonight.
> Dear Buys, tonight you'll snuggle up to your wife . . . to any or all of your wives. I know what's wrong here. We have to bleed the horses as soon as they fall ill. Bleed them well.

That evening we devise a new plan. The Tambookies will have to wait until we've got fresh horses. Ngqika has horses. We must shoot an elephant. I volunteer for this. One of us will take the tusks to Ngqika as a gift to show we are still his chums and we don't at all think that he's crazy and dangerous and we have true as God all this time merely been trekking after elephants. A few of us will then follow the man with the tusks into Caffraria and filch the Caffres' horses while Ngqika and his captains are receiving the guest. Nobody faults the plan. There is no other plan.

The next morning most of the company walk up the mountain to witness the great bloodletting. We are halfway up the mountain when we hear branches snapping as some creature comes charging down at us. I've got my gun at the ready; as the shrubs open up before me, it's Ngei who blunders into me and collapses. I make him stand. The man's body is covered in arrow wounds. The Hottentot convulses and vomits on the ground in front of him till he can't breathe any more.

He stands for a few moments with his hands on his knees and gasps and then he vomits again. He comes upright and clings to me. He starts babbling in his own language and in Dutch and nobody understands a word he's saying. He sees Kemp and totters towards him and falls on his neck and says something again and drops down dead at his feet.

The scumbags can't be far! I shout.

I run up the mountain to the horses.

I come upon the body of another Hottentot, also grazed with the arrow wounds that spread death through a human body within a quarter of an hour. I shout at the men further down the mountain to load their rifles, calamity is upon us. At the place where the horses were kept, I count fourteen carcases riddled with arrows. A few of the large bodies are still sighing and groaning and don't know they're dead already. I chase away the over-hasty vultures. After a long search we find three horses and two stallion foals indulging in the juicy grass stalks that will shimmer with dew for a while longer in the shade of the mountainside.

With our horses gone and dead we decide that in future we'll keep close to the northern border of the Colony. Unless you're an animal or a Bushman you need decent transport and bags of munitions to brave the untamed other side of the border. On 30 March we strike camp and trek west by north. That night I sit up with Glider, my beautiful, dear, beloved and faithful bay who has held up through it all, but is now also ailing. Before daybreak I shoot him. Yes, I cried.

It's a cold April in this arid land when we arrive at Haazenfontein. The veldt shrinks back under the frost, but there is enough water for a desert people and it is high here. Some people say all the rivers of the country have their source here.

The wretched Kemp is shivering with cold and fever, but on Sunday morning he's ready with three sermons, one for the Dutch, one for the focking English and then catechism for the Hottentots. The man's flame is not quenched, but it seems to me as if he's still not recovered his health after the major stomach ructions of a while ago.

I trek into the Colony on the ox-cart to find out from the Tjaart person – Field Commander van der Walt, I have since been informed – what my chances are for a pardon. Since I can no longer rely on the goodwill of the Caffre king, I'm starting to test the waters of the English temperament at the Cape so long. Kemp writes a pack of letters for me to take along. There is one to Van der Walt asking him to send his wagon to transport Kemp to the Field Commander's farm in Tarka, from where he'll arrange transport to Graaffe Rijnet. Then also a moving plea pertaining to my outlaw status.

In the course of the night before my departure a few hyenas tear our last horse to pieces and thirty jackals come to devour what the hyenas and a lone lion left behind. By morning even the bones have vanished. All that we find is a piece of skull with one eye regarding us milkily.

I rejoin the nomadic tribe in time to watch in wonderment a host of locusts swarming past northwards. A thundering immeasurable cloud, a mile wide and how many long. The leading hoppers descend and settle and devour everything that grows, to fall in again at the back when the cloud has streamed past darkly and deafeningly. The larvae have hatched in the frontier districts and mounted the wind and will rage forth until they've exhausted themselves or been blown into the sea. As they move they leave eggs behind and new storms arise. Never resting, they carry on hopping until the very dust is alive. I hear stories of how such swarms cross rivers, the floating drowned form a bridge for the rearguard. They smother the fires the farmers make to staunch them by hopping into the fires in their thousands. Those that don't get burnt move on.

The little lost band draws up and even the oxen turn their yoke-burdened shoulders to gaze at the locusts, how the things that were still larvae only the other day now denude the course of their migration

of all that human or animal could eat. This track will remain visible
for weeks, as if a monstrous harrow has moved across the land.

We trek on through plains full of wildebeest, bontebok, springbok,
jackal, leopard, wild dogs and my red dogs with their new wild
blood, even more savage. At the foot of the Bamboesberg we swerve
south and then west to cross the Colony border once again through
a defile in the mountains. On 27 April we stop at a place called
Schapenkraal.

~

My days with Kemp draw to a close. Van der Walt had given me a
letter for Kemp in which he says that the missionaries Read and Van
der Lingen are already waiting for him in Graaffe Rijnet with a wagon
at the ready. Van der Walt also offers his own wagon to fetch Kemp
from us. Kemp writes back and thanks the zealous Van der Walt for
his wagon. He also asks that, if possible, Van der Walt should bring
along mission money to pay Kemp's travel companions for their trouble
in bringing him this far. I still don't divulge to Kemp that the so-called
Christians that he now wants to pay were the selfsame thieves who
at Ngqika's place systematically robbed him blind.

~

Esteemed voyeur, do not begrudge me a break in my narrative. I have
no desire to tell you what Kemp and I spoke about that night when we
could have a last dispute in peace. See, my old friend is also somewhat
cryptic on the subject in his diary of 30 April:

> By the mercy of the Lord I got an opportunity to converse freely
> with Buys on the concerns of his soul.

There by the fire we were honest for once, with each other and
especially with ourselves. We prattled for a long time about God and
soul and that which no man ever dares utter to another or to himself.
Our conversation took us to places far beyond the limits of the permis-
sible, places that will never be revisited in daylight. If you want to

know more, you can damnwell think it up. Go on, go as far as your imagination can take you. Believe me, that night we went further.

~

On the 6th of May 1801 Van der Walt turns up with his wagon and the money Kemp asked for. On the 7th they're gone. I shall never see Jank'hanna van der Kemp again.

While I'm helping him load the wagon, I filch a little bag of letters. I'll melt them down and cast bullets. The words of the press will spread through this land as my friend hoped. They will be lodged in many hearts and brains and I'll assist a horde of Heathenish souls to escape from their mortal dungeons, so please it the Lord of missionaries. Amen.

7 – 8 November 1814

1

Where once my houses stood, game parks and hunting lodges now lie. Where once I lived, you don't live. My ferality has seeped into the soil. Where I staked my claim, where I pissed on the corner posts of my yard, there your bricks and your tar don't grow.

It is early morning, my house is dark. If you want to see where you are, open the narrow casement window. Bang open the stuck shutter; the wood warped last winter. The light flows down the wall, over the floor. The window frames the mountains, all of the outside hovers before the window opening; then the landscape washes in, imprisoned in the room. The darkness inside frames the light on the dung-covered floor. The floor anchors your feet. *This* is the first mark we make on earth, the place where you scrabble open a seat for yourself by the fire. Once the soil around the floor has been trodden flat, the dance can begin. And see, the wall is a floor rising up. The wall frames the window. Walls divide up the floor, walls create rooms; as soon as there are rooms, time slows down. The wall separates us from the world and it creates a new world, a framed world. Indeed, the wall separates, thank God. We can coexist as long as the walls remain standing. The floor and walls and windows choose one another and separate one another and share one outside and together they bring about a last partition: a roof. In this country roofs are seldom flat; where else would the coffins go? The roof is dried rushes; it is cool; it burns easily.

Do you hear the termites in the wood of the frames? The yellow-wood door frames are their mansions with a thousand rooms. They were here first. You are standing in a long house with one room opening into another. You are standing in the kitchen. Are you surprised that *this* is your entrance – the hearth? Open the back door. With the opening and closing of windows and doors you rule the routes of the wind. Against the outer wall is piled a heap of rhinoceros bush and hopbush for firewood. Can you still smell the bread in the built-out baking oven?

The kitchen is my wife's nest. See, the lanterns are calabashes into which she cut holes for candles. See, the last two porcelain plates are hanging against the wall, the relics of what my neighbours call civilisation. And you don't besmirch civilisation with animal fat and sweet potatoes. The tin plates in the little wooden cupboard that I hammered together. The bowls of wood, the basins of earthenware. The cups and saucers mostly broken by children, by jolting wagons and by temper tantrums. Run a finger over any object here and you won't find any dust. The copper gleams and even the wood strives to shine. She polishes every ladle and spoon until the things start sharing their own intimate light with her, as if they lose all happenstance and become more real. Every fork is inexorably here and hers. The house is brought forth from her callused hands. She takes care. She rebuilds the house from the inside. And I can hardly hammer together a rickety table. Her long fingers burnish the house to life every day anew. It is her house, it is egg and nest, it is country and universe. Every few years I tell a Hottentot to limewash the outer walls.

Peek into the pantry, but keep your paws off my biltong. Look up, the purlins are festooned with bowls and tobacco. Do you see the massive ridge pole of mountain cypress? It's the only wood in the house that has not yet invited in the termites.

Step out of the kitchen into the back room. In the evenings we eat here. Step warily in the dusk, one or two of my offspring are always playing or sleeping here. My wife sets only forks on the table. In my world everyone carries his own knife. My blade has worn thin with whetting. Open the shutter, otherwise you'll bump into the little table and six chairs that were in the house before us. Two of the chairs are held together by God's grace and tolerated only for the sake of their beauty. They have been eaten hollow. A solid fart would reduce them to the dust whence they came. The furniture mirrors the house back to itself. The table is a floor on the floor. It is furniture that your body brushes against most often and not the floor and walls. Furniture has a more intimate knowledge of your body. Furniture brings the outside inside, because until recently it was still trees and driftwood. Furniture is the outside that has been sawn and planed and varnished. You will fit, but I have to stoop under the reed ceiling. Just as well *my* table does not stand here.

Down the narrow passage, hardly room for a decent pair of shoulders, but the celling vanishes here and a man like me can keep his head upright between the roof trusses. To the right the two bedrooms. Keep going. Inside are hide rugs and cots strung with thongs and hide. For the rest you have no business here.

You are standing in the front room, the front door next to you. Do you see how my wife has decorated the threshold with peach pips? The rifle above the door. The broom in the corner. The mattresses against the wall, stuffed with shrubs and klipspringer hair.

Open the front door. I couldn't have made these wooden hinges. Allow me to flick the termite off your arm.

See, the great white stinkwood with the branches and twigs that ramify and ramify out of sight. When in the bare winters I sit under the tree and gaze heavenward, the delicate branch-deltas make the sky seem like a sheet of crazed glass.

Look around you. Before you lies the bare yard. The turf walls that used to surround the homestead six feet from the house, the stone turrets with the loopholes on the four corners, those I all flattened when I moved in here. In these kloofs there's no point in barricading yourself against the Caffres and the Bushmen. If they come, they come. Nobody's going to hear you screaming here. All that the barricades do is trap the creatures invading your home and make them more bloodthirsty. No, your house must have a clear prospect. If you go out by the front door and you're still not outside, there's something amiss. Build your house in the open, so that you can see what's happening around you. If Omni-I am nostalgic for these kloofs, I like reading about how other people lived here: As you build your temple, says one Couga sage, so your gods will be.

Walk around the house. Careful, you've almost stepped on the lizard. My wife keeps the animals outside, but the chickens and ducks and pet lamb roam not far from the back door. You wouldn't say so to stand here looking at the place, but the house grew out of the soil. The sandstone from the hills and the clay from the earth. Go and have a look at the stone kraal. Whoever built it knew that stone has a grain like wood; he knew the stone's propensity. A stone reveals itself under the hammer. The Couga is the breeding ground of stones, say the Hottentots. But the house no longer has any dealings with nature. It's the whitewashed – yes, washed whiter than driven snow – homestead of the legendary Coenraad de Buys, citizen of the Colony, married, father, grandfather, rent-payer. You can laugh, go on. Like a hermit crab did I move into another man's house, did I withdraw from the world. Every house is a shell. A rectangular house on a surveyed and measured farm. Without marker stones there will no longer be a Colony and to the devil with the Colony. But without boundary markers also no farm, no house, no room, no bed with a pillow resting against a solid, whitewashed wall. Limestone is dead animals. Crushed, desiccated animals; desecrated shells. Shells that have been pulverised, ground, puddled by the subterranean violence; by the fearsome heat of the earth's innards. Dead, compacted animals, I, Omni-Buys, read the other evening in a book of French verse. Truly, sometimes when I think back to this place, my throat constricts, words fail me and I am reduced to echoing the words of others.

You've been through my house, the inside and the outside I have shown you, but you have not found me there. The house over there belongs to Maria and her children and that other one is Nombini's shack. The one further along is where my flame-haired daughter Bettie lives with her white husband and my whitewashed grandchild. I managed to defend her honour against Ngqika's attentions until we left Caffraria behind and she could marry Jan the Christian. Jan the most boring man on this earth. Jan who will cherish her. Jan who, unlike me and Ngqika, is content with one wife; Jan, for whom she is all women. In any case. Go and see for yourself by all means, those little houses are smaller and perhaps not so tidy; if you've seen one house, you've seen most of them. In those houses, too, I am not to be found. The huts you see against the western hills are where the workers live; it's far from the homesteads, but over there they catch the morning sun in the cold winters.

This yard will be coming to life soon and then you'll have to stand aside. Come and stand here by my shoulder, here where I'm sitting at my table under the white stinkwood on this already sweltering day. Come and stand at the table that I made, almost eleven years ago when I moved in here. The table with the crooked joints and the uneven top of mountain cypress. I went and chopped down the cypress tree myself. Almost sixty feet high that giant towered. Sawing it up and hauling it back was a business. One of the legs is a stinkwood beam, another of yellowwood and the other two are ironwood beams. This table that I built for my family, big enough for all the children and their mothers and their appendages. The table that, come hell or high water, refused to go in by the door. The table that has been standing under the tree for almost eleven years and is rotting gradually from beneath and is being devoured from the inside by the termites that do not tolerate any kind of structure in these kloofs. Under this table there is no floor, just the soil, the sand and stone ground down by my

235

own feet. Here next to the tree I picked up a fossil, a shell, slumbering in its own shape. Come stand here by my side and watch the proceedings.

~

See, my wagon is standing ready for its team. Twenty or so rifles, munitions, six elephant tusks, hides, a tin full of beads, anything to barter with there where money loses its value; the necessary coffee, sugar, corned meat, sweet potatoes. Brandy. My little trunk of clothes. I'm ready to shake the Couga dust off my feet.

> Pack your bags and be gone, Buys! Long Piet Ferreira sneered
> at me the other day at the cattle sale.

My other neighbours shuffled their feet and looked the other way and offered no demur. Sometimes your enemies have a point. The last thing I was to do as citizen of the goddam Colony, the act that would sentence me to the desert, was when at the beginning of last year I went and spoke the truth about my neighbours.

In front of me on the table the mad traveller's book is lying open. Next to it a loaded musket. I sit still. The rasping of the termites in the table top audible under my hands for a moment. Two of my lads come running across the yard. The baboons in the hills are demented, yell at the children and thump their chests and the stones with human fists. The big one's mouth is foam flecked. Gawie is barely six and trips yowling over his feet. Windvogel's half-grown cuckoo-child, Windvogel the younger, wakes up under the lean-to of the cookhouse. He looks up, rubs across the downy clumps of his first beard, shouts at the boys to fall flat. He shoots and kills the foaming ape and sits down again on his arse, hat over his eyes. I shoot another one that's trying to abscond behind the rocks.

> Father, those teeth! It wasn't us, Father! Dirk shouts as he runs.

Gawie clings to me. I release myself. I scold them. Dirk is eight already, he should have known better. He must go and fetch the cane. They know very well one doesn't tease baboons. When the two have calmed down and have done with admiring the welts on each other's backsides, I send them bustling to round up the Buys clan.

I reload the gun. Even the baboons are going berserk in these kloofs. The rampant boredom. I thank the Lord for my wives. A bored man feels lonely very quickly. Here among the kloofs there are quite a few old bachelors. And on the frontier women were not always to be found for the asking. There were stories in the more remote areas of a gentleman or two who took tips from the baboons and sometimes anointed a sweet melon as wife. Like the baboons these Lotharios, according to report, also ate the evidence afterwards, either from shame or hunger. And in those parts there was a farmer – not to name names – but they say that he never took a wife. Never even a bit of up and over on the sly. Visitors started remarking that the little orphaned baboon he'd adopted was prancing about the yard sporting a starched white bonnet.

The book is lying open on a map of the interior. I know it's a map, because I've seen the previous ones. Saw how the landscapes with each successive map dematerialise further into hallucinations. The maps of somebody who should rather have stayed at home.

The hassle with my neighbours was merely the spark in the powder keg under my butt. My arse had been itching for a long time to trek. It's as if my guts and my arsehole throb along with all the world; the contractions and then the expulsions, the coil and release. The whole world breathes in and out and I along with it; I can no longer hold my breath. How can a man sit still if the peristalsis of God's creation makes his rear end crawl with all the cramping up and letting go? My houses, my farms, my citizenship of the Colony, all of it frames the wild wide chaos out there. The stone markers at the corners of my farm, the house walls of my families, the beds of my wives – all frames. You stake out the boundaries of your house so that you can have a view of the stars. Provisionally. Until one day the frame of the house explodes with the movement it cannot contain.

~

This morning I call a meeting of all my people.

> I'm trekking tomorrow morning at daybreak. Those of you who want to come along, stow your stuff on the wagons if there's space for it.
>
> Where are we going, Father?
>
> We're blundering north, my child.

I sit at the table and watch the yard starting to teem. Around me at first the botheration and altercation; then my people start scurrying to get their belongings onto a wagon. I write letters to my comrades to go with me, into the wilderness. It is the year 1814. Eleven years is a long time, but at times it feels no longer than a sweaty morning.

My wife comes walking towards me. She comes to stand in front of the table, her hands and eyes on the table, then she walks around to where I'm sitting and comes to stand next to me, doesn't make a sound. I get up. She presses me to her.

> Are we coming back?
>
> No.

My wife's name is Elizabeth. She wears a white woman's frock. I love my wife. We are married. Yes, I, Coenraad de Buys, two years ago went forth to get married in Swellendam in the sight of the Lord our God and the minister and congregation. I gave her a name and recorded the name in the register: *Elizabeth born 1782 in the land of the Makina, behind the Tambookies*. She has a way of looking at me. Her mouth and eyes and rounded blushing cheeks compose in a way that makes her at such moments the most beautiful woman I've ever seen. Oh, her mouth.

You've not missed all that much in these eleven years. When Kemp decamped for Graaffe Rijnet I went back to Ngqika to sort things out between us. In Caffraria rumours arrived, roundabout and richly embroidered, that the Christians who had lived at Ngqika's place with me had once again become a nuisance in Graaffe Rijnet. Once again the stories that I and thousands of Caffres were planning to drive the English into the sea. My son, the king of the Rharhabe, received me

238

with open arms; his mother was less overjoyed to see me. I wasn't sure whether we were still married; I wasn't sure whether she hated me or whether I was merely nothing to her. I went to sleep with her one night, and we performed sexual acts because there was nothing to be said. Her arms were even fatter than when I'd last laid eyes on her. She sat on top of me and her upper arms flapped like the wings of a wounded bird and she was thinking of other things. I don't think she noticed when I spurted in her. It was all over between us. Even that night I was jealous. I had been Maria's first and only. Nombini had from time to time had to lie down under old Langa and had also treated herself to Windvogel. But those two pricks I'd known and those I had brought to account. My women were *my* women. The other little Caffre maidens over the years had been mere lumps of tender flesh. Yese was as old as I and she lusted as strongly as I and she lay with whoever she wanted to lie with, as I did. I can never forgive her.

My people and I left the place with the blessing of the king. We trekked eastward for weeks as far as the Mambookies behind the Tambookies, and there I saw Elizabeth. She then had another name; don't ask. It's *her* name. Let it be. She played with my children as if she were a child again herself. I was in love. She immediately made friends with my Bettie and she constantly said her name: Elizabeth. Elizabeth. She liked the way the z and the th tickled her succulent red tongue. I spoke to her father and cast before him beads and cattle and tusks and hides and everything his wrinkled heart desired and took his daughter and named her Elizabeth. I moved back to my son, the one and only king of Caffraria.

When my shaft is inside my Elizabeth and her hands claw at my back, I whisper that first name of hers. The sounds throb like sighs and sobs in my throat, as if her name could only be sounded from the mouth of somebody who is coming.

What do you want to do with the stuff that doesn't fit onto the wagons? Elizabeth asks.

Not my worry.

We must burn it. We must burn it all down. It will look so beautiful.

Oh, her mouth.

~

While gathering my stuff before daybreak and loading it onto the wagons, I once again come across the traveller's book at the bottom of a wagon chest. Fish moths have been eating at it. Something wet has leaked onto it and permeated it. The pages are swollen like carcases in summer. I set the book aside and finished packing.

The first few pages cling together. I carefully ease them apart. On the first page is the title, *Het reizen door het binnenland* . . . Travels in the Interior. The rest has been scratched out, and underneath it, where the name of the author would have been, something seems to have gnawed a hole in the paper. At the top of the page a second, later title has been written in large, hurried letters: *Flatus Vocis*. I wish Kemp had been here to translate. When I'm not writing letters, I page through the scribblings of the madman while my family is packing and carting out furniture.

The book is full of maps. The first few are meticulously drawn. Around the Cape the scale is accurate, the mountains and rivers traced in different-coloured ink, every name of town and landmark written in and the red line of his route dotted eastward. The road ahead is white and empty. It must be difficult drawing a map of a region belonging to no one. The rivers still floweth where they listeth. They don't yet bear names: they only make noise. On the dotted line a small figure on horse-back, the traveller himself also part of his own map. Further along in the book the maps become fewer and stranger. The man is travelling up his own arse; on the later maps, north is always ahead of the little horseman, no matter which direction he's travelling in.

I page on. My eye falls on a female thigh. On this map dragons and piles of skulls proliferate instead of rivers and mountains. In the top right-hand corner is the pelvis of a woman sitting with legs spread as if arising from the map. He draws so well that I start drooling. Her right leg frames the top edge and her calf caresses Mozambique. From the colossal cunt like a sublime black sun slithers the serpent's tail on which, between the pale scales, is written *Gariep*. The traveller didn't know how rivers flow, because this Gariep serpent is slithering up into her. If you look closely, you see a little forked tongue peeking out of her navel.

Maria comes waddling over the yard. I press her to me, my little old wife, nowadays even shorter, all belly and dugs. She struggles free with her knotty arms, punches me in the chest and rages on, scolding and scuffing. When she calms down, I ask her whether she's coming along.

Where else am I supposed to go if not following you, Buys? She shakes her head and regards me with her hide-and-seek eyes and grabs me around the waist, her head in my belly. She stuffs a yellowed sheet of paper into my hand.

There, you're going to have to pin this to your hat so the Christians don't shoot you.

My pardon, the rescindment of my outlaw status; my citizenship. It is from this piece of paper that I now want to escape. Maria is a cunning vixen. She's handing me this thing so that I should reflect on what it's cost me to be able to squat here in peace for eleven years. Maria does not throw the bones of my fate, but packs them out all too neatly and then persuades me that I've done the throwing myself.

It was like that wayback time again, she says, when we were living by the sea and you just lay around. You're not lazy, not a bit. When you get like that, then you play dead, like a thing lying in its hole waiting to bite.

She is my first wife. She's known me from always. I've long since ceased to have any defence against her. I look at the paper in my hand. Yes, I fought a long time for this sheet calling me Citizen. But in the end it cost nothing more than sitting through a long goddam meeting.

2

I was with Ngqika when the Batavians took over the Cape in 1803.
I was shouting at and shrinking from my wives when the letter from
Lieutenant-General Janssens arrived on one fine day in June. The
new governor asks me to meet him in Algoa Bay. Apparently I can be
of great help in the negotiations with Ngqika's indigenes. Janssens
flatters as only a bureaucrat can. He appeals to my help as a friend
of my country, the Dutch colony in South Africa. Would like to ask
the man in what sense a colony is a country; more of an anthill, if
you're asking me. He writes that he's convinced that I'll rush to his
aid – *since I suppose that the welfare of the Country in which you were
born and in which you spent the greater part of your life will always be
dear to you.*

He had a point there: I do flatter easily. I send a Hottentot back
and inform him that I'll meet my honoured governor at such-and-such
a drift on the Fish River on the agreed-upon date. I tell Ngqika that if
we can win over the new authorities, they may well be less of a nuisance
than the focking British. Ngqika is not having any.

I saddle my horse, along with three Polish deserters from the
ninth Jägers battalion, an English deserter and a few of Ngqika's
strongest captains, and go and pay a visit to the governor at the drift
border crossing, where he's been dismounted for a few days. On
14 June Janssens' uniform is without a wrinkle, his buttons buffed
that morning. I'm sure he's been rehearsing his welcoming address
every morning to the little ears of the few hippopotami that haven't
been massacred yet.

Janssens is as friendly as he is strict. He has a firm handshake and
looks me in the eye more squarely than any landdrost or official that
I've yet come across. He has either nothing or plenty to hide. He's
almost of my height, but his shoulders are less stooped than mine.
His nose and neck are long, the corners of his mouth permanently
turned up, as if he finds the world amusing. I ask him to meet my son

and king in five days' time at the Kat River. The king feels threatened
by his enemies and doesn't want to venture so far from his home.
Janssens surveys the bunch of deserters with me. I plead on behalf
of Ngqika that the deserters will surrender themselves, but that the
king would regard it as a great honour to himself if they could be
pardoned. Janssens orders them to be manacled and sent to the
Cape to be tried there.

The governor tells me that he has met the other Caffre chiefs and
what a cock-up it was and how they stank. He says that they refuse
to move across the border before Ngqika surrenders me. They say
Ngqika is a thief and a murderer and they think he is under my
thumb and furthermore also in cahoots with the Colony. I say that
Ngqika for his part has gripes about the rebel chiefs who steal from
him and the annoying offensives they launch against him. We reach
an agreement that I'll try to persuade Ngqika to make peace with the
rebels and that I'll clear out of Caffraria if it will bring about peace
among the Caffres. Janssens presents a few gifts to Enno, Ngqika's
son-in-law, the biggest of the strongest captains, and we decamp back
to the Great Place, the Poles and the Englishman with pale faces and
fettered feet watching us leave.

∾

The wagons fill up quickly. My family scurry around, rinse bowls, fold
clothes, wrap crockery in cloths. My stuff has been packed, I can say
good bye to the Couga in my own time. I page through the *Flatus Vocis*,
look at the pictures of unicorns. He writes that he saw the unicorns
in the caves where the Bushmen danced. He says that if it was drawn,
there must be such creatures; Bushmen have no imagination. He
hears stories of an animal the size of a gemsbok, with the spoor of a
zebra and a single horn on the forehead. Here, too, in the Couga,
there are many stories meandering around in circles, unrecognisable
when they return to source. Here, too, in the Couga, there are Bushmen paintings. In the open caves of the Braam River, in the deep

ravine, there are many paintings. If you want to see them, you have to swim through pools between narrow and high rock faces, as if you were being born again.

~

Ngqika's messengers go and request Janssens to send soldiers to meet the king with a wagon or cart for his fat mother who wouldn't be able to manage such a long walk. Janssens sends the cart and a few officers and on 22 June they await us in the road. Ngqika rides out ahead of us on an unsaddled horse. The stallion stops when it sees the colonisers, inspects them. Ngqika asks me and the advisers whether it's safe. He whistles and his retinue of more than a hundred and fifty comes into motion. Yese clambers into the cart. Ngqika and I remain on horseback and the rest follow on foot.

Janssens meets us with all the pomp and circumstance he could rustle up. In a clearing between the bushes, on the lush grass next to the river, with dense forest and rock faces around us, there he meets us. The neat rows of soldiers' tents on the grass plot with the Batavian flag fluttering in front of the big tent of the governor. The wagons and goods concealed against the background of brushwood.

On one bank of the Kat River the lines of white tents in the green grass with all the showy formality, discipline and complacency of Europe. The Waldeck infantry is drawn up in a rigid rank. Their blue coats like a wave threatening to break; the blinding line of bayonets fixed to the muzzles of muskets towering over so many shoulders. From somewhere at the back the cannon salute erupts, then the beat of the drum binding every boot to the measure of the drill. On the opposite bank the prancing horses and the sign language of flashing sabres raised aloft in the fine-boned hands of officers. Here in the narrow pathway, between the sabres, the governor awaits the king of Caffraria.

My Xhosas: tall, naked, red cloaks floating free; the assegais shinier than bayonets. They walk ceremoniously, sombrely. A different discipline, dictating that you skewer your foe face-to-face, not mow him down at a distance.

Ngqika rides at the head, his advisers walk behind him, and behind them my Yese in a white robe. She has descended from the cart for the arrival and walks out in front of the horses. She's sweating. I can see her nipples shining through the cloth. She licks the moisture from her lips.

To one side a little chap sits sketching the whole story. Perhaps you know the painting, may even know the painter's name was Paravicini. Well, it was hot that day and nobody stood still and he wasn't looking everywhere equally attentively. The occasion was, for instance, not at all such a dour affair as his sketch suggests. As soon as the two groups sniffed each other's horse shit, the officers immediately greeted the young king, and jokes were soon exchanged. We streamed into the camp like a lot of rowdy sons whose mother has summoned them in to supper.

In the camp the king dismounts, swallows his smile and is conducted to the governor's tent. When he meets the Dutchman, my son extends his hand and with great dignity shakes the hand of the governor, as I taught him. The governor and his officers can't keep their eyes off the Caffre king. My king enjoys the attention. You have to laugh, reading how that lot describes Ngqika. As if they're singing songs of praise with both his balls in their cheeks.

The king, Yese and two of his wives are ushered into the tent. The Dutch find it hot. The side flaps of the tent are thrown open. Promptly the tent is mobbed by the officers and Christians gawping at the proceedings. They stay away from the far end of the tent where Ngqika is standing, because behind him, beyond the boundary of the tent poles, stand his advisers and captains and behind them, in a semicircle, sit his hundred and fifty warriors in their blood-red mantles with assegais at their feet. One of the officers strums a mandolin and another sings a folk song. The king talks to the Dutchmen. Everybody laughs and nods and carries on shaking hands.

The king and his family and I are invited for supper at the governor's table. I am proud of my son. He doesn't know the food and he doesn't know the knives and forks, but he learns fast. The women struggle. Ngqika likes the strange rich meat sauces and he appreciates the wine. With every new dish set before him he sends a portion over his shoulder to the taster. When he is satisfied that it's not poisoned, he makes a great to-do about the culinary skill. The governor thinks he likes the food so much that he wants to share it with his people. We don't disabuse him with the truth.

Janssens says the trek to the Kat River was arduous. The road was bad or non-existent, the streams many and not easy to traverse. But game was plentiful. He boasts about the thousands of pounds of meat they shot in those five days of travelling. Ever since the first stone was cast, man has learnt to kill at a distance. I'm starting to wonder whether the new musket bullets don't increase the distance unduly. When you can no longer see a creature's eyes when you shoot it, you start weighing meat by the pound.

A day's journey away from the Kat River Janssens' party came across a few farmers from Bruyntjeshoogte. They were in pursuit of the Caffres who had stolen their cattle. They'd caught up with the thieves and retrieved their cattle and shot two of the Caffres. Janssens tells the story hesitantly, anxious that this incident could further sour public relations. Ngqika shakes his head and smiles broadly, his gob stuffed with beef. No, he says, he can find no fault with the actions of the farmers.

The thieves got what they deserved, says the king in Xhosa.

Welcome to the other side of your border, General, I interpret.

Ngqika's wives pour themselves more wine and clink glasses until the red juice makes the starched table cloth look like a battlefield. Janssens raises a hand for more napkins. He wants to know from me whether all the colonists, that is to say Dutch Christians, are as terrifying as the crowd that travelled with him. He tells me that when they were outspanning at the Sundays River, one of the Christians was sleeping on a wagon. A freshly slaughtered sheep was suspended from the wagon to bleed dry. The carcase attracts a hyena that starts eating the sheep from below. The farmer stealthily takes his gun and pushes the muzzle down the carcase into the hyena's mouth and blasts away the creature's head. I want to say that the Christians hereabouts are mostly about ten feet tall and spit fire and can get women with child at a distance, but the governor is droning on excitedly. He tells of the forests through which the road winds at times. The troops of monkeys yelling at them when they pass under the trees. The colonists then nimbly scramble into the trees, as if they themselves had long tails and four hands. They grab hold of the monkeys and break their necks and roast them. Some of them are cute enough to be kept as pets, until they steal food and are then also roasted.

I prefer dogs to animals with thumbs, I say.
Janssens stops chewing, regards me quizzically.

Most colonists of my acquaintance aren't really great tree-climbers, I say.

~

While paging through the traveller's insane book, I stroke the dog at my feet. I have two dogs about the place, big black creatures with long tails and even longer legs. The price tame animals pay for lounging about the house with full bellies is that their owners baptise them with unpalatable names. Unless you deserve your anonymity, you are expected to leap up and wag your tail whenever you hear your name. Until they prove the contrary to me, I call the yard dogs Janssens and De Mist, after the two functionaries who barked so loudly but could get nothing bitten.

I still sometimes see the pack of stray dogs when I'm in the veldt, and at night their eyes gleam on the edge of the clean-swept yard. Yes, they're still around, with the bodies of the young ones more and more favouring hyenas. But they keep far away from civilisation, as if they are scared of contamination. When Janssens and De Mist smell them, the tails are between the legs and they come and lie whining by my feet. Hear my song: Dogs are the descendants of the first wolves who could tolerate humans for long enough to be fed by them.

After rattling on in every detail and with the necessary Latin nomenclature about the build of the wildebeest's penis and thereupon the structure of the Hottentot women's nether lips, the traveller also tells about his pet monkey. The dumb creature scoffed all the insects the traveller had collected, including the pins he'd stuck them down with. The traveller laments the loss of the many hours he spent taming and training the monkey, as well as the wasted hours spent ordering and classifying nature.

I abandon the plaint of the failed scientist to lend a hand where my youngest sons are struggling to lift the large cooking pot onto the wagon.

~

Ngqika's wives are sozzled after the second glass of wine and laugh raucously. At their feet lie the shards of their glasses. At the Great Place they are queens, but here you see them for the spoilt little tipsy girls they are. Janssens gets up before the dessert and excuses himself. I hear him muttering outside about the damned stink. He is back soon with a handkerchief soaked with sweet perfume that for the rest of the evening never hovers very far from his face.

The Xhosa ruler can't stop enthusing about the pretty uniforms of the occupiers. Janssens says he has just the thing for the king. He'd wanted to hand over the present at the end of the meeting, but why not now. An officer is beckoned up and returns minutes later with a new uniform. Ngqika touches and caresses the lapels and wants to put on the thing there and then. The meal is forgotten; a gaggle of officers help him into the uniform. The garments are hopelessly too small for him; his forearms and calves almost totally bare; immediately a rip down the spine. The king disengages himself from the eager hands of the soldiers and goes to parade before his warriors in his new apparel. They egg him on. The too-short sleeves and trouser legs make him seem even bigger and stronger. He delights in how the soldiers gawp at the Caffre king bursting out of their largest uniform. As soon as he notices the admiring exclamations and glances starting to taper off, he takes off the uniform, but he keeps the hat with the feather and the cockade on his regal head. Now he demands Janssens' voluminous cloak, but this is blushingly refused. Even the governor finds it hard to say no to Ngqika. He promises to send him a cloak just like his.

After supper Ngqika disappears to his wives in the tents that have been prepared for them. Janssens disappears to his paperwork. I wander about among the soldiers gathered in groups around fires. At a fire smoking dismally they offer me wine. Most of the pipsqueaks in the circle have hardly started shaving. They break green leaves off a cycad and throw it on the flames. Not used to making their own fires. They talk about all the game they've seen. On the dry plains on the other side of the Sundays River there were buck by the thousands upon thousands, even a lot of quaggas. In one day the governor's hunters shot fifty-four buck that they call mountain buck and many more that they didn't count. They tell about buck moving in herds of thousands, how beautiful it was to see these hosts fleeing before the horses of the hunters. They tell how these antelopes leapt, as if they were flying rather than running, animals who in their flight sought to break away from the earth and the slaughter. I say we call them springbok. The soldiers say that makes sense. Now they know what they were hunting. I drink their wine and teach them the names of plants and antelopes and all kinds of other things they will be devouring here. A captain tells of the white antelope in the herd of three, no, he swears by the only God, surely *four* thousand grey buck that on another day sheered past them unrelenting and vast as a glacier. I ask him about glaciers and believe nothing of what he tells me. The captain says the governor immediately wanted to have this rare snow-white buck and a handful of the younger men set off in pursuit. The antelope stood out from its fellows and they separated it from the herd, which now all looked alike and indistinguishable. They surrounded the white rarity and tired it out until they could capture the animal with their bare hands without firing a shot. You can go and have a look, Janssens gave that white hide to Monsieur Perron who on his return from the South Sea Islands stopped over at the Cape. Perron donated it to the Museum of the National Institute of Paris where it is daily being gawked at by Parisians, indistinguishable in their powdered wigs.

When the moon is high, I wander to Yese's tent. I stand outside and prick up my ears. I walk back to the fires.

∼

Maps are as old as mankind. Ever since the first scrawlings of the migratory patterns of game on the walls of caves we have been drawing lines and living within them. Every line becomes a knot that tightens around you. On the map now stretched out on the table before me, the writer has abandoned the power of knowing and binding. Rather, here in the middle of the *Flatus Vocis*, he starts opening up. Layer upon layer of ink, a black sea of experiences and routes and fever dreams. Only here and there sketches and words glimmer through, the map as crammed and incomprehensible as life itself: rivers, mountains, huts, kopjes, screams, birds, clouds, earthquakes, fire, Christians, winds, the horseman himself, states of mind, sexual organs, graves, corpses, gallows, sea monsters, smoke, laughter, Heathens, sunsets, dust, seasons, predators, battles, quarries, stars, elephant trails, yowls, grass, water maidens, mud, thorn trees, bushes, ageing, outcries, stone, young girls, sand, wagon routes, leaves, tortoises.

∼

At sunrise Janssens is standing in front of his tent waiting for Ngqika so that the interview may commence. The king is late, as is the divine right of kings, and I keep the governor company. Janssens goes to sit down in the cool tent, starts paging through his paperwork to get his facts straight for the day. I smoke. He says he believes in two things: that the Caffres must be driven out of the Zuurveld and that, when every Caffre in the Colony is on the right side of the Fish, the colonists living among the Caffres, people like yours truly, must also clear out of there. All intercourse between Christian and Caffre must cease. That is all that will make this country work, he says. Look at you spluttering in your coffee.

Janssens tells me of the trouble the rebellious Hottentot Johannes Stuurman is stirring. The Hottentot uprising is making everybody uneasy, he says. The farmers are scared and are starting to shoot or clear out. Even Van der Kemp can't manage to placate these wild Hottentots. Old Klaas and his comrades are too wily to be circumvented. All that will work with such a Hotnot, he says, is bribery. Janssens sighs exaggeratedly and when he looks up, I feel compelled to sigh in sympathy. He touches my shoulder, I his confidant whom he does not know from Adam. Then there is the dreaded Ndlambe, he says, lying this side of the Fish. Also the Gqunukhwebe, the Mbalu and the Dange are digging in between the Sundays and Fish Rivers. It is for these reasons, he says and sighs again, that he's undertaken this journey, to bring peace and prosperity to us here in the eastern districts.

Thank God for those he has set over us, I say.

He leaves his work for a moment, looks up at me and then carries on underlining notes. His quill is new. Not a drop of ink is spilt. I open my knapsack and take out *my* papers. A multitude of letters and petitions that I've been keeping for the last few years, precisely against such an opportunity as this. In the pile that I unpack on his desk is a petition listing the injustices perpetrated upon me and my fellows by the focking English; also two letters from the Reverend Ballot urging me to return to the Colony and two from Van Rensburg describing how he's trying to mediate my case with the authorities.

And what is this? Janssens demands without looking up.

Paperwork, General. It shows that I behaved myself under the

Caffres. That the fo– the English and Maynier blackened me.
My name, I mean. I am still as white as the lilies of the field.

More red than white, Mijnheer Buys, he smiles while starting
to rifle through the letters.

I read the look in his eyes. He is polite, even cracks jokes, but behind
that curved-up smile I see the distrust. I am a prominent gent here
on the other side of the border, charming but dangerous. Something
for the museum or the gallows, but not something to walk about freely.
I plot and scheme with the Caffres. My existence is not exactly con-
venient for the Colony. The Christians hate me, all the chiefs except
Ngqika hate me. My fellow rebels, even Hannes Bezuidenhout, call
me a good-for-nothing and a shit-stirrer when they are questioned
in Graaffe Rijnet.

How do you feel about coming home, Mijnheer Buys?

Home?

Back to the Colony? A farm in De Lange Cloof?

Home? I must go home. My days with Ngqika are numbered, that I
know. Everybody knows it, except the king. I say I would like to go
back to De Lange Cloof if it suited them. Janssens says it suits them
exceptionally well. He wants me to go and tell his commissioner-
general, one De Mist, what the Caffres are all about. I can see him
making a mental note to warn his pal against me as soon as I've left.
Later, as Omni-Buys, I'll read the letters of this fellow with the
flapping epaulettes, how he, shortly after our conversation, calls me,
Khula, the most dangerous man in the Colony.

∾

How does one go home, I wondered that day and am wondering again
today. Nombini is standing next to the nearest wagon. Look how pretty:
she in the hand-me-down dress that Maria has made her wear these
last few years – Godalmighty, woman, cover yourself. Can't you see
the place is full of half-grown boys? She who stands on her toes, the
calves showing. Under the dress her breasts still hold their shape,

those majestic nipples spring to attention for the breeze. She is ageing beautifully. She is quieter, keeps herself to herself, and still, after all these years, doesn't know how, when I gaze at her, the world around us ceases to exist. She places her birdcage on the wagon, carefully packs it between two crates, wrapped in a blanket. She plaited the thing years ago for an orphaned weaver bird that she raised. She looked for a long time at the weaver nests hanging from the trees in the yard. She plaited her cage in the calabash shape of the nests. So that the little one should feel at home, she said. When the bird grew up and escaped, the cage housed other little birds that had fallen out of nests or broken their wings. In the last year or so the cage has been hanging empty in her house. The revolving shadows of the straw lattice form patterns against her walls.

Each one of my wives' homes looks different. Nombini doesn't often allow me into her house. She says I walk and talk too loudly. Her nest can't take it. Her house is full of trinkets, delicate little things that she and her children make. If you see the house, you'll think it's a hodgepodge, but it contains unfathomable patterns and refrains, as fragile and intricate as the spider's web spun in every corner. I stay away.

Have you seen how birds build their nests? Humans can do everything except build a bird's nest. Humans are always less at home in their houses than animals. Birds build nests without tools, it assumes shape from the inside, like a shell. The bird presses and stretches the material with her breast until it becomes pliable. The nest takes the shape of the bird's body. The female hollows out the nest and eases back the walls constantly until they become soft and warm. The house is her passion. Every blade of perfectly plaited grass in the nest has been pressed back innumerable times with laboured breath, with heartbeats. A pressure from inside, a physical, dominating intimacy. The nest is a burgeoning fruit challenging its limits.

Nombini makes sure that the cage is settled snugly in the wagon. How does one go home? I'm on my way once again, after eleven years during which I dwelled mainly in Elizabeth's house, sometimes slept

253

over in Maria's house and now and again could go and lie, pussyfoot, on Nombini's plaited rug. My shelter, my shack on Shit-face Senekal's farm, that hole in the ground, was that my home? My first and only home? To that I can't return; it's been covered over, the wattle rotten. How I catch myself whistling again the tune that I used to warble in those years while lying in my jackal lair.

I go and stand behind Nombini, my chin on her shoulder, while she's fitting her plaited and painted knick-knacks in between the guns and flour and powder and sugar. I place my hands on her little pot-belly, which after little Windvogel's birth has never tightened again. I whistle what I whistled when all those years ago I lay gazing at my wattle roof with unseeing eyes, my prick in my hand, the world small and the stars close by.

∼

The interview is stately, more ceremony than conversation. Ngqika, having shed the uniform and at home again in his little animal skin loincloth and cloak, sits next to his mother and four of the oldest advisers. Janssens sits on his own on the other side of the table. I and the Bethelsdorp Hottentot Platje, who is interpreting for Janssens, are seated on either side of the table. The riempie stool is too low. I have to get up every now and again and walk around the table to stretch my legs. The tent flaps have been opened again, the retinues of both parties are seated outside. When there seems to be no end to the talking, the audience gradually drifts away as the winter sun warms them into drowsiness.

The governor starts proceedings by announcing the reason for his journey: Peace is possible only if each holds to his permitted bank of the Fish, as it pleases the VOC, the focking English, the Batavians and God the Father himself. Ngqika assures him that it is a great pleasure to lay eyes on the ruler of the Colony. He says he's always been a friend to the Christians. That is exactly why the Caffre rebels are taking up arms against him in hordes, from all directions from which the winds blow and the sun and moon rise and set. Can you hear me sweetening the king's words with honey so that they can slither sweetly and slickly into Janssens' bony ear?

By afternoon the interview is still dragging on. Janssens knows only one tune: Ngqika must see to it that all the Caffres move east of the Fish. Ngqika turns to Yese and the elders. When the whispering gets heated, they go and stand in the corner of the tent and talk as if they were alone and the governor far away in the Cape. Ngqika looks at me pointedly and says he has no control over the renegade Xhosas. But since he lives east of the Fish in any case, he himself has no problem respecting the border. Janssens nods, satisfied. What exactly he's so damned pleased about, heaven alone knows: Ngqika is offering him absolutely nothing.

I can't believe my ears when Janssens asks whether either Maynier or Bresler ever attempted to incite Ngqika to attack the colonists sheltering with him. My fabrications have actually floated all the way to the Netherlands and back. Ngqika looks at me and then starts to recite the little rhyme that his Khula whispered into his ear years ago. He says Maynier did indeed send him gifts four or five years ago and informed him that if he attacked and wiped out me and a few of my fellows, he could keep half our horses and all our cattle.

> Maynier wanted all our sheep, I add and Platje looks at me and looks away. And the king says he's incapable of betraying his friends, I embroider forth.

Janssens glances askance at me, before, after an eternity, starting to rifle his notes again for a next question.

Janssens is nobody's fool, he can see I'm interpreting myself and not the king. My ventriloquism makes things dangerous for my son. I noticed during last night's meal already: As soon as Ngqika starts talking politics with the governor, his words become conflated with my stories and distortions and moods. While the two carry on negotiating, I hold my peace, as far as possible.

The last item on the agenda is me myself. Behold: I am interpreting the negotiations regarding my own future. Ngqika says he is prepared to chase all the Christians at the Great Place to their own side of the Fish; all of them except Khula. I know his country and I know the Colony and he needs me as mediator. Janssens digs in: I must get out of there and back to De Lange Cloof and my legitimate family. I could remain Ngqika's friend, as long as a river ran between us. I interpret and for the rest keep my trap shut.

On that day I was a few years past forty; I was sick of hiding from the bunch of Christians and Caffres who on both sides of the border wanted to skin me alive. Believe me, a pardon and a plot of land on which I could plant and forage for more than one season did not seem like an unattractive proposition. A house with walls not built of firewood and wattle, not too bad either. Janssens was highly excited to extricate me from under the Caffres. He even promised me an escort, in case Ndlambe or suchlike obnoxious Caffres were to ambush me on my way back to the fusty embrace of the Colony.

Ngqika signs the document of their agreement. They agree that Ngqika will recognise the Fish River as border. The acknowledgement that he just happens to live on the other side of the river apparently affords Janssens great joy. Ngqika is given more presents. Tobacco, knick-knacks, ornaments. For later delivery there are European cloth, cloaks, a horse with a fancy saddle and bridle and a two-wheel cart. The king distributes whatever he doesn't want among his subjects. He gives the governor four magnificent oxen. In the late afternoon he sets off on his own to bid the governor farewell. The coxcomb king struts through the ranks of the soldiers, his red cloak fluttering, his assegai glittering and the tricorn hat with the white plume firmly and dapperly displayed on his head. The two of them shake hands and embrace and shake hands again and neither can get enough of the other's back-scratching. Janssens sets off for Graaffe Rijnet, there to be told that France and the English are once again at war. I trek away with the

Caffres, back to the Great Place for one last time to set my house in order before settling down in the long kloofs from which I tore myself away so many years ago.

I was proud, yes. Of myself. The governor, the king, the soldiers and warriors, they were all in my hands. I was the only one there who could speak decent Dutch and Xhosa. I knew the fears and perplexities and purposes of both sides like nobody else there or since. The Dutch wanted me there as interpreter and that was what I would be to them. When they sounded me out about my relations with the Caffres, I was as vague and hazy as a Lange Cloof morning. As soon as you realise you're being used, the game gets interesting.

That sketch of Paravicini is quite charming and not too badly botched, except for two things: Ngqika was on horseback. And I was there, there in the midst of it all. My voice was the voice of both sides. I talked with myself, negotiated my freedom and my confinement with myself in two languages.

∼

A week or so later Cornelis Faber returns from Graaffe Rijnet, where he'd gone to barter two wagonloads of timber. The authorities stopped him in the dusty main street and told him that if he or any of us dissidents put as much as a foot in the Colony without having bidden Caffraria a last farewell, we would be arrested on the spot and dispatched to the Castle.

Come September Ngqika still does not want to let me go. He says it's unsafe for me to trek back to the Colony past Ndlambe's hordes with my womenfolk and children. I'm in no hurry. The Colony is delivering angry letters; Ndlambe and the other Caffres on the Colony side of the Fish don't want to move back over the border before I've left there. The rumours I hear about myself make it difficult for me to look in the mirror and see anything. In Caffraria I am Khula, a man with wives and children and cattle, like all the other Caffres. In the Colony I'm a ten-foot monster with eight arms who makes the earth

quake when I break wind. Four Christian friends turn up at my
house with a wagon and a lot of guns and help me to move back to
De Lange Cloof.

Yes, I took a proper leave of Ngqika. We talked for a long time,
I embraced him like the son he was to me. He cried. I took leave of
Yese too. With a formal handshake and a bow like the gentleman I am.
My jaw was clenched; she looked past me.

At Bruyntjeshoogte Faber and the English deserter Jan Naader and
I come across Captain Alberti, the commander of Fort Frederick. We
assure him that there are now only Caffres left in Caffraria. He starts
asking questions and I can see the man is not going to be fobbed off
with the usual commonplaces. But too many stories, and not all of
them equally true, are even more useless than platitudes. I talk a heap
of shit and somewhere inside I hide nuggets of truth. Do you see how
he looks me up and down for tokens of honesty, while I'm betraying
Bentley and Bezuidenhout and the Lochenbergs? How I blab out
everything about their plans to flee to Delagoa Bay? How they're only
waiting for powder and bullets from the Cape? To the devil with them.
If I have to behave myself, if I have to go and strap myself into demure
good-neighbourliness, how come they get to go and savour succulent
tropical women? And as is the wont of his ilk, Alberti all too labori-
ously records the absolutely nothing that he is the wiser:

> I must admit that in this matter I was discomfited. Coenraad
> de Buys is too little to be trusted to enable one to make use of
> anything he says, and who knows what moved him to tell all
> the above.

～

I'm sweating. See, the demented wanderer also has maps of the
heavens in his *Flatus* book. One with all the Christian constellations –
Orion, Leo, the Southern Cross and suchlike – daintily traced out with
the names attached. Then there is also a map of the constellations of
the Caffres and the Hottentots and the Bushmen, as told to him:

Orion's belt here becomes three dogs chasing three pigs. A crocodile with a star in its jaws. The seven sisters become a man with a spade. Things like that. And then a map with the stars, only stars, no lines connecting them to form an animal or a story. Hundreds, thousands of bare dots spread over two pages. Underneath the first of these dot-speckled pages is written: *Make an object that only becomes visible after you've looked at it for a while*. At the top of the next page: *Go into an empty room and make a list of its contents*.

∾

In 1803 we trek through the extremities, back through the Zuurveld, back to De Lange Cloof. Farmlands are on fire. Houses are on fire. Almost half the farms have been devastated, a third of the Christians have moved away already. Orchards and vineyards are gravid with rotten fruit. Maize fields have been trampled and are still smouldering. Corpses hang from blackened trees. Everywhere the vultures and the crows and everywhere the dogs. The fleeing farmers are on their way, God knows where to, in battered half-empty wagons. Torn cloth fluttering like white flags where it no longer covers the wagon's bamboo ribs. Smoke and wrath, stubble, dust and emptiness.

3

In the Couga, at the back of the Attaquas Cloof, farms are named after heart's desires. I settle on d'Opkomst, the arising, my gift from the authorities, my thirty pieces of silver. My Uncle Jacob lived here in the 1770s, after that his brother-in-law, then my big brother Johannes, up to more or less 1790, they say. After that the place was in a Scheepers' name for a few years. And now I. We. This farm's gates, too, are now locked to you, reader; this land, too, is in your time, in the time of Omni-Buys, a game conservation area. The traces of ruins can still be seen in the grass, but it smells of baboon piss.

D'Opkomst is a frontier farm. On the edge of the Couga, the furthest east of the farms. When I moved in here, the farm was in the Swellendam district, a year or so later in Uitenhage, and nowadays, apparently, I'm living in George. New borders for new districts with new names of new bureaucrats are forever moving the farm around, even though I don't exactly feel the earth moving here under the tree.

On Brandhoek next door lives Doors Minnie, Christina's grandson, my step-nephew. We don't talk much. Especially not after the fellow went and married a Ferreira a few years ago. To the other side lies the kraal of the selfsame Stuurman who caused the Colony so much shit with his rebellious Hottentots who fought alongside the Caffres. He was apparently also given a few morgen to put a stopper on his gun and his big mouth. Seems to me the Batavians post everybody who gives them a hard time to the Couga; in these kloofs you can go ahead and swear and shoot and nobody will be any the wiser. If the black hole in the Castle is full, there are always more remote farms to be distributed. Here where sight and sound vanish without a trace.

When I set foot here, I immediately went to greet big brother Johannes on his farm not far away. His wife wouldn't allow me into the house. I went to look for my brother in his fields and we shook each other's hand and after smoking a pipe we didn't have much to say to each other. We promised each other that we would visit regularly and not become strangers to each other again and that I would come and show him my wives and children. I did not see my brother again.

~

With our first spring in the Couga I decided one morning that my wives should have a birthday. Not one of them knows on which day she was born. We don't observe birthdays. Nor the children; we write the dates in the front of the Bible. We'd hardly been here a few months, everyone under one roof, in what is now my and Elizabeth's house. They are sitting in the kitchen; Elizabeth fills the kettle with water. Maria doesn't interrupt her story. I say that tomorrow is their birthday. I say we must have a great feast. I hug them where they remain sitting at the table. I say we must start preparing. I'll provide the meat, they can start preparing the vegetables and the pudding so long. I send Coenraad Wilhelm and Philip out with a new gun. They are more or less twelve, are quite competent hunters already. I get the hell out of the madhouse, go and sit at my table, under my tree. I'm drawing up plans for the farming lands. I make sums for seed. The activity in the house is loud, but not a peep from the womenfolk. Normally all three of them talk at the same time. I'm pleased that they get on so well together.

The following noon the table groans under the weight of meats and potatoes and green stuff and sweet potatoes. I say let's carry everything out to the outside table, it's a beautiful day. I bring out the wine. I tell Bettie she must keep the children occupied, I'm making a feast for my wives. I fill their beakers with wine. I address them, how beautiful they are looking today, what good mothers they are, how much they mean to me. I make the jokes and we all laugh. We laugh when Nombini knocks back her wine before the toast has been proposed. We laugh when Maria takes umbrage and throws a handful of pumpkin at me when I say that it's not cooked through. We laugh when later I miss my chair in sitting down. We laugh when Elizabeth gives every-one a present, me included. For me she's wrapped two new flintstones

261

in a cloth. We laugh when she says: for our husband and hunter.
I suspect these are from the flintstones I acquired last month. I don't
remember very much more of the afternoon. I wake up with my head
on my arms, at the head of an empty table. Somebody has placed a
lantern next to me, cleared the table. My flintstones are wet with
dew. I go and crawl in behind Maria, my arm like a tendril around
her body. I press her to me, my head in the hollow where her
shoulder turns into neck and her frizz is turning grey. She takes hold
of my hand, removes it from her breast.

Many happy returns, my wife, I say against the lobe of her ear.
Dearlordgodinheaven, Buys, she says.

~

Eleven years later I'm sitting and counting my furniture. At the back
of the *Flatus* Whatever there are blank pages on which I now make
lists of what is on the wagon and what is still to come and what can
remain. The book is also full of lists. The traveller lists the contents
of his wagon chest, so many shirts, so many trousers, too few shoes.
Bible, books with Latin titles. He keeps a scrupulous record of every
animal that his party shoots. He distinguishes between those
shot to be eaten and those killed to be painted and analysed and
immortalised. He divides animals and plants into Latin classes. One
of the lists has been scratched over, the page torn and over it all, in
fresher ink, a messy scrawl: *We fear not being able to say everything,
therefore we make lists.*

I gaze out over my farm. On the verso of the faded lists I write my
own. This is what I'm taking with me:
3 wives,
a whole lot of children and their lice hopping from head to head,
4 Hottentots,
7 Hottentot youths,
6 Hottentot women,
7 Hottentot girls,

not a single slave,
2 heavily laden wagons,
1 ox-cart,
innumerable regrets,
2 horses,
24 trek oxen,
121 heads of cattle,
46 sheep,
108 goats and
all the brandy I can carry with me.
And this is what I'm going to set on fire:
4 muids of barley,
35 muids of tares,
4 000 vines,
1 leaguer of wine,
etcetera,
1 barn and
3 homes.

~

Hardly have I shed my shoes under my new bed or De Mist summons me to the Zondaghs' farm, Avontuur. Apparently he wants, as Janssens promised, to see me to sound me out about the Caffres. I want to get the chit-chat behind me and on Old Year's morning 1801 I am in the saddle long before daybreak. My horse is a no-good mare that I rode out of Caffraria. I named her Maynier. All the way over the mountains of the Couga I lash the hell out of her to see how soon I can ride the thing to death. By afternoon I leap off Maynier and land on Zondagh's farm. I touch her up where it hurts; she kicks Zondagh's slave who has come to cool her down.

There's quite a to-do on Avontuur. Every blessed farmer in the area is standing around smoking in his Sunday best. Everyone has a petition under his arm or a complaint in his bosom that the Netherlander must be apprised of. I haven't even greeted the owner of the farm, when I've acquired a tail. A cheeky little chap with frills up to the chin and a cow's lick of a fringe introduces himself with fingers that crunch in my hand.

> Doctor Martin Hinrich Lichtenstein, he says with a German accent.

> Doctor Coenraad de Buys, I say.

The thin lips under the strong nose cleave open in a laugh.

> I feel as if I know you already, Mijnheer Buys. You are a much talked-about man in the Colony. And now I must hear that you are also a doctor?

> Nowadays you are all seeking my advice against the Caffre plague. A proper bloodletting is the best medicine.

The fellow smirks excessively and repeats my joke to the next farmer, who blows smoke into his face. I am told that Lichtenstein is the medical officer of the Colony and schoolmaster to the children of Governor Janssens.

Matthys Zondagh the younger is taller than his father, old Matthys, with whom my Uncle Jacob had such a shindy. He is friendly and asks after my family, of whom I probably know less than he. His wife, Adriana, comes bearing rusks. She's a bit on the thin side, but there is still enough there to get a grip on. I am introduced to Commissioner-General Jacob Abraham de Mist and his half-grown daughter Augusta – little breasts with plump nipples rubbing against the thin cloth and making your mouth water, but otherwise pale, with transparent lips and a snub nose so high in the air that you can see all the way into her skull.

When the coffee has been imbibed, the host and the women are left behind in the sitting room. De Mist and a few of his right-hand men lead me to the dining room with the big chairs to talk. The commissioner-general's eyes are deep-set, his mouth a scab under his nose, the lips cracked and bleeding behind the lumps of spit clustering in the corners of his mouth. His jacket takes issue with his paunch. From his farts I deduce that he is a vegetable muncher. He asks me about my days with Van der Kemp – apparently the two knew each other in the Netherlands when Kemp was a soldier. De Mist is so affable, it makes me puke. I want to bawl into his face, I am guilty! I am guilty, set me on fire and devour me. Skin me alive, oh Lord, but deliver me from these misconceived philanthropists. My hands wander over the armrest, my fingers start tracing the delicate wood carving. De Mist and company ask the strangest questions; at first I think they are playing the fool, until I see the expectant frowns when I hesitate to reply.

Can I get hold of some of the Caffre maps for them?

Are some Caffres the slaves of other Caffres and how do they decide who are slaves?

How are the negotiations between the Bushmen and the Caffres progressing?

How do I see the Christian's place in Africa?

What I said, I can't remember. What I wanted to say, was: There is no peace to be made here; there is nothing to be understood here. The only revolution here is that between dust and fire, the only equality the levelling of the land by the elements, the only fraternity a function of a common enemy or a shared disgrace. The only liberty the one that comes from surrendering to your fate.

I give them what they're looking for, I paint the Caffres as the innocent children of nature that the enlightened gents want to see. The more I keep my trap shut, the more they nod in agreement, fill in my silences with what they want to hear. De Mist cannot understand that our people on the border can't see the border, that it's just a river, full of mud, dangerous, or sometimes a parched ditch. I tell him about Caffre politics, who's quarrelling with whom, last I heard. I add on and leave out; what does it matter; what do I know? Lichtenstein takes minutes. Now and again I catch him looking at me as if he wanted to measure me up and sketch me like a felled giraffe. I smile at him and talk to his boss. I am friendly and unruffled. I push out my chest.

I keep my cramping hands under the table. The German records everything. Sometimes I lose the thread of my argument, much more interested in the contours of the carving against the table legs. Whoever carved it can talk to wood as these people can't talk to Caffres and farmers. De Mist wants to know whether I suffer any remorse over my past.

> So far I've got away with everything.
>
> You don't feel guilty?
>
> Those who call me guilty, *have* to stone me. For their own survival.
>
> I do not understand, Mijnheer Buys.
>
> If I'm not guilty, they will reproach themselves unto their dying day.
>
> Reproach?
>
> Yes, because they never lived, merely farmed and prayed and paid. I am a free man, a noble savage. I sign my own name.
>
> I write my own fate. My seed I sow far and wide.

Etcetera all afternoon long. Goddammit, you surely know, even this I don't believe a word of, but oh, you should have been there. You should have seen what I could see: the way they bought every bun I baked, all this libertarian shit. I am modest and friendly and then, every now and again, I drop a little pearl, something straight from the boudoir of that dissolute marquis of whom old Kemp told me. How they hung onto my every word, how they couldn't wait for me to shock them with my free spirit. The priceless way in which my audience choked on my choice buns.

~

When we adjourn, I ask Zondagh who made his tables and chairs. He beckons to a slave and whispers something and the slave vanishes. He says we must wait a while, then he'll introduce us to a man like no other. The slave returns with his hands full of guns. Then he leaves again and returns with two chairs and a bag full of locks and a leather bag full of tools that he unpacks on the table next to the polished guns. Only then do I see the man standing in the doorway. He is slender and bowed, his skin pale from working indoors. Zondagh introduces the man as Gildenhuys. An elderly woman leads the man into the room and shows him a chair to sit on. He inspects us all, smiles broadly, shakes his head, but doesn't make a sound. His long fingers move in the air and the woman makes similar movements. The man nods.

Gentlemen, I introduce you to our Gildenhuys, says Zondagh. Zondagh says Gildenhuys was born deaf and dumb. He developed his own language along with his sister. The two understand each other perfectly, but for the rest he is cut off from the world's eternal chatter. No wonder he seems so friendly. Zondagh proceeds to display the man's handiwork to us. The bolts and locks, the breech bolts, the woodcarving. The chisels and hammers, the saws, long and short, each made with the most exquisite care. Craftsmanship such as I have never seen. Zondagh prattles on about the man to whom he continually refers as Our Gildenhuys. Gildenhuys himself shows his handiwork with evident pride. He even performs a demonstration, there in the dining room, in which he engraves an aloe on a piece of yellowwood plank that Zondagh has brought in. Then we are led out to go and inspect his smithy. Elaborate metal carvings are suspended from the walls. I can see Gildenhuys has had to conduct this tour countless times. I realise why he does it with such readiness. Yes, he *is* Zondagh's Gildenhuys, the farmer keeps him like a tame monkey to impress his guests with his tricks. But Gildenhuys himself is the main beneficiary of the situation. He can live in the midst of all this wealth on the richest farm in De Lange Cloof, while being free to practise his trade in peace. Apparently he taught himself, an inborn feeling for taste and quality. There is a meagre supply of patterns in circulation in these parts, and most of the shapes and ornaments are of his own creation. A careful and patient giftedness. He plays along with Zondagh's show, because here he can do whatever his dumb heart desires, in his own time, without the pother of a pot that has to be kept boiling. Without being sized up out there every raging day and having to justify his existence to his neighbours.

The show is concluded with Zondagh's insisting that his Gildenhuys must show us a few words of his sign language. His sister's callused fingers talk rapidly with her brother, this man with whom she shares a silent life. She tugs at the heavy dress dragging on the ground. She makes a short speech about her brother's secret language. How he might be deaf and dumb, but knows no lethargy and boredom in his occluded world. He is indeed a weird fellow; the figurines he carves are all from another world, or on their way to an unforeseeable else-where. The gestures he thought up himself also entertain the audience. He makes a horse gallop with the two forefingers of his right hand on the flat of his left palm. But it is his word for Hottentot that makes De Mist roar with laughter: He presses two thumbnails against each other, as one squashes a tick, and then looks up for the expected reaction. Zondagh must have in the past instructed him to keep this gesture for last. Nothing makes the high-ups laugh like the recognition of their own misanthropy in the countenance of an innocent man.

Gildenhuys with his soiled and supple fingers is left behind in the smithy with his sister when we adjourn for a cocktail of genever before the evening's festivities. Augusta's little legs are trembling under the silken dress. She says she must lie down, the sun is making her light-headed. I look at her and she looks away.

≈

I remember Kemp's eruption so many years ago when he rattled off the names of God, how the listing and the shouting exorcised dark things within him. While piling hay around the houses with my children and the labourers so that they will flare up more readily later on, I mumble the Couga things, the Couga names I'm taking my leave of:

> Yellowwood, assegai wood, ironwood, candlewood, stinkwood,
> stink cat, wildcat, rooikat, rooibekkie, red rhebok, red bishop,

red hare, red alder, white alder, white-eye, white stinkwood,
white sugarbush, krantz sugarbush, broad-leaved sugarbush,
ganna bush, bramble bush, yellow bush, taaibos, slangbos,
salvia, sour grass, sweet water, water mongoose, rock pigeon,
rock martin, house martin, hippopotamus, porcupine,
pincushion, piet-my-vrou, chat, dassie, the distant snow,
spring hare, spekboom, keurboom, waboom, wagtail, wild
wormwood, wild olive, wild hemp, guinea fowl, genet, the
gentle rain, turtledove, loerie, barn owl, butcherbird, sugarbird,
spotted mousebird, pied starling, pied crow, black-backed
jackal, maned jackal, ring-necked raven, ratel, these accursed
people, baboon, bee-eater, honeyguide, heather, broom, bread-
fruit, bulrush, buchu, blue goshawk, blue wildebeest, here
and there a bluebuck, grey-winged francolin, grey rhebok,
steenbok, bokmakierie, kiewiet, kokkewiet, klipspringer, duiker,
lammervanger, pig's ear, monkey apple, mountain cypress,
mountain reed, mountains, valleys, milkweed, mint, mitre aloe,
bitter aloe, things that from afar look like flies, elephant, Cape
lion, Cape pheasant, fish eagle, bateleur eagle, tea tree, leopard,
sandstone, stoep-sitting, soil, stones and stones, my uncle
Jacob, my brother, my bed, my table, my farm, Philip, my
dear dead son Philip, zebra.
Oh the abysm of lists, of a life abandoned.

∽

In what I take to be Zondagh's bedroom, I am standing at the window
gazing over the yard. Festivities have flared up. Flames from the muzzles
of guns light up the farm at short intervals. The farmers started the
shooting, but De Mist's dragoons are quick to join in with their guns.
The new year is upon us. Answering shots are heard from neighbouring
farms. He is handy with his mouth. His hand is around my shaft with
the knob on the inside of his cheek and then again all the way back
to his tonsils. In between he keeps mumbling and I understand not

a single word and press his head against me to silence him. I start throbbing; he tries to pull away; I spurt, filling his gob. He chokes.

Now let me hear what you've been so busy scribbling about me. Lichtenstein translates his German into Dutch for me. I make suggestions: It's not necessary to mention how fat Yese is. Does he have no manners? She's a queen. Cross out. My rheumatism is nobody's business. Cross out. He reads some more. More is crossed out. Another few suggestions. He adds and crosses out. When I'm satisfied, he has to read the German as well. I like the sounds: the hard edges and sharp contours tempered by the soft burr. There is a splodge of my seed on his frills. He doesn't know about it.

You don't have to believe me, but this is how I helped write the paragraph that would be quoted and translated countless times; the most complete extant description of my appearance:

Die Vorstellungen, die uns das sonst oft vergrössernde Gerücht von diesem seltsamen Menschen im Voraus gegeben, wurden bei seinem Eintritt vollkommen gerechtfertigt. Seine ungeheure Grösse (er misst fast sieben Fuss), der kräftige, schön proportioniert Bau seiner Glieder, die ruhige Haltung seines Körpers, der zuversichtliche Blick, die hohe Stirn, seine ganze Miene und eine gewisse Würde in seinen Bewegungen machten einen höchst angenehmen Gesamteindruck. So mag man sich die Heroen der Vorwelt denken, das lebendige Bild eines Hercules, ein Schrecken den Feinden, das Vertrauen der Seinigen. Was wir nach den Beschreibungen nicht in ihm zu finden erwartet, war eine gewisse Bescheidenheit und Zurückhaltung in seinen Reden, eine Milde und Freundlichkeit in Blick und Miene, die durchaus nicht ahnen liessen, dass der Mann so viele Jahre unter rohen Wilden gelebt, und die mehr noch, als seine Reden, das üble Vorurtheil, das wir gegen ihn mitgebracht hatten, hinwegnahmen. Er gab bereitwillig Auskunft über die Gegenstände, wegen welcher er befragt ward, vermied jedoch sorgfältig, über sich selbst und seine Verhältnisse zu den Kaffern zu sprechen. Dieses schlaue

Ausweichen, oft begleitet von einem schalkhaften Lächeln, in welchem der ganze Ausdruck des innern Bewusstseins seiner Kraft lag, und in welchem deutlich zu lesen war, dass nicht die Furcht seine Zurückhaltung verursache, sondern als verschmähe ers, die leere Neugierde der Frager auf Kosten der Wahrheit oder seines persönlichen Rufs zu befriedigen, machte uns den Menschen noch interessanter und steigerte unsere Theilnahme vielleicht zu einem höhern Grad, als es die Erzählung seiner Schicksale gethan haben würde.

You can say that again.

When I went outside, I saw that the New Year's festivities, which had started quite demurely, had in the natural course of things got out of hand. This suits me well; I am absorbed unseen into the pell-mell. I drink with the farmers and try to corner an all too nimble little slave girl against the stable wall. She's quite game, but then plays hard to get. I let her get away; my Sturm und Drang is by now bobbing in the belly of the German.

~

Elizabeth stands behind me, rubs my shoulders, peeks at what I'm reading in the *Flatus Vocis*. She bends over me, her stomach pressing against the back of my head. She pages back until she reaches the sketches of the unicorn. She says, Hey, it's an eland with a single horn. I say No, that's not what he wanted to draw. She asks what kind of a creature it is. I tell her about unicorns, the fables that travellers come to find here. And how, when they search hard enough, they find the lie that they yearn for.

Why don't they draw our place the way it looks?
Oh, my wife's mouth. See the corners curling up when she talks, the lips thrusting out slightly when she listens.

What will they do if one day they come across their stories in the veldt? she asks.
She doesn't wait for an answer, runs into the house. I hear a banging

271

and plaster falling and then she's back with the rhebok horns that were still hanging in the passage this morning. She breaks the horns from the plank on which they're mounted, brandishes one straight horn in front of her.

Come, Coenraad, let's give them a unicorn.

We go and dig up the white foal that died last week. The grave isn't deep, the soil is still loose. After a foot or so our spade strikes the carcase. It smells of putrefaction, the worms are already hard at work. We pull the foal's neck out of the ground. Elizabeth sits down cross-legged at the side of the grave. She holds the head between her legs while I nail the rhebok horn between the foal's wild and liquefying eyes. The younger offspring leave their packing and come and stand around us and prattle. Elizabeth says the diggers will see the nails. I send Piet to go and find a broken harness. He returns with a bridle in a cotted mass, the bit rusted to bits, the leather cracked and torn. We bridle the unicorn foal, push the bit into its mouth. We harness the fable and cover it up to be dug up and written up by travellers who dare to follow in our footsteps. I hug my wife next to the freshly despoiled grave. We laugh at our mischief. I hold her until she wriggles free to go and pack the last stuff. In the lap of her dress the stains that leaked out of the foal, like the dry blood of pomegranates.

∿

When the sun stops climbing and slowly starts sinking back to earth, my offspring become more and more excited about the move. Maria and Nombini grumble between themselves and avoid me as far as possible. The wagons are just about fully laden. The wagon tilts are tentered. Near Elizabeth's house a duck is paddling another in a puddle. The one on top dunks the other one under the water and the fornication doesn't stop even when the bottom one has drowned. I summon two of the labourers and tell them to round up the trek oxen so long. There's no end to the duck. I sit down and watch the shebang.

∿

The next morning at Avontuur, the first morning of 1804, I have break-fast with the Zondaghs and De Mist at long tables carried out under the trees. Lichtenstein says he's keeping busy at the Cape. He writes articles about the anatomy of ostriches and the epidemic of tummy-run in the Cape barracks. He tells me about the map of the Colony that's he working on. He tells me about the voyages he's planning, the uncharted regions to which he's looking forward – trips across the eastern border and perhaps even northwards to the Bechuana. He tells me about ships in bottles. He's not even a quarter of a century old, quite wise for his years, but blind to the disappointments awaiting him. He knows the plants and trees and game of the country as I know them. The handshaking ensues and Zondagh gives me a package of rusks and peaches to take along.

For the women in your house, he jokes.

I look at Adriana and she looks away. The commissioner-general passes wind when he mounts his horse, on his way further along De Lange Cloof; on his way to pit his freethinking ideals against the everlasting mountains where the echoing crags are mute.

4

Maria bangs a little trunk down on the table and grumbles back to
the packing. Old letters that have not been thrown away. Would she
have preserved them for all these years? I know nothing about this;
I don't hoard. A few from Christina from years ago. I open one, but
before I can read a word, the handwriting makes me keck. I chuck
the goddam trunk from the table, get up and trample the whole lot
into the dirt. You, who most assuredly have never in your precious
life shot a buck, you and your kind curse all that is a man. Just look
at the bloodthirst, the callousness and the heedlessly escalating
devastation, you say. You raise your sons like the daughters of governors.
Listen to me: Rather look at the mothers. Every son with a gun or a
spear or a prick in his hand has a mother. Every son sees his mother
in that moment when everything blanches white with rage.

A month or so ago I rode across to my uncle Jacob de Buys' homestead
on Diepe Cloof. I was getting ready to take my leave of the haunts of
Ferreiras and their ilk. As a child nobody in the house talked about
Uncle Jacob the jailbird. By the time he was released, my father was
dead already. I met him once or twice, but he and Christina never
had much to say to each other. With the Senekals, too, he didn't mingle.
While I was keeping myself scarce here in the Couga, I never saw
him. My family had brought it home to me very clearly that my half-
breeds and assorted women were not welcome on their doorsteps.
Before decamping for ever, I wanted to smoke a pipe or two with
my uncle.

Aunt Catharina opens the door, glances over my shoulder to see
whether I've come on my own. One eye is full of the milk of blindness,
but she can still see quite enough. She shows me to the kitchen where
Uncle Jacob is sitting with his coffee. He is old, well over seventy,
but he's still sitting up straight and his beard still hangs full. When

he sees the calabash of karrie I brought, he empties his coffee out over the half-door and holds out his mug.

Goddam, child! That Caffre porridge has put marrow in your bones. Just look at you. I heard that you'd moved in hereabouts. Thought you might come and show your face.

I'm here now, aren't I?

He drains the karrie, holds out his mug again.

Pour for us. As I always say, only a Hotnot woman can make karrie. Katrien tries, but she's too much of a Christian for this devil's piss.

While we're sitting with her in the kitchen, Aunt Catharina prepares food. Uncle Jacob is complaining about the people who are all bundling up here on top of one another.

A man can't move any more, the lot cluster together so much, sometimes six families squatting on a single farm. A few years ago you had to ride an hour or more to see your neighbour, now you can't sit on your pot in peace, or somebody bangs down your door.

I agree and check to see whether his table is as full of termites as mine. I knock on the table top, the wood feels solid. Uncle Jacob drones on.

The beasts of the field can no longer walk the old trodden ways. Nowadays the rabble shoot at anything that catches their eye. And all this fighting, all the veldt stinks of people. The animals are starting to walk other trails. The pathways are getting fewer and fewer. There isn't room for us all.

He tells of berserk elephants breaking trees. He hears stories of a few young bulls attacking a rhinoceros and mounting it and then killing it. He says an elephant servicing a reluctant rhinoceros is a sight nobody should have to witness.

Heed my words, he says. The animals are becoming ever more bestial as the child of man becomes ever tamer.

Aunt Catharina shakes her head and serves calves' cullions and belly and jacket sweet potato.

275

After the meal Uncle Jacob starts rummaging for old clothes in a chest. He says I must take the stuff that is too large for him nowadays. He says he's shrinking away. I thought my uncle was strong when I saw him, but when I look through his old clothes, I see how big he used to be. The jackets he produces hang loose on my shoulders. While he's making me try on a pair of trousers or such, I make him tell his story. He was a legend in our house, even though my people didn't speak of him. The horse's mouth always adds flavour to a story. He tells eagerly and gets thirsty quickly. We move back to the kitchen, where the karrie awaits us. When my aunt starts grumbling, it's to the stoep, where the sun is starting to wester.

~

Jacob and his Katrien were hardly married or they fled Granny Elsje's domain. Uncle Jacob says his mother was a hellcat, they were at each other's throats ever since he could reach her neck. He and Aunt Catharina in due course returned to the family farm, with his mother observing their farming methods with a snide sneer. One day they had another altercation. He walked out and tied a Hottentot's hands to a rafter and his feet to the chimney posts and lashed the living daylights out of the dumb creature. While the labourers were carting the body away, Granny Elsje snarled across the yard:

There, that's good, that's how you should all be treated! Shortly hereafter she moved in with Uncle Petrus. Even years later, when she was ill and harmless on her deathbed, Uncle Jacob kept his distance.

I was more terrified of that woman and more furious than at any host of Caffres, he says.

Granny Elsje was a harridan, but Uncle Jacob was himself not the easiest man to get along with. His neighbour, old Matthys Zondagh, apparently one day climbed into him with a dropper, after a dispute over a deserting labourer. In 1772 Uncle Jacob and his friend Van Staden go and lodge a complaint in the Cape about the violence inflicted upon them by the Swellendam landdrost. The bailiff has them arrested there and then. Apparently the landdrost had in the meantime written to the Cape and said that the two farmers had sworn at him and abused and pushed and shoved and hit him. That Jacob had threatened him with a loaded gun. The two so-called dangerous subjects are locked up, without a trial. Two years later Uncle Jacob is so weakened and sickly that his wife has to go and nurse him in the Castle.

Unexpectedly, he guffaws and tells how the Cape people were always looking for dead dogs to dig into the soil when they wanted to plant a new tree. Apparently made the tree grow more quickly. He spills karrie on the stoep and curses and laughs.

> Whenever somebody started digging a hole in front of his house, all that was dog kept its distance. Because a dead dog isn't always to be found, says my uncle. Then you start looking out for the neighbour's dog that yaps non-stop.

For two years and seven months he and Van Staden were detained and then released without a trial or a blush or a by-your-leave. He was exempted from quitrent on his farm for the period, but when he returned to De Lange Cloof he was ruined. Aunt Catharina had had to manage the farms and the Hottentots on her own and on top of it had had to go to the Cape herself to nurse him. Ever since, any field cornet or heemraad or landdrost or clergyman or goddam pen-pusher has had to cajole or threaten with the Cape artillery before my uncle would allow him anywhere near his house.

When I rode away that evening, with him standing on his stoep shouting drunken benedictions after me, I knew I had no need to see him again. We had talked our talk; we could now muck on each to his own little pile of stones.

You can go and check in the books and you'll see that the old devil became a member of a church for the first time in 1815, more than a year after our visit, after I'd left all Cape borders well behind me. Had his courage forsaken him at the last at the prospect of braving the Lord on his own and without the benefit of clergy? He could actually have postponed the churchgoing for a while longer; tares tarry on. He survived his wife; goddammit, the old scoundrel survived *me*. He only went to the tall trees in 1826, at eighty-nine, in all probability wielding a dropper.

∼

With all the commotion around the house the birds have cleared out. Apart from the voices and the bang and clatter you hear only the cicadas. If you listen well, you can follow their tune. They don't sound just one note. But that you only hear after many hours of sitting and listening. They say you lose the seed of freedom when you can no longer be bored. If freedom is to be measured by boredom, I'm the freest man in the Couga.

They say that at Tierkloof there's a mummy nestled in a cave. They say it was a Hottentot king. His biltong-body is covered with honeybush and waxberry. They say he has beads made of seashells around his head. Two funerary stones with ochre paintings by his corpse. The old ruler is dead and desiccated, but apparently as whole as the day he submitted his spirit to his strange god. That is what the Couga does to a man. It wraps you up and dries you out and embalms you here for ever in your cave, on your farm, in your body.

For eleven years I whistled the same tune when going to the cows in the morning for the milking; for eleven years another tune when walking back from the fields. Eleven years the same weaverbirds in the tree above my head, the same noises of the night. Eleven years I studied the routines of the veldt and animals and people around me and in the end got ensnared in them. To be embalmed in this way is not always unpleasant. My house was not only what happened between its walls. It was also the sounds of the outside: the tunes of the region, the shouting at each other and laughter and sometimes the singing of my wives and children; my out-of-tune whistling in the veldt. A man can feel at home in refrains.

Listen, the wondrous tinkling of Elizabeth's dinner bell as she carries the crate full of household goods past me. Imagine, my wife and I and our two lads, Gabriël and Michiel, assume our normal seats around the table in the dark, cool dining room. I say the prayer I recited every day, at lunch and dinner. Gawie teases his brother Midge and we tuck in. Chine, pumpkin and samp, steeped in the gravy that I sound her out about every time and that she smiles chastely about every time and says a woman does not deliver up her secrets. A man can come to love refrains.

~

The porcupine quill in Aletta's hair catches the sun as she takes down the last of the laundry from the line. I remember a day, two years or so ago, when I, Coenraad Buys, went and committed myself to a refrain that I was all too fond of, the meals that three times a day descend from nowhere upon my table. The sitting down to the tables laden with pots of meat, the leading in prayer and the licking clean of the dishes, especially the lying down after the meal, every melody of this I know well. But the false notes in a kitchen are an obscure business.

My children left for the veldt in the early morning to trap something meaty. They return with four porcupines and a hare. Porcupines don't dig holes, they dig pits. To get the thing out of there is always a pother if you can't smoke it out. Jan's arms are red when he dumps the creatures on the kitchen table. A porcupine can't walk past a bush without gobbling a mouthful; stay away from its belly, it's too bitter to eat. If you have stomach trouble, then you dry that belly, grind it up and infuse it over boiling water like herbs.

Believe me, never offer to help a woman in the kitchen. She'll first of all make you stand around like a fool and yell at you, and when you no longer know where to stand or what to say, then she'll put you to work.

Close your trap, dammit, it's fly season. And pass me that knife, says Maria.

She allows nobody else to take a knife to her meat. She grabs the knife from my belt and cuts out the arseholes. She believes a porcupine arsehole shouldn't come anywhere near a flame, it spoils the flavour. On commando we were never so fussy. We ate everything, arsehole and all, but nobody was ever lauded for culinary skills. She hangs the carcases over the flames. She stuffs the knife into my hand.

Come on, Buys, if you want to be useful, deal with those quills. I wait until the quills are on fire and then scrape them off. She pretends to be chopping vegetables, but when I look around, I catch her, hand on the hip, supervising me. The last quill is done. I pass her the meat.

Pick up the quills, the whole ones can go to the daughters for the hair.

I bend down and start picking up the quills.

Come on, like that you'll be here all day tottering like a heron. She shoves me out of the way and is down on her knees and scrapes together all the quills and passes them to me.

The broken ones can be chucked out, the whole ones to your daughters. Get on with it, then!

I clear out and first stand outside swearing and chuck the broken ones down next to the house and give the rest to Aletta.

Buys! I'm waiting for you!

She's standing in the doorway with a bucket.

Go and bring the water to the boil.

She disappears into the house again; I stoke the outside fire. When I go back in with the boiling water, the meat is lying in a bowl, steeping in vinegar. The backs of the porcupines have been flayed open. She calls this the mealies – with the quills removed, the flesh looks just like a dark-coloured mealie. She pours the boiling water over the mealies and scrubs them white. She stuffs the porcupine mealies into my hand.

Go hang them against the breeze, she says. And don't let them get bruised.

I go hang the lumps of meat like laundry and get myself out of there.

280

By four o'clock I hear her approach from a distance. The backs can be taken down. I bring in the meat and have to chop beans and peel potatoes while Maria is preparing the pot. She throws in the porcupine ribs and tails. The mealies are the best meat. Those she will fry with the hare when the pot meat is almost done. I throw the vegetables into another pot.

> That's not nearly enough, Buys. How many mouths do you count?

I didn't count. I start peeling again. She throws a few unpeeled potatoes into the pot. When the tails are done, the mill appears on the table and I have to mince tails. The half-cooked ribs go onto the coals along with the hare and the mealies.

Before the meal is dished up, there's yet another story. Every offshoot gets his own plate of food. To serve a meal is apparently quite a complicated business. This one is short of more meat than that one, that one more beans than the other. Dirk is cutting teeth and gets only soft meat. Jan is too thin and must get an extra bit of hare. I'm too stout and don't get any ribs. Aletta's stomach is playing up, she gets bread and black tea. The unpeeled potatoes are for the daughters: peels are said to make your hair shine. I start mumbling something about the suckling pig's coat that isn't exactly blinding.

> Shut up, Buys! Go and call your children, the food is getting cold.

No man can conquer the wilderness *and* the kitchen.

~

Uncle Jacob and I are not the only ones to get ourselves into trouble. Our whole family has problems with bosses. My big brother Johannes, too, had to go and see the Batavian landdrost because of the curses and slaps he levelled at Veldt Commandant van Rooijen. So it's probably understandable that the neighbours weren't too pleased when yet another Buys – a Caffre lover and Caffre copulator at that – moved into the district. Buyses should be sown as sparsely as possible. As soon

281

as there's a whole clump of them in one place, the strife and court cases start up.

Under my neighbours, whom, the Lord knows, I never loved as myself, I was known, in those first years in the Couga, as Outlaw Buys. They won't let me buy on credit and don't want me in their homes. The Ferreiras of Elandsfontein especially slander me every chance they get. Long Piet makes no secret of the fact that he thinks I'm something sticking to the sole of his shoe. His cousin and wife Martha is one of the local bitches who refer to me behind my back as King of the Bastards. Behind *her* back everybody calls her Mad Martha; that lady is impossible to get on with. When I have to call in at Elandsfontein, she receives me cordially, serves her universally celebrated milk tart, asks interested questions. Piet and I settle our business as soon as possible in order to be spared the sight of each other, but Martha insists on offering another cup of coffee. I feel like a child in her sitting room, as if between slurps of coffee she's waiting for me to break something. As if she's deliberately placed her most precious saucer in my hands, because she knows my hands are too rough for porcelain. The saucer cracks in my hand. She smiles at me.

If that rabble want to tattle on about my colourful clan, then that's all right by me. I'm not ashamed of my family. But all the talk about the price on my head is starting to irritate me. I'm a free man, dammit. Not free as a bird, but free like these accursed burghers around me who are born free and in all freedom expire on the same plot of borrowed ground. May the very stones cry out my citizenship and if not the stones then at the very least the goddam landdrost. I ride to Swellendam, only to be informed that I have to ride to Uitenhage if I wish to speak to my landdrost. Swellendam has washed its hands of the red Couga clay. I collar a scrivener and make the man sit down so that he can write. I dictate a charming letter to the authorities to make sure that I can bestride my farm as a free man. The fellow has to rewrite the thing three times before I am satisfied with my petition:

I shall not elaborate upon the causes of my general decline, the

ruinous tendency of my many households. I shall also not bore
you with the adversities with which I have had to contend in the
last decade. I am furthermore not vengefully inclined towards
those who were the cause and engine of my adversity. I am only
thankful that Providence has granted me the strength to endure
it all, as well as the blessing, after so many years under the Heathen
nations, to be allowed to return to the land of my birth under the
rule of those who have been appointed over me by the Batavian
government.

Were I, however, to remain peaceably among my countrymen,
I beg to inform the Commissioner-General that during the
dominion of the English I was declared an outlaw, and a hundred
rix-dollars offered for my body dead or alive. I have long since
forgiven this murderous onslaught on my life, but it would greatly
please me if my pardon were to be announced in as public a
manner as my being declared an outlaw. Let it be proclaimed
that I returned to the Colony with the full knowledge and
permission of the highest authority at the Cape, here to end my
days as a peaceful and obedient Burgher under the aegis of the
laws of the land.

Find enclosed herein a copy of the Notice of 14 February 1789
declaring me an outlaw.

The Burgher Coenraad Buys.

The bureaucratic machine reports back that my pardon was
included in the general amnesty declared on 1 March 1803, to
everybody arraigned by the English for political misdemeanours.
My return to the Colony occurred not only with the knowledge of
but in express instruction from the governor, and I would be permitted
to lead a free and unhindered life among other inhabitants as long as
I behaved in a respectable manner. The decree of outlawry is hereby
officially rescinded. A copy of this resolution will be sent to me so
that I can have it registered at any drostdy as may prove necessary.

Do you also smirk when you read how the terrorists of one authority are accorded amnesty and declared freedom fighters by the next succession of wigheads? Do you also want to cry out: The past is not dead, it's not even past?

For the rest of the Batavian rule I keep my trap shut and make myself small and grant my fellow human being his terrestrial happiness. I have a few children baptised and do my best not to commit adultery, nor to kill anybody, nor to steal, nor to bear false witness against my neighbour and also not to covet my neighbour's house, his wife, his manservant, his ox, his ass and not even his ever so comely maidservant.

In 1806 the focking English overrun the Batavians. We had all remained hopeful that the Cape would become Dutch again, as soon as peace was declared in Europe. But believe me, Couga-Coenraad's world was small. The Bushmen who now and again filched a sheep were more of a nuisance than the Bushmen-of-the-Sea.

When in that year I once again had a yowling child in my lap and had to be told how the Ferreira snot-noses execrated my brood for outlaw half-breeds, I'd had enough of Mad Martha's cinnamon-sugar reign of terror. I got to hear stories of how Martha assaulted her house-maids. Stories that she'd thrashed a few of them to death. Some of them had previously been Kemp's catechumens. I write my old friend a long account, in the hope that he can engage his power as colonial spokesman of the Lord to harrow the Ferreiras. I hear nothing from him, till five years later I am summonsed to testify against my neighbour's wife.

∼

I sit apart at my daughter's wedding. 5 August 1809, Swellendam. Mists swirl about the town. Bettie is marrying Johan Sowietsky. A bland and blond fellow; wouldn't harm even a mosquito. Not very many of the groom's people have turned up. The few who have made it into the pews gape at us open-mouthed when we walk into the church. The Sowietskys are a pallid bunch, the older generation's Slavic accents still weigh down their words. The father and mother know what their son is letting himself in for. They came to exchange pleasantries soon after Jan came to beg me for the hand of my daughter. It's the rest of the family that's sitting there muttering and mumbling under their breath and smirking at my colourful little tribe filling up the pew behind me. The minister drones his drone and the church choir wauls worse than the yard cats in August. Bettie and Jan mutter a few little nothings at each other. She's looking lovely. Elizabeth and Nombini helped Maria to stitch the dress together. My wives are a band apart. Then the ring is on my daughter's finger. Not one of my wives wears a ring. There is a ceremonial shaking of hands such as I last witnessed at Avontuur and then a drinking of tea such as I have never witnessed. The tea is weak and lukewarm, but this crowd fling it down their gullets as if it were the abundant streams of nectar or virgin piss or whatever of the New Jerusalem. The tarts are not inedible. I have to dissuade a few of the younger offspring from the cake tables with the flat of my hand. You'd swear I never fed the rascals. After the cake and tarts have disappeared, my children play in the dust. The older sons stand with me and smoke. The eldest and Elizabeth's little ones I know well, but the lot in the middle, I don't really know about them. Piet and Aletta and little Maria and Windvogel the younger. I wasn't at home much when they arrived. They didn't pick up my scent while they were still lying shut-eyed squealing and shitting. I am the husband of their mothers; I am not their father. Nombini stayed for as long as she had to; there she is now, walking down the street on her own, on her way out of town. We'll pick her up when we head home. She doesn't last long among people. She has the two children by Langa but they steer clear of me. Then there's Windvogel's lad, who is now my lad. But nothing of our own.

Jan comes to light his pipe with us outside the church hall. He's been calling me Father since we came out of church. I tell the men what I read years ago in the *Flatus Vocis*. How the Portuguese explorers plant crosses all along the coast. How our explorer arrives at a kraal where the people think the cross on the rocks is an altar of fertility.

How the men sneak off to the stone cross at night and, believe me, stand there and rub themselves up against the cross and return home full of hope to service their wives. Nobody laughs.

Bettie can't get away from the clucking women around her. She waves at me. I take my son-in-law aside. I tell him Now listen well. I list a series of atrocities that I shall perpetrate upon him and his extended family if he should mess with my Bettie. I tell him I like him. He has manners, especially with the womenfolk. He knows what an exceptional creature Bettie is; he worships the ground her feet tread upon. I tell him Keep it like that. He nods and gulps and says Yes Father. As you say, Father. When he walks away to his friends, I call him back.

> Jan, I say, always remember: Do as I say and not as I do.
>
> Yes, Father, of course, Father.
>
> Well, then, that's all right. Those pals of yours want to ply you with strong liquor. Let's go and see whether they have enough for an old man's thirst.

The young crowd don't keep up for very long, then they hive off to go and drink elsewhere at their own pace. The Sowietskys also get going by late afternoon. Jan remains shiny-eyed and upright. We walk across to Bettie where she's sitting red-eyed in the corner of the little hall with Maria. I hang on to Jan, his puny shoulders only just support me. I let go of him, lose my balance and grab at Maria and Bettie. With a hand on the shoulder of each and a tongue that slurs in their ears, I say Jan is a man after my own heart. I say Bettie deserves such a man. And Maria says:

> Yes, my dear child. You deserve better than me. Your Jan will stay with you. He's not a rover, I can see that. You can't make a rover stay at home. With him you do as with a baby. Ever since we've been farming at Opkoms, your father has had to have his teat or his bottle, otherwise he bawls or tries to run away.

I settle next to Maria. I put an arm around her. She doesn't resist. We look at our daughter. I watch how Jan treats her. He touches her slowly and gently. When she was small, nobody was permitted to touch Bettie. As she grew older, that didn't change. The boys couldn't get near her – even Maria and I had to keep our hands to ourselves. Nobody, till this pale and blond Jan. He is tall and strong, but carries himself as if he's smaller than she. I look out of the window at how he presses her to him where they think we can't see them. How they kiss. He touches her as I touch Elizabeth's special cups, as you touch a lamb that has to be gentled out of a ewe. You hardly touch, but you make sure that you have a grip. I watch what Jan does and I try the same with my hands on Maria. She looks at me as she hasn't looked at me for a long time, just for a moment. She gets up and pours the last of the tea.

∼

As long as my brandy casks don't run dry, the peace at Couga endures up to and including 1811, a shambles of a year in my life.

The year kicks off with the wedding of Coenraad Wilhelm, but this joyful occasion is soon forgotten in a nitpicking about river water. I've been renting a pasturage farm for two years, De Doorn River, from Marthinus Menderon, but the Heynses complain that I use up all the river's water before it reaches their outspan. They go and moan to the heemraad and really abuse me in the plaint and I have to get away from there. They must take their water and squirt it up their clenched arseholes.

De Doorn River was one thing, but then came the bother with the Hottentots. Commandant Linde decides that each Hottentot who does not have a contract with the farmer he's working for must be called up for military service. The bunch with their shiny muskets and showy hats come prance with their equally shiny horses in my yard. When I can't show them a single contract, they take my Hottentots from me. My children and I and their appendages try to feed and harvest and care for the cattle and the crops, but goddammit what's the use and why.

On top of that, the Second Caffre War was raging at the time. Graaffe Rijnet's landdrost, Anders Stockenström, was in action at Bruyntjeshoogte. The story goes that Stockenström left there just before the New Year with twenty-four men to talk tactics with Colonel Graham. At Doringnek on the Zuurberg they ran up against a crowd of Caffres. Stockenström regards himself as friend to Caffre and Christian in equal measure. He dismounts with no gun in his hand and goes to negotiate with the Caffres to let them through. When he gets back to his horse, they are surrounded and the Caffres murder Anders and seven other burghers, also a bastard interpreter, one Philip de Buys, my dear, dear son Philip.

In 1812 burghers not resident in the districts of Graaffe Rijnet or Uitenhage could choose to donate money for the safeguarding of the border against the Caffres rather than to perform military service. I paid for my younger sons; Coenraad Wilhelm paid for himself. I'm not sending my blood to the slaughter again. Death is sure to sniff you out in due course; no need to go looking for her.

When I, Omni-Buys, rummage through the archives, I find that my signature by 1811 looked very different to when I moved into the Couga in 1803. Where once a man would sign his name with care, believing as he did that he had just cleansed that name of all blot and disgrace, in later years he will scratch and stab at a piece of paper with the nearest quill to hand, from anger and frustration, because he realises that you can rid yourself of everything except your name. That it is your name that brands you as scapegoat to be driven into the desert. I had a name, and no matter how I signed it, it refused to allow me to find peace between the beloved baboons and aloes of the Couga.

≈

Omni-I sees you all standing in the Couga with your sunburnt necks taking snapshots of my farm. Sometimes one of you will enquire which route I would have taken, through the kloofs and over the mountains. In your time the main roads are tarred, criss-crossing the land, like the lashes of a whip. Do you know that these were once elephant trails, these national roads? Your mountain passes were designed by antelopes and elephants. You merely came to cast the tar and set off the dynamite and bury your prisoners of war next to the road they made. There are many routes out of the Couga. The roads have always been there.

My wife Nombini is not being difficult; she's merely holding herself apart. She lives her life on the edge of the household. She will sit with us and laugh at the table; she will laugh as long as it's necessary. If Maria or I lambast her she listens with bent head. When the chastisement ends, she straightens that long neck and goes off to do what she wants to. I can talk to her about things I would never mention to the other two. She listens to me, she doesn't judge; she guards my secrets. Whether she is indeed listening to my outpourings – in Xhosa or in Dutch – and if it's of any moment to her, that I don't know. Her life is something unknowable and regards me hardly at all. I'm an incidental, like a bothersome knee, something she thinks of only when it hurts.

When the Hottentots were still on my farm, they constructed an impressive system of canals to conduct water from the kloofs to the farmyard. Nevertheless Nombini persists in fetching, late every morning when the sun has seeped its warmth into the rocks, two pails of water from the river. The river is just here close by, in the evenings you can hear it rushing, but the woman stays away for hours with her pails. Three years ago I went to spy on my wife one morning.

Nombini with her pails comes out of her house in a daze, eyes staring straight ahead. She marches across the yard, almost steps on little Dirk who's sitting building a kraal for his clay oxen. She strides into the veldt, me following. She keeps next to the river for a while, then she puts down the buckets on the bank and turns away up against the incline. The bushes and grass at her feet are green, but the trees around her are huge black spears, charred by last year's fire. She walks fast, steps lightly and constantly looks about her, searching. The pathway she is following from the river is narrower than any antelope trail. She stands still, steps out of the path, picks up a stone and places it in the path and walks on. I don't get close, just see at an angle how she touches her back, over the cloth of the dress she never looks at home in. How her hands find the bow of the laced-up dress, pulls it loose and how she steps out of the dress when it falls free and gets snagged in a sugar bush. See, her buttocks are two beating hearts. Once again into the bushes, once again the stooping and groping on the ground, once again the stone placed in the path and then on again. On with the path, overgrown since the buck no longer walk here, or forged open in the wilderness by something smaller and lighter. I get to the first stone in the path. It's a tortoise turned on its back. So too the second one. She walks as if she's urgently on her way somewhere, until she stops and bends down in the bushes and turns up a tortoise to lie kicking the air helplessly. Then she takes to the path again resolutely. I stop counting after the twentieth turned-over tortoise. She stops. After an hour's walking she stands still, gazes in front of her for a while, turns around and comes walking toward me. I shrink away just in time behind the nearest milkwood. I lie knotted together behind the bush until she's walked past me. When she's some distance away, I stretch myself and fart the fart I had to hold in. I carry on along the path, want to see what made her turn round. The road stops. Where she came to a halt is where the path peters out in front of a collapsed anthill. I turn around. For the first time my farm is out of sight. I walk back, following her. The tortoises are gone. None of them are left lying in the path. I catch her up; see, over there she's bending down in the path. She picks up the tortoise, puts it back on its legs and walks on. The tortoise starts walking along the path towards me. Behold: It's not an antelope trail that she and I are walking. It's a path she's trodden for eight years. Every day for eight years she's walked until she can no longer see the farm; every day she turns over every tortoise she comes across. Then the walk back, turning over the tortoises again and before the last bend putting on the dress again. I put my foot down before the tortoise waddling towards me. See, there she is, next to the river again, the hem of her dress soaked in the stream. She fills the buckets with water and walks back to the homestead. I pick up the tortoise and place the dumb creature down on its shell and follow my wife, back home.

~

I'm sitting with the book again, ticking off the last supplies on the lists. When the most important things have been ticked off, I make another list in the light of dusk. *This* is what I had to contend with here in the Couga:
bluetongue,
women,
children,
bloat,
Bushmen,
anger,
leopards,
gallsickness,
church councils,
heemraden,
heartwater,
Mad Martha,
liverfluke,
baboons,
comfort.

While I'm trying to think of more mortal enemies, Elizabeth appears in the yard. She's been in the veldt gathering medicine for the journey. While living in the Couga I was at home most of the time. No revolutions or journeys of exploration or flights from authorities. I was with my wives and children. I saw the children growing up and the wives growing old. I did what I could around the house, even though I'm still not of much use with a hammer or a saw. My hands curled up more by the year, felt slightly less, cramped slightly more. I taught my sons to ride and to shoot. I taught my daughters about the plants and herbs in the veldt. But Elizabeth is the true doctor in the family. She knows a plant or an infusion for every complaint and her ears prick up when the people of the area tell about their cures. Over the years I've also learnt some cures by which the people of these valleys swear. I write them down in the back of the book, tear out the page and stuff it into the chest with Elizabeth's herbs:

infused rue for fever;

wild dagga as prophylactic for colds, flu, wheeziness, gallstones;

infused goat's dung or nettles for measles;

bread poultice for blood poisoning;

candlewax and lamp oil for chapped feet;

infusion of pomegranate peel for worms;

wormwood and the juice of sour figs for squitters;

warm cow dung and vinegar for open sores;

rhinoceros bush for pain in the side;

infusion of buchu or false buchu for bladder and kidney ailments;

smoked bitter apple or poison apple for toothache;

a few drops of rabbit piss for earache;

warm bran in a sachet for pain relief;

blue soap and sugar mixed with spit for boils; and always remember:

keep your trap shut and know your place and

wrap infections in warm cat skin.

There were cures for everything, except staying young and sitting still.

5

The sun sidles in under the leaves of the white stinkwood and catches me from the side. I take the *Flatus* book and seek shelter in Maria's house. Before the long trail claims me, I want to linger here for the last time. It's been months since I was in here. I see my children outside. Maria and I no longer really sleep together and we don't eat together. As I step into the house, two clay dolls crunch under my feet. The gloom inside is cool. In the eleven years we've lived here, Maria gave birth to her last two children. Bettie was hardly married and out of the house when Eliza was born. Maria was missing her eldest child and wanted another Elizabeth. She was still upset that I'd named my wife Elizabeth as well, but she kept to Eliza for the little one. It wasn't long before the confusion led to everybody's calling the baby, who kept on making knocking noises with her tongue, Toktokkie, after the tapping beetle. After Doorsie's birth four years ago – Theodorus in the Cape's books, after my friend Kemp – Maria stopped bleeding. Is it her blood that makes a woman attractive? Now and again we still laugh and talk through the night, but sometimes I remain soft and wrinkly when her barren lap brushes against me.

Maria's house is smaller than the other and her children now tally eight, not counting Bettie, who lives on her own, or Philip, who is dead, or the other boys who are doing their own thing. Her house is disrupted with periodic bouts of tidiness and uproar. It's the children's sleeping quarters, their playground. She can manoeuvre the exuberant chaos in a certain direction, but the whirlwind itself she does not try to stem. The children clutter and litter until one day she bawls them out and lets fly under them with those paddle-hands of hers. Then the little rascals start sweeping and cleaning while she sits outside smoking and blowing smoke rings with conviction. After that it's a palaver trying to find anything in the house. The little darlings pack everything away, but not where it was before. They wipe up where they've spilt, but with hands and cloths that are dirtier than the spill.

293

Behind me against the wall there is a muddy streak where a little hand tried to rub out a drawing. Most of the more important furniture has been carted out to the wagons. I take it that the furniture and toys still standing around here are destined for the flames.

In a corner looms the throne the children built me. The chair is decorated with pieces of copper wrapped around the backrest with thongs. Behind the backrest ostrich feathers radiate like a black-and-white halo. I drag the throne to the centre of the room, so that I can see outside but also take in the house around me. Janssens is furiously digging up something outside, he yelps excitedly with his snout full of sand.

Where I open the *Flatus Vocis* the traveller is whingeing about the sleeping arrangements of slaves. He says the slaves at the Cape are short and weak because the creatures mate like animals in the slave quarters, where men and women lie together. Their reprehensible masters allow them to perish in the mire of Heathendom, he says. For strong offspring a European should have a hand in the breeding, says our researcher. Not that a hand has ever impregnated anybody, Mijnheer, I want to add. Then I realise where I'm sitting. On the throne of the King of the Bastards, which my own offspring made for me as a gift, egged on by the gallows humour of their mother, my first love. A European hand! He can go to hell! Not one of my children is as strong as those of Ngqika, Mijnheer the crazy rover.

On the next page our expert on the nations of the earth opines on the subject of the Hottentots. By nature, he says, they are not too far from white. But as soon as a child is born, they rub the baby with oil and place it in the sun and repeat that every day so the little one can bake brown all over. The sun has baked my tribe of half-castes as well; those born whitish are now also brown – the whiteness visible only in the places that the bathwater alone sees. And the bath does not see them very often.

According to the traveller, the Hottentots break the baby's nose so that it should lie flat against the face. Oh, for God's sake! As he grows older, the Hottentot allegedly carries on anointing himself with oils and fats until eventually he is pitch black. This, apparently, they do to make themselves stronger. Hence, according to him, the Caffres and their strength. Wonder what would happen to the numbskull if he should ever ask Ngqika whether he is also a sun-baked Hotnot?

I plonk the book down on my throne. Food for the flames. Janssens notices me and stops the digging. He comes to fetch me to inspect his excavation. I stroke my immense dog while he's digging. A dizzy spell makes me sit down. Janssens licks my face. The ploughing paws suddenly deafening, as if they're harrowing at the back of my head, there where things should have remained buried.

～

If it hadn't been for Kemp and his new pal Read's damned philanthropy, I might have ended my days in the Couga. If only I hadn't written him that letter. No, not even you will believe that. I'd have trekked my trek sooner or later anyway. In any case. The two missionaries squat in that shithole Bethelsdorp and invite all that is Hottentot or Caffre to come and moan about the hidings the farmers administer them. They believe every word and write it all down and post it to England. Cradock is instructed by the focking British Minister of Colonies to investigate all fifty charges by the missionaries against the farmers. De Swarte Ommegang – The Black Circuit, our name for that circuitous court – gets going in 1812 and meanders about between Graaffe Rijnet, George and Uitenhage. Preachers have always thought that if you confess hard enough, it will set you free. Farmers slap and thrash their workers. It's always been like that. It will damnwell always be like that. The strong ones trample the small ones, the small ones get stronger with being trampled, until they can trample themselves.

Initially I'm aggrieved when I hear about the Ommegang, until I'm told that there's also a whole list of charges against Long Piet and Mad Martha. I am summonsed to go and testify in George about the stories that I peddled to Kemp. Many thanks, Kemp, for this last gift. Oh, Martha, I thought, now it's my turn to trample.

~

The summons was still lying right there on the table where I read and left it, when I got news of Kemp's death. In December 1811, so the people say, the old man gave up the ghost in the Cape.

Lord knows, Kemp, I bade you farewell ten years ago at Schapen-kraal. What mourning was to be done, I mourned then and had done with mourning. We had our own lives to live. I came to squat here. Now I am told that in your sixtieth year you acquired a lovely little slave girl, fourteen years old, and set her free, her mother and brothers as well. Married the overjoyed maiden. They say she was rounding out with your fourth child when she bent over your deathbed to make sure that the blanket was covering your long body properly. Dear old Kemp, I was witness to how the crafty woman-flesh of these parts, dark and tender, led you into temptation until seventy times seven every day. Yea, verily, for once and for always and damn me, at last, you permitted yourself to yield. And what a yielding it was! I don't mourn you, Jank'hanna, I rejoice *with* you. My friend who is dead for ever.

~

The evening before I'm due to set off for court, Maria and Elizabeth and I are sitting at the kitchen table. They want to know where I'm heading. Coenraad Buys setting foot off his farm is a great event these days. I tell them about Mad Martha and the tales doing the rounds. How she bullies and beats her labourers to death. Maria snorts:

But, Buys, you're a fine one to talk.

Nombini is standing in the doorway. I notice her only when she turns on her heel and walks out.

Maria, that mad piece of shamelessness must not get away with such cruelty.

You yourself have been to court because you maltreat your
workers.

I was not found guilty.

Only because you and your pals chased off the landdrost.

I want to start protesting, then Elizabeth gets up.

I'm going to bed, Coenraad. You must travel well tomorrow.

Sit for a while longer, wife, I say.

The Coenraad I married wasn't scared of his neighbour's wife.
Maria gets to her feet, spluttering.

Sleep well, you two turtle doves, she says as she leaves.

∾

A pheasant calls from the other end of the yard. The dog's snout perks
up out of the hole, its ears erect. He wants to take off, then I grab him
by the scruff of the neck, drag him back to the hole. I push his head
into the loose soil.

There, I say, you wanted to dig. Now *dig*.

He digs up a bone and trots off across the yard, flaunting the chewed-
to-a-pulp treasure in his mouth.

∾

On 4 January 1813 the Ferreira trial has been running for two days. I
walk into the little hall. George's new drostdy, the ancient posthouse,
smells of wood oil. There they sit, the whole accursed ruck of them.
Every soul in the district crammed in here. The air is saturated with
sweat and spite and silence. And in the dock Mad Martha Ferreira,
fortyish, stocky and strong, broad shoulders, rhinoceros hide. No tits
to speak off, two dried-up dugs under the dark frock. Eight children
have emerged from under that frock to date. The muscles in the forearms. The knobbly hands. She is tidy. Even here in the courtroom the
audience whispers of her milk tart. The lashless white eyes don't blink
and don't let go of me. Long Piet is younger than I, but looks older,
bowed down prematurely under those eyes of Martha's. There was a

charge against him as well, that he had trampled a Hottentot youth, Kleinveld, with his horse, but the corpse was without any blemish and Piet was not summonsed. He is here as support for his beloved wife.

On the bench with its hopeless carpentry the worthies L.C.H. Strubberg and P.L. Cloete shuffle in their seats in boredom. Landdrost A.G. van Kervel is the plaintiff. G. Beelaerts van Blokland is the prosecutor. The atmosphere is strained, first names too intimate, only initials are tolerated.

Eleven charges. Seven dead by her hand, four mutilated. I slide into the back row. My fingers cramp into claws when I see the grimace around her mouth. She smiles at me, at the whole court, while checking to see who all turned up for the performance. I know that grimace. As the lips curl up for the laugh, the cheeks compress the eyes into smug slits. It's a laugh that as a child I saw often. It says I am pleased you did that, Coenraad; I am pleased you went too far. Now I have licence to flatten you. Because you are not respectable. Martha is not pretty like my mother, she doesn't know how to swing her hips. But they are of the same stock. The quiet violence of respectability. This white woman with the bearing of a lady, educated as few women of her class are, schooled and trained and addled, every hair pinned up and covered up; the compression of the corset curdling and compacting everything inside it. Good morning, my dear mother. I smile back.

For four days I sit and listen to the plaints, waiting for my turn to be called. For four days I look at her before I get to say my say. The Hottentots stream into court and confess and cry and malign the Christians. Martha sits and listens. When the proceedings are adjourned, she talks softly to her husband and at times laughs behind her hand at whispered jokes. The Hottentots in the witness stand look bewildered, each one more so than the next, as if they cannot comprehend that a court could listen to them without hanging them afterwards. Some talk at length, others just cry. The witness stand warms up with the bums of the wounded and the chancers. One or

298

two speak their testimony like rhymes learnt by rote; I recognise phrases from Kemp's catechising. Kemp knew how to train a Hottentot.

Watch her closely when the mad madam defends herself. She hides her big hands under the witness stand. She feigns gently, contemplatively, demurely and serenely. Civilised. She is aware of herself and of everybody around her. She answers two hundred and forty-eight questions. The only thing in this courtroom that is not under her control is her left foot that almost inaudibly knocks on the wooden floor.

> I discipline my workers, she says, because I am a precise
> woman, very set on my work.
> And the title Mad Martha, how do you feel about the name?
> I know very well that they call me Mad Martha, but that is
> without foundation. I am no madder than others who are
> obliged to deal with Hottentots and Blacks. Still, I know I am
> standing before just judges and in that I trust.

And in that vein the she-wolf talks herself out of a corner.

∼

The Ferreira clan were banished from Algoa Bay in 1803 already, precisely because of all the stories that their farm labourers spread about even then. Piet and Martha move to De Lange Cloof, to Dieprivier, the farm of Piet's younger brother Naas. Three years later they settle on Elandsfontein, where they are still squatting behind their fortified turf ramparts, breeding like mildew.

Here in George the scandals of Algoa Bay caught up with the miscreant of a woman. At Fort Frederick, so the people aver, the slave woman Manissa was lashed every day with a sjambok, once an eye was taken out. Manissa goes to gather wood and does not return. Martha follows in her footsteps and returns without the slave. Half an hour's walk from the homestead they find a spoor of blood, a bloodspot, a piece of taaibos wood, drag marks, the small footprints of Martha and a bundle of wood tied with Cape tulip.

Martha Ferreira:

> I did not chastise dear Manissa. Perhaps once gave her a few
> well-deserved lashes across the back. The woman had the
> Mozambique disease. She died of red diarrhoea, Your Honour,
> the blood stool. Night before her death I nursed her. Old Esau
> buried her.

Roosje and her child Hendrik left Kemp's mission station to go and
work for Martha. At Dieprivier Roosje developed a dry cough and the
consumptive disease. She couldn't work any more; she was beaten
every day with a stick or sjambok. One fine day she runs away from
the cookhouse. Martha is hot on her heels and beats her and hits her
in the back with a rock so that she falls down in a ditch and dies next
to the kraal. She was buried and three weeks later Martha and Long
Piet left Dieprivier.

Mad Martha:

> Roosje was a poor, sickly creature, all skin and bones. I doc-
> tored her with goosegrass and sowthistle, but nothing could
> staunch the consumption. We buried her as is the Hottentot
> custom in a kaross and a rug.

At Dieprivier Martha sends little Hendrik, Roosje's pride and joy, to
go and fetch calves. It starts raining and snowing and he can't get back
over the flooded river. The Hottentot Geduld finds him after three days
in the veldt behind a rhinoceros bush, rigid with cold. Back at home
Martha puts the child's feet in a pot of boiling water. He can't feel that
the water is boiling. He just sees steam. Martha treats the sores, wraps
the boiled feet in cloth and one by one the toes start dropping off.

Mad Adder:

> When Geduld turned up with the boy, I dosed him with warm
> wine. Added crushed tendrils of sour fig to warm water and
> warmed Hendrik's little feet in it. I put a poultice of barley on
> his feet to draw out the burn. I did my best. I did though once
> take a paddle to the child's head because he swore. That I am
> sorry about, Your Honour.

What is it to me that the woman Bitja went to collect wood at Dieprivier and that Martha caught up with her and gashed open her eyebrow and lips? What business is it of mine that when the lunch meat was spoiled one day, Martha cut the housemaid Lys' arm with a knife? What does it matter to me, I'm waiting to face the mad bubonic bitch myself.

≈

I settle myself in the witness stand, push the table forward to create space for my legs and my wrath. That woman puts me off my stroke so much, I'm not my normal eloquent self. I stare at my scruffy shoes, the chafed ankles, my trousers that don't reach where they should. Not that the other Christians in the hall look any better. But the cloak of respectability is not upon my shoulders; the panoply of white conformity I do not wear. Everybody examines me as if I've crawled out of a hole. My voice is hoarse, my oration brusque.

Coenraad de Buys:

> Your honour, about five years ago a raggle-taggle Caffre and two women turned up on my farm and complained about the Ferreiras. I can tell you today only what I wrote at the time to my honoured friend, the late Jank- . . . Doctor van der Kemp. The Hottentot woman Griet left Doctor van der Kemp's mission station to go and work for . . . er . . . Mrs Ferreira. Martha, Mrs Ferreira, apparently beat her and stoned her. Griet's body was full of running sores and after a while her hands were no longer worth anything. She died in front of her straw hut and two women dug her in. That is what I know, what I heard.

Goddam Martha:

> In her last days Griet complained of a hard band over her navel. She said she was drinking snake venom for it and at full moon I saw her wandering about muttering. Then she fell down in the door of the hut. Her belly was swollen. Even Mijnheer Buys would not have looked at her twice.

The rabble laugh.

And Rachel? Van Blokland asks.

To the devil with Rachel, I want to shout. I want to see Martha hang until her eyeballs pop and her tongue swells up like a rotten fish. Coenraad de Buys:

> The woman Rachel was one of Kemp's Bethelsdorp Hottentots,
> a reborn child of our Lord, who went to work for that . . . for
> Mrs Ferreira. The phthisis made the woman spit blood. So
> I am told. Mrs Ferreira is alleged to have beaten her to death,
> and, so I am told, dragged her a hundred paces to her straw
> hut and, I swear that *that* is what I was told, that night set the
> hut on fire. Apparently Rachel was buried the next morning
> in the vineyard.

A Hottentot succeeds me and says Martha burnt down the hut only two weeks after the thrashing. Another one nods conspiratorially in my direction and to hell with him too. He alleges that Rachel was burnt alive. Yet another says that it was a high wind that brought the fire.

Crazy Clap-cunt:

> Little Rachel suffered from the fever for a month and com-
> plained of a stitch under her right teat. I nursed that daughter
> of Ham. Gave her candles to burn at night when the sleep was
> elsewhere. The wind was strong that night: I pray that little
> Rachel was asleep when the flames overwhelmed her and she
> returned to the bosom of our Father.

I am excused, but Martha's meagre smile does not let me go. The room around us vanishes. It is just she and I in the courtroom, on earth. I stare at Martha, how she tugs at her dress, irons out the wrinkles on her lap with the back of her hand. With one ear I hear how Long Piet's labourer Esau buys himself the slave woman Steyn as wife. How Martha beats her with sjamboks, broomsticks, jukskeis, and heavy objects. The flesh that rots with all the bruising and starts to fall off the woman's body. How with swollen and rotten arms and head she lies senseless. Esau was not allowed to visit her but he went to say good bye to his wife in secret. She died and her body was just gone.

When the young Hottentot Hans comes to speak in person, he does not look up once. He knows as well as I that once you look into those eyes, you've had it. When he was eleven or twelve he did housework at Elandsfontein and minded the children. He says when the children were naughty or cried, Martha beat him with river bush canes, brooms and jukskeis. And then nursed him.

One Hottentot after the other comes to testify that Martha beat one Abigaël so badly that the pus oozed from her wounds until she died. The story has many endings. The story has one ending. Abigaël died in Algoa Bay. She died in Dieprivier. She died at Elandsfontein. Abigaël is dead. Mother Martha, ungodly goodness personified, says the woman died in childbirth of red diarrhoea.

The Hottentots in borrowed Sunday best say that when old Mina one day botched a piece of embroidery, she was beaten till she was blind and her eyes pulp. They say her wounds stank to high heaven. The end of this story also takes many forms: Martha hit the woman behind the head with a plank while she was sitting in front of her hut. She is dead. Martha beat her with a yoke. She died in a ditch. Black-hearted Martha who could have been my mother:

> Mina was old and small and poxy. Her whole body and face covered with the red scabs of the shame. The woman couldn't work in the house any longer. No person could be expected to face such a sight. Mina henceforward worked in the garden.
> I didn't touch the woman; the pox was the end of her.

On one point only everybody is agreed: Mina's grave at Elandsfontein was shallow. The dogs dug her up.

The only charge on which Mad Martha was found guilty, was that of the blow to Hendrik's head. She had to pay a fine. Outside the courtroom the Couga Christians surrounded her and shook her hand

and hugged her. I walked past them and somebody snarled things at me. From the centre of the circle she waved at me.

~

I gather the Buys clan so we can set fire to the farmyard together. A father, after all, should worship with his family. The lot finish off or abandon whatever they were doing and walk across to where I'm starting to light the firebrands, but I myself stumble around, I fidget and fumble. My head is sputtering – stories about Martha, about the Couga, stories in the traveller's book.

Oh, the stories doing the rounds in the Couga. Old Jan Prinsloo who haunts his farm, Wolwekraal, over there. They say he wanders about at night among his horses looking for souls to devour. Skinned and roasted by his labourers, he walks, red and liplessly grinning, around his old yard in the kloofs. Apparently tied a few pregnant women to a wheel and beat them to ribbons and killed their husbands when they wanted to resist and then all hell broke loose on the old horse breeder's farm. Some say his labourers consumed old Jan after roasting him, others say that he ran all aflame to the stables and arrived there ablaze.

Are Martha's victims already wandering about around her house? Are her maids awaiting their chance to skin her alive one night? I wish her such an eternal wandering, without skin or lips, for ever surrounded by her ghosts. Shall I write Prinsloo and Martha's stories in the back of the book? My own nightmares? Shall I supplement the wanderings of the vagabond scientist with monsters of my own so that they too can be consumed by fire? Is there room for more ghost stories in a book that aspires to science and constantly bogs down in horrors?

It's truly dangerous to get embroiled in stories. Take, for instance, this *Vocis* affair of the traveller sitting rotting under that tree, so many wagon trails ago. He boarded a ship and landed here with a fresh quill and a large flagon of ink and wanted to write down the world.

One fellow came to commit Africa to writing and went mad. At least he found peace under the tree. His book survived him; did his book murder him? Something tells me the book is dangerous, contagious. As soon as you pen that first sentence, you're up to your neck. Well, *Flatus*, may you find peace in the flames.

I plant the torches in the ground around me, light one from the other. See, here the Buyses come walking up across the yard. My family, my Buys clan, laughing, their faces glowing when they enter the circle of torchlight. The stuck-up neighbours can chase us away like rogue dogs, but we won't cringe and roll over, we won't bare our bellies to anybody. A lizard scuttles away before their feet, into a stone crevice, to stay behind and to live on tomorrow as if we've never been here. Oh, the indomitable lizards of this land.

One last story I want to share with you, so that I can exorcise the accursed book once and for all, is the one where our *Flatus* friend recounts his experiments with a leguan. He tells how he caught a medium-sized leguan, about two feet long of body and three of tail, along with her two young at Agter-Bruyntjeshoogte. He grabs the leguan behind the neck so she can't bite. It's a tussle to keep control of the animal. He wants to kill the specimen as soon as possible without mutilating the body. He takes a darning needle and stabs the thing repeatedly in the heart and the head. The leguan waddles off. The scientist's Christian host undertakes to polish off the animal. He grabs hold of her and squeezes her hard by the chest a few times, ties her legs together and hangs her by her neck. Two days later the leguan is gone from the gallows, but lingers about the farmyard, apparently exhausted after her tribulations. The traveller and the farmer now devise another plan. The traveller has a cask full of brandy in which he keeps other specimens like snakes and smaller creatures. They catch the leguan again, once again tie up her legs, so that she doesn't lacerate the other specimens with her sharp claws, and dump her into the brandy. The Mijnheer *Vocis* tells how he holds her under with both hands, how she struggles in the brandy and doesn't suffocate in the spirits as he'd expected. How she after a quarter of an hour is still showing signs of life, still refuses to be analysed, and then gives up the ghost. You must descend to hell, Christina and Martha and all your kind! Unless you drown me in brandy, I, Coenraad de Buys, Khula the Great, shall also not perish.

∼

Toktokkie takes a torch from me and walks up to the only home she's ever known.

6

Fire can never be wrong. The flames sing as they devour. Two houses on fire, with us in the centre of the yard, between the two altars that are also sacrifices, to nothing and nobody; my children's eyes sparkling. Each one of the fires an animal that consumes everything that was once born; the fires grow until everything has been devoured and then start consuming themselves. It shines like a paradise, it burns like hell. It is plenty and pain. It is a feast and an apocalypse. The fire lives fully in sparks and sudden flickerings. It is weightless and the arch-enemy of gravity. See! See the houses burn! If we must vanish, let us vanish completely! Let us destroy our life here with a fire without measure or equal! That obliterates all tracks! That annuls citizenship! That wipes land tenure off the face of the earth! That extinguishes surety to the end of goddam oblivion!

The Couga existence finds its consummation in this moment when the roof timbers come crashing down. In the fierceness of the destruction I see the one and overriding proof that I have indeed been here, did indeed try to live like other people. At this moment when the roof collapses on the floor and the flames leap up from the ground to far above the walls, I relive every day of eleven years.

Maria's house is burning. Elizabeth's house is burning. Nombini said her house would not burn, the veldt had to claim it. I went to help her remove the window frames and doors so that everything that walks and crawls and flies can nest there when we're gone. Bettie persuaded Jan to come along, but when he heard of the house-burning he said we'd at last taken total leave of our senses. He is standing here next to me with my flame-headed daughter in his arms. I can see in his eyes reflecting the heat that he now understands.

～

After the Swarte Ommegang, the Circuit Court, the last of my friends turned their backs on me. Mad Martha had two milk tarts delivered.

I fed the things to the suckling pig. I was sure the tarts were poisoned.
The pig rooted around in it with its snout and snorted and planted a
huge turd in it. Well done, thou good and faithful servant.

In August the Cape is surrendered to the English. Every time the
mob up there start shooting at one another, our Colony is passed
around like an orphan between guardians who can't bring this unruly
child to heel. Under the focking English I shall not abide. Among
these Christians I shall not abide.

It's simple: If you have to leave, you have to leave. There are fewer
choices in life than you think. To be honest, if you're not welcome in
your neighbourhood, you can forget about feeling at home. For eleven
years I tried. Fifty is behind me; if I'm not a citizen by this time, I'm
not suddenly at eighty going to be greeted with open arms and
unpoisoned tarts.

It's grown late, but even the little ones are still awake with excitement.
In front of us the houses are still smouldering. I've made a fire; the
women are preparing the last meat that must be eaten before we leave
tomorrow. In the light of the fires the aloes against the incline come
to life. They are standing sentry or surrounding us for the onslaught,
who can tell. In front of me De Mist is lying asleep, almost in the
embers. Stray sparks scintillate in his coat. The strong spirits in my
belly still my insides. The boys around me all hunker around the fire,
elbows on knees, heads in hand. Nobody taught them to sit like this,
that is how children have sat by fires from always and into all eternity.
I smoke my pipe. Ruminating by a fire you find that the frailest
twig reddening and furling up recalls the volcanoes and pyres of old.
The blade of straw blowing away on the wind shows us the way to
our destiny.

Toktokkie comes to sit next to me with her straw doll and the
Flatus Vocis.

Father left this in the house. I rescued it from the fire.

308

Thank you, Tokkie, but I gave the book to the fire. It's yours if you want it.

Thank you, Father.

She grabs me around the neck, lets go quickly to get to the book. She tears out pages and folds animals that she arranges around the fire. One by one they catch fire, the elephant, the buck, the duck, the horse, the lion, the little men. A folded-up page falls from the back of the book. She folds it into a flower and hands it to me. I put it to one side and discuss arrangements for tomorrow morning with Hannes and Dirk and Windvogel. Toktokkie is back with a pin and fixes the folded flower to my chest. She comes to sit on my lap and soon gets lost in dreams that make her little feet kick out. I sit with my children around and on top of me; my wives are lying in a bundle on the other side of the fire. Far away I can hear the red dogs calling. It is peaceful around the fire with my sleeping people. Peaceful at last, now that I know it's all coming to an end. I sit drowsily watching the wind blowing the soot from my houses into the veldt.

∿

Like friends, the game has also got scarcer by the day. In September of this foul year of our Lord 1814 the hunting laws have become so strict that you must go and kowtow to the landdrost for every damned rabbit you want to shoot.

Authorities draw lines on maps, because authorities need farmers, not hunters. As soon as you own land, you surrender several years of your life. There is too much at risk. You have too much to lose. You invest too much in the land. Over the seasons you tame her, you harrow her into fertility. You have too much to kill for, too much to die for. Hunters live longer than farmers.

I take my sons along when I have the chance to go hunting. You learn to know nature through hunting. You can walk around and collect and take notes, but you don't learn as much as when you walk the veldt with a gun. The source of knowledge is desire, and hunting is an overpowering passion. If you want to get to know a klipspringer, you must taste it. You become as one with every potato and sweet potato you eat. Even God had to be made flesh the better to be able to taste. And the better to be able to hunt. God is constantly hunting us. He is the great collector. We hunt as we are hunted.

≈

The Caffres say the day does not break twice. There are no new beginnings. But there are places that have not seen me. As soon as I settle down on the wagon chest, a wind escapes me. I swallow deep; I feel dizzy. How it stinks, the blockage that made a responsible citizen of me. I erupt: it is exhilaration. I crack the whip. The oxen come into motion. We trudge through the kloofs towards the open spaces. My view shall no longer be occluded by mountains and by trees. My eyes are seeking an uninterrupted prospect; I want to see the earth unfolding to the horizon. A landscape that you cannot fence in, cannot break up into smaller divisions, cannot divide up into manageable gobbets of sense. An expanse in which you can't make yourself at home. I'm letting go, I grow smaller in a breadth that grows greater. I want to range far until I become a dot and vanish.

The last stars are still hanging in the sky when the sun starts showing itself. The paper flower drops from my chest. I squash a last termite underfoot. I hand the whip to Maria next to me on the wagon chest. I fold open the paper. It's a last map. Or, at least, parts of the scrawlings look like little bits of map. The folds of Toktokkie's flower draw new boundary lines on the ink lines. I fold in the four corners, trying to reassemble the flower. When the points meet in the middle, I see a meticulous map of Swellendam. Like the wanderer's first maps, fine and precise. I fold the corners over once more. The surface now much smaller, with a next map appearing, this one of the whole Colony. Once more I force the corners together, decipher the traveller's last riddle. Now I see the whole of Africa. It becomes more difficult to fold in the corners. The scrap of paper gets smaller and my hands struggle to hold it. After the next folding over there is a small terrestrial globe. When I fold the corners in once more, the little block of paper now almost as thick as it is wide, a tiny die lies in my hand, on each face the dotted stars of the firmament.

1814 –

1

Beyond the border of the Colony everything is always only outside. Even in your wagon tent at night the dew and wind shudder through the chinks, the cold cuts all the way into your rheumatic bones. Nothing can be stitched up close enough to keep the outside out. After a few weeks you smell like the veldt, you curl up at night like an animal. If you sit on horseback for long enough, you sometimes hear sounds streaming over your lips from deep down in your throat. On the trek time functions differently. Yesterday is just as clear and impossible as tomorrow. Today an infinite succession of fainting spells, flashes and compulsions. The force of the world obliterates you.

Look into the compound eye of the fly on my arm. The whip cracks; the fly zooms away over the plains. *And the earth was without form, and void; and darkness was upon the face of the deep.* Your books, reader, speak of a primal bang, that first crack of the whip, the first wrathful bellow. See, a jagged lightning bolt; the zigzag route of a fly; the world appears.

The first crack of the whip, and the cosmic oxen lurch forth into the furthest reaches. Things start stirring. Dense and warm and close beyond all measure, with lightning-swift expansion and cooling down. The cosmos explodes out and open.

Elementary particles start burgeoning. Sweltering; the particles buzz unpredictably. That which is and that which is not collide ceaselessly until there is more that *is* than what is not. More dust than nothing. The Transorangia or the beginning of time? You might well ask.

Criss-cross through time and space, Fly. Look with all your eyes. Make your lenses arc into infinity. The whole conglomeration grows older and colder. Flitter your wings until you become a blur of motion. Can you feel things starting to attract one another? How glutinous gravity descends on creation? How it wants to put an end to all the flying around? Your wings grow sticky and heavy as you acquire mass. Gaseous clouds congeal and become stars and constellations and milky ways. Be careful where you flutter, the universe is filling up.

Everything was closer together in the past. Close to the hearth of the universe it is colder and slower. I see you smirk: the universe or old Coenraad Buys? But see out there at the extremities! There the cosmos itself scatters. Flitter your wings! Far away from where things float loose and lone, far beyond the silt of gravity, stars shoot apart. The farther away, the faster they shoot. They tear away from one another because the distance between them expands. The space, the nothing, between them grows, without the stars themselves moving. Sometimes it is distance that moves, not us. Fly away, impossible Fly!

And God said: Let there be light! and there was light. You, Fly, speed through time, faster than light, but we here on the wagon, our light is not fast enough to catch up with that which is ever shooting faster and further away from us. The future we will never see. And also the light of primal things has not reached us yet. Heavenly fires long since extinguished will still shine forth tonight. We live in the light of dead stars.

You glide forth, but slower; movement becomes more arduous. The primal bang and everything fires up, but ever since then everything is a tying up, tidying up and dividing up. Shoot into a rocky crevice. See how things down here mutter and sputter until they grow gravid. Whoosh up, away from the iron core, up from out of the molten magma, through the melting amniotic fluid of fire, the semi-stone semi-flame slowly solidifying, away, upwards, through time and rock formations. Shoot over the waters, the substratum that arises from under you and dries out, over sand and stones, over the earth's crust where continents slowly tear apart and collide.

See, everything finds its place and name. *And God called the light Day and the darkness he called Night.* The pinnacle of the Great Tying-up: the organisation of organs into organisms. Ha! The particles and gases congeal into creatures, later mutate into humanoids. The life that chains you to the soil, so fast that you no longer want to let go. Your wings carry you further through time until you have to dodge rocks fatally plummeting to earth. Ice and dust fall into the sea from the backs of meteorites and the spark of life flames up. The tails of creatures start to twitch. In that small warm puddle full of salt and light and currents God breathes his breath into us. His breath stinks of ammonia.

Everything that lives and breathes is a stranger on this blue clod. Earth tolerates life, but she did not give birth to it. No wonder you can't settle down. No wonder you never feel at home. No wonder you're forever wanting to fly up and away. Go then, ascend and survey the wide expanses: you'll find no fatherland. There are tracks in the sand and stories about the tracks and for the rest only longing and wind.

Careful, old Fly: God – or the focking governor, through whichever of your multiple eyes you care to look – sets nets around the chaos. The compressed nothing has exploded in time and space and ever since God and governor have tried to reclaim every cubic foot and moment. If you want to get away from gravity, you must trek across the Gariep. Not even the gulls can get airborne in the Cape any longer. Begone, World!

See, a fly settles on the third-last ox. The whip cracks. Fly across the Gariep.

Shoot through the eighteenth century, across the rust-brown plains beyond the Great River. Sheer across the vague spider's web of light in the night. Little clusters of people around fires; the fires far apart. Sometimes knotted together like the nodes in shallow roots. Nomads extend themselves across the plains, they cling to openness.

Rush on, to the second half of the century. Do you see the dens of robbers down there, how patiently they wait to attack suddenly? Are you also thinking of the flicker-fast tongue of the lizard? Do you see the plains devouring and growing in all directions? It's the freebooters that make the open spaces grow: as soon as you kick off your shoes, they're on top of you. The robbers create the open spaces as the plains create them. Fly lower and see how the grass and bushes burgeon after sudden rains. Do you see how the shepherds on the open plains migrate, following the sprouting of green grass tufts? It is not a country, it is mere soil. Something to wedge your feet into.

Fly where you will and see how everything becomes and decays. See how innocent. See, it's all a game on a level board. Create and destroy; becoming, outward, eternally. The robbers and the plains. Do you see the lovely tension? Like that of a bow, a lyre.

Settle on any living body in any year and see the deserters and the runaway slaves and failed farmers and freebooters and Hottentots and Caffres and Bastaards stream across the border and see them screw each other senseless and into new incarnations. Settle on any jacket and see how the Colony's rags and tatters and gunpowder and lead and ways of doing have already begun to sully also this soil.

Circle the valleys beyond the Gariep and see the raids intensify, how the looters band together in ever larger gangs and flatten settlements, hundreds by hundreds of marauders with enough lead for the whole damned Africa. Take care not to be swallowed by a vulture. Fly higher and see the plundering causing a flood of refugees to well up and stream eastward, all along the great Gariep that Christians are now starting to call the Orange, after the colourful name of a royal house.

You've been flittering since for ever and you will know: The Colony has always been there. It starts up anywhere if you don't guard against it. The Colony burgeons from nowhere, always already in full bloom where yesterday there was nothing, like a poisonous flower in the Karoo.

The Colony's borders explode, blast open in the direction of the Transorangia, there where the nomads roam and rob and shoot off into the cosmos at their own speed and at the dictates of their own desires. Fly in between these roilings and ructions and reports and silences all the way to the day when the Second Colony traps the drifters in the crucible called Klaarwater, the place of clear water. Settle with your proboscis on the shoulder of a missionary and smell in him the fetid fused power of church and state. Do you feel how his chill breath cools and congeals everything that boils and bubbles and battles?

Walk on the missionary skin. Smell with the hairs on your body. Do you smell the rotten food and old excrement and half-chewed bones that tell you that there are people stuck here? Do you smell how their shit and sweat seep into the soil, how the diseases start breeding and the walls start pressing? Do you smell the sweet tobacco and civilisation in the missionary's cheek? Do the little hairs vibrate when you smell his fear? He who here, hundreds of miles of barren plain from the border, prepares the people for civilisation with his droning, drawling voice. He who wants to wash every Bastaard white as the driven snow and outfit him with British vestments; the pious panoply of diligence, regularity and cleanliness. Shepherds who should cease their wanderings and rather, to please God, sit down on their arses by their orchards and munch cabbage on the little stoeps of their European stone cottages – solid, safe and square. Do you see, beloved Fly, who only deigns to settle on that which stinks, how the stone solidifies into church and Klaarwater becomes Colony?

The cattle farmers and robbers still follow their routes as before, from one fountain or watering hole to the next. They know every well, outspan there only to leave it behind again at the break of day. Did you see, ancient Fly, all those many years ago, how the Bastaards and

317

the Koranas and the Bushmen could stop at these fountains, one after the other? And do you see, Fly of yesterday, how by 1803 the Griqua State assumes possession of the line of fountains? The line of survival points extending for fifty miles, south-west and north-east from Klaarwater: Klooffontein near the Gariep, through to the wells of Rietfontein, Witwater, Taaiboschfontein, all the way to the northernmost point and Ongeluksfontein.

Fear not, Fly, there is still plenty of refuse and remains for you to suck at. I understand you. I myself also fear the peace of the Colony much more than the constant wars outside its gates. We, the desert brigands, carry the mark of Cain with pride on our scorched heads, like plumes in our hats. Do you see me down there, Fly? Do you see me trek, how I can only truly settle when I'm in the saddle? The looters overrun the farms with their neatly squared little gardens. Enraged, they trample the beans and watercourses. The Colony, as you know very well, will vanquish them – *us* – and write up the history. Before there were Colonies there was no history, merely geology.

Fly over these plains one last time and seek the heated herds, the fiery flocks that keep erupting outwards like fragments of creation, faster and further, before the Great Coagulation that is always panting icily down our necks. Fly forth and come and settle on my cheek here where, somewhere in the Nieuweveld, I am shaking the hand of a man named Danster.

We left the last of the wagon tracks behind us so many days ago. There is no end to the Nieuweveld, the New Territory. There is no horizon here, only a haziness where the soil starts liquescing and the sky dusts over. The hordes of little table mountains make me crack my whip over the oxen; we're not yet far enough away from the Cape. The skin around my big toe is purple, it looks putrid. The trek is dawdling and in the evenings I want to scream when the kaross touches my toe.

The gout started at fifty. The pain comes at night. It's the glow in your foot that wakes you up. The big toe feels swollen and dead, but if you dare touch it, you gnash your teeth. It doesn't recede till dawn. Over the next few days the sore subsides. On such days I stay off my foot.

I abandoned the Colony in the company of two northern sheep farmers, David de Kooker and Hans Opperman, two louts whose eyes sparkle when you say Elephant Tusk. And every day since then more souls join us. Any lost or fed-up wretch who sees our wagons and horses and guns gathers up his own little bundle and signs up. Quite a few runaway slaves, deserters, a bunch of Hottentots, a few Caffres and windfall women, succulent new bodies that I take as concubines. Together with De Kooker and Opperman's families and my Buys clan we make up a fine little flock, sometimes up to a hundred, sometimes I stop counting at twice that; a small army on the march to oblivion. Nombini runs away one night. I catch her the following morning and tie her to the wagon until she calms down. For weeks we roam around. Then we get stuck at one watering hole for months. In the mornings, when the attacks subside, the skin around the toe itches and then peels off.

When, one evening at the butt end of 1814, we were outspanning, the Redcaffres were upon us. I kick at the buggered-up disselboom, then the shouting is everywhere. We are surrounded. Caffres, all of them painted red and naked under leather karosses greased with red ochre and fat. Assegais, but also a plethora of guns, shiny in the setting sun. Three hundred or so of them, on horseback, on oxen, most of them on foot. The Redcaffres, the Blootcaffres, the bare Caffres. Among them also quite a few Hottentots and Bushmen, most of them in Christian clothes and every single one with a Colony gun. Ever since arriving in the Nieuweveld I've been hearing stories about this gang of plunderers. If half the stories are true, few of us will see the light of day tomorrow. I'm ready with the double-barrelled flintlock, then I see the smiles. These Blootcaffres aren't picking a fight. A flamboyant little chap alights from his ox with sharpened horns and comes to meet me.

You are Buys and I am Danster the Dancer. We must eat and
    drink and smoke and talk, he says in fluent Dutch.
I shake his hand with a flabbergasted and cramping hand.

Danster is wearing a tricorn hat with ostrich plumes fanning out,
a blue jacket with the epaulettes and polished insignias of rank of a
captain in the Waldeck cavalry, gold rings and pieces of copper on
a richly festooned thong around his neck. On his feet brand-new
top boots that reflect the sky. All that marks him as one of the Blootcaffres is his mask of red ochre. Under the clay his face is deeply
grooved, the eyes dark unfathomable gashes. On his upper lip a
moustache that he twirls obsessively.

I make a proper fire and get out the brandy and introduce him to
Opperman, De Kooker and my wives. The two farmers don't have
much to say and go and stoke their own fires. Danster tells his tale
and I tell mine and in between we drink.

Danster laughs incessantly as if he finds the world a joke. Every so
often he gets up and stretches his legs with odd little shuffle steps
and then sits down in a different place next to the fire. He doesn't
really hang on to the thread of his story. His thoughts cavort and tussle
with each other, like my pack of feral dogs that nowadays scavenge in
our wake on the abundance and superfluity.

Danster says his name was once Nzwane. He says he's the younger
brother of the old stud bull Ndlambe. Under his moustache Danster
sports a crooked grin. Initially he speaks more Xhosa, but as his
biography leaves Caffraria behind, the narrative becomes ever
more Dutch.

He tells how, after the turn of the century, the Colony guards
the eastern border day and night with the new British money. How
the Rharhabe, nowadays the lapdogs of the focking Empire, expand
and extend their territory to the Fish River, till the smaller tribes no
longer have a foothold. Like pimples they are squeezed out from one
side by the index finger of the Colony and on the other side by the
thumb of the Rharhabe, northwards. Little detachments of Caffres

hive off to the Gariep in search of ivory and freedom. They remain Xhosas, he says, they wear their clothes and speak their language, but they also learn to live and to loot like the people of these parts. He says here you have to look twice some days to see who is a Xhosa and who is Oorlam or Bastaard or Christian.

In the hurly-burly of the Gariep River he baptised himself Danster. Here you have to make a name for yourself, he says. Your old name you leave behind in the Colony. You find a name and you blow it up as large as you can, with all the sound and fury at your command. The next prick you come up against watches his step, unsure whether you're dangerous or crazy or both.

I tell him about my years in De Lange Cloof and Graaffe Rijnet and Caffraria and the Couga. Throughout my chronicle he nods and grunts in affirmation, as if he's heard it all before. It's only when his hat falls off his head after a vehement nod that I realise that he is paralytically pissed.

He says he was a son in the House of the Right Hand of the Rharhabe, but he took his small gang and went tusk harvesting along the Baviaans River in the Winterberg up to about a quarter of a century ago. After this his name traced a criss-cross course between the Gamka River, the Cape, Bushmanland beyond the Sneeuberge as far as the bank of the Gariep and back to the Colony, away from the Bushmen and the droughts. In the Nieuweveld the gang rented themselves out as farm labourers until they could buy enough guns to hunt elephants and make war. By 1800 they were armed to the teeth and back in the Gariep.

Initially Danster's gang keep themselves to themselves around a great fire that towers over all the others. As the evening wears on, my Hottentots and Caffres start mingling with them. This crowd breathes new life into a company that in the last few months have seen more than enough of one another. And most certainly tonight new life is being breathed into quite a few young laps under and behind the wagons.

Together with Jager Afrikaner they plunder the Colony, the Bechuanas and the Koranas until there's a squabble and Afrikaner abducts all the women and children of the Danster gang. Danster takes revenge with his depleted gang, but Afrikaner is too strong. They manage to rescue only the women; the children have to be left behind with that abominable Hotnot. Danster flees to the Gariep River islands and later back to the Langeberg where they'd lived originally. There they join forces with the gang of Olela, a dethroned chief, and Gola, a son of Langa's.

> That time was honey, says Danster. Nobody could stand up
> to us. I was captain, nobody talked back at me. We were
> Xhosa and Bushmen and Korana and Christian, any man
> with his own gun or spear was welcome. We traded in sheep,
> tobacco, ivory and brandy. And by trading I mean taking,
> he says.

When the night turns cold and the fire burns low, Danster wriggles himself into a thing somewhere between a kaross and an overcoat, assembled from rags of cloth and hide. The cloths were selected with an eye to their gaudiness and to their degree of shine. In the flames the cloak scintillates in reds and yellows and blues like suns and stars perpetually exploding.

> Only the Bastaards we steered clear of, he says, primed with
> genever courage.

With Klaarwater they didn't meddle; the mission station had too many guns and horses. But the rest of the Transorangia got hit hard. Klaarwater's missionary, Anderson, was reportedly so terrified of Danster that he even went to the Cape to beg Baird, the acting governor, for protection. Danster leaps up and trots around the fire and falls flat on his backside with his boots in the coals. The fine tissue of betrayal and honour wears thin. Danster falls out with Gola and Olela and moves back to Caffraria to recruit a new gang.

It is late at night when with slurring speech he tells about the time he was eventually caught. For sheepstealing he had to go to the Castle.

Caledon loaded him and his followers on a ship to Algoa Bay to be posted back to Caffraria from there. Somewhere between Fort Frederick and the Fish River they overpower the soldiers and escape. He rustles up a gang anew and by 1811 he and five hundred men are back at the Gariep. He says they looted sheep and goats and cattle. The Briquas, the Batlhaping, as the lot call themselves, apparently were given such a hard time that eventually they quit that muddy ditch called Kuruman and went to squat at Dithakong. He says every single marksman in his gang could trade a man's eyes for bullets from a hundred paces, even more. He swears, he says.

Just before he rises to his feet one last time, just before he then stagger-dances, just before he falls face first in the sand, and just before I cover him with his coat of many colours like one who is dead, he jumps up, comes to squat before me and grabs me by the shoulders. The dark slits where his eyes should be are pure flame:

> Once, Buys, for three days on end we kept shooting and
> murdering and bleeding and pegging it and the only ones
> sleeping were the men dressed in dust. But by the evening
> of the third day the sea of cattle belonged to us, as far as the
> eye could see, and the ground we could no longer touch,
> because we were dancing on corpses.

Maria says we have long since become too ingrown into each other to let go now. We're together till we keel over, she says, but her body is no longer mine. Children we are no longer vouchsafed, and since leaving the Couga I have rounded up a veritable herd of young buck for myself.

> Godknows what you want, Buys; I'm no longer playing your
> game. If you want to start something, you can go and lie with
> your Caffre women.

On evenings like last night – when she knows I'm too drunk to get anything done, other than crawling in behind her buttocks and to start

323

snoring with kneading hands around her breasts – she still allows me
to lie with her.

When we wake up, Danster and some of his pals have settled in
before a fresh fire, getting water on the boil. With these reprobates by
our side the wilderness will stand aside for us as we trek past. No
animal or Bushman will henceforth venture near us. Danster jumps
up when he sees me. He is certainly not much younger than I, but he's
slept off last night's brandy like a young man. I pick up my hat from
where it's lying next to the wagon, dip it into a basin of water, and
pull it down over my eyes as far as possible. From beneath the small
and merciful lean-to above my eyes I see that Danster is this morning
wearing the Sunday suit of a missionary, complete with the tight-fitting
little hat the men of God love so much. Underneath the jacket the
red-smeared chest peeks out. For a moment the spectre of a sunburnt
Kemp standing before me. I wonder how many outfits the fellow has.
The black trousers tucked into the top boots.

> Buys, get your people into the wagons, then the Reverend
> Danster will go show you where the elephants graze.

We skim ahead across the Transorangia, along what the people here
call the New Gariep. Danster is a miraculous guide. I know these
hereabouts merely as stories and rumours, a wild and wide world
beyond the laws of the Colony, but still under the eyes of the missionaries, ever wakeful and lidless. I have some idea of where Klaarwater
lies. Somewhere to the north-west of Klaarwater lie the home farms
of the Afrikaner robber clan. South-west of Klaarwater lies the new
mission station for the Bushmen, Tooverberg. Further to the north,
I am told, dwell the docile Bechuanas with their hordes of cattle,
waiting to be overrun. Danster has criss-crossed this area, he knows
which wagon trails are dead ends, which watering holes have been
poisoned and where the Bushmen and leopards lurk. What's more,
I can talk to him for hours without dozing off in the saddle. Opperman

and De Kooker can only drivel on about stolen sheep and their difficult wives.

To relieve the tedium of the journey, Danster and his crowd and I sometimes go and harass the London focking Missionary Society where they're trying to convert the Bushmen at Tooverberg. On our first plundering raid we charge into the settlement and scatter the people. I scratch around in the missionary's hut and appropriate a beautiful herneuter knife that the fellow has hardly used. The knife cuts a deep notch in the leather when I test it against the sheath. Something catches my eye. Through the window I see somebody standing in the doorway of the little school building. None other than goddam Master Markus. How in the devil's name did he end up here? Is the slab of misery following me? He is standing motionless in the off-kilter door-frame, looking at the pillage raging around him. His shirt tucked in, without a wrinkle or a sweat stain. I lift my gun, keep his mug in my sights and walk up to him until the barrel is resting against his head.

What are you doing here, Schoolmaster? I ask.

I am teaching school, Mijnheer.

You don't recognise me.

You seem familiar to me.

I am Coenraad de Buys.

How do you do.

Do you in all truth want to tell me that you've never heard of Coenraad de Buys?

I have heard of you, Mijnheer. I am Markus Goossens.

I prod him in the face with the barrel.

Stand aside, Schoolmaster.

This is my school, Mijnheer. Here you don't enter.

The fellow remains standing and I remain standing. The gun is getting heavy.

Excuse me, Mijnheer, he says. I have work to do.

He turns on his heel and shuts the door in my face. I stare at the closed door. The gun wavers in my hand. Behind me a converted Bushman yells in the Dutch the schoolmaster has fed him. I turn around to the screams of pain; the plundering sucks me in and I forget about the shut school door until we ride off with the looted cattle. Then I never forget it again.

In the course of the next week we go and filch a few sheep every day and round up the little shepherds. Danster, who takes care to wear his Sunday best on such days, delivers eloquent sermons, so flagrantly blasphemous that I scan the blue heavens in terror. Danster converts quite a few Bushmen and they join our flock of sinners.

(One morning De Kooker is nowhere to be found, but his wagons are bedded down in the sand and his family are making their morning coffee. His wife says he says he's coming back.

> He said the children and I should trek with you so long,
> Mijnheer Buys. He didn't say when, but he left a pocket of
> ammunition for the Caffre Danster as down payment to lead
> him back to us, as soon as he wants to come back.

This fellow we won't see again, I think and look at his wife and she looks away.)

On my outings with Danster I also smear myself with clay and wear a handkerchief over my nose and beard, so that at a quick glance no bugger is going to see a Christian. North-east of Klaarwater, near Campbell, I unload my people and go looting with Danster.

The pious converted don't have a chance. The survivors can only forgive us, because the ways of the Lord are not for us to know and whatever. Danster takes his leave and moves north to go and strip the Hardcastle mission bare. With him as guide my knowledge of these plains, my herds and particularly my army – my nation – have increased considerably. The names Buys and Danster lure all that is robber and deserter. As long as he and I don't molest Christians or put our paws into the hallowed Colony, the Colony's little sweaty hands are tied. My red dogs come to scavenge as soon as the battlefields fall silent. The vultures have to wait for the remains of the remains.

The first days of 1815 we spend trekking towards a fertile tract of land at the convergence of the Harts and Vaal Rivers. Rumours from the Colony reach my campfire. Danster and I are said to be gallivanting with the looting and heresy beyond the Gariep. Somewhere a little bird must have chirped. I don't lie awake at night wondering why Opperman, his bedraggled little wife and snot-nosed kids chose to excuse and absent themselves in a hurry just now – that very same little goddam bird must have informed him that otherwise I would have sped him on his way with a horsewhip under his traitor's arse.

At a remove I hear also that the landdrost of Uitenhage, one Cuyler, is warning his counterpart in Graaffe Rijnet, nowadays a Fischer, against me. I am apparently a 'dangerous character'. Cuyler is said to have suggested that they should go and take tea with the Bezuiden- houts – at present burghers of the Baviaans River, I am told – to fish for information regarding yours truly's address. With this calibre of clerk the whole world goes to pot! I'd give anything to see the Bezui- denhouts bringing out their best cups for the focking misters.

I am a rich man, but my toe torments me most nights and my hands swell and cramp. If the pain keeps me awake at night, I prick up my ears at the rustle of every bush outside and expect the end. Janssens, my dog, succumbs to the damned ticks. A fortnight later old De Mist stalks stiff-legged into the veldt and does not return. At least Danster and his rapacious Caffres are back soon and there is merrymaking again around the fires in the evening. If you're living with Danster, you dance till you fall, drink till you drop and sleep till you get up. I don't really dance. We plunder and smuggle. We get richer and fatter. I know who my friends are on this earth: they are the enemies of everyone else.

～

They say you know a man when you've walked a few miles in his shoes. Bullshit. You know a man when you've ridden a few miles on his horse. In his saddle, in February, on the banks of the Harts River. In his moleskin breeches.

I scratch my crotch and search for something to shoot. Game has been scarce these last few weeks. Strings of Klaarwater Bastaards cross the river every day and trample the antelope trails. They don't mess with us, but the groups get bigger and more and more of them flock together in one spot. Danster regularly dispatches a few red-painted scouts to cast an eye. The Redcaffres report that at night the people talk loudly and angrily around the fires.

I ride to the river to have a drink of water. I lead my horse through the bushes and reeds. Downriver an unearthly swearing erupts. Women's pelvises and God's wrath collide and explode and make love in extended sentences of Dutch such as I've never heard. My eyes are not what they used to be, but I could swear I see a straggling of people standing and yelling on an oasis in the middle of the river. I ride up to them.

The river is shallow, but the bottom is invisible. A wagon's wheel can get stuck between rocks under the muddy water. The wheel can break if the startled oxen try to dislodge the wagon by force. The wheel is particularly liable to break if it's burdened with a whole damned forest.

I wade into the stream. I greet the people: an old Bastaard, a young one with a hump like an ox, an old woman and four little girls in dresses of the same blue cloth. On the wagon towers a luxuriant jungle with the lushest dagga trees and tobacco, the dagga heads downy and rust-coloured. The bushes protrude over the toprail, and tease-tickle the water. In between the dagga arises mouthwatering golden tobacco. See, the Flying Gardener has built a scaffolding on which is perched a second garden with the taller plants. The four poles on the corners of the wagon are hidden under the lush growth of the trees. The poles keep the upper storey up, full of shallow bowls of soil in which the trees are planted. So not the forest that I observed from the bank, but two gardens, neatly packaged for transportation.

When the young Bastaard notices me, he lowers his hump and clumsily manoeuvres the gun around his shoulder and into his hands and takes aim at my forehead. My gun is on my back and my hands are in the air. The children have stopped crying. Everything except the river is dead quiet until I'm standing in front of them, up to my waist in the water, with an extended hand wavering in the air before the hunchback. He lowers the gun and takes my hand.

The little band is quite amicable when I introduce myself. I help the men to wiggle loose the broken wheel. Two felloes sink, two spokes float away, the whole damned wheel is river fodder. We lift the wagon so the oxen can haul the other three wheels through the stream. It's a bloody business. Two of us have seen better days, the marrow shrunk in our bones. The young Bastaard is a lean lad under the hump, one who swears with vigour rather than grips with conviction.

They tell me that they're moving away from Griekwastad, Griqua-town. I tell them I don't know such a place. They say it's the new name for Klaarwater. The lad is not built for Colony uniforms, so now they're clearing out. I say, wait a bit, begin at the beginning. The old man doesn't swear as colourfully as his son, but he spins a good story. In between the wagon-lugging and tripping over my own big feet – the pestilential toe is throbbing again today – I am informed that all that is pot is boiling over at the mission station.

The oldster tells that Brother Campbell – the very one after whom the Campbell station is named, apparently a bigwig in the focking Missionary Society – went on a tour two years ago to all the little cherished flocks here at the foreskin of Africa. Apparently never braves the daylight without his little parasol. He visits every mission station and pronounces blessings as appropriate. Of course names a godforsaken town after himself. When Campbell ended up in Klaarwater last year, the light of Heavenly inspiration struck him like a migraine. He hears the people calling themselves Bastaards. And, what's more, quite proud of it. Surely that *cannot* be, *must* not be. He is profoundly insulted, in his own being, but especially on behalf of the wretched dumb Heathens themselves. He assembles the little congregation and allows the Bastaards to choose themselves a name. Somebody remembers a name

329

from his ancestors, Griqua or some such. By teatime every Bastaard, Korana, Hottentot and Bushman at the station has been dubbed a Griqua, and by suppertime Klaarwater is called Griquatown. The mouth of God's envoy drools with fervour. Right there and then he devises a constitution, as you can read in the writings of our learned ameliorator: *In the history of the world there was no account of any people existing and prospering without laws*. Thus do you create a pedigree, a nation and a state in one afternoon.

On dry ground we examine the wheel properly. There is not much to be salvaged. Smashed to the nave. We break off branches and devise a sled for the buggered axle tree to rest on. They say they still have some distance to travel. To family awaiting them. About half a day's journey from the Buys nation and the Redcaffres. With all our yelling every blessed buck and hare this side of the Gariep has been scared off, so I offer to accompany them for a while. A travelling garden of smoking materials is not something you behold every day.

With his mouth behind his hand, as if the stones had ears, the lad tells me about Griquatown's missionary. Focking William Anderson: was on the point of getting married, but then opted to come and live with the Gariep Bastaards for almost twenty years instead. The lad says Anderson must be over forty, but he has no wrinkles from shouting or laughing.

One of the little blue-frocked girls starts bawling to her mother. The old father sees to her with a reed cane while interrupting his eldest and only and deformed son with a tirade about the Society.

> The missionary is the eyes and ears and lips and I'm telling you Whiteman also the teeth of the Cape. God take their teeth and curse their spit!

Go and see for yourself in the archives how these bureaucrats could hone their words. In 1809 the Lord focking Caledon writes to Anderson that every possible assistance will be rendered him by the Cape, not because God's word is being brought to the Heathens, but on account of the mission stations' *most beneficial effects in recalling the*

Natives to habits of Industry and Regularity, without which it will ever be impossible to bind them in Society. Behold, we put bits in the horses' mouths, indeed!

The father and the hunchback son keep interrupting each other while we make a fire at dusk. They tell me about the crazy Hottentot who came to preach at Klaarwater. Kupido Kakkerlak was his name, Cupido Cockroach. The lad says Anderson was fulfilled with Heavenly wrath when the Hotnot broke into song between the huts every night at nine o'clock until the whole congregation bleated along with him. The wauling then carried on till the next morning. Anderson was highly upset that, while some were singing, there was also much talking and laughing, which according to him would open a portal to impurity and immorality; and that it bred, the morning after such exuberant nights, a certain slothfulness among the flock. Anderson says he has no objection to singing, but does it have to happen late at night?

> A congregation that get too carried away with the Lord sometimes forget to work their fingers to the bone, says the oldster.
>
> Goddam phthisis-tool! I shout.
>
> My spirit also pukes with a joyful noise, the hunchback pipsqueak affirms.

They say that Kakkerlak did not last long in the State of the Griquas and apparently soon left for Dithakong. The Hottentot missionary sounds like a rare bird, indeed. Sorry I never met the fellow.

The old woman throws a few sweet potatoes into a pot and there is a scraping of porridge for everybody. She sits watching us eat. Her hands in her lap have a light tremor and her lips smack along with ours, as if she can taste what we're tasting. When we've done, she scrapes the leftovers into a dish for herself and doesn't look up until she's licked her dry-twig fingers clean.

The oldster's name is Jannas van Riebeeck. He asks me why I'm laughing. I walk to the river with Jannas and his boy-child. The moon floats on the water like a blown-up carcase. Jannas wets a bit of soft clay soil on the bank and kneads it till it's tacky. He breaks a stick in two and gives his son one half. They sit opposite each other and push the sticks into the ground. They drill towards each other until a narrow tunnel connects them. He lies down with his ear on the hole and his son blows into the other hole. Jannas feels the air in his ear and nods: the tunnel is open. He pours a bit of water down the tunnel. He presses a plug of dagga into the hole and lights it. His son is on his stomach, his mouth on the other hole; he smokes the herb through the earth artery. The lad smokes till he's had enough, then he offers me the earth pipe. The smoke hits hard when it shoots up from the earth to the back of the lungs. I cough, spit the sand out of my cheeks. The hole is plugged again until all three of us are silly and satisfied.

Back in the camp Jannas is heavy hearted. Apparently Anderson has been instructed to round up all deserters – criminals, slaves, Hottentots or Bastaards – who have escaped to the Gariep and to post them back to the Colony. The wretched man couldn't arrest a church choir. In addition he has to send twenty young men from Griquatown for military service in the Zwartveld. If the people refuse to give up their sons, they may no longer trade legally with the Colony.

> You see what my lad looks like. He can plough a bit, but he's too crooked for a gun.

I thought the little woman was asleep, but her kaross comes to life and sobs.

> They also no longer want us to plant dagga and tobacco, Jannas continues. There are vegetables only in the garden of the Lord. But our Lord doesn't have to hawk for a living. Not with all those pearls in his crown.

The scorpion that's come to warm itself at the fire is claiming my attention. I block his route with a twig and start a duel.

> I'm a hawker, says Jannas. My leaves are my livelihood. I don't know about slaughtering and milking, but I know everything about everything that you can stuff into a pipe. My trees are

my flock and I'm their shepherd. If the law says a man can no
longer be what he is, then it's time to clear out. If the law says
you must sacrifice your crook-backed son, then it's time to
clear out. So then I took my garden and I cleared out.

The young hunchback is poking about in the pots for another scraping
to eat. Words fail me. The old man carries on talking. I let him be.
The scorpion's sting darts out and retracts. Its tail casts big shadows
in the branches. The world shifts and shudders in the flickerings of
the flames, without outline. The scorpion ducks and attacks. Tomorrow,
in the pale light of day, everything will seem merely what it is. But see,
now, the fulgurous shadows of the flames. See, the little red scorpion.
See how nimble, and then he's gone. Just see the moon. See.

2

The three-wheeled wagon causes trouble all the way until at sunset we reach the outspan of the Griqua deserters. The wagons and tents are empty. Around a great fire the people are sitting and standing while a Bastaard in a Sunday suit is addressing them. It seems as if we've arrived at a church service, a church service with remarkably many guns. Jannas and I walk up while his people unload their stuff with his family.

The Sunday suit is full of fervour, a slick-tongued minister who preaches the perdition of religion; the church one in which the congregation damns itself to hell.

> Brethren! We shall wait until our nation has congregated here by the Hart. We shall wait until the Hartenaars are a mighty nation! We shall wait for the time to be ripe and we shall march upon Klaarwater and we shall descend like a plague and we shall grab the gunpowder from the grasp of the missionary and we shall shoot Anderson in the head and we shall shoot that self-appointed Griqua Kok in the kneecaps!

The people applaud him. He holds up his hands.

> Brethren! Think not that I am come to send peace on earth; I came not to send peace, but a sword.

A new Moses who smashes the stone tablets of the law to shards and comes from Sinai with a musket in his hand as a message to his people.

> For I am come to set a man at variance against his missionary, and the daughter against her slave driver. He that loveth missionary or government over his freedom is not worthy of his freedom! And he that taketh not his gun, and followeth after me, is not worthy of the name Bastaard. He that findeth his life with Anderson and Campbell shall lose it; and he that loseth his life for the sake of freedom shall find it!

The people yell their accord and fire shots into the air and give vent to strange hymns.

To hell with the laws, to hell with the missionaries and to hell with their religion. And I said unto the missionary: You can tie me up and make me abide, but you cannot make me work. Before they came among us we looked well after ourselves and after they have left, we shall once again look after ourselves. And brethren, I say unto you today: We have no need of those crows and their god! My soul is hell-bent! To burn! To burn, brethren and sisters!

He concludes his sermon by holding a Bible aloft. He drops it at his feet and sets it alight.

I look for my travelling companion, but Jannas has left to join his people. His wife and his children and his garden stir him more than speeches. But I am a man of the word. My skin prickles; my hands cramp into claws. My breeches tent out. I like these people and their rage and the little Bastaard maiden who is fluttering her eyes over there.

≈

I wake up on top of her, hitch up my breeches and make myself scarce. I get something they call coffee by a fire. I listen and look. The preacher walks past and I follow him to the back of a wagon, where a conclave of greybeards are conferring. Guns, polished bright and never been used, displayed against the wagon. The fug from their pipe smoke is as thick as their conspiracy. I listen, I look; then I let fly.

I hear myself talk. I feel my legs straightening themselves beneath me, I see myself standing and orating in Graaffe Rijnet, by now all of two decades in the past. I tell them they are a free people. They are not the scullions of any focking Englishman's laws.

Campbell disowned you to the government, I thunder. It is he who wants to collect your sons for the government. Your sons are not taxes. They are not rents. Think well, men. Your sons are not white. They will never be treated like the Christian children. The focking Britons are not looking for soldiers. They want to feed your sons to the cannons. They bring learning and

customs like false gifts, like blankets full of pox. They teach
you to write so you can fill in birth registers. So that the sons
of bitches can see how many sons your wives bear. They say
they are proclaiming the Word of God, but brethren, beware
of the focking Englishman's inscriptions. They are not
inscribing you in the Book of Life. They are penning you
down in the Books of the Cape.

I ask for a sip of water, wait for the old men to calm down. Then in
my tempter's purr:

English, focking English, is not a language. A man can talk in
a language. Focking English can only be obeyed. It's a language
for making sums. Your names are the numbers. If you must
starve in the wilderness, why not on your own terms?

I tell them they are a nation in their own right, strong enough to
defend themselves. If they want to barter, I say, they must come to
me, I shall be their missionary. I'll mediate for them with the frontier
farmers for their cattle and dagga and rounded-up Bushmen. I say
I'll see to it that they're paid in gunpowder and bullets:

We shall go forth from this place like locusts, brethren, we'll
pillage and take what we can, while we can for as long as we
can. Until our names are breathed around every fire. Until the
fat of the land is oozing from our lips.

The old men listen and smoke and nod. I ride out of their camp
with a full belly, an emptied ball-bag and a brand-new gun. I feel
twenty years younger. Revolutions are more fun than ox-roasting.

An aside: My gracious accomplice, this land is one of robbers and
raiders. When I'd hardly moved into the Couga, Coenraad Bezuidenhout and Cobus Vry had already understood that the northern border
yields more profit than the eternal squabbling at the Fish. Nowadays
there's a soldier skulking in every aardvark lair next to the river. If you
want to hunt elephants, they wrote to me, you must betake yourself

to the Bastaards. I heard of missionaries who traded so many tusks that they could leave the lost souls to find their own salvation, and retire in comfort and ease in the Cape. On my Couga farm I started gazing into the distance. Bezuidenhout and Vry went to stir up trouble near Ongeluksfontein, and absconded with as many cattle, sheep and Bushman children as they could herd. Some say that they also helped to spread the first smallpox epidemic in that area. Those two were never exactly partial to bathing.

When at last I ventured north of the Colony, all you heard were stories of other looters. This here is a land of robbers. Selah. What would I not give to be a fly on so many walls? A fly on the wall of Jan Bloem, the German deserter from Thüringen who fled the Colony after murdering his wife. A fly on the cheek of Pieter Pienaar, the Hantam farmer and pass builder who meets up with Bloem in the Namaqualand and tells him to go and look after his farm on the Gariep. Who shortly thereafter, with his family, Bloem and a lot of Koranas and Bushmen, starts looting Briqua cattle and children all along the river as far as the Langeberg. A fly buzzing around the heads of the brothers Kruger, counterfeiters who escape from Robben Island and move in among the Koranas, become, along with the Bloems, well-known frontier thugs and nowadays lie in wait on the northern border to plunder wagonloads of ivory. A fly has to be on its guard around the Afrikaner clan. They say that Klaas Afrikaner and his people are brutes such as this country has never seen. They'll relieve you of your wings in no time. Klaas Afrikaner, the Oorlam Hottentot who goes to work for the selfsame Pienaar in order to avoid military service. Pienaar sends him also to the Gariep as cattle-herd, and here herding cattle includes stealing cattle. The Afrikaners who on punitive comman-dos against the Bushmen apparently dispatch over six hundred souls.

A fly on the cell wall of the Pole Stephanus, a counterfeiter who prints paper money for himself. Who saws open the cell door with a rusty nail. Who goes to hide out with the Zak River missionaries until they find out who he is. Who passes himself off as a prophet in the

Transorangia. A prophet who delivers sermons and then vanishes in a cloud of gunpowder smoke. His followers on their knees before his new religion, part Hebrew and part Greek and wholly dedicated to him. Until a farmer recognises him and he cuts the farmer's throat and goes to rob and reave with Jager Afrikaner. Stephanus who wants to escape on board a ship on the West Coast but meets and kills a pen-pusher on the way and the ship that sails away and he who gets lost in the interior until one day he too finds himself at the wrong end of a blade.

~

Thus far the gadflies of the veldt, but what about the houseflies? A wall-eyed fly on the bedroom walls of these frontier thugs, every single one a bigamist who gads across colour boundaries. Pienaar who is said to lie with the women of his Hottentots, also with Klaas Afrikaner's bitch, until the young Titus Afrikaner slaughters Pienaar and some say also his wife and children. Jacob Kruger with his five wives, a Briqua woman, a Rolong and a Korana or so. Bloem, the old bugger, has some ten wives, a Bushman and one of each of the Korana tribes, a Taaibosch, a Kats, a Links, a Springbok and suchlike what-nots. I'm telling you, a fly on my bedroom wall I swat flat, but I no longer have a bedroom. Damn all walls anyway! Any case, here in the Transorangia I and my assorted women are not as conspicuous as in the coy Colony.

~

The Bastaards who come to me seeking an opening in the smuggling trade are down at heel. Civilisation has done them no favours. They rob to peddle. They are woebegone and angry. Not only at the Cape and its missionaries, but also at the gravy-grubbing families, the Koks and the Berendses, the Bastaard nobility appointed over them by the missionaries. These are young blades, with the wrong surnames, or the right surnames but the wrong in-laws. They're no longer Griquas but Hartenaars, the people of the Harts River. Every day more Koranas and Bushmen join them, and everyone is handed a gun, a horse if there's one to spare. They mutiny against the authorities, against their brothers and fathers who are still living as subjects in Griquatown and planting vegetables. One half of the Griquas want to grow old on the stoep of a square house. The veldt bulbs, the mealies, the sweat of their brows. The other half know the Transorangia is no country to grow old in. These Blasboere, coffee-coloured farmers, become Harte-naars, there to dare or die. The blood, the glory, the radiance of their countenance. Apart from the speeches they don't speak Dutch within earshot and don't mention focking English. They no longer greet each other with How are things, because Things are really shit and thank you, everyone knows it only too well. Look it up, later generations of Griquas would call these young blades The Patriots.

I loot and laugh and drink and hunt with them. Maria and Elizabeth brew vast cauldrons for the hungry patriots. I introduce the Hartenaars to the frontier farmers on the Nu-Gariep and the Ky-Gariep with whom I trade. The men embroiled in the Colony are looking for cattle and ivory and labour. For a Bushman and a head of cattle they pay with brandy and gunpowder and lead and sometimes a second-hand musket. The shortcut to money and a feathered nest on these plains is the weaving of a robber's nest. New trade routes are traced that will never appear on any map, but in the sand you can see the wagon tracks cutting ever deeper. Farmers who used to call in at Griquatown to barter goods for cattle now come to talk to us.

The farmers tell us that things are going awry with a vengeance in the mission state. Since Anderson's return from the Cape, the town has been emptying out. In Griquatown they no longer build houses. They plant dagga and tobacco that they can trade, rather than mealies and pumpkin that are only good for grazing. Those who don't defect to the Hartenaars are chronically on the wagon trail bartering and trading with Christian farmers. When I enquire after Campbell's constitution they lift an eyebrow and ask Whose constitution and what does it constitute?

Oh, just see the violence on the Skietgeweergrens, the Frontier of the Shooting Gun. The new arrivals and their despair, the chancers and those lost beyond redemption. Rapacious rapscallions. All welcome, dregs of crushed communities give birth to new gangs, melt away into other mobs. Mercenaries, warriors, looters, nomads, vagrants, fugitives, pilgrims, who's to tell. There are two races here, farmers and looters, and they interbreed like the blazes. Beyond the Border we're all Bastaards, all feral dogs.

If war persists, people keep moving. They don't sit still for long enough to congeal into Colony. Families turn into gangs. The rules prevailing here are the same as those at the dogfights of Graaffe Rijnet. In these swinish stables a discipline different to that in the ordered military lines. See, here we operate with eternal blackmail, forfeiture or betrayal and a series of ephemeral perceptions of honour. You take, as I told the congregation, what you can, while you can.

Don't get me wrong. I was on my way out, away. I peddled ideals so that I could smuggle ivory and guns. If the missionaries were to quit Griquatown, the government would get the hell out along with them and I could do business to my heart's content. And if Anderson were to hive off, the only route to gunpowder and guns would be through me and me alone. He who does not know me will not inherit the kingdom of gunpowder.

~

If you want to plunder a mission station, you must be more terrifying than the Lord Almighty. See, we rise up over the horizon. We bear down upon Griquatown. A horde too vast and improbable to be contained in the compass of an eye. See, the shards of glass and mirror and copper and iron around necks and arms and on shields, blades and barrels, these all catch the light and shatter it into innumerable impossible suns and our enemies cannot abide our countenance. A legion of abhorrence, hundreds of us, visions of terror astride on horseback, on mules, on warhorses – my sons and I on the fastest horses booty can buy – airborne nightmares, naked or half-naked or garbed in antique vestments almost Biblical or in animal hides and adornments of silk or the leather of the Christians and the fragments of uniforms still stained with the blood of the previous owners, tunics of defunct dragoons, tasselled and fringed cavalry jackets, one with a top hat and umbrella, and a naked red-painted Caffre in white stockings and Danster in a virginal bridal gown and some in tricorn hats or crowned with thongs and feathers and paint, skins of lions and leopards flutter over speeding shoulders, one wears a peeled-open leopard head like a bonnet, Sunday suits like a host of the resurrected, Caffres naked and scarlet and a few vigorous Bastaards in flapping swallow-tailed coats all of them on charging oxen with their horns low and sharpened and a deserter with a washbasin as knightly breastplate strapped to his chest, the tin dented from the blows of other days, and see, my Bushmen racing along on the ridges who will tighten the noose and my red dogs, my half-hyena dogs swerving criss-cross through the undergrowth, raging and snapping at the Bushmen and horses while loaded guns now sprout from shoulders and eyes narrow in faces motley and comically smudged and smeared and painted like a company of clowns on horseback, yes I could die laughing, and see, we yowl and roar maniacally and we open fire on them like a horde from Hell more abhorrent even than the fire and brimstone of Christian Reckoning, skirling and shrieking, clothed in smoke like those phantoms in regions beyond certainty and sense where the eye wanders and the lip shudders and drools.

Oh God, shouts Anderson the focking missionary.

∽

If you want to get to know a man, you have to study his national bookkeeping. Every pedlar and looter has to know the secret economy of the Transorangia. In these days it's easier to smuggle the teeth of chickens than the tusks of elephants. Even here in the Gariep the beasts have just about been shot out. The scarcer, the more valuable

341

in the Colony. We barter with the Briquas and Barolong. You don't barter with the Briqua before they've harvested. If you arrive there while the plantings are still standing in the fields, they ask What are we supposed to see with your mirrors? Our fire doesn't need your tinderbox. Our snot sticks to our forearms just as fast as to your hand-kerchiefs. Your knives are blunter than those we forge ourselves – so they snarl at us. But at the Briqua harvest festival we barter our tobacco for a heap of ivory.

You buy a sheep in the Colony for two rix-dollars and go and barter it with the Briquas for an elephant tusk. You take this tusk to the Colony and sell it at one or two rix-dollars per pound, and a good tusk weighs anything up to a hundred pounds. I hear of missionaries who traded four wagonloads of tusks with the Barolong for two hundred sheep and a few beads. There are fellows around here who in two years make three thousand rix-dollars from smuggling tusks. If you can survive two journeys with tusk-laden wagons between the Transorangia and the Cape – if the Bushmen and the fever and the lions don't get you – you can retire to Tulbagh on a wine farm with all the slaves and wine that your heart desires. Believe me, our own dear Anderson himself once traded more than two hundred and fifty rix-dollars' worth of tusks for twenty rix-dollars' worth of beads. A focking missionary's swindle can cost you much more than your immortal soul.

~

My flocks are big, my children grow tall. I am a rich man and replete. In the mornings and evenings my hands claw up, my legs grow ever more rigid, but for the rest this old reaver is fighting fit. 1815 is a good year. The Buys nation waxes apace: Apart from Danster's Caffres many of the Hartenaars wander into our camp and don't wander out again. Escaped slaves pour in from all over. A few English and Scottish soldiers desert to me; warriors from neighbouring tribes desert for exactly the same reason: they see our feasting and the fat around our mouths. Even a few Bushmen, sick of surviving in the hunting ground as the hunted, come and offer their knobkerries and their knobbly limbs.

I'm in the saddle or out in the open all day, yet my belly is getting ever more at odds with my shirt with every night's feasting. Oh, the lamb cutlets. As my flock and my prestige grow, so too my collection of women. I look after the women who have borne my children, those who are with child; also those I assail with lust every now and again, and the girls I pick out of the herd because I can't stand the thought of any other man touching them. In the evenings I eat with Maria and Elizabeth and my children. At night I lie with Elizabeth. Nombini doesn't run away any more. She and her children clear their own campsite. Bettie bears a child. It's the last fat year of my life. By the end of March 1816 the lean ones are already gnawing at me.

News travels slowly beyond the border. At first rogue rumours that you have to dam up and filter, until a single story, complete with head and tail, seeps through slowly and clearly. The first I hear is that the focking English have hanged Cornelis Faber. The place's name is Slagtersnek, the Ridge of the Butcher. The story reaches me circuitously and too late. Freek Bezuidenhout, brother to Hannes and Coenraad, has an altercation with a Hotnot labourer and when he refuses to appear in court, a pack of pandours fusillade him in a cave on his farm. Hannes stands next to the grave with old Willem Prinsloo, Faber, who's come from Tarka to bury his brother-in-law Freek, and a handful of other fellows from the old days of Graaffe Rijnet. The bunch get boozing and Hannes calls for revenge. He calls the Christians and he calls Ngqika's Caffres. The Christians come, Ngqika stays away. It's almost funny to hear that I reputedly went to Caffraria with Faber to plead for Ngqika's support. But I don't laugh. If I'd known, I'd have been there. And would have been dead by now. The rebellion perishes in its cradle. They shoot Hannes when he refuses to surrender. Faber and four others are sentenced to death. Five men stand on the trapdoor. The trapdoor drops and only one rope holds. One noose breaks one man's neck. Four ropes break; four men hurtle to the ground.

Bewildered and half strangled four men stagger to Cuyler and plead for mercy. The dead man is taken down, the noose is tested. I pray to the distant Lord that it was Cornelis, that he got the strong rope. Because see what happens now: four men, one at a time, one after the other, after the other, after the other, are hanged with the good and faithful rope; the strong rope holds every blessed time. Thank God for the government.

∼

There are days here next to the Hart that the sky is impossibly blue and my toe forgets all about the gout. On such a morning I go riding until I reach a stretch of grassland, out of sight of the camp. I take off my shoes, so that the damned toe doesn't chafe. I take off my breeches, so that the scuffed leather doesn't tear. Shirt, underclothes. I jump up and down, limber up the limbs. Then I run.

I pant, the phlegm in my throat thwarts me, I spit out morsels of this morning's pipe, strings of brown drool flutter in my wake. The earth races from under me. Knees creaking. My heart batters my breast to bits, eyes are watering, toes take hold, feet follow, strides stretch and stretch, hands flick like fins through the thick ooze of air. My head low, my eyes shut; head raised, the world appears, chest burning, suffocating. Then I no longer need breath. The whole body a lung and sweat, in, out, outside inside. Calves contract, spring open. Ankle tendons stretch and knot up into my loins. I am beautiful. I am perfect. My breastbone cleaves open the world. Every muscle contracts into a knot, stretches as far as it can and further. The wind sings through my bones, hollow as the bones of birds. Heels slap against my buttocks, a hand slaps at my ear. I am as wild as God himself; I outrun death, until I stumble and crash down.

The phlegm has been burnt away. A string of drool in my beard. I sit down, legs stretched out in front of me and long. I sit forward, touch my thighs, scrabble the sand out from between my buttocks. What is this thing they call Buys? In the running things were not so clear. I start getting up and twist my ankle. Back onto my arse I sink back into my body; I am a thing that feels its ankle throbbing. Back behind the impermeable prison walls of skin. The greasy burden of cast-off clothing here to one side. My own weight in water and bone – ever sinking under the weight of how I ended up in this body. Dropped from some heaven like a black horse, a bad horse. Did we think up the sky so that we could fall out of it?

See, me, Coenraad de Buys: naked. No marks other than scars. My body disjointed, not merged together with markings and tattoos. The hairy belly. The crumpled penis. The grey streaks in my eyes. The womanly ankles down there. My body is stranger than the body of anybody else. More at home with the least known body under any kaross than with this blinding bareness in the sand. I get to my feet, dust my backside. My body is as open as a plot of ground. I scratch at the mosquito bite. My bald spot scorches. I jam my hat onto my head firmly. The long grass; the sun blanches the sky. The white clamours in my ears. My hands touch and feel my sides. My skin scares me. All this skin. Pleated, folded again and again like a good blade. Unfolded. Skin, through and through and in every orifice: the mouth and ears, the nostrils and the arsehole. I fart. My jacket with smoking materials in its pocket is lying over there.

You are a free man if you can sit naked on a rock and light a pipe. This world, stretched out around me. I inhale the smoke. While I'm holding my breath, little waterfalls of smoke stream from my nose. Nothing remains inside. This world with its sun and universe, its rocks, its beehives, its beasts, its mirages.

When I was little, there was only a Buys-thing, the Buys-thing-playing-with-knucklebones-on-the-stoep-after-lunch-thing. That chunk of caterwauling back yard was the Buys-thing. The more my body gives up piecemeal, the more absolute the split: the idea of Coenraad de Buys, Omni-Buys; and an old man tottering into hostile territory. Two figures that never look each other in the eye.

These Buyses in this world: the fossils, the stripes of the zebra, the humanoid beasts, Maynier's pretty waistcoats, the exact number of petals of that precise protea, the furrow of a bullet through a forehead, the ghosts of rainbows, printing presses. A time when I could run when I wanted to. The snakeskin of the other day, Nombini's face while she's breastfeeding, a blade of grass and the cow ruminating it. The eye that moves while you read what I recite. With my thumb and my index finger I remove a thread of tobacco from my tongue. I jump up, run until sight and sound are lost in fury. I put on my clothes and ride back to the camp on my horse with the back and the hooves, the bit and the mane.

The camp is just over the next rise when a large dappled stallion thunders past me. See, it bolted after its rider was shot. The Bastaard in the saddle is lying on his back with his feet still anchored in the stirrups, the flies a sticky black mass around the corpse and the horse. The stallion is crazed; the dead weight on its back won't let go. I chase after it; try to corner it; it shakes its withers, rears up on its hind legs, tries to rid itself of its directionless rider. The eyes are empty, the mouth is foaming. It has seen too much of people ever to allow one on its back again. The horse runs off, comes to a halt some distance away. I grab hold of my powder horn; a large female leopard appears from the undergrowth, close to the dappled horse. I bridle in my horse's fright, I load my gun. The leopard is not here for me. The rider dances furiously on the horse's back. From how far away did she smell the horse's weakness on the wind? The horse's eyes show white, it leaps away. I shoot at the leopard and miss. The stallion's frenzy lends it a last spark under the arse. When the leopard brings it down presently, the delirium will enclose him against the pain.

～

The Hartenaars remain sheep of my flock as long as I feed them guns. I am their contact with the Colony for whatever they want to barter. I am their missionary. They plunder with me and I with Danster. Our tents cover the plain like the pestilential sand.

Twenty months after I arrived in Griqualand their visits become less frequent. I am no longer accorded quite as warm a welcome to the Bastaard camps. They are damnwell managing without me. I ask a few wretches on their way to Griquatown to buy me munitions from the Reverend Anderson. The focking missionary laughs in their faces. The Hendrikses and the Goeymans, two families who cherish grudges against the missionaries like pearls, threaten – with a prod or two from me – the station itself, but that doesn't put bullets into our barrels either. The news that De Kooker is on his way back was of course hogwash. For a while I hope that the message was wrong, that the misbegotten afterbirth Opperman is on his way; I'll stuff that two-faced typhus-tool's greased head up his fart-hole. Grietjie, De Kooker's wife, needs to be consoled vigorously when the road remains empty. She is white as a porcelain saucer, with the body of a voluptuous young Caffre woman. She wets my shoulder with tears and I touch her bum. A week later news arrives that De Kooker has moved in with the field cornet. He waits until I'm out hunting and comes to snaffle Grietjie and her brood. So, too, that bum and that bastard disappear from my life. I send the two English deserters to the Colony for powder and bullets. We soon learn that all they achieved was to be transmuted into turds in the innards of a few hungry lions.

I myself trek to the Colony with a whole lot of cattle and looted Bushmen and barter them all along the border. By the end of June I'm back with a wagonload of guns and lead and powder. Early in July Danster and I trek to the Hartenaars. We clamber on the back of the wagon, I tear down the tent. Danster and I stand amidst the chests of munitions; we harangue them vigorously. We are on our way to the Barolong on the other side of Dithakong, we bellow. We are going to strip them bare. Every man who comes along gets a gun and ammunition. We all share in the loot. The lot of them mutter and mumble and meet. In the evenings Danster and I sit by our own fire. I take the wagon further up the Hart, to Makoon, the chief of a group of Koranas. They're not yet as settled and staid as the slothful Hartenaars. Their shelters are temporary, their blades sharp. Their horses are better fed than their women. Robbers to the depth of their beings, especially in the pitch-black beads of their eyes. Makoon's Koranas say they're going along with me. When I ride into the Hartenaar camp with this lot, all of a sudden any number of Hartenaars want to come along. Perhaps. Perchance. Possibly. When by the end of August at long last all the talking runs dry and everybody is satisfied with how many heads of cattle he will possibly be able to loot, there is a feasting to be done first. A week later we hit the road with conviction, having drunk ourselves into valour and screwed ourselves into oblivion and all set for blood and riches. Three gangs are trekking together: Makoon's Koranas and I, Danster and his Redcaffres and the Hartenaar heretics. Every single one with a Buys gun over the shoulder.

~

In the veldt the bones bloom lily white. I shoot the most beautiful gemsbok that's ever walked God's earth in the neck. It collapses gracefully. We ride on. I shoot two quaggas and a few springbok to keep my barrel warm. I shoot at the rock piles of the Hottentots and think of the baby that died. I shoot an ostrich, a duiker and four wildebeest because there's nothing else to shoot.

We come across a small Korana settlement and ride on. We want to get to the little company of Barolong west of Dithakong. Rumours are rife that their cattle have doubled in number in this last year. But see, a few miles on the other side of the Korana huts stands a sea of cattle. This we can't pass by. One of Danster's men goes to scout. There are two cattle-herds. Both on horseback, both armed. The one a Korana, the other a huge Caffre. It can't be that easy.

We – the horde of hundreds that we are – spread out and surround the cattle. The bald-headed Caffre charges his horse through our spread-out line and bridles it the moment he is behind us. There he sits, motionless. His head is shaven and long, too long. I keep an eye on him and more particularly on the distance from his hands to his gun. I'm itching to shoot. My toe is giving me all sorts of hell. My hands take turns cramping up. The Korana herdsman's horse staggers in the middle of the congested herd. The Korana's finger tenses around the trigger, the bullet slams into a rock and ricochets into the heavens somewhere. Next to me somebody returns fire. The herdsman's head gushes roses. Our horses trot up closer, tighten the noose around the cattle until they calm down. In the distance the people of the settlement stand and watch us rounding up their cattle. They stand for a while contemplating our numbers and our guns and then turn round and return to their huts. The Caffre on horseback is still sitting where he was sitting. His gun is resting across his neck and shoulders, his arms draped over the weapon on either side, as if crucified into judgement. Conceited scumbag.

I wave at a few of Makoon's warriors and we trot nearer, each with a gun aimed at the Caffre. He is big, mid-thirties. His head looks so long and bare because where his ears should be there are only two little holes, like on either side of a bird's head. I tell him in Xhosa to throw down his gun.

      Speak Dutch, Whiteman.

      Throw down your gun.

      Don't you have any respect for a firearm? he asks.

He tosses his gun at the nearest Korana, who catches it mid-air. I tell him to get the hell off his horse. He dismounts, walks towards me with the reins in his hand. Danster wants to know why I haven't yet shot this piece of ooze.

      My name is Arend, says the Dutch Caffre. Joseph Arend.

      I am Coenraad de Buys.

      Your name travels far and wide.

      Believe me, everything you've heard is true.

He looks me up and down, an Eagle by name and nature, then at the Koranas on horseback with us, then at my army that has already started driving off the cattle.

      Is it always so easy? he asks.

Is what always so easy?

Looting cattle.

You say no only once to a gun.

Is that all you do?

Is what all I do?

Rustling cattle.

I hunt elephants.

I'm coming along, says Arend.

He ignores all the guns aimed at him, turns around and jumps onto his horse. He starts cantering away. When we don't move, flabbergasted at this scoundrel who seems so eager to get shot, he turns around in the saddle:

Come on! Before those miserable Koranas see us jabbering here! It's *their* gun and *their* horse that I'm damnwell carting off here!

Arend kicks his horse where it hurts and the creature speeds off.

We can't have a cattle-herd running away from us, says Danster and takes off after him.

I swing my rifle back over my shoulder and unlace my boot so that the toe can breathe more easily and follow my henchmen on horseback.

At the outspan I choke Arend's story out of him. We celebrate our windfall-herd and slaughter a few of the Korana cattle. He drinks along with us and laughs loudly, but when I question him, he clams shut like a mule refusing to take the bit. Danster and Arend share a joke. Danster grabs him behind the neck and they bump heads in a friendly sort of way. Arend gets up and goes for a piss. I open my breeches next to him, wait for the rivulet, which nowadays flows in its own time, drop by drop and painfully. He gazes in front of him, speaks softly as if I weren't there.

That misbegotten Boer took my ears because I wouldn't listen. He wanted to take my nose as well because it was too high up

in the air. So I ran away from his farm to the Great River. It was
the beginning of this very year. It's far from the Sneeuberg.
Seventeen days I walked and chewed the bark of thorn trees.
On the seventeenth day I caught a guinea fowl and devoured
the thing – bones, feathers. A guinea-fowl beak you have to
chew here towards the back, otherwise it jabs you in the cheek.
The rivulet stutters from my yard, doesn't even wet the sand.

After two months of mucking along like that, one day I stumbled
into a Korana kraal next to the Gariep and fell over and got up
eleven days later from the reed mat on which I'd passed out.
I trekked along with them to this place. I herd their cattle and
they hide me from the Griquas.

Why would you want to hide from the Griquas?

I'm told they catch slaves and send them back to the Colony.

Back next to the fire he's all affability again. Laughs and swears
and talks about the weather and women. He is, after me, the biggest
man here. His skull-like head and scarred body and eyes that don't let
go keep everyone on their toes. Danster's little slits observe him every
now and again, but he dishes up a second and a third helping of meat
for the new friend. Arend knows when to tell a dirty joke, before caution
turns into distrust.

It's only Arend and I left by the glowing ash. Too lazy and drunk to
get up out of the fire-warmed sand. I take off my shoe and press my
foot into the cool sand. The thing is once again so swollen that it's
peeling. If I keep my hands over the coals and the brandy to hand,
they're less inclined to cramp. I try again.

What was the son-of-a-bitch's name?

Master Burger. Andries Burger.

He spits.

Were you with him for a long time?

I'm told I came into the world in the Cape, but ever since I can
remember I've been part of his household. He apprenticed me.
I'm a thatcher and a builder. If I'd been free I could have gone

351

and started a home in the Cape or Stellenbosch and rounded up a little Malay girl. Burger even rented me out one year to Reverend Campbell, a man of God . . .

I am familiar with him, yes.

I had to show the Reverend Campbell around those years when he came to tour all his mission stations.

Sounds as if Burger left you to follow your own head.

A man hits harder when a possession starts leading his own life. If you want to start behaving like a free human being, your boss must make you less than human.

Then he takes up the knife.

Then he skins you.

Two days later we plunder the Barolong and shoot three and wound one and take all their cattle. We trek east for a while and go and barter some of the cattle with the Briquas of Dithakong for knives and tobacco and beads. Beyond the Gariep beads are money. Danster looks all too fetching in his Sunday best with the dried blood on the collar. I use the opportunity to warn the Dithakong people against the focking missionaries, the agents of the government, the robbers of spirits and customs. The brother of the Briqua chief, Mothibi, is all ears for my heretical tirade. We ride past the ruins on the kopjes and enquire from the people and nobody knows who used to live here. Now I read as Omni-Buys that it was their own ancestors who split and carted and stacked those rocks. But how, after a few generations, is anybody to recognise himself?

The return journey is slow with all the cattle that have to be driven. One night the Bushmen try to get to the herds. We catch a few of the creatures to go and sell in the Cape. Arend says nothing and stands watching the business. When he walks over to where they are sitting roped together, nobody breathes a word. When he cuts their throats one by one, one and all are silent.

Back next to the Harts River the cattle are divided up. The Harte-naars claim their due. Shortly afterwards they crawl back to Griquatown tail between the legs. Quite a few of the Hartenaar gang come and join me. Most of them Bastaards, but also a few Koranas and even Bushmen – Bushmen prepared to trade their own people. Anderson receives the prodigal sons and blesses them and what do I know. Peek into the old books and smirk with me at the way the authorities take Anderson to task for our little outing to the Barolong: *These atrocious murders had been anticipated from collecting so many indolent and ill-disposed people together where there was no sort of social compact to restrain them.*

The Briquas must have taken my heresy to heart, because when the missionary Evans turns up among the Dithakong with his red neck and glad tidings, the captains kick his arse. Mothibi's brother was apparently on his way to my camp with this welcome news when Bushman arrows turned him into a watering can.

In the mission letters I am of course the one to blame for all these events – I, *a Colonist long known for his rebellious Disposition and bad habits, who has for many years been a very Distinguished Character among the Disaffected on the frontiers.* Well I never. Such flattering words should surely be embroidered and displayed in the hallway.

Danster treks on to loot as no man has ever looted. Alliances with people like him never last long. He dances through the world to his own tune. While you're dancing along, you share the force of the whirl-wind, and then the dance is over. He bids farewell with an exuberant string of blessings and filth. The last you see is his gang like a dust storm on the horizon. With him gone, the days drag more slowly; even my gun's firing under my ear sounds distant. Most of the Hartenaars desert me to return to their vegetable patches. They are brought to their knees by guilt and pray voraciously. The looted cattle are returned to the Barolong. Their worthless souls, *those* they return to focking Anderson.

3

The Hartenaars who wanted to clear out have cleared out. I am told that Danster is keeping up the good work under the mission stations with his guns. I and my boys feed our horses and oil our guns and then it's back to Dithakong. We hunt elephants in the territory of Mothibi's Briquas. Coenraad Wilhelm and Johannes shoot a fair number. Windvogel the younger and Piet are also dab hands at hunting, but it's son-in-law Jan who surprises everybody with his shooting skill. Ever since we trekked across the border he's been all too eager to learn to hunt properly. He asked questions ad nauseam, but he took the advice to heart. He remains the calmest of men, but the moment his cheek feels the butt of a gun his eyes harden and he ordains what will live and what will die in the world in front of his barrel. Every day in the bush he picks up a shiny stone or mottled leaf. Back in the camp he gives Bettie a treasure for every day he's been gone.

We trek for three weeks to Thabeng in pursuit of the depleted herds and Elizabeth gives birth to a son and the Lord knows I've run out of names for my offspring and we baptise him Baba. At Thabeng, along with Sefunelo's Rolong-Seleka, we pile our wagons high with tusks. I mediate a short-lived alliance between Mothibi and the Seleka for an expedition against the Bakwena. I, my guns, my horses, my sons, Arend and a few of the most battle-ready men in my retinue join up with Mothibi's three regiments.

We wake up in the veldt where the spring of 1817 bleeds over everything like a ruptured artery. We trek into the triangle of mountains between Paardeplaats, Hartebeesfontein and Schoonspruit. The bush is too quiet.

The attack starts from on high. Assegais drop from nowhere into soft rumps. Man in front of me is too slow. Arrows. Blood in my face. Arrow in my shoulder. In front of me he disappears under a rock; his legs jerk as if he's dancing. Now the rocks rain down. The Bakwena are sitting high up and behind the rocks and they roll the gigantic

boulders down on us. We retreat, flee. They pursue us. In front of
me warriors are tripping over corpses. My people and I get away. The
Seleka soon vanish into the mountains. The Briquas don't know
the mountain defiles and kloofs and are decimated. The Bakwena
trap them in a steep ravine and carry out a major massacre.

On the return Mothibi first calls in at Thabeng to plunder the Seleka
as a token of his disgust at the defeat. Sefunelo's Seleka wreak havoc
under the Briquas. I had told Sefunelo of Mothibi's plans. Mothibi
slinks back to Dithakong and undergoes an excessive conversion.

~

Sometimes you cling to memories, but to no avail. They crumble like
sandstone if you touch them, then just the dust in your hand. Sometimes Omni-I reads a scene in a book and it feels as if I remember it
from my own, erstwhile life. As if other people's lives capture something
of my life, moments of which I can recall – the content of a conversation, the fly on the brim of my hat, but not the words.

I remember that Arend and I had been waiting under a tree on the
banks of the Gariep since sunrise that morning. See, the river stretches
out in front of us for ever and always. See, we're waiting for a farmer
from the Colony. He wants to have a talk. He has guns and I have
ivory. Even though it's open and empty as far as you can see, there are
many eyes on the river. With us are six extra horses with saddlebags
for the flints and gunpowder that he's offered as appetiser. Here you
don't want to get caught with a clumsy wagon. I've stood the elephant
tusk we lugged along against a tree.

The farmer said he wanted to talk by this tree on this day. He said
we'd know which one. The big flowering camel thorn where it seems
the river wants to bend but then doesn't bend, some distance to the
west of the wagon trail. He said the tree stood on its own. He said
on 1 August it would be flowering golden as the sun. Arend and I are
sitting under the spreading crown, in golden bloom as the farmer
promised. It's as if you can hear the branches above our heads branching

out. To one side there are the ribs of an ox protruding from the sand. There's a stone in my shoe.

You're right. It's too much for one man, says Arend.

He is silent. Then, suddenly cheerful:

Probably no point in giving up now. We should have done it years ago.

My feet are swollen. I can't get the shoe off my foot.

Goddammit, stop your jabbering and help me with the damned thing.

We were men of renown, there in the beginning. Now it's too late. They won't even arrest us. They'll shoot us and leave us lying in the veldt like those bones over there.

I tug at my shoe.

What are you doing?

I'm taking off my shoe. You've never experienced such a thing? You should take off your shoes every day. How many times must I tell you? You won't listen.

Help me.

Does it hurt? he asks snidely.

Does it hurt? The earless Caffre wants to know if it hurts.

Yes, nobody ever suffers except His Excellency Buys.

Does it hurt? I mock him.

Arend pushes two index fingers into his ear apertures.

The pinkfoot-Boer wants to know?

Every tug at the shoe sets off a sharp stab of pain at the back of my head. I manage to take off the damned shoe, look into it, turn it over, shake it, look on the ground to see if anything fell out; feel inside again.

Well? Arend asks.

Nothing.

He takes off his hat, rubs the sweat from his stubble-scalp. I scratch between my toes.

One of the thieves was saved. At least that's half, the skull-head mumbles.

356

What?

Supposing we repented. Confessed.

Confessed what?

Never mind.

I smack the back of his head. Above us the bark of the young branches is smooth and reddish brown, but the trunk against our backs is deeply grooved and grey.

Dammit, Arend. *What* is it now?

Two thieves, crucified on either side of the Messiah. One . . .

The what?

The Messiah. Christ.

I'm leaving.

I get up. Arend sighs, twirls a twig after an ant lion in his tunnel. I flop down next to him again.

If you want to chatter about the Bible, then rather the Old Testament. The deserts, the wars and the women. The gangs with the countenances of lions.

You should become a psalmist.

You should bugger off.

I'm just thinking, he says. The apostles, all four of them were there by the cross. And only one reports a thief saved. Why believe him rather than the other three?

Who believes him?

Everybody. That's the story.

People are baboons.

I get up, limp away from his chatter, gaze into the distance with my hand shielding my eyes, gaze in the other direction. Arend peeks into my shoe and drops it and spits. There is nothing here. Nobody is on his way. A giraffe sticks its neck over the horizon and then sinks down again into the other side of the world.

Well, should we get going? he asks.

Yes, I think so, let's get going, I say.

We don't move.

Two-inch thorns grow in pairs from the trunk and branches. At the base they clump together, thick and gnarled. The big Caffre walks to the ribs towering up out of the sand. He breaks off a rib, examines the dry marrow.

Where do all these corpses come from? he asks.

These skeletons.

You tell me.

That's true, I tell him.

He walks to and fro and kicks the sand, tracing a spoor behind him with the rib.

We should have thought first. Thought what we were getting ourselves into. All the shooting and fleeing. All the dead.

At the very beginning. Then I thought, and weighed things up, yes.

Arend sits down. The afternoon sun bakes the flowers so that the sweetness cloys the air.

Have you given any thought to what you're going to do with all the money? he asks.

What money?

The money we're going to get in the Colony for all the ivory. How many tons haven't we gathered, gathered and bartered for guns and gunpowder to shoot more elephants. What are you going to do when you're a rich man?

Buy more guns.

No, Buys, I mean when we've done hunting and looting.

His eyes mist over with gazing into the mirage.

I can see it, he murmurs. I'm going to buy a farm. In the Cape or Tulbagh or Stellenbosch, any place with mountains and vineyards and shade. A new hat with a red hatband stuck with ostrich feathers. A suit of clothes that glitters when the sun catches it. First of all I'm going to build a pantry and stuff it full of kudu loins and legs of mutton and sweet potatoes and pumpkin; tobacco and biltong in the rafters. Then a wine cellar under

the house to keep the wine cool. A dam full of brandy. Then a
stoep on which I can sit and smoke and talk. Then a bedroom
large enough for three white maidens and me in the middle.

His gaze sharpens into focus again.

And you, Buys? How big a bed are you going to build? What
are you going to buy first of all?

Buy more guns. Buy more horses. More gunpowder. More lead.
More flints. More guns.

But what are you going to do with it all?

Loot more cattle, shoot more elephants.

I stuff a plug of tobacco into my cheek and start chewing vigorously.

You're a difficult person to get along with, Coenraad.

So let's go our separate ways, I say.

You're always saying that, but you come and sit by my fire
every night.

The conversation evaporates like our sweat in the sand. Each one
sits thinking of the last man he shot, the last wound he stepped on.
A breeze I don't feel on my body stirs the feathery leaves around us.
I lick my finger and stick it in the air. The tree feathers are still
immediately.

Voices of the dead, I say.

I remember the stories of my childhood. On these plains you have to
keep talking if you don't want to think.

They rustle like wings, he says immediately, almost as relieved
as I to escape his memories.

Like leaves, I say.

Like sand, he says.

Like leaves, I say.

For just a moment the draught moves through the branches again,
but now also over my face. Then it's gone. We remain silent together
and separately.

They're all talking at the same time, Arend resumes after a
few moments.

Each to himself, I say.

They whisper.

They rustle, I say.

They murmur.

They rustle, I say.

Silence.

What are they saying?

They are talking about their lives, I say.

To have lived was not enough for them.

They must talk about it, I say.

To be dead is not enough for them.

It's not enough, I say.

Silence.

They rustle like feathers, he says.

Like leaves.

Like ash.

Like leaves, I say.

Long silence.

Say something, will you.

I'm trying, I say.

Long silence.

Specks appear on the horizon and we load our guns and dig ourselves in and wait for what we hope is the farmer. The specks grow into people. It's not the farmer. It's four runaway slaves who almost trip right over us. They've escaped from their owners and ended up on the same wagon trail as Landdrost Stockenström – Andries, the son of Anders – and his retinue. Who are on their way here. We thank the slaves for the forewarning and offer them horses and a safe escape and get out of there. My swollen feet cramp in the stirrups and my fingers cramp around the reins and God damn the farmer who was late.

A few Bastaards turn up at our camp on the Harts River and say they're also fleeing before Stockenström. I say Find yourselves a place to lie down. Their bed rolls remain tightly coiled behind their saddles and the horses are not unsaddled and they're a bit too interested in everything around them and the following morning they're nowhere to be seen. I pack my stuff and trek north to a Barolong kraal at Khunwana.

In every flower there is a bee with feet full of pollen and a sting. The air is filled with the bleating of lambs and young goats. The calves suckle their mothers dry. The last shred of moon burns through the tent. The shadows play on Elizabeth's skin like seven veils. She sits on the edge of the mattress, combs her hair with her left hand while her right hand is handling me somewhat reluctantly so that I should leave her alone till this afternoon. She is close to a hundred strokes with both hands when there is a yelling outside. She's a dear good wife and tries to bring things to a head quickly, but oh well, it's a struggle nowadays. With breeches tenting out and rapidly subsiding, I go and see what's the matter.

A Bushman woman is howling like a hyena on heat. I have to shake her by the shoulders a few times before I'm told that she went to fetch water when the dogs started barking. She saw the men and the horses and the guns by the watering hole. I grab my gun and lace up my breeches properly and bawl Arend awake. We leap onto two of the horses that are nowadays kept saddled in rotation.

At the watering hole the gang are sitting on their haunches drinking with their horses. Quenching their thirst before coming to kill me. We tether our horses to a blackthorn and walk through the undergrowth and out into the open and I have to clear my throat before they look up. I recognise the droll little cocksucker who jumps up and points his gun at me and says I must give myself up. I inform him that there are already two guns trained on him. Cornelis Kok gulps and looks at his pals and sees their empty hands and their pale visages.

You came looting cattle with me, Kok. You got rich yourself. So why so full of virtue now?

These are other times, Buys.

I'd forgotten how shrill the little guy's voice is.

It's two goddam months later, you dog's dick! I shout at him. I did you people no harm!

There's no longer room for you here, he shouts back. Your time is past. We're taking you to Stockenström. With you in the Castle's pit, we can carry on with our lives, be safe from your kind.

If you shoot me in the back, Bastaard, you'll be safe in neither heaven nor hell nor any damned mission station.

Arend and I turn around and walk back to our horses. Three of the newly converted geldings fire at us and miss by a mile and I tell Arend Just keep walking and a fourth shot splinters a branch in front of us. Arend swings around and shoots a Bushman hanger-on in the shoulder. The commando behind us falls silent. We charge back to the camp as if death itself is biting our butts because it is.

There's no time to flee. Everyone who can get hold of a gun ensconces himself around the camp. The women and children cower behind tents and wagons and rocks and screens and bushes and anthills. An hour or so later I see Kok's pudgy-cheeked countenance peering out of the undergrowth. I take aim at my leisure, can't wait to pull the trigger. Arend puts his hand on the barrel, shoves the gun down to the ground firmly. Kok beckons another Griqua catechumen closer. They whisper and I see what Arend means. They are scared. There are twenty, perhaps thirty of them, and we are an army, an army of whites and Caffres and Bastaards and Hottentots and Bushmen, pissed off and armed.

We're coming back, Buys!

The squeaky little tremolo calls in the wilderness as Kok and the other Stockenström acolytes trickle away. Weeks later I receive the glad tidings that my corpse is once again worth a thousand rix-dollars to the Colony.

Stockenström's little commando didn't get very far, but there will be others. My life beside the Hart is over. With the price on my head I no longer dare venture onto any wagon trail. Nobody dare sell me gunpowder any more. Once again as free as the birds of the heavens, as free as my friend Arend, the pared-down slave. I spread my outlawed wings and by October I'm fleeing before rumours of a second commando seeking my blood and bounty, but it never turns up. When summer and the cicadas descend upon us searing and shrill, I'm building a house at Thabeng. The kraal is perched on the hills, surrounded with springs and hartebeest, abundant as the grazing. When in later years the Christians come to mine gold in the area, they'll name their town, as is the custom, for what they can see: Hartebeesfontein, the fountain of the hartebeest.

The people come and complain to me about red hyenas with ridged backs that are biting their calves.

What are you coming to me for? I snarl at them. Do I have dominion over the hyenas of the wild?

Sefunelo's wobbling double chin could make one wonder if his mother was a turkey and he was hatched from an egg, but alas not. The double chin is his own achievement, his reward for his percipience and prosperity. He allows me to shelter with his Rolong-Seleka on one condition: My magnificent herds remain mine as long as I and my horde remain at Thabeng. Should I leave him, my cattle remain behind in his kraals. To show that I'm settling here, I build a house of stone. By 'I' I mean to say Arend. I lend a hand, but Arend says which stone goes where. See, the first white man's home in the trans-Vaal. While we're building, I tell myself that I don't miss the Couga. The women create a vegetable garden, big enough to feed the Buys nation and quite a few Seleka. Sefunelo eats my mealies and inspects my house and calls me his friend. If from time to time I go off to linger or loot among the Hurutshe and the Ngwaketse and all that is a Kwena kraal, he is the one who sees me off, my concubines grumbling and grousing

in the background. And my wives don't turn up either. Lord alone
knows what's going on in Nombini's head; Maria eternally scolding
around the house like the general she is. She says she has a household to husband against famine and failure and has no time for my
games. Elizabeth stays with me in our stone house.

~

I keep trekking. You leave marks behind you, stains of experiences
that stick to you again every time you walk past them. Every time, in
those eastern frontier years, that I rode past old Langa's kraal, I was
struck with blindness and my mind's eye did the seeing: that day
I went to fetch Nombini. The way she looked at me while her people
were being manhandled and murdered in front of her, how I lost her
before I could steal her. That kopje in Bechuanaland – this I've never
told anybody – where I shot off the Caffre's nose, and how he laughed
as he fell. And the deadly Yese – this I've babbled about ad nauseam –
how I lay on the plaited rug and stared at the reed roof of her hut
and thought of the men before me who had lain with her on that
exact patch of compacted soil. Things too good and too terrible to
be reminded of: the blue dread of the mountains, the terror of the
plains; the wind through the golden veldt, as if rippling muscles
were playing under the earth's grass hide. The little bit of fur and the
wound in the cleft of every woman. Eland. Lions. My red dogs. Quill
and ink. Elizabeth's mouth. The fat around my children that I scrub
off and the navel cord that I fold double and knot and cut with a
whetted knife. Baobabs. Glider. Arend. Danster. Gun and powder.
Bezuidenhout. Kemp's ruined feet. Maria. Windvogel. Those little
blue flowers. Elizabeth in our stone house. You keep trekking, pursued
by your life.

The day has been long and tonight this old body is nothing but aches
and pains. I lie watching Elizabeth slowly peeling off her layers of
dresses. My wife, this lady of the wilderness. She still dresses up every
day, in dresses that refuse to get threadbare like Maria's.

All three my wives cost me dearly. For Maria I gave up my white family. For Nombini I gave up Maria. After that thunderstorm where Nombini sat playing with the porcelain dish, Maria was never again really my wife. And Nombini never grew closer to me than that night. She remains the stolen one, the prisoner of war; the one who turns over tortoises, who plaits birdcages. For Elizabeth I had to give up my children – with the four that she and I were to line up I was at home more often, sometimes played along, plucked a decent clay-stick, even plaited a straw doll or two. The children by other women were left behind. I was never there; I was a prick and a progenitor, never a father. My fire-haired Bettie who is now a woman herself. What will become of her in this bedlam? For Elizabeth I'll renounce everything; she is my mate. And have I mentioned her mouth? To the devil with the past and to hell with the future: see, my wife is unlacing her bodice.

We laugh too much to get much kissing done. I chase her around the two small rooms; she flutters away ahead of me. I can hardly get hold of the hem of her dress. In the front room the brood are lying in a heap pretending to be asleep. In the bedroom I press her against the wall. Her face in my hands. I can but look at this person. She polishes my flabby and hairy belly as if it's the most precious copper. My prick shrinks into itself, my toe starts throbbing. She kisses my bald patches. I let go of her.

   Come on, my old ox. Come and lie by me. Just hold me.
Our legs twine together. I press her to me until her eyes say it's hurting. I rub across her dear wrinkled buttocks, the skin hanging loose around her chin. I ask how one person can be so soft.

   It's you who knead me, Mijnheer.
She touches my crotch; still nothing. We kiss. She licks over my closed eyes. She sings softly while like a female baboon she forages in my chest hair for fleas. I scratch her back while she's telling how she tied Baba and Jan to each other with a thong today when they hit each other. After the two of them had to put up with each other all afternoon with three legs and no arms they are once again great friends.

Besides, they learnt about slipknots, she says. She plaits my beard
with the selfsame thong in three thick strands, with soup bones at
the lower end:

Now the ancestors will quail before your countenance, my
wild white warrior.

She hunkers on my chest and starts undoing the soup bones from
the red-and-grey beard. I say, Let it be for a while. Her arms shoot
out above her head; an unearthly cooing and clucking and growling
emanates from under her ribs. She falls on me and kisses me all over
on my peeled cheeks and forehead. I erupt and grab her and turn her
over and then everything functions as it should. My wife and I, we
are a series of eruptions. I explode, I vibrate on my own, like a sound
that's lost its tune. I stir, buffet, calm down, come back, vanish, with
no more pattern than the flight of mosquitoes.

My old and raddled body is no longer mine; if she touches me there,
if I touch here, our bodies become a single thing, more absolute, more
separate than ever. Our bodies become a place, a place of touch,
a smooth place of a thousand bodies. We are one and we become many.
We fold until only skin remains. Nothing remains of man and woman.
Everything is real and useless. The one thing and the other touch and
swerve here on the verge of the inside-out, the I-you, the verge where
one skin touches the other, where pain winks with pleasure, where
the whole body becomes hide, no deeper organs; nothing is penetrated.
We are invulnerable, we are for ever. I love her. There is no love without making love. And every hard shaft demands an infinitesimally small
measure of love. Here where everything that can open and shut in our
bodies folds open and slides shut, here the frontier of what I am and
where I am trembles, before I transmute into something else.

A few thrusts, then I spurt, an eternity later. It is as if my heart contracts, my blood pours out and fills up again. I am still Buys, I become
Buys, without returning to Buys. I overflow. She smears my seed over
her stomach and pulls me down on top of her.

See, Buys clambers off her, gets up to get rid of a cramp. He sits down in front of her, grabs her feet and opens her legs, sidles closer, the little hairs on her calves against his old man's saddlebags. He rubs over her thighs and gazes at the folds of her sheath. He stares and stares and sees an exact and absolute vision of death, a perfect yearning that cannot be fulfilled without blasting bodies apart and with that this vision. His eye cannot settle; it slides along the swerves and lines and niches and follows the farewells and retreats. She wants to cover herself, awkward with being examined like this. He wrestles her hands away, says what he has to say to calm her down. He gazes and gazes. He sees how she smells, how she tastes, how she sounds. There is nothing here to understand. Everything is exactly what it is and unstable. She does not move, but it feels as if what he sees vanishes between two blinkings of his eye.

Listen to me carrying on. Please pardon this old varmint. She is the first woman who can talk to my body, the first one who can cajole this convulsing carcase and patiently invite it to talk back. All my life I've been blindly pursuing my prick, until at long last the here and now of her. But see, tomorrow I'll see a bobbing pair of never-seen-before buttocks, and believe me, then I'll butt in again, searching for something I've found already.

Can't get to the bottom of this business. And it's *then*, as old Kemp said, that the long lists ensue: poking pairing pushing mating, frigging, banging, coupling, covering, fertilising. Loving. Hunching humping jumping bumping banging bonking. Sleeping with, making love. Flipping binding bundling screwing scrubbing shagging shtupping; penetration fornication copulation, coitus congress carnal knowledge; deflowering, dallying; tupping treading shafting nailing ramming ramping rumping pumping rooting rogering. Oh, what the hell.

~

Gunpowder and clothing run out if you're in hiding. The Colony, after all, is closed to me till the goddam Second Coming. I lift up mine eyes unto the kopjes in the east, from whence cometh my help if not

from the Portuguese. Arend and I talk and draw maps in the sand.
I decide that Arend and Coenraad Wilhelm will go and look for
gunpowder in Delagoa Bay. They'll cross the Drakensberg at the
Olifantsvallei and they'll find the Portuguese town of Inhambane that
I've been looking for for such a long time and they'll return with
gunpowder and clothing and riches. I and a few men travel with them
as far as the Molopo River and somewhere in March 1819 I shake
the hands of my son and Arend and trek on to the Hurutshe capital
Karechuenya in the Tshwenyane hills. The Bastaards with me say
that Karechuenya is at least as large as the Cape and much cleaner.
They say Karechuenya is the richest of all the Caffre kraals. If a
portion of their riches could find their way into my pocket, that
wouldn't come amiss. Sefunelo isn't going to make me rich. Perhaps
my horsemen and guns, my name, could be worth more at Karechuenya
than at Thabeng.

~

See, all the veldt is aflutter with brown butterflies. They cluster on us
like flies. I take off my hat, flap them away, the grey horse under me
shivers its mane. The one nameless mount follows the other until it,
too, is speared or arrowed or simply dies like all tamed animals in the
interior. I press my hat back onto my head. Then the tapping on the
inside of the sweat-moistened leather, the scrabbling in my hair. I lift
the hat and a butterfly erupts.

The sand is dark red, the dust kicked up by the hooves, rusty. The
people we travel past seem calm and long-suffering, as if the soil has
been saturated with blood and has nothing more to demand from those
who set foot on her. The grass is yellow, the trees lush and green and
the sky so bright it scorches my eyes.

We approach the settlement from the east. Peaked huts like the
armour of a lizard extend over the surface of the two highest hills in
the area. A colony of kraals on the kopjes, and in the low-lying areas
wild olives and marula and tambotie as far as the eye can see. See, the

gigantic wild plum tree on the slopes of the steepest peak, the teeming southern peak of Karechuenya.

This is the Caffre city of cities. Such a multitude of people I could not have imagined. Some people say there are sixteen thousand souls living here, others say twenty thousand; I don't try to count them. The Bastaards say Karechuenya means See, here be baboons; apparently used to be a colony of apes before people started piling up the rocks.

I trek through their pasturage, the herdsmen wave at me. Their flocks like an undulating brown sea over the hills as far as an old man can see, and then the unknown expanse. Every few yards the veldt looks different, but mainly overgrown and impenetrable. You have to watch your step or you fall into one of the fountains that spring up here as only stones can in the rest of this vast expanse. A one-eared dog keeps running in under my horse's hooves, the dumb creature excited to the point of peril. I take a gulp of water from the knapsack, spit.

The Hurutshes walk to meet us. They say chief Senosi lives on the southern peak in the kgosing, the royal district. Chief Diutlwileng lives on the plateau, the northern district where the biggest cattle kraals are situated. Both are children of the daughters of the deceased king. Both rule over their own people, each on his own hill. Senosi lives on the royal hill and we must meet him first. I have the wagons outspanned at the foot of the southern hill. The town's children descend upon us. I unsaddle my horse and walk up the hill with the welcoming committee. See, the women here walk with their shoulders thrown back, their breasts like soft battering rams.

The northern district is not visible from Senosi's hill. What one can see from the hill is a plain bordered by hills extending in front of me for a hundred miles. Between the high stone walls people are teeming. The stonework is the best I've ever seen, square and strong but fine and artistic; no hole for a louse in between any of the cut and stacked stones. The neighbourhoods are divided up into wards, each ward with the divisions of ten or so families, each division a ring wall as high as I myself on my toes. In every camp is a large hut for sleeping, as well as one or two smaller huts. Above a foot-high stone base, which keeps out the wind and the crawling creatures, the residences are of wood, the roofs of reed. Large man-height monoliths in front of some of the kraals and in front of the huts of the most prominent residents. Each camp has its own grain store, ten feet high, raised from the ground on stones and with a thatched roof. Stone mills and fireplaces in front of the huts, generally also with a small kraal where the slaughter animals are kept. Most of these yards are enclosed with a low stone wall. Here and there even a narrow and upright stone doorway in front of a hut. The door rests in a groove cut into the flat stone on the threshold. In the evening the door slides shut and in the morning the door slides open. Large spiders spin and descend and ascend in every tree. Never have I seen so many leopard skins. The people wear and drape the skins as I use cattle hides. Large skins. In this area the hunters are more plentiful than the prey.

I meet Senosi at the kgotla, the meeting place compacted by many feet. He is large and serious. He jokes when it's expected of him, but without conviction. We shake the necessary hands and he invites me and his closest advisers to his hut for beer and kudu. He listens with one ear and rubs his arms and chest with both his hands, so that after a while I look away.

Was he merely caressing his oiled arms, or was it fate that he felt prickling on his skin? Could he have guessed then that this gigantic town and all its people would be razed to the red ground barely three or four years later? That his arms and his walls would not be able to withstand the hordes of the difaqane?

A high wall with large upright white rocks at its entrance encloses Senosi's yard. Inside are four huts, a large one for him and his arms, two smallish ones for his wives and a fourth small one for storage. His wives are pretty, but Senosi is more concerned with the bulging of the veins on his forearms when he balls his fists. His beer is good and strong, and as the afternoon lingers on, his wives get prettier and prettier. The kudu meat is young and succulent. To stop staring at the chief's

muscles and especially his wives – who giggle archly when the calabashes they're bearing spill beer on them – I enquire with feigned
interest after the white and polished stones. The oldest adviser says
the white quartz is scarce. It is the colour of the place where the spirits
dwell. Only he with the requisite importance and daring to chat with
the dead and the spirits, plants a stone like that at his door. While I
live will I praise the Lord, just to be allowed to slurp up the foaming
beer from between those breasts.

The wagons blunder around the slope of the hill and down into the
kloof. Around us the vegetable gardens and lands, and forges burning
all day. We outspan and start clearing a plot of land next to a spring.
The Hurutshes take one look at my kraals of branches and a few days
later there's a whole gang in the camp building stone kraals for my
cattle, and five huts for me and the men with me.

Two or three weeks after I've moved in between the wild figs and
the umbrella thorn, the sorcerer comes to call. Wrapped in a kaross
cloak stretching to his ankles and with his woolly headdress the man
looks as if he's expecting snow at any moment. His eyes are milky and
peer into another world. He's come to bless me and to safeguard my
camp against the worst of the evil spirits. He lives on the hill with
Senosi so that he can be with his ancestors. The ancestors, he says,
live in a cave on the south side of the hill. He says the chiefs also go
to the cave to discuss the urgent affairs of the day with the ancients
of spirit. He says the ancestors like giving advice, but you have to
beware of the snake with many heads that also lives in the cave. The
lights that one can see at night close to the cave are the eyes of the
snake gleaming in the moonlight. He says there on that hill you feel
the nature spirits and the ancestors in your blood. This place is holy.
The sorcerer strikes the nearest log with his stick. The nature spirits
roam all over, he says. He says you can't see them with your ordinary
eyes, but they are in every stone on the hill and also here in the
forests of the kloof. He says one of the thickets on the hill is his alone
to enter. That is where he dances for rain, where he pleads for rain

371

with the god he calls Modimo. He says he dances up there where it's high so that the ancestors can hear him. But it's by the waters here in the kloof that the real holiness dwells. Every blessed drop of every fountain and waterfall and pool and puddle here is holy and can heal. He says I'll see yet, every day there are sick and careworn people who come to seek out the waters here near my camp. I walk with him to the nearest pool so that he can collect his rain medicine. He says that what the water spits out is the medicine against the drought. He fills his bag with the scum that the water vomits out on her banks – twigs, leaves, moss, mud and a whole school of tadpoles. I take off my boots and soak my sore feet in the water. Today only one kind of holy water is going to be of any use – the kind you find in a flagon or a vat, not in any holy puddle.

In the course of the next few weeks I get to know the mighty city of Karechuenya very well. I go to explore the northern district of chief Diutlwileng. This district is divided into two neighbourhoods with a narrow clearing between the two. The northern section is slightly smaller, but more densely populated. Diutlwileng's dwelling is sur-rounded with other largish huts, the kgoro, where the chiefs reside and near to them the other nobility. A large cattle kraal, the lesaka, easily two hundred and fifty by a hundred and fifty feet, occupies the centre of the settlement. In the evenings they drive some five hundred cattle into this stone kraal next to the kgotla. The construc-tion here is not of the same quality. A different kind of stone here, but it also seems to be newer, as if Senosi's dwelling had been built by an earlier breed of people who had a better understanding of the secrets of stone.

If you've seen one kraal you've seen them all. Even stone walls are not a rare sight. It's the sheer size of this place that amazes me. I wander around for days with a dropped jaw and a toe protesting against the long-distance walks. I've never been to the Cape; the largest town I know is Swellendam. How so many people can live together in a single heap and not tear each other to pieces passes my humble understanding. See, from the kloof I gaze up at the hills at night and at their fires like stars.

I go and bother the smiths and their forges. The cone-shaped forges encircle the neck of the hill like a string of beads. The clay ovens are more than six feet high, twelve feet or more wide. The tunnel on the surface that runs into a fire and then shoots up into the chimney. The blowpipes on the sides to keep the flames alive. Over the fire an earthenware bowl has been fastened, filled with iron ore, charcoal and quartz sand. I squat next to the smith and light my pipe and scratch myself and regard this lot until the iron appears from the crucible of the earth oven, gets thrown into a bowl of water, and sinks. Grains of cold purity.

The next day I'm back and the day after that. I watch the man melting and beating and shaping copper and iron. I barter beads and ivory for copper earrings and necklaces for my wives who are far away. One morning the man turns up at my tent where I'm sitting grinding coffee. Morning, I say. Moro, he says. He takes out something wrapped in hide out of his bag and puts it down in front of me and steps back and waits. I abandon the coffee and pick up the bundle, open it. I pick up the long cleaver with the wooden haft, cleave the air a few times, thank the man, who laughs broadly and walks off.

Go hunting, walk to the camp, go chatter with the elders, walk back to the camp, walk, walk, walk. Walk past the lion house: the pit dug deeper than a white man's grave, the wall, higher than a white giant like me, stacked around the pit, the observation tower on wooden stilts behind the pit. The warrior with his assegais and his chameleon eyes guarding over the caterwauling kids in the pit. The women leave their little ones in the lion house when they go to the lands. Here the warrior guards them against the lions and leopards and golden eagles. See, the sweet thorn, see, another camel thorn. I sit down and take off my shoes and there's nothing there to salvage. I fling them into the tree and the thorns grab the laces and there they dance to their own tune free of the weight of my damned feet.

Amazement also has its limits. Even immensity gets boring in the long run. My chronic ailments do though allow me to mount a horse often enough and to go and shoot a few beasts. The elephants develop a taste for lead and make for my guns like moths to a candle. It is truly a land of milk and honey and copper and meat and even vegetables if it must. I am quite happy here and the young girls quite accommodating. But my gunpowder is running out, my rifle oil has run out and my only shirt is a discarded leopard skin with holes for the arms and a thong around the paunch. I sit next to my wagon and pick the peeled skin from my toe. What was it that that pen-pusher wrote about me? *A very distinguished Character among the Disaffected on the frontiers.* Focking English. Disaffected. I know *affected*. My heart is not stone, after all. But *disaffected*. If something no longer affects you, I assume. But more than that? Dissatisfied? Dissatisfied *because* it no longer affects you? Focking English. Focking disaffected. I look up at the hill and its majestic city. Focking disaffected. The stone kraals and my cattle. The open-hearted people who walk past and wave. Focking disaffected. The necklaces, the panga, the pile of ivory here next to me. The fly on my breeches. Focking disaffected. My blue swollen toe and its peelings. Focking disaffected.

∼

Arend and Coenraad Wilhelm find me still encamped at Karechuenya. On this winter's day I'm sitting on the kgotla with a few Hurutshes making hunting plans. I've wrapped a large kaross around myself. The wind blows through the holes in my leopard skin. Arend picks up a pack of linen from the wagon and tosses it at my feet.

There, we almost got killed for that. Cut yourself a cute goddam gown.

Arend has a different story every day, but today he seems serious and his black eyes don't let go of mine. He sits down and makes Coenraad Wilhelm sit down. While Arend is telling about their journey, Coenraad Wilhelm chews vigorously at a blade of grass and nods and grunts affirmatively and looks at the ground. Arend tells that way beyond the Vaal they came across a lot of Bokwena who live to the east of the Kwena-Modisane. The people were welcoming when they heard that Arend and Coenraad Wilhelm are also on friendly footing with the Hurutshe. Their elders fed them bowls of milk and told them all about a community of Macuas, white people, on the coast, just a bit further away, about two days' journey. They drew their own maps in the sand, pebbles and twigs were mountains and rivers and kraals. They said that the whitish people live on the far side of a wide water that they cross on floats. Arend believes that they were talking of Delagoa Bay which lies on the other side of the big Matola River. He says the Bakwena sold them the linen.

That far they trekked and no further, because the rivers were in flood and the land was awash with blood and corpses and crows. All the way from here to the Drakensberg, says Arend, one continuous and continuing war between everybody and everybody. Arend says he was sad: if the wind blew in the right direction, he could smell the gunpowder in Delagoa Bay. A few days far and impossibly far.

I listen and look at my son, emaciated after the journey. I look at my bare paws and the little heap of cloth lying before us in the red sand. We'll perish here. Our clothes will wear through until we walk about naked like the Caffres, and when the last gunpowder has been shot out, we'll be hunted like the beasts of the veldt, just another little straggle of pale Bushmen who beg and steal until we starve or get mown down or get sold to a Christian farmer. Arend gets up and shakes the sand from his breeches and says he's going to bathe. As he walks away he takes off his shirt and Burger's old lashes still criss-cross his back like faded writing. I get up.

Let him be, Father, says Coenraad Wilhelm.

I catch Arend up from behind and grab him by the neck and throw him to the ground. He is up immediately and fells me with a blow. One of my Hottentots appears from nowhere and pushes his musket into the runaway slave's mouth. I struggle to my feet and spit out a tooth.

A few of my Bastaards and Hottentots come running and I say Tie him to that pole. Arend utters no word, doesn't protest. I lash his back to pieces, old scars gash open again. I lambast him for a rotten slave and robber and ask him where he's hiding my Portuguese gunpowder. I carry on whipping until the whip feels like lead and then I start whipping with my left hand until everything in me cramps. Arend is quiet and when I look around Coenraad Wilhelm is gone. I tell my men to untie him and walk off.

Late that afternoon Arend comes to find me. He says his belongings are packed. He's leaving now. I ask him where to. He says his cattle and ivory are waiting for him at Thabeng. I needn't worry, by the time I get back home, he'll have left, back to the Hart. His composure is terrifying. His shirt is weighed down where the blood seeps through on his back, but he's walking up straight.

> Back to the Hart? The commandos will get you. Have you taken leave of your senses quite apart from your goddam ears?
> Those Christian bastards are after the price on *your* head, Boer, I'm just another disfigured runaway slave, says the Caffre as he walks off: We all look the same.

Arend is gone and him, too, I'll never see again. Find him in your pages and you'll read how he went and settled himself next to the Hart with his ivory and his cattle, how Campbell summoned him in 1820 to be his guide again, this time in fact to Karechuenya. How he fled before the Mantatees and afterwards pursued that lot again along with the missionary Moffat. In 1823 he was present at the great battle of Dithakong. Then he robbed the missionaries of Kuruman of their tobacco and vegetables. In 1828 he and his three children moved there. Arend looted and raged along with me against the Colony, but yet wanted to be accepted by the Cape civilisation. He used to say that he was thinking of his children. His offspring I never laid eyes on. Did he hide them from his fellow reavers? He said his children shouldn't grow up in the wilderness and get lost as he did. That, and, in spite of the robbing and boozing, he never turned his back on his Lord. After all, you keep your eye on someone who carries lightning bolts in his hand, he said once. His soul was always the Lord's, but his body still belonged to that scoundrel Burger. Through the mediation of the traveller George Thompson, Arend could manumit himself for a thousand five hundred rix-dollars. Arend built Moffat a house and church at Kuruman. He'd always wanted to be a builder, and single-handed church-building makes up for a whole lot of guilt. He and his children were baptised on 1 May 1829. On that day he was confirmed as Moffat's first convert, and henceforth he would be known not as Arend, but Aaron Joseph. In 1849 he delivers a parcel from Moffat to Doctor focking Livingstone-I-presume at Kolobeng. He told his children how he and Livingstone had debated, discussed the right kind of thatch and the sturdiest rafters. That the man had no clue what he was talking about. Aaron was seen in 1850 in the interior and people apparently hunted with him along the Botletle River in 1851. And then he wanders away from under our reading eyes, might it have pleased his Lord, on a destined day to find rest, aged and contented, his children with him, in any place with mountains and vineyards and shade.

～

One afternoon two days after Arend's departure I walk to the nearest stone wall and hammer my head against the stones until it's bleeding profusely and then keep on hammering and they say I shouted but of that I don't know anything.

4

Rumours of my death are plentiful and some nights I start believing them. Every night when I wake up to piss, my limbs cramp, my toe throbs. But the breath of life persists, albeit gasping.

That damned Sara, old Kemp's favourite convert from our days with Ngqika, apparently nowadays goes around every mission station telling how I wandered among the tribes murdering and came to grief. And read for yourself: When Anderson heard another rumour, that I and my people had been murdered in the Zoutpansberg, he believed it with all that was left of his heart and soul, and wrote about it to everybody who might be interested.

If I'm not dead, I'm a chief. I wake up at Karechuenya, but the world says I'm dead. See, I'm sitting on my backside on the dusty assembly place of the Hurutshe sharing my beloved sweet potatoes. But the world says I'm living with the Bapedi of Blouberg where I'm pals with their chief Sekwati and they call me Kadisha and I rule as supreme chief with bow and arrow. Am I misremembering? Was I there for a while, on the track of dwindling elephant herds or the even more elusive Portuguese? Who knows; how can you keep track if even your name slips out from under you?

What the buggers do get right is that my gunpowder is running out fast and that I, yes *I*, Coenraad de Buys, descendant of the Huguenots, big-game hunter and revolutionary, of late, would you believe it, in an idle hour practise the tensing of a bow and the flight of an arrow. What they also get right is that my name drifts ever further from me, that the rumours of the death of what is called Buys are perhaps not so far-fetched. When last did anybody call me De Buys, when last Coenraad, and forget about Coen. Among the Pedi I am apparently Kadisha. Also here in Karechuenya Buys is a thing of the past; here, too, I have been dubbed a new name: Moro – my greeting to one and all when I brew my coffee in the morning. Morning I say; Moro they say. And go ahead, laugh when you read that *moro* later, after my actual departing of this life, becomes these people's word for coffee beans. A greeting, an echo, a goddam dish of watery coffee.

≈

One of the Hurutshe women is pregnant with yet another little Buys slip of the prick. I have to tread carefully around the toes of all the chiefs. When they request me and my guns, my horses and men, I do not refuse. Diutlwileng and his warriors lead us to the Tholwane River and Lotlhakane where the Malete live. Diutlwileng says they are a thorn in his flesh, this bunch of refractory tributaries. We shoot them and stab them and burn down their settlement. Some say the Malete were hereafter placed under Senosi's forceful control and everything was in order again. Others say the Hurutshe couldn't scatter them. I wouldn't know. I saw people bleeding and huts burning. My gun-powder had run out. I left the place. I didn't start this quarrel and didn't see the end of it either. Merely went and shot out my last munitions on a bunch of strangers. All that I gained from the palaver was another name. Later I would pretend that I didn't care a fig or a fart when I heard that the Malete called me Diphafa. A rich name, this one: it can apparently refer either to the feathers in my hat, or it can mean Great Vats of Beer. I imagine that the sound of a blow against a beer vat sounds like the crack of my rifle or my roaring when I chase up my men. Or, let's be honest: perhaps the slim young warriors had laid eyes on my majestic beer belly.

≈

In October, when spring is blooming and pollinating into summer, I miss my wives and trek back to Thabeng. Arriving there, I find that Maria and Nombini have moved in with Elizabeth. When I come riding up, the three are sitting next to each other on the stoep, each with a pipe in the mouth. They blow rings and mutter and no one gets up when I unsaddle. After a week or three I can no longer endure being in that little house with the three witches. One at a time they

379

are lovely, but together they turn into a three-headed dragon. I whisper into Elizabeth's ear and the following morning she and I and her children are on a wagon and gone. We trek south and arrive at Matloangtloang, the kraal of Moletsane and his Bataung next to the Sand River. Moletsane is ill and summons me immediately. I give him one of Elizabeth's cures. Thanks be to God he recovers; out of gratitude he tries to keep us there. I'm no physician and from that place, too, we move, some distance to the north and west to Lehurutshe, where we are safe and welcome with the Hurutshe. I don't lay eyes on a single elephant. Without tusks there's no gunpowder. In due course we trek back to Sefunelo and Maria and Nombini and the children, all the children, blessed as I damnwell am.

My house in Thabeng is solid and secure and Elizabeth keeps it clean and neat. The vegetable garden cultivated by the women of the Buys nation is lush and fertile. But here I can stay only because and while I have guns. Every gun is worth a hundred warriors, as I persuade every chieftain. But without gunpowder a gun is just a blunt stick.

My Caffres and my Bushmen manage with their assegais and arrows and knobkerries. But my sons and Bastaards and deserters and Hottentots want powder for their guns. The Buys nation is nothing in this country without shooting materials. Every morning my sons and I teach ourselves to shoot with a bow and arrow. We improve, but a blind Bushman is still a better shot than we. Sefunelo must notice that the air is clear of powder fumes these days; he looks the other way when I approach. I get the cattle-herds to count my cattle every night. I could get a wagon going to the frontier farmers to beg gunpowder, but every Christian is nowadays wary of being seen with me. And life here also goes on. There is guarding to be done. There is hunting to be done. There is eating to be done.

One of the Scottish deserters, an uncouth fellow with the name of Buchanan, is on guard duty with me one evening. We sit by the fire and peer into the bushes for hyenas or Heathens. The Scotsman's nose grows in all directions, apparently broke it every weekend in the pubs of Edinburgh.

Fuckin cold out tonight.

We sit. He pours the last powder from his horn and loads his gun.

Shit. I'm out. Fuck. Ye have some powder to spare?

No, I say. Nothing left to spare. But some left to shoot.

I pass him my powder horn.

We should make our own bloody powder.

Something scurries in the undergrowth.

An shoot the shit out of this fuckin country. Make a pile, a fuckin mountain of powder. We just leave it here with a few flints and bugger off, an the fuckin savages can blow each other up. We come back an take what's fuckin left. Shit.

He spits. I let go of the thong I've been whittling.

Buchuman, I ask, where find you the recipe for powder?

Five pounds nitre, one part charcoal. Two fuckin thirds of a part brimstone.

Brimstone? From the Bible?

From fuckin volcanoes.

No volcanoes in this land.

Hot springs too. Same fuckin thing. Wherever the fuckin earth tears an boils an retches.

And where come you on this wisdom?

Our captain was a cunt about the military science shit. Had to learn everything by bloody heart. Had to be able to build a fuckin cannon from scratch. In the field. An with field he meant the fuckin jungle.

You can powder make? I ask.

Buys, I can fuckin powder make. Much as yer bloody black heart craves.

~

When, at the dawning of the day, we start enquiring, Sefunelo's people talk of the waters that steam and heal, less than a week away on horseback. I saddle up after lunch with my sons Piet and Dirk, the four Hartenaars who still have strong horses, Buchanan and his friend Lusk, the other Scottish deserter. We get going, as they indicate, north and east. We ride the horses for all they're worth and don't sleep. On the fifth day we see a cloud of steam rising up from the earth in a boiling morass covered with bulrushes. The mountains are beautiful here, big and blue and all over. We hack away the bulrushes and find the source. The veldt is teeming with animals. It's as if the elephants know we're running out of powder. They taunt us, bathe right in front of our noses. The Scotsmen scratch with their knives at every stone in sight and curse and don't find any sulphur.

The Ndebele Caffres who live here speak a language I don't altogether master. The one walking in front explains that the place's name is something like Boiling-Boiling or The Pot that Boils. They invite us to their kraal for the night. They are friendly and share their beer, a beer such as I've never drunk. Before bedtime fists are flying. At first we fight with each other and the people laugh. Then Lusk ups and punches a Caffre in the face and everything grows quiet. The Caffre gets up and dusts himself and everything grows more quiet. He must be some captain or other, and pride now badly hurt. In our hurry we forgot to bring along an interpreter on this journey. The conversation that ensues is short and nonsensical and we clear out.

We wake up in the veldt with Kortman the Hartenaar shouting that the Caffres are upon us. The leading Caffres are on horseback. Our own horses are exhausted and won't last long ahead of them. We race a mile or four and then I gesture my men up a steep kopje. The hill lies stretched out in the veldt like a dozing lion. We scramble up the hindquarters, between the shoulders and then a steeper incline, through the lush mane of bush up to the sturdy crown.

The Caffres on horseback congregate at the foot of the kopje and wait for the others to catch up. When the entire kraal's men have surrounded the kopje, they start slowly crawling up. Buchanan says Fuck the fuckin savages and lets fly. Piet and Dirk also fire and somebody hits a Caffre and he staggers and falls over backwards and rolls and disappears. The Caffres retreat and remain sitting at the foot of the hill. When night descends on us, they light fires around the kopje, with our single fire on the peak. We sit and laugh about the mess. Even though we don't have enough gunpowder to shoot them away, their immense respect for the wonder-thunder of our fire-shooters keeps them at bay. We laugh and we smoke and we go to bed. The next morning the Caffres are still sitting there. We wander around. A bit further down the ruins of a former city, the red stone walls flattened by the baboons. Iron furnaces. Earthenware shards. Buchanan kicks over the last unbroken grain bin. By afternoon we realise that our water is not going to last long. Evidently the Caffres know this already. On a barren hill so close to the sun it won't be long before we perish of thirst. All they need do is wait for their parching revenge.

By the second day we are no longer laughing. The Caffres are going nowhere. We are not sure how many of them there are. Most of them are sheltering on the lee side of the hill. Between the nine of us there are five leather water bags, not one of them full.

I ration the water. The bags don't move out of my sight. In the mornings, afternoons, evenings and at bedtime I distribute small drinks of water to man and horse. On day four we are still besieged. The Caffres are still quite comfortably settled. Now and again they snarl some snide piece of shit at us in their incomprehensible language. I instruct the men no longer to irrigate the bushes on the hill; henceforth everybody has to piss in the empty water bags. When the bags are full, every single one of us empties his bladder into bowls or any hollow object that we've carted along. No drop of piss is wasted.

On the seventh day we rest like our Father, too tired and dehydrated to stand up straight, sunburnt and worn out. The last drop of water was drunk a day ago and of rain there is no sign. Lusk takes a sip of piss and spits it out and wipes his tongue clean with the flat of his hand.

Dead at fuckin thirty, Buchanan grumbles. Ye must be fucking kiddin. Since the day I crawled out of my ma's pestiferous cunt an killed the bitch I haven't done nothing worth a long warm shit. Nothing.

Lusk slaps the back of his head and sits down next to his expatriate comrade. The mocking Caffres seem rather sick of the game themselves, but we hear from up here how the humiliated bellwether stirs up the crowd.

I stand on a rock face. I look down on the larger part of the besiegers. As if all of creation combines for this single moment, the eighth day breaks all at once. Believe me, a single beam strikes the rock face – this exact rock face – and bathes me in fire. I fill my lungs with air and thunder a roar down upon them. When I have the attention of one and of all, I address them from there in a hotchpotch of Caffre languages. I hope they will understand a word here and there. I shout that I dispose over magic powers. They mock me. I pour a bag full of piss out in an arc in front of me down the depths. They are silent. I shout that I'm making water up here. I shower down another bag of piss. I bellow and bluster that, should they be of the opinion that we beleaguered are running out of water, they can spare themselves the trouble of guarding the hill. We have so much water that we could quench their thirst as well. I toss two more knapsacks down the slopes so that the piss splashes on the rocks down there like fountains, sparkling in the sun – as the people of that area will tell you to this day. The Caffres are silent. Then they run.

≈

I hear you protest, reader: It was Gabriël who poured the last water or bags of piss down the hill. It was my children who were trapped there and it was their clever ploy. It was twenty years after my death. *That* is why Buyskop, Buys' Hill, is called that today, not because of me, but the next generation of Buyses. But hear this: Listen to the talk of the people living there today next to the hot springs. Listen to who *they* say stood on that rock face that day. The hell with the history books. In local lore it was I, Coenraad, who stood there that day thundering at the Caffres, a smelly water sack in my cramping hand.

Any case. Go and wander around on Buyskop. Do you see what remains of the focking English's blockhouse? Follow the dirt road cutting between the stone walls. Among the last traces of primordial stone kraals you'll see the chipped-away rock face. The unfinished blocks of sandstone scattered around. A century after our siege the Christians come to cut the red stones for their Union Buildings. Cart it off in wagons to Pretoria. If you should ever find yourselves at the Union Buildings, sniff at the stones. You may just catch a vague whiff of Buys piss in the walls.

~

Fed-up and hungry we struggle down the kopje, minus one horse. We swill ourselves silly from the fountain at the foot of the hill. Nobody pursues a sorcerer. We travel on without disturbance through the night following rumours of more hot-water springs a day's journey or so along. Just before dawn somebody shoots something; we devour it half raw before setting off again.

The following afternoon we see steam rising up from the hills in front of us. Buchanan kneels on the rocks next to the simmering water. He beckons us nearer. A streak of sulphur surrounds the eyes of the boiling springs. Strange bright yellow flowers growing on stone and smelling of rotten eggs. We scrape off the glittering brimstone with our knives and chop it fine and throw it into the saddlebags and get away from there. We take a wide detour back to Thabeng.

Sefunelo is planning a plundering expedition. He says I and my guns must come along. He says he doesn't look after my wives for free. I say he must wait a few days, we're making the fire for our guns.

Buchanan gathers the Buys nation and says Tonight we're going to look for a cave where bats live. It's Doors and Michiel who find the cave, an hour's walk from the camp. They see a spurt of bats streaming out of an overhanging rock face. Run back to the camp and light the torches to summon everybody back. Buchanan, I and the two children walk to the cave. Buchuman looks around and nods. He stamps his foot hard on the sand floor, places a white stone next to the footprint. If the print is still here tomorrow, he mutters, we have to keep looking. At dusk the following day he walks to the cave and comes back and says the print next to the stone is almost gone. He says that when the tracks disappear so quickly, the soil is rich in saltpetre. The following morning we are standing in the cave and scooping up the floor of the cave and throwing the sand in bags lashed to the pack ox. Above our heads hundreds, thousands of bats are hanging asleep. Now and again one craps on us, but for the rest they take no notice of the shit stealers.

Back at the camp Buchanan instructs a few of my Hottentots to go find the nearest willow and to cut it down. They have to burn it and make charcoal. As finely ground as the charcoal that wily women smear around their eyes, he says. He calls me and Lusk and says:

An now, boys, I'll show you the fuckin alchemy of nitre.

We build a lye pit, which Buchanan calls a hopper: a solid funnel with a trough at the lower end. The two Scotsmen drill holes in the planks and carve wooden pegs, nail the frame together with a wooden hammer. I find a thick log and with a small hatchet chop a deep furrow along the length of the trunk. The V-shaped frame of the funnel is balanced on top of the trough. We pack twigs along the bottom of the funnel vat, and scatter straw on the twigs and along the side planks to seal the pit.

The soil from the bat cave is poured into the lye pit until it's almost full. We empty buckets of water over the soil to leach it of its saltpetre salts, or, as Buchanan refers to it affectionately, the mother liquor.

The mother liquor drips down the sides of the hopper and into the trough. I call a few children and they skim the decoction from the trough into the pots and calabashes and Buchanan says Pour again. They keep on leaching the same liquid through the bat soil, to dissolve all the saltpetre in the shit.

> Captain sayd ye have to keep leaching till the solution's thick
> enough for a fuckin egg to float on.

To one side we stoke a fire of camel thorn. Buchanan says you use
only hardwood for the ash you need here. Once the logs are burnt out,
I leach the ash in a vat. We add the ash decoction to the mother liquor
until there are no more deposits of white curds. Lusk puts the solution
into kettles and makes a fire under them. Buchanan keeps an eye and
adds a dash of oxblood to the boiling mixture. Fragments of whatever
float to the top. The surface of the kettles starts foaming like beer.
While it simmers, Lusk keeps skimming off the foam and flotsam.

By evening Buchanan says it's boiled long enough. I feel intoxicated.
The Scotsmen are grinning too much. I suspect the crazy clouds from
the kettles. I ask Buchanan why they call it mother liquor. He laughs
and grabs my sore shoulder and says Well it shure as shit ain't the milk
from your ol' ma's teets and I say What knows you.

We empty the kettles through cloths. The foam and the bits of solid
matter remain behind on the cloth. As it cools, fine, bitter, needle-
shaped crystals form on the cloth.

> Fuckin nitre, says Buchanan.

We skim off the crystals and lay them out on cloths to bake dry in
tomorrow's sun.

The next morning a crowd gathers to witness the critical mixing.
The ground willow charcoal is spread out on a torn-open bag and next
to it the mound of ground saltpetre crystals. We spread open a blanket.
I help Buchanan add the charcoal to the saltpetre and to mix it. Then
we add the sulphur. We squat and blend the stuff with our fingers,
guarding against too much friction, so as not to be blown sky-high.
Buchanan gets up and dusts his hands and knees over the blanket
and takes off his shirt and breeches. I stand up and retreat from the
mad Scotsman and look at the crowd, my nation and Sefunelo and
his nation.

> My captain said ye piss on it, it airs it out, he sayd. Make it
> stick together like cookie dough, he sayd. Didn't fuckin question

the captain, the man spoke true in all else. An so, Buys, yer piss
be the secret ingredient.
I open my breeches and stand with my pizzle in my hand. I think of
printing presses.

Break the seal, Buys!
Buchuman crawls on all fours in front of me into the pile of precious,
stinking gunpowder meal.

Lusk, bring forth yer staff an piss, my friend!
Lusk is at hand immediately, and his prick has no problem. The torrent
next to me calls forth my own water as well. At our feet Buchanan is
kneading like a demented baker with the piss splashing on him and
the meal turning into dough. He hollers for more. Presently there are
other streams next to ours until the baker shouts For fuck sakes rein
in yer cocks. The filthy black meal stinks like a hell of unmentionables
and overripe eggs.

The crowd is as silent as a single congregation. Buchanan arises
from the dough. He glistens and he stretches himself and every muscle
tenses, with the sun a halo behind him. Then he kneels next to his
brew and watches it drying and every now and again pokes around in
it with his knife. Nobody leaves. When the dough has been baked dry
and become gunpowder, the Scotsman gets up and takes a pinch of it
between his fingers. He walks over to a little fire where a few Caffres
are sitting cooking something and he tosses it into the coals and new
flames explode. He throws his head back and screams something word-
less or Scottish and the congregation gasps for breath; then all rejoice.
Buchanan walks into the crowd and somebody hands him a kaross to
cover his shame. In passing he touches my shoulder.

Thanks be to ye, Buys, I fuckin needed this day.
He disappears into the background, never again to emerge from it.

Bring your horns, men! I shout.
My men file up and hold out their empty horns and receive from us
the life-giving powder, like crazed communicants.

5

All year long Sefunelo has been sitting on his posterior blunting his assegai with looking at it, but as soon as my gun can shoot again, I have to shoot where he aims. We go to plunder the Bakwena on the Harts River, but don't come away with very many cattle. The locusts have already stripped their lands bare. Believe me, the Bakwena round up the ravenous pestilences, pound them fine and then make flour of them. The Bakwena are tall, with hawk-shaped faces. They see us coming from far away. The warriors are hard and hungry and fight like men who have nothing to lose. The people's stone walls collapse. Sefunelo loses his best warriors.

The defeat is of course my fault. When I get home and bash open my head against the door and yank the thing out of the doorframes and decide to move on, I must accept as my portion that I will forfeit my cattle. So that's said and done: once again I possess nothing on this earth. There isn't much that I want to take with me. Accordingly I leave my host, apart from my flocks of almost one-and-a-half thousand, a wagon to temper his temperament. See, another house ablaze. I leave Thabeng behind me. This place that I am leaving, that I totally renounce, perdures absolutely in my absence, absolutely itself.

We trek past people who are spreading themselves wide over the open veldt. They drive game to a vast plain full of pitfalls. Buck and zebras and wildebeest tumble in and disappear and break their bones at the bottom of the pits, where they lie bellowing and waiting for the death blow. We ride past people who build their huts in underground caves to escape the eternal warfare on the surface. We gape at people who live in huts on stilts, since the surface has been usurped by lions and desolation. We trek past the horizon. In March 1820 my family and I are once again settled in the kloofs next to Karechuenya. I introduce the baby born in the meantime and her mother, the young Hurutshe woman from last spring, to the rest of the family. We trek past all sense of family and connections. I am told that Campbell is on his way to subjugate the Hurutshe and their majestic city to the power of quill and ink. I greet the people who have been good to me. I load the Hurutshe woman and the baby into the wagon with us and in April make shallow tracks from there and am gone.

~

Sweet thorn, rooibos, the tallest giraffes these eyes have ever beheld, the spots darker than those in the south; blue wildebeest, red rocks. A black bird-creature that spreads its wings around itself like an umbrella, the deep and bright blue under the wings flashing forth a lure to the fish. Monkeys, red buck, tambotie everywhere. See, a young giraffe with the umbilical cord still dangling like a second, unnatural pizzle. Warthogs. The vulture toying with its food. The sighing and groaning and huffing of hippopotami. Zebras, the fish eagle's plaintive call. Black and brown stones. Whirligig beetles. Long after dark still the copper glow between the undulating kopjes. Even the sun is sometimes scared of following its fate to the bitter end.

~

Makaba, the dreaded warrior chief of the Ngwaketse, invites me and my nation to come and stay with him. He shuttles constantly between Kanye, when peace reigns, and the hills a few miles to the north, when things get heated. The hills are barricaded, like his eyes under his beetling brow, and from there he wages war against the surrounding world. He gathers splinter groups of other tribes like the spoils of war, the Buys nation merely the latest addition to this assembly. He offers his friendship to the Briquas and the Hurutshe, and when they distrust his smile, he attacks them anew and with renewed vigour. He loots women and prisoners of war and these, too, are inducted into the community. When Makaba doesn't seize what he wants, he barters with his neighbours. Tobacco, hides, feathers, ornaments and tools of copper, iron and tin. And ivory, always ivory.

Like everybody else in this desert, the Ngwaketse barter women for cattle and cattle for labour and loyalty. The more cattle and women you have, the richer you are. Once I, too, was rich like he. With Makaba I eat and drink myself to ruination. My gut grows and my muscles shrink. I don't walk around if I don't have to. In these days I have a seizure. The cramps take over, one of these days very soon I'm going to crumple and shrivel up like a dried-up chameleon. I lie down for a few days and when I get up, my left leg is stiff. For a few days my left hand refuses to obey me. Elizabeth swears she won't tell anyone how I struggle in bed.

Buchuman's home-made gunpowder in my horn gives me fresh marrow in my bones. As long as I'm seated in my saddle, nobody can see how stiff my leg is. My sons and I and my army melt bullets and we are at Makaba's side when he goes to plunder the Bakwena and Malete all along the brown waters of the Madikwe.

~

The first shot cracks. See, that one feels with both hands where his lower jaw used to be till a moment ago. We're massacring them; from all sides we descend on them. A first flight of arrows and spears. People fall and lie pinioned to the ground like impaled insects. Then the horse-men charge. See, here right in front of me: blood pours from the nose and ears of the naked Caffre; he rocks on his feet, brandishes his knob-kerrie at the sky and at the flies. Then I am on top of him and over him with four horseshoes. Throats gape; blood vomits from these new laughing mouths. To one side a wounded Caffre is rammed by two warriors and then beaten to a pulp with knobkerries. Lusk and Buchanan anoint a cow with lamp oil and set light to it and drive it shrieking through the straw huts. The cow drops down and lows and her eyes roll and somebody kills her with a cleaver. Son-in-law Jan stands on the edge of the kraal with a few guns. A Hottentot next to him reloads while he takes the weapons from the loader one by one and takes aim and shoots a distant person. Two assegais meet and sheer past each other in Buchanan's belly and he pirouettes and dances for a moment, comically and unconvincingly, before he drops and dies. Shots, smoke; people perish as well as a child or two who get in the way. My horse stumbles and dies under me. I'm on my third gun already and have to reload. I stoop into a hut and sit crouched up in the dusk and ram in the bullet while the woman and her children cower wailing in the corner. I take aim through the door opening and flatten a Caffre and load the other two guns and once again walk out to face the blood-stained daylight.

After everybody who wanted to take issue is dead and the vultures have alighted around us, we round up the women and children and cattle and trek back home. Jan rides next to me, his eyes misted over, his mouth open and empty. He retches. Vomit on the flanks of his horse. He wipes his mouth. Rides on.

> I'm going to the Colony, Father, he says after a few miles. I've spoken to Bettie.
>
> That is in order.
>
> I do not want to take your daughter from you.
>
> You look after Bettie well.
>
> I am glad Father understands.
>
> That is not what I said. You are the one who seems to understand something of all this. That is why you have to get away from here.

The tracker and interpreter is called Vyfdraai. His tongue knows the clicks of many languages. Makana's people say that their grandfathers said that Vyfdraai was sitting in wait for them way back when they arrived at their dwelling place. Even then he was as old as the stones. He has for ever gone without a name. For ever they have called him just Vyfdraai – a kudu bull too headstrong to die. They say his flesh is biltong already and he hasn't bled in years. Vyfdraai shows us where the elephants roam. See, the gigantic bull, the trunk that yaws skyward and the dust that he sprays over himself. Jan is the first one off his horse.

He is mine, Father.

Go get him, I say.

He loads his gun, another one, and walks towards the bull. The bull's ears flap, it lowers its ears and raises its trunk. The trumpeting and then the charge. Jan waits until the elephant is right in front of him, fires at the centre of the forehead, hits; the bull retreats. He seizes the other gun, fires again. The elephant crashes to the ground, the front legs crumple first, the head hits the ground. The animal grazes the ground dying and breaks branches and uproots a tree and comes to rest by Jan's feet. A few men clap hands and applaud him. Jan ignores us, drops his gun and walks to his horse, takes out a hatchet and walks back to the carcase. He hacks at the left tusk without a word. We watch him, we let him be. He chops off the tusk. Now he starts hacking away at the hind foot. He starts weeping and when he gapes open his mouth threads of snot and drool web his lips. Vyfdraai takes the hatchet from his hand and starts hacking further at the foot. We escape the perturbation and lend a hand with chopping up the elephant. Like proud new fathers or hairy and terrible midwives with bloody forearms and with the fat still on our fingers we load the tusks and feet onto the wagon and leave the rest of the elephant to the creatures of the veldt.

~

I wash the slaughter off me and walk to Bettie's tent. I perch my daughter on the horse in front of me as of old and we ride into the wilderness. We sit down by a broad and quiet stretch of river. See how the fish eagle cleaves the water and with a fish in its talons soars up again. It's only on sitting down that I realise how tired I am. There isn't much to say. I ruffle her hair, that beloved red bush that charmed the entire interior. I kiss her on her forehead and tell her I'll miss her. That if one day I return to the Colony I'll teach my grandsons to hunt. She says that's Jan's job. I say I'll teach my granddaughters the names of the wild flowers. She says that what I taught her, she'll teach her daughters in turn. I ask her what then remains for me to come and do. She says I must come and take off my shoes on her stoep and soak my feet in warm water and gaze across the yard and tell her all the tall tales of my exploits. I ask what shoes. She says I must come and lie and brag as old men do and fart in company.

What is that tree? I ask her.

Tambotie. Everybody knows that, my little father.

And that one?

Knobthorn.

I have no more to teach you, my child.

One day you must teach me how to say good bye.

The trick is not to make any promises.

She hugs me and cries a bit and then I lead the horse with her on its back to the camp. I make sure that my daughter has a proper seat on a horse before I let her go. She sits in the middle of the saddle. Stirrups on the ball of her foot, heels down, knees in. Reins light in the hands, as if she's holding two chicks.

Maria cries when she hears the news. That night I lie up close to my wife. We tell each other stories about Bettie. We make sure that we remember each anecdote in the same way, so that our child can become a proper story.

A day or so later Bettie and Jan's wagon is loaded. Why do I think of that pestilential schoolmaster when I see the two children riding off? I wonder if Jan and my Bettie will find the peace they long for in the Colony. I wonder how that goddam master achieved his calm, how his equanimity can make him so strong. Strong enough to shut the door in the countenance of Coenraad de Buys. Have never come across the prick again, but I'm sure you'll never find Markus Whatsisname chopping up an elephant all a-blubber. To the devil with him. Be damned and be gone, all schoolmasters! There goes my daughter, riding away from me for ever, back to the country of stoeps and old men. I kick the nearest stone and curse my toe that shoots a pain all the way to just this side of my damned knee.

∼

I'm on my way from the cattle when I hear Michiel shouting by the stream. The boys are playing at clay-stick. Two armies on opposite banks, smeared with the same clay clustered in lumps at the end of their sticks. My son jumps yelling from behind a bush and hits Segotshane – one of Makaba's little bullocks – square in the chest.

> Buys, your clay is full of stones! the Caffre prince shouts in his language.

> Get gone, dog-dick! Michiel fires back in Dutch.

He and Segotshane are nowadays off in the veldt all day and get back to the kraal in the evening with sly smiles and skinned knees and keel over on the nearest kaross. He presses a handful of stones into the ball of clay, and with a resounding Begone, you utter goddam villain! his willow cane shoots the clay bullet with enough force to draw Segotshane's noble blood. The other little Caffres gather in no time. Stones and clay and spit spatter and scatter all over. I grab Michiel by the scruff of his neck and drag him to one side.

> You mother is going to wash that gob of yours with soap tonight.
> Yes, Father.
> What is your battle plan?
> Father?
> How are you going to bugger up the other side? I ask.
> We just pelt each other, Father.
> No, dammit, man. Come, get those blackies together so that I can tell you about battle tactics.
> Father?
> The science of strategy.
> Yes, Father.

The little chaps stand listening, heads bent. They scrabble their sticks in the sand. I hear the mumbling. Michiel blushes, pretends the nearest tuft of grass is demanding his total attention. I instruct the children in strategy.

> You have to charge out from *those* and *those* bushes, I say. Do

you see that bit of sandy soil where the stream is shallow? If you can occupy that terrain, you have a crossing to the other side, you can surround the attackers, trap them against their own screens.

The little bantams stand counting their toes. The gang on the other side yell and jeer at us. One of the cheeky snot-nosed Heathens shouts something about my paunch. I grab Michiel's stick from his hand, press a piece of clay around the point, and switch the little mocking monkey between the eyes.

The meeting scatters, the war now once again at full pitch. My men find the crossing I told them about, but so do the enemy. The lines clash and mingle and soon it's a free-for-all. Ten-year-old fists fly and the sticks are now just sticks. If there is any throwing, it's with stones. My toe is playing up again today; the hands are also not that wonderful at aiming the stick. I alone have to play by the rules. I can damnwell not pummel and pepper the children as they're doing to each other. To them I'm just as much a part of the battle and perhaps the only adversary – the white man, the fat man, the old man. I trip, the damp clay sags under me.

The first one is on top of me and then the next. I'm lying under a heap of wriggling and squealing boy children who fell me like an exhausted elephant. They scramble over me, tug at my hair and beard and then tackle each other. My Midge is in between somewhere, now and again I spot a familiar arm or a pair of green eyes. My last linen shirt tears. Somewhere under the children I stop wriggling. I lie back in the river clay, close my eyes. Never have I heard Midge laugh like that. Never ever have I played like that with my own brood. It's not too unpleasant.

~

Makaba says Stockenström and Campbell are poking about, sniffing the air for any smelly rumours about him blowing about. I am paramount chief here, he says and spreads his arms and sticks out his belly:

They are welcome to pay me obeisance, but they dare not send me messages as to how I should lead my people. We dispatch two messengers, one of his men and one of mine. They tell Campbell Makaba invited me to stay with him in exchange for two or three herds of cattle, but when I turned up here, he gave me only thirty head of cattle. So I was supposedly highly upset and did not want to accept the measly number of cows. Makaba sends me two oxen to slaughter. According to the customs of the Ngwaketse these sacrificial animals say that I am his prisoner. Every time I want to escape from his trap, two more slaughter oxen arrive, saying Not so fast. Campbell swallows the story like Stellenbosch sweetmeats. So that when the messengers invite him cordially to visit Makaba, he stays well away, scared that he also will be detained here against his divinely established will.

Behold, I neither slumber nor sleep. There are noises in the night. If I as much as put my nose out of the tent, I always and everywhere carry at least three guns with me. I have taught Elizabeth to load them. If the attack comes, I need only fire while she reloads. For what it's worth: This anxiety and sleeplessness story is all true and real and I make sure that the men convey it as it is to Campbell. Instead of the message conjuring me up in his mind's eye as an unpredictable and terrifying bogeyman, it moves the bloody dodderer to pity me. Apparently he enquires with great concern about the extent of my fear and misery. When they tell me this, I feel as if every vein in my body is going to explode. I am not miserable! I want to shout at the shit-slobbering minister across the vastness. I am not afeard: I am able-bodied!

Apparently Stockenström also spoke of wanting to set eyes on me. There was even talk of a pardon if I could provide him with useful information regarding the interior. A pardon for a road map, provided that recent malfeasances have not proved me unworthy of his mercy. Begone, viperous wretch! The bugger never got hold of me. So sorry to disappoint him.

I'm living quite comfortably with Makaba. With all our looting I'm building up a respectable herd again, but my army is dwindling. The pox-afflicted cowards desert me, at first one by one, then in droves. I'm under the thumb of Makaba with little more power than one of his captains. My men want to get rich. They want to trade ivory with lazy frontier farmers, not blast away their precious gunpowder for a Caffre chief's empire. Anyway. You take what you can, while you can.

See: This is October 1820 and I'm on the back of my last horse, a large stallion of burnished copper. Along with Diutlwileng's Hurutshe my people and I rustle the cattle of the Ngwaketse and I shoot out my most precious gunpowder on the cattle-herds and warriors of my recent ally, my comrade, the dreaded Makaba.

Another friend betrayed, another wagon laden and away we go, back to Lehurutshe, and here I want to stay. We lay out farmlands, we extract water, we sow what there is to sow. The horses have all died by now.

One morning, hardly a month after we've finished sowing, two of my dogs lie impaled in my kraal. The Hurutshe Caffres who greet me amiably during the day steal my cattle the moment the sun sets. The dogs fend off the thieves with their lives night after night. Soon I've had enough of this. One fine night I have the dogs tied up. Doors and Doris are on guard in the kraal. I give them one of my last powder horns. Doors is ten and Doris has just turned seven. It's not long before they spot some bodies in the bushes. Two Caffres climb into the kraal. Doors knows pretty well by now how to wield a gun and he rounds up the two chancers. The others disappear into the night. We unleash the dogs and they charge after the others. I push one of the Caffres up against the branches of the kraal. I ask why they want to take my cattle. He says the command comes from the captain. He's heard that I want to trek to the Bakwena. I curse the Caffre onto his knees and Doris is at hand promptly to keep him there. Doors keeps the other one quiet with a gun to his head.

Doris, today is your day, my son, I say.

Father.

Shoot the bastard.

I keep my gun trained on the kneeling Caffre while my son gets the better of his shakes. Doris rests his gun securely against the Caffre's forehead.

Shoot, child, don't think.

Father.

The Caffre is crying and Doris is crying and Doors also starts sobbing and I ask the Caffre if he's telling the truth and he says yes.

Shoot, I say.

Doris gapes at me open-mouthed; I shove him.

Goddam, child, have you no ears?

The gun kicks in my son's hands and the top of the Caffre's head splatters against the kraal wall. Doris' face is spattered with blood. I chase the other Caffre back to the captain with the message:

On this day I'm trekking, you god-cursed villain. If you're
planning to do anything to me, you'd better come now.

We haven't yet done inspanning, when we see them seething down the hills like ants. We fasten the last yokes securely while the Caffres surround us. The oxen mill around between the wagons and the Buys clan. There's no space to move or think. The Caffres move in upon us, the noose starts tightening. I ask through my interpreter what they want. They remain silent and come closer. I ask them who they think bears the guilt for the blood that flowed last night. They remain silent. The interpreter, a nervous creature with a big mouth and little limp arms, flings his assegai into the ruck. He hasn't properly recovered his footing after the throw when he has a Hurutshe assegai in his shoulder. I drag him into the wagon and pluck out the thing and tell the daughters to minister to him with Elizabeth's concoctions. I take up all three of my guns and climb out of the wagon and walk in among them and start firing and around me I think I hear other shots ringing out and when I come to my senses, ten Caffres are lying dead and the others are in full flight and I chuck away the empty powder horn and we finish the inspanning and I crack the whip.

∾

The following evening we arrive at Kolobeng and the Bakwena of paramount chief Motswasele. Only some ten Hartenaar Bastaards and runaway slaves are still trekking with me. The rest of the company is connected to me by bonds of bastardised Buys blood.

The kraal is just about deserted. An old man says the people are out trapping game. My sons and I walk into the veldt to introduce ourselves. Just outside the kraal we find the Caffres walking in a huge circle as far as the eye can see. The Caffres furthest from the kraal come closer and closer. The animals tire themselves out running hither and thither. Even the women and children walk up to the exhausted animals and beat them to death.

A few days after we encamped at Kolobeng, Vyfdraai peeks into my wagon tent. I ask him where he's come from, how he knew to find us here. He says he's going to unroll his sleeping mat under the wagon if it pleases me. With him you don't ask questions.

We eat the Bakwena's melon and millet. My red dogs laugh like hyenas in the night. One or two come to scavenge food when the camp is dozing in the afternoon. We sleep behind the six-foot stone walls of the Bakwena. I remember stories that these stone workers are the descendants of the people who built the palaces of Solomon's concubine, the Queen of Sheba. The queen of Africa who spread her legs for the king of Israel; the wise king who carted off her treasures in royal caravans so that his buttocks could recline on ivory and his lips could sip the table wine from golden goblets. Of gold and ivory and Biblical riches not much remains, but their melons are sweet as honey. And they don't mess with my goddam cattle.

∾

Today, I tell my people, we're hunting for a new pair of breeches for me.

Last week I was watching a clump of grass quivering by my feet and then being sucked into the ground. Vyfdraai is in attendance, ancient and sturdy as a baobab. He says it's a mole rat. I say I don't know such creatures. He jabs his assegai into the ground, a foot or so from where the grass disappeared into the earth. He digs around the planted assegai until he's opened up the tunnel. I come closer. The tunnel is not deep, four or five inches, but wide, more than twenty-five inches in diameter, if I had to guess. Vyfdraai says he has seen tunnels more than half a mile long. At the tip of the assegai sprawls the thing. More rat than mole, if you were to ask me. Almost eight inches long, short sturdy legs, a tiny tail of not more than an inch. Vyfdraai yanks the mole rat off the blade and places it in my palm. About ten ounces. The fur is thick and short and soft. Almost as black as the tunnel. On the back of the head is a snow-white spot, hence the Dutch name of *bles mol*, bald mole, I guess. A repulsive little monster, but its fur is softer than any hide I've ever handled. As with other moles, this rattish beast has no ears. Little blue eyes peer unseeing from under heavy eyelids. Vyfdraai sticks his finger into the mouth and shows me the big incisors with which the mole rat tunnels. Behind the teeth are flaps of flesh like lips. My informant tells me it's so that the soil shouldn't spill down its gullet when it's tunnelling.

That night I lie awake dreaming up a pair of breeches of soft black fur with white spots. I can feel in advance how it drapes my legs, how gently the saddle bumps my furred backside. When I get Vyfdraai on his own again, I ask him how one could get hold of a whole lot of the mole rats. He says they live in colonies, he says easily forty to a nest. He says the nest isn't just there for the taking, it's eight feet under-ground. You have to catch them when they're active, when they're tunnelling after the rains.

When I saw the thunderstorm starting to gather this morning, I knew my breeches were lying in wait for me buried deep, there where the grass disappears into the earth.

Today, I tell my people, we're hunting for a new pair of breeches for me.

The rain sets in, great drops thud on the sand like fists. Every man and his mate find a stick or spade or axe handle or any blunt object that can hit hard, and follow me to the moles. I spread a tarpaulin in the rain and make a fire under it for the firebrands later. See, we're a bunch of twenty or so armed men and women standing and staring at the ground.

The tunnelling starts. Molehills spring up, grasses and flowers sink away. There's no end to the rain. I curse, but Vyfdraai says it's a good thing, these rains. He burrows open a molehill. The waters of the heavens quickly flood the tunnels, the deluge drives the first mole rat to the surface. Vyfdraai clobbers it with his knobkerrie. We follow his example. Dig open the heaps, let in the flood, wallop a fleeing mole or two. Vyfdraai tosses the mole rat at my feet.

We must find the queen, he says.

Queen?

Vyfdraai says in the depths of the mole rat nest there are only one male and one female who mate, the others are celibate workers. If the queen falls, then the whole colony scatters.

What is a home without a mother? I ask.

He says when the whole lot disperse like that over the open ground, then every eagle and jackal in existence appears, and most of the little beasts are devoured. As soon as the queen cops it, they're all buggered. It's not for nothing they live underground. Above ground the creatures have never had a chance. I think of my jackal's lair in Shit-skull Senekal's yard. I smell once more the snugness, being cherished in the belly of the earth.

Vyfdraai and I kick open mole hills, jab sticks into the ground to find the tunnels and follow the tunnels to where they converge in one spot. I hand out firebrands and on all sides my people start smoking out and finishing off the vermin. We dig down to the shallowest tunnel and ram in the firebrands. I daydream about the smoke surging through the tunnels, ever deeper, into the store rooms, over the little ones lying asleep, all the way into the throne room. The mole rats swarm out, hordes of the creatures.

There's the bitch! Vyfdraai shouts.

He scurries after a little fat one, clearly pregnant and clumsier than her slaves. Never thought such an old goat could still streak. He slips in the mud, gets hold of her and flattens her with his knobkerrie. It's a massacre. Around me the yells and blows as we all exuberantly squash the forty or fifty, the goddam army, of mole rats.

With our bloodthirst quenched, we start gathering and skinning the moles. The skins are thrown on one heap, the carcases on another – a heap of crumpled fingers of giants, with teeth. When the sun starts setting, we make a mole rat casserole. The meat is fairly edible. You have to cook it for a long time and add some of Elizabeth's leaves.

My wives and daughters bray the skins and prepare them, and it's not a week or see, my new mole-rat-skin breeches. I put them on and strut around in them and wait for their reactions. Nombini and Elizabeth don't say much. Toktokkie and Aletta think it's lovely. Maria laughs herself off her feet and has to sit down.

My good Lord, Buys. You're getting to be more of a clown by the day. Look at your tomato nose and the spotted breeches.

Ai, my husband.

She gets up and hugs me and kisses my cheek and walks off grinning. I stand a polished dish against a wagon wheel and inspect myself from my belt down to my feet. To the devil with you all.

∽

Here I stay and from morning to evening my sons and I practise until we've mastered the bow and arrow. I cut arrows until I have two quivers full, grease a few bowstrings well with fat. My moleskin breeches are already balding on my backside from all the sitting around, but they still keep the contents inside and warm. The rest of my wardrobe is karosses and thongs and raw hides. Buys, the Esau of Africa, attired in the skins of many creatures.

My hands cramp me awake. I tie up a few karosses in a bundle, take two bows, the two quivers of arrows, the extra strings and tie the whole lot to a pack ox. I hug Maria and Elizabeth and a few of my children and kiss one or two here and there. Elizabeth gives me a tied-up parcel with biltong and herbs for the rheumatism. Maria sighs and mumbles something and Nombini is nowhere to be seen.

I get onto the ox and head north by east and go in search of the country of the Ngwato.

My body aches too much to sleep and every day I ride for as long as the ox responds to the quirt. Alone on this endless plain a man thinks too much. Your thoughts wander far afield and return and then start chasing their own tails. I sniff at my hide attire. My sweat regenerates the sweat and blood of the previous owners of the hides. Am I my skin or do I have my skin?

In the long nights my red dogs howl around me. I catch sight of them every now and again. They keep their distance, wary in the wake of this hairy thing that looks like Buys, but smells like an uncouth concoction of creatures.

Next to my little fire I look at the stars, I look at the black bushes in front of me, I think back a long way. As soon as I try to think ahead, it's just the flames and the bushes. I must go further, forward, to the horizon. But the horizon remains the border. There is no ultimate haven to look forward to. After every horizon another arises from the plains. Three days later I no longer think of anything. I hear my breath, I feel the belly of the ox beneath me rumbling, I smell the sand the hooves dislodge. The white sky and the anthills under trees. When of an afternoon the ox tires, I don't walk on. My bare paws are not callused enough for this seething sand. I taste the melon and the last tobacco. See, I poke my prick into the moist and warm nostril of the ox.

After eight days, not far from the Tswapong hills, I find the Ngwato and their kraal. I get back onto the goddam ox and ride back ten days to Kolobeng and fetch my people and load the wagon and trek north and east back to the Ngwato.

A day's journey from our new hosts the wagon wheel breaks, smashed to accursed smithereens. We drag brushwood in under the wagon and haul the ramshackle thing until the people spot us and help us along the last stretch to their huts. As we trek with the broken-wheeled wagon and the Heathens pushing and pulling and pothering at the overladen waddling house, the whole contraption breaks up more and more until towards the end of July 1821 we limp in between the fires of the Ngwato with a heap of firewood and splinters on two wheels and Chief Kgari comes to meet us laughing and shaking his head.

I want to get to the Portuguese, to Inhambane, to the land of linen and gunpowder, but with this wagon we're going nowhere. The women like it here and complain when I talk of trekking on. While my sons and I try to fix the wagon, I tell the Hartenaars to devise a house in the meantime. Wattle-and-daub houses are no more than square huts and the Ngwato don't take much notice of the building activity, but a house on wheels remains an oddity for them all. For the first week or three we work on the wagon every day. The thing has to be rebuilt from scratch. After a month we get to the wreckage hardly once a week. When we hammer away at the wagon there's always a crowd of curious lookers-on. Sometimes they're already sitting waiting for us around the wagon wreck when we come walking up with our hammers and saws.

The Ngwato call me Kgowe, the first mohibidu, red man, they lay eyes on. Vyfdraai says Kgowe means To peel with a knife. My skin is sunburnt and sore, yes, I'll grant them that. Where the hides don't reach it does indeed look like flayed flesh. I have been stripped of skin and name. No longer white, red. No longer Coenraad, Kgowe. Whoever I am, I am at home here. For a month or so, I totally forget to rebuild the wagon. But still I want to get away, out, further. Inhambane I call my distant horizon. *That* far, I know by now, I'm not going to make it. But if you want to drag a whole lot of people with you into oblivion, you'd better give the nothingness a name for them to cling to.

I go hunting and overnight at a Birwa kraal. I lie with a young woman who carries on as I've never seen before. I let her do her thing for as long as I can hold out, which isn't long. The next morning I can hardly get back into the saddle and she waves me good bye and her people stand staring at me sourly and silently until I've vanished over the ridge.

My sons start itching to trek. We hammer away at the wagon with renewed vigour until it's standing on its own four wheels. Everything that needs to turn we lubricate with all the fat and all the oil we can find. A month later an old Caffre and the young woman and a few assegais come to visit us. The old man is her father and wants cattle from me because his daughter is pregnant. He is sent on his way with three heads of cattle and the daughter cries with joy and hugs me and I shove her away and go and pitch another damn tent.

Elizabeth is also pregnant again and full of nonsense. When she says she's feeling flu-ish I go off to find something for my hands to do rather than listen to the whingeing. She says her head and throat are sore. Maria says Elizabeth is feverish, she must lie down flat. I leave her in the cool house to feel sorry for herself. In the blazing sun I go and make the last adjustments to the wagon.

A day later she can't get up at all. She says she feels every muscle in her body because every one has a different kind of pain. She starts puking and shitting. The sorcerer says she has the yellow fever. I sit with her through the night and try to cool her with wet cloths. Nombini and Maria take over when I drop off to sleep. We keep her moist, but she gets hotter and hotter. What is water and what is sweat we can no longer tell. Her body is like fire in my arms and then she starts shaking with cold shivers. My wife turns yellow. I am red and she is yellow and never are we the same.

The sun is hardly up, or the wagon is loaded with Elizabeth in the back, wrapped under the softest hides and karosses. She is delirious and talks nonsense and cries and sleeps and dreams. I go to say good bye to Kgari and we hug each other and he wishes me strength. He says Come back when your wife is hale again and your son has been born and may it be a son. I say Till we meet again and here are some cattle for your trouble. I go to find Vyfdraai to tell him we're on our way. He is nowhere to be found. Realise only then that I haven't seen him for days. The immortal kudu has already found his own way.

The young Birwa woman comes to the wagon to say something and I don't understand a word of it. I think she's saying that the child's name will be Mmegale, but what do I know and what do I care. I shout senseless nothings from the wagon that the waving people hear as farewells and we ride into the rising sun.

~

My Omni-head spins when I read how the missionary Wheels Willoughby is later to allege that I died of the yellow fever in the Tswapong hills. You should see those hills. It's a piece of Eden in the midst of this wilderness. East of Palapye the world rears up, forty miles by ten. More than a thousand feet above the plains the lushness luxuri-ates. The mountain range is wise and silent with antiquity. They say it's been standing like that since the Creation. The hills fold and frown with the deep and rich countenance of sandstone, quartz and iron.

I can see how my wife and I, overwhelmed with the feverish yellow and hallucination, help each other off old Glider at the foot of the hills. We fold back the dripping branches, step into the forest, clinging together to keep each other upright. I see how we're too hot for clothes. Alone and forlorn we strip each other of our last rags. Our feet in the crevices step on the cold shards of vanished people. See how in the dusk we scrabble open antique foundries. We stoke a smoky fire with the wet branches of the trees above us. She speaks in hushed tones to her hallucinations; I snarl listless insults at mine. Fragments of copper melt anew and form rivulets among the coals. Sputtering sparks shoot

up. The red-ochre drawing on the overhang lights up and cools
down and vanishes. We no longer speak. We share a fever dream with
resigned smiles and tears, eruptions of laughter and rolling around in
the damp grass. Branches break in the thickets as buck take fright at
our exuberance. A leopard calls comfortingly from its tree. In the morning we are weaker and the world hazy and who knows whether we are
really seeing the parrots. Their green bellies and the yellow markings
on the wings and foreheads against the lead-grey bodies. I hold my
wife's hair as she vomits against a tree. I wipe her mouth and give her
water from a stream and kiss her long until overtaken by dizziness.
We wake in the late afternoon with the butterflies around us. She grinds
her teeth as they touch down upon her. I chase away the riot of colour
from her. On the forest floor around us the wandering shadow of the
spread wings of storks. We taste the waterfall on our lips before we
see it. I sink down and she pulls me up. When the green curtains open,
we shower together for a last time. Dassies lie in the splashes of sun
on the stones. I hold my wife tight while she murmurs nonsense and
hearing and seeing fade out. I wake up next to the lagoon. She is dead
in my arms and cold as water, her eyes distant and clear as the river
stones. The frogs are deafening, then suddenly silent. I do not get up
again. The green closes in around me. My body becomes heavy and
somewhere I hear a black eagle call. My mouth for a last time on her
unanswering lips.

Those green hills are not granted to me. I lash the oxen to bleeding,
but faster than their fastest they cannot go. Here behind me in the
wagon my wife shudders with cold in the sweltering summer. Too weak
to chase off the flies caking around her encrusted mouth. Next to her
Maria and Nombini have fallen asleep. So many nights of caring and
waking. How far away could the Portuguese be with their miraculous
medicine? Arend said they were barely two days away from where
he and Coenraad Wilhelm had to turn around. We should have been
there by now. Where and when does this accursed continent end?
Where are the boats and the breakers beyond all this dust? I must go

on, forward through the red sand and thorn trees, to the trackless Portuguese, or at least the river. Any godforsaken puddle in which to bathe my wife.

6

The Limpopo flows wide; the hippopotami yawn. The crocodiles snap at one another with listless violence. We trek for five days along the bank and try to keep Elizabeth cool and to break the fever. She has a miscarriage. The wagon is covered in blood. I scrub the planks clean. I find clots of what could have been my child. Life drains from her through her womb. She is no longer yellow, but grey. Her scream freezes the blood of everyone except her own and then she is dead.

$\sim$

In the midst of the night noises of the veldt I lie on my back and look at the stars. I must have slept, because I wake up. All of creation staggers before the sun that scorches over the world. When I reach the camp Nombini offers me a bowl of water. I must have drunk it, because suddenly it is empty. I call the boys. We cover her, tamp down the soil, haul river stones and pile them on top of her.

How long have we been sitting here on our arses? Days? Weeks? The veldt is flat, the soil is red, the grass yellow, the bushes green, the trees bear thorns, the horizon is white, the sky blue and deep and so godfor-etcetera. Strange nests like plaited yellow whirlwinds hang from the branches. Thump the tree and you hear the Babel of twittering from the dark tunnels, but the residents never appear. Anthills clamber up the trunks. Nombini. Cracked clay of a watering hole. Maria. Children, all the children. Baobabs quiet as palaces. Eland. Buffalo. Snores. Herds. Stampedes. At dusk the distance flames up. I imagine mountains in the mist.

$\sim$

My people are asleep. I'm sitting on my own, stoke all the fires in the camp with new wood. I sit. The six fires surrounding me flare up high, the camp as bright as day. Above me the black velvet night, the white holes in the canvas flicker like stars. The undergrowth creaks. Then:

410

a herd of eland charge through the camp, in between the fires, the sweat on their flanks, every fold and muscle illuminated. The sacred antelopes in the daylight here with me with above us the pitch-black night, as if they sheer outside time and season and reason and between worlds and through all reality and dream. Behind me the undergrowth creaks again to admit the eland.

~

On a morning like all the others Maria shakes me awake in the wagon. She wants to know what's the story with Nombini and me.

　　How should I know, I say. Is she haranguing me again where
　　I can't hear?
Maria says Nombini disappeared in the night. Maria says she woke up to the sound of crying when Nombini said good bye to her children. Then she was off with a little bundle of food under her arm. I ask why Maria did not stop her. She says I know very well there's no arguing with that Caffre woman:

　　You try to stop her once she's got an idea into that head of stone.
Maria says Nombini mumbled something about a godalmighty nest she wanted to go and build, that she wanted to climb trees before her toes are blunt with walking. I fall back onto my bed. At the back of my head something rattles like a bead somebody is spinning at the bottom of a porcelain dish. I lie and wait till Maria takes umbrage and stalks out.

~

The ants march in a line to the grubs, pick them up and haul them to the shoulder-high anthill here next to me. I carefully pick up an ant, put it down some distance from its comrades. It scurries back at once to the file and falls in. I bend over to pick up another ant: my breeches tear. The arse-end of my mole-rat breeches in tatters. My beloved breeches, you stinking scoundrel! Oh godless traitor! I tear off the breeches and leave them to the ants to drag into their

subterranean kingdom. To the devil also with breeches. I walk back
to the camp to devise a loincloth for the ridiculous and crumpled bell
clappering between my legs.

When the next morning I wander into the veldt with my bow and
arrows and a kaross around my shoulders, hat on the head and a buckskin around my hips, Maria and the children grin at Buys the Bushman.

You must hope and pray you don't bump into your pals today!

Maria shouts after me. They'll sell you to the nearest farmer!
I walk on, too angry to shout back. The sun scorches my lily-white
legs. It's only later that afternoon when I'm doing battle with a thorn
in my ankle that I realise how long it's been since I've thought of shoes.
Then I think of Kemp, of spotted breeches and mad maps. And I wonder
how the nest is progressing of the woman who never was mine.

~

A day, a week later. I walk to the wagon. Whence the headache? For
months now not a drop of liquor over my lips. Something smells of
burnt feathers. My heart thumps my chest to pieces. The world reels.
I stand still, hands on knees. Puke. My legs give way under me. I try
to get up. I fall and have a fit. An outcry:

What in godsname, Buys?
Somebody slaps me. An eye flutters, opens. Maria offers me water.
The water tastes wrong; it spills on me. I bite my tongue and it bleeds.

~

They stand around me. Mealtime before the wagon. Baba touches
my face.

Why did Father's face droop like that? Is his face going to
drop off, Aunt Maria?

Let be, child, says Maria. Come on, stop it.
Baba wipes the snot off his lip, sits down to one side.

Can you feel if I touch here? Maria asks. Lift up your arms,
Buys.

412

I lift them above my head. I keep them there. The left arm floats down, even though it feels as if I'm keeping it up. Maria makes me sit up. A big plate of food in front of me.

Come, eat, you're sick with sadness.

I'm hungry; the food drops into my lap. The left hand doesn't want to function.

What are you saying? Speak properly.

She feeds me. Swallow, dammit, swallow. Around me the chattering of children. My understanding slips in and out.

Shh, now. Chew. There you go. Swallow.

She wipes my mouth. She pulls the bespattered kaross over my head. The left arm gets stuck in the hide. She jerks. It tears. She cries. She's gone. The children prattle. She's back, plonks down a mirror in front of me.

There, see. See what you look like now.

A face lies before me on the table. Dirty beard. Red and grey. The skin red and peeling. The left side sags down, the mouth gapes open to the left. The left eye half shut, the eye looks the other way. I smile. The mirror smiles on the right side, on the left everything droops undisturbed, a string of drool hovers in the beard.

～

They don't leave me in peace. If I get up, there's a child or a thing under my slack-side armpit to support me. Windvogel the younger gives me a baobab crutch. Beautifully carved and oiled, but goddammit! Are you wishing me dead now, bugger, I berate him. He understands not a word I say and hugs me and says it's a pleasure. God damned in every blessed heaven! At mealtimes it's a great entertainment for every-body to feed me. At night Maria lies curled up under my armpit – such a thing hasn't happened in years and years. She snores. I sit more than I lie. The swallowing doesn't work when I'm lying flat.

They wash me, even though I'm not dirty; they cart me around, even though I'm perfectly at home where I am. If I object, they pretend not to understand. If I hit out at them, they think I'm having a fit. Then the bunch of them *really* pity me.

~

Wake up one morning with the wagon shaking under me. I struggle upright and peer out of the tent flap. Maria is sitting on the wagon chest cursing the oxen on their way. She stops the wagon when she sees I'm trying to shift in beside her. When she's satisfied that I'm securely settled, she cracks the whip again. A fly settles on my cheek. The wagon stops on a rise. You can see far in every direction. With the help of Jan, the wagon leader, she gets me off the wagon and sits me down on a flat rock.

> I've been mucking along behind you for a lifetime, Buys. And you just can't sit still and stay there. I get old and grey and all that I could hope for all these years was to sit with you. To sit and look at the world.

She settles herself next to me.

> Now you will sit on your arse. So keep your trap shut for a change, then we look to see the end of the bloody road.
> No end, I say.
> What?

I practise the word with my tongue before I speak. I speak slowly, take my time with every sound until it's lined up right to climb onto the breath from my lungs.

> No end. Never ends. Always another.
> Lordgod, Buys.

She slaps my shoulder. We sit peering into the distance: trees, bushes, anthills. The yellow grass.

> You'd better not leave me with the children of your lost Caffre women. I've walked after you too far. So don't go and commit some godimbecile stupidity now.

I say something. When it's emerged from my lips, it's incomprehensible to both of us.

We sit for a long time, now and again she starts saying something, then has second thoughts. Eventually:

> But if you . . . Oh, Lord, *when* you decide you want to go and muck in somewhere again, for sweetheavensake just take this along.

A leather pouch has found its way into my lap. It looks vaguely familiar. I fiddle with the thong with my right hand, don't manage to open it. She takes it from me and unlaces it. I peek into the pouch with my good eye. Kemp's lead letters that I stole when he pushed off. Never had the heart to melt the stuff for munitions as I'd intended. Left it somewhere and forgot about it. For all these years she's been keeping it.

> And you're going to need this as well, you old bandit.

From a fold of her dress she conjures up a powder horn, places it in my hand. It's chock-full of gunpowder.

> Thought I'd hide the last bit of powder until it became really necessary.

She is silent, then smiles:

> Thought that way I'd at least be saving the lives of a few poor Caffres and elephants.

She starts laughing at herself, stops instantly and puts her hand on the horn that is still clutched in my hand. We sit peering ahead of us.

> My speech is spoken, she says.

I don't know what to say. We sit staring across the plains for a while. Then she gets up, dusts her backside.

> Well, then, up you get. That crowd of Buyses must be dying of hunger by now.

~

The next day I indicate to the boys to stoke me a fire. I hold out the pouch of Kemp's letters to Baba and make him understand that he has to start melting so long. I drag my good-for-nothing foot to the wagon.

Rummage in the chests looking for my bullet moulds. Back at the fire Baba is nowhere to be seen. He's chucked the letters into a pot, stood the pot in the flames and cleared out. Goddammit, I should have thrashed the little shit more often when my hands still could. I make sure my lame leg is firmly planted, bend over the fire and get the pot out of there. The letters are starting to run. I put the pot down in the sand. Want to sit down, then my leg gives way. I knock over the pot into the fire. I strike the ground and kick and shout. The children turn up instantly, they spoon the bits of lead they can rescue out of the coals. The rest of Kemp's letters will, like his sermons, become part of the ash and gravel and strike nobody. The lead pebbles will lie here till one day an ostrich pecks them up and shits them out again undigested somewhere else.

I sit down and start pouring the drops of lead into the mould. I think of Geertruy under the tree, of me practising letters with a quill. *Zijn en hebben*. Being and having. I am nothing. I have nothing. My heart is empty. I scratch under the loincloth, count my two balls. From them my uncountable seed that fell in places not all of which I know. Who comes after me will bear my mark and signs, a red beard somewhere, perhaps a voice that can incite people, one day a man who can shoot well. And that is all.

After an eternity I manage to cast four bullets. That will suffice. How far can the damned Portuguese be? I get all three my guns lifted, want to go and inspect them in peace somewhere, away from prying eyes. I don't manage a good grip, drop them just as Johannes spots me.

> Father must get in out of the sun. Come, let's go and sit by
> the wagon.

He inspects the guns. He takes aim with one, nods. Takes out the flint from another and places it in the chosen gun. Then he replaces the breech with that of another gun. He cleans the barrel. He polishes the butt while looking at me all the time. He sits with the gun in his hands, examines it, then hands it to me.

> This one will last, Father.

He gets up and walks to the tent where his wife is trying to soothe their baby.

Toktokkie comes to feed me water. One of the little ones waves at me. Right in front of me is a blurred blot, only at the edges does the world still contract into focus. I turn my head slightly to place the child from the corner of my eye, and then the little creature is gone. I feel the threads of spit spinning webs in the sagging corner of my mouth.

In the afternoon I hone my stolen herneuter with one hand, the whetstone clenched between my knees. I go and lie in the wagon. Lie on my back gazing at the crooked frame that I was supposed to fix. Aletta scrambles into the wagon, complains of mice in the food chest. I doze off, don't dream, wake up from the heat. Outside Midge and Gawie are shouting at each other. Sleep overwhelms me again. Wake up with Toktokkie and little Maria tickling my feet. I yell at them. Maria comes in, rummages around, arranges things around me and doesn't look at me and speaks no word and is off the wagon again and gone. I get up. Sit down again. Peer at where the wagon tent is chafed through, the sun that sidles in there; the dust that drifts into the column of light and only then becomes visible, in drifting creates patterns and constellations and breaks up and vanishes as soon as it floats out of the column. A fly walks on my chin, over my lip and into the sagging mouth. I swallow. I go and sit outside and listen to the hurly-burly around me. I prune my toenails.

~

As the sun starts gathering water for the night's drought, I call my people together.

> Tonight we're all eating together, I keep on saying until they
> understand me.

Maria snorts in the background. I ask her if I can have a bit of sugar on the sweet potatoes. Just tonight, I know there isn't much left.

> What are you saying, Buys? Talk so I can hear you, she says
> without looking up from the cauldron.

I repeat. She doesn't reply, stirs the pot with conviction. I go and sit at the makeshift table in front of the wagon. The undergrowth snaps just over there, not far from the camp. Animals on their way to the watering hole. I watch the children scurrying around me to carry food to the table and sit down one by one. The half-grown ones at the table, the little ones on the ground. They tease and mock among themselves; here two boys on the verge of fisticuffs, there a granddaughter in tears. In between a continuous buzz of laughter. I can't feel my face; I don't know if I'm smiling. Maria feeds me if I get too excited and spear my flabby mouth with my fork. Oh, the roasted fat, the pink flesh. My every earthly possession for a last dram of spirits. Oh, Maria's sweet potatoes.

What exactly and how much I said to them, I can no longer recall; with my sagging mouth they would in any case not have understood very much of it. I remember that I told them about Inhambane that can't be too far away, while scrutinising each one of them with care to burn each little mug into the back of my eyes. Some say I had more than three hundred children, more than three thousand grandchildren. *That* fertile I couldn't have been. I hope not. The troop here with me is in any case nowhere near all my offspring. Bettie is gone, the baby dead; Philip dead. What do I know of what happened to the others. But this little lot in front of me, they are here. Even Windvogel the younger. See, the young men who are big and strong already, as I once was, each with his own wife and wives and children. My grandchildren. The daughters who look like their mothers. The little ones with the busy eyes and stick legs who still have to grow into being human. Aletta and Eliza, my Toktokkie, fiddling with a pressed flower under the table. Piet, Dirk with the black eye, little Maria, the big men Johannes and Coenraad Wilhelm. Johannes' wife, another goddam Christina, is breastfeeding the baby. Coenraad Wilhelm's wife, Katrien, is lending a hand with clearing the table. Doors, ever frowning like his namesake Kemp. My beloved Elizabeth's offspring, each one with that expression of hers around the eyes: Gabriël and Michiel, my Gawie and Midge, the two rapscallions. Little Doris, more taciturn and more dangerous by the day. Little Jan. Baba, the little man for whom there were no names left over.

~

You must not believe everything that Midge was to tell later; he was always a handful. But something scratches the Omni-Eye of this Omni-Buys when I read Michiel's recorded words:

> He was sorely aggrieved over the loss of our mother, and in his grief said unto us, that he would leave us there, we should not proceed further into the land, and also not go back. He said also that the white people would eventually arrive. The Lord would provide for us.

~

When is Father going away, why can't we go along, asks Gawie.

We're going along, the little ones chirp.

Coenraad Wilhelm gets up and walks away, Maria is washing dishes, Dirk gazes at me with a look I don't understand. Then everybody starts chattering and asking questions at the same time. They must have understood enough through my drooling and slurring. I claw the battered Bible closer.

Let us read, I say.

Everyone is silent at once. They look at each other, examine the table top. I stroke the leather, feel the pages, quite possibly the last paper these dead fingers will ever touch. I open the book, search for my place, and begin:

> And the first came out red all over like a hairy garment; and they called his name Esau. And after that came his brother out, and his hand took hold on Esau's heel; and his name was called Jacob: and Isaac was threescore years old when she bore him. And the boys grew: and Esau was a cunning hunter, a man of the field, and Jacob was a plain man, dwelling in tents.

419

I look up. They don't understand a single word dropping from my gibbering jaw, but each and every one nods piously and with eyes wandering elsewhere pretends to be listening.

> *And Isaac loved Esau, because he did eat of his venison: but*
> *Rebekah loved Jacob.*

~

I lie behind Maria. Here, at long last, it is not necessary to forgive her her lack of mystery. Tonight it is the familiarity of every wart and mole that I seek out with my mouth. I drink from them as from a colony of breasts. Tonight her gurglings and snorings drone beautifully. I don't close an eye. I want to make sure my fingers remember every part of her. The sweat at the back of her knees, the smell of her grey frizz, the shapes of her ears. I touch her, but my fingers are dead. To feel her skin I have to sniff her body with my snout, my hands mere front paws, hard and calcified like hooves. In the early hours I get up. She pretends to be sleeping.

I struggle to fasten the buckskin around my hips. Throw a kaross over my shoulders. I scrabble in the pot, wrap the leftovers in a cloth. Slip the herneuter into the loincloth. I sit by the cold embers, smoke a pipe. I wrap hides around my feet, try to tie the thongs with one hand and give up. Johannes comes out of his tent with a baby on his arm, looks me in the eye, soothes the child at his breast, stoops into the tent again. I keep looking at the tent. Nobody appears. I tie a bundle of karosses to my back. It's too heavy; I drop it. Against the wagon lean the bows and quivers. For that you need two damned arms. I take up my gun, the very last powder horn, the pouch with four bullets. My right leg drags me to the brushwood. One of the dogs charges at me, licks my calf, won't leave me. I chase him away quietly, but the cur lingers on behind me. I throw stones at him until he stops and then trots back to the camp.

In the Tswapong hills I wanted to die. Here at the edge of the camp, where the bushes close in, my second death then, the demise of my name, of Coenraad de Buys. Adieu, Mijnheer de Buys. Till we meet again, Khula, Kadisha, Moro, Diphafa. Het ga je goed, Kgowe. Farewell, Coen. All that still lives is my raddled body; all that can still die is my woundedness.

7

See, here we stand. I, the Omni-Buys who has bewhispered you to
here, and you, my reader. Further we cannot go. Here we have to take
our leave of the man-beast Buys. He is no longer I; he is apocryphal.
See, he gazes at the slumbering wagon and tents. The stars are on fire,
the moon is meagre, the sun already inexorable on the horizon. He
limps on, turns around again. Maria has not emerged from the wagon
yet. She is still lying with her face to the side of the tent, her eyes open.
You try to catch up with him. My hand to your chest stays you for ever.
We see him walk away against the half-light of early morning.

~

*The dogs smelled the weakened creature from far away. The soil has
been baked hard, he leaves no tracks. They follow his familiar stench
until they see him, this thing with the dragging gait. They see him
stumble along the grain of the earth, his left arm swinging to its own
measure, the left leg sinew to sinew alongside. His paws are bleeding.
Before they trot off to where they can smell the quaggas, the pack greet
him as they have done for generations. After a moon's milky filling and
draining they come across him again. He shuffles along bent almost at
right angles, the gun in his claw all that keeps him upright. He mutters
to himself, does not hear his knife falling behind him and staying there.
He stops only when he sees the red dog. He does not move while the dog
comes to sniff at him. When the pack see him again half a moon later,
he's prowling on all four paws, the gun and powder horn dangling under
his belly. His fur is hanging loose, his knuckles bleed. He scans the
world of brushwood and distant cawings. The dogs fell a waterbuck and
devour it and forget about the crawling loner. At daybreak they sniff out
the bush pigs and guinea fowl. They find him prodding and devouring
the insides of a frog. He peels pieces of bark from dead trees, stuffs the
teeming crawling creatures into his mouth. His claws find roots in the
sand. He digs and pulls and gnaws. He hunkers with a root in the cheek,*

peers lazy eyed at the bushes and does not see the dogs. His nostrils dilate. The red dog breaks through the branches; the creature's head turns at an angle. For a moment they regard each other, then they both growl. The pack recalls the red dog. The man-beast has not moved yet; he keeps on gazing. The moon is full again and still in the sky with the morning sun when he comes upon the dogs at the watering hole. Their heads are buried in an eland. The red dog looks up, its hyena-like snout red and dripping. His head drops back into the carcase. With a last shot fired into the air, the monster scatters the dogs. They peer out of the undergrowth at how he descends upon the eland, how he tugs furiously at a hind leg trying to tear it off. He falls forward, head first into the guts. A gnawing and growling sounds from the belly of the eland. When he catches his breath his head is wet, a strip of flesh dangles from his jaws. A dog snaps a branch. He turns his head, he sniffs, his jaws let go of the chewed flesh. He looks up; they are everywhere. They tear away his hides, tear out his hair, tear off his skin; drive their claws into him. Their canines hook onto joints; the bones break. They tear open the body. The red dog grabs a chunk of meat, devours it to one side with his cubs. The dogs devour him; then they devour the rest of the eland. Later they lie in the damp sand next to the watering hole, their tongues smacking. A bitch kecks, vomits out a morsel of bone, gobbles it up again immediately. The cubs snap at each other. When the sand is baked hot, the pack trot into the veldt in search of the slender strips of shade of a thorn tree. At dusk they will trek on.

∽

See, there he vanishes into the bush now. Did you see? Because that was the last sighting of Coenraad de Buys. But to be dead is not enough. Like molten letters I linger in the gravel without eroding. I am the thistle. The piss in the stone of the Union Buildings. Like a pack of dogs I renew myself constantly. You'll never be shot of me.

Addendum

The way you imagined this exceptional man on the basis of often
exaggerated accounts turns out, upon meeting him, to be entirely
justified. His uncommon height (nearly seven feet), his shapely limbs,
his excellent carriage and the confident look of his eye, his high forehead,
his whole mien, and a certain dignity in his movements, made a most
pleasing impression. So one might want to imagine the heroes of
antiquity, a living image of Hercules, a terror to his enemies and a
pillar of strength to his friends. What the descriptions had not led us
to expect was a certain modesty and reticence in his conversation, a
mildness and kindness in his looks and mien, which could not in the
least have led you to suspect that the man had for so many years
lived among untutored savages, and which, still more than his words,
contributed to remove the prejudice we had conceived against him.
He willingly gave information concerning the subjects upon which
he was questioned, but carefully avoided elaborating upon himself
and his relations with the Caffres. This sly reticence was often
accompanied with a sort of wry smile, that spoke of the inward con-
sciousness of his own powers, and in which was plainly to be read
that his forbearance was not the result of fear; it was rather as if he
scorned to satisfy the vapid curiosity of his questioners at the expense
of truth, or of his own personal reputation. This rendered him all the
more interesting to us, and probably excited our sympathy much more
than the relation of his story would have done.

Original German quoted from: Lichtenstein, Hinrich. 1967 (1811).
Reisen im südlichen Afrika in den Jahren 1803, 1804, 1805 und 1806.
Volume 1. Stuttgart: Brockhaus/Antiquarium. 344–345.

Acknowledgements

On the tracks of the historical Buys I consulted, among others, works by the following authors: John Campbell, Max du Preez, Richard Elphick, IH Enklaar, OJO Ferreira, Herman Giliomee, Peter Kallaway, Martin Legassick, MH Lichtenstein, Andrew Manson, Roelf Marx, Noël Mostert, Neil Parsons, Nigel Penn, Gustav Preller, AE Schoeman, JT van der Kemp, PJ van der Merwe and HG Wagner.

   As far as other quotations, references and rewritings are concerned: Omni-Buys saw it all, read every word. He eats as he reads. As he plunders mission stations and cattle kraals, so he plunders the texts of others far and wide in order to tell his own tale. Should you then in his retelling stumble across the remains of other authors, notably Samuel Beckett and Cormac McCarthy, regard it as the homage of a scoundrel.

Glossary

biltong: cured and salted meat, either venison or beef

blesbok: a South African antelope, named for the white blaze on its forehead

bokmakierie: (onomatopoeia) a southern African shrike

bontebok: a southern African antelope, named for its pied ('bont') appearance

buchu: an aromatic herb, used in medicinal concoctions and for distilling brandy

burgher: a free citizen of Dutch origin

Colony: (in this context) the Cape Colony

cloof: see kloof

dagga: marijuana

dassie: the Cape hyrax or rock rabbit

disselboom: the stout central pole of a wagon, to which the draught oxen were yoked

drift: a causeway or ford

drostdy: the seat of the local landdrost (q.v.)

duiker: small southern African antelope, named for its plunging motion in running

eland: the largest of the antelopes, considered sacred by the San people

gemsbok: oryx, one of the fastest of the antelopes

genever: Dutch gin

hartebeest: a common southern African antelope

heemraad (plural heemraden): an assistant to the landdrost (q.v.)

herneuter (knife): a long hunting knife, normally carried on a belt

Hotnot: (pejorative) an abbreviated form of *Hottentot*

jukskei: the stout peg securing the yoke to the neck of the ox kaross: an animal hide, cured to form a blanket or garment

keurboom: a small southern African flowering tree

kiewiet: (onomatopoeia) the southern African plover or lapwing, named for its harsh cry

klipspringer: literally *rock jumper*, a small southern African antelope

kloof: a ravine or steep valley in the fold of two mountains

knobkerrie: a stick with one rounded end, used as a weapon

kokkewiet: (onomatopoeia) the bokmakierie (q.v.), a green-and-yellow shrike, named for its characteristic call

kopje: a rocky hillock

kraal: a village of southern African indigenous people; also an enclosure for cattle or sheep

kudu: a large, handsome gazelle with long spiral horns

laager: a circle of wagons in the open, usually for defensive purposes

landdrost: under Dutch rule at the Cape, a magistrate

lobola: bride price paid, usually in cattle, to the father of the bride

loerie: attractive bird with brilliant crimson-and-green plumage

mealie: a head of maize

Mijnheer: Sir (literally *My Lord*), polite form of address; when prefixed to the surname, equivalent of *Mr*

muid: a dry measure for corn etc.

nek: a saddle or declivity between two hills

Oorlam: a semi-nomadic mixed-race tribe

panga: a long, flat-bladed cleaver used to cut brushwood or sugar cane

piet-my-vrou: (onomatopoeia) the red-chested cuckoo

poort: a defile between two mountains, often with a river running through it

quagga: a now-extinct zebra-like quadruped

ratel: the honey badger

rhebok: a small southern African antelope

riempie: a narrow thong cut from a cured animal hide; often used to plait the seat of a chair or bench

rix-dollar: from the Dutch *rijksdaler*, imperial dollar, a unit of currency used in the colonies of various European colonial powers

rooibekkie: literally *little red beak*, either the waxbill or the pin-tailed whydah

rooikat: literally *red cat*, a type of lynx or caracal

slangbos: literally *snake bush*, colloquial name for various types of bush with medicinal and sometimes poisonous qualities

spekboom: literally *fat tree*, a southern African succulent, also known as the elephant tree

spoor: the track of an animal

springbok: an abundant southern African antelope, named for its habit of jumping when alarmed or pursued

spruit: a small watercourse, usually dry, except in the rainy season

steenbok: literally *stone buck*, a small southern African antelope

stoep: a raised platform or verandah across the front of a house

Strandloper: literally *shore walker*, nomadic indigenous people, related to the Bushmen and Hottentots

taaibos: literally *tough bush*, applied to a variety of bushes and shrubs with tough branches and bark

veldt: the plains, open air

veldwagtmeester: literally *country guard commander*, a rural commander of a military unit

VOC: Verenigde Oost-Indische Compagnie, the Dutch East India Company, possessing quasi-governmental powers at the Cape and other Dutch possessions; dissolved in 1799

waboom: literally *wagon tree*, the *Protea grandiflora*; its wood was regarded as suitable for the felloes of wagon wheels

PUSHKIN PRESS

Pushkin Press was founded in 1997, and publishes novels, essays, memoirs, children's books—everything from timeless classics to the urgent and contemporary.

Our books represent exciting, high-quality writing from around the world: we publish some of the twentieth century's most widely acclaimed, brilliant authors such as Stefan Zweig, Marcel Aymé, Teffi, Antal Szerb, Gaito Gazdanov and Yasushi Inoue, as well as compelling and award-winning contemporary writers, including Andrés Neuman, Edith Pearlman, Eka Kurniawan, Ayelet Gundar-Goshen and Chigozie Obioma.

Pushkin Press publishes the world's best stories, to be read and read again. To discover more, visit www.pushkinpress.com.

=====

THE SPECTRE OF ALEXANDER WOLF

GAITO GAZDANOV

'A mesmerising work of literature' Antony Beevor

SUMMER BEFORE THE DARK

VOLKER WEIDERMANN

'For such a slim book to convey with such poignancy the extinction of a generation of "Great Europeans" is a triumph' *Sunday Telegraph*

MESSAGES FROM A LOST WORLD

STEFAN ZWEIG

'At a time of monetary crisis and political disorder… Zweig's celebration of the brotherhood of peoples reminds us that there is another way' *The Nation*

THE EVENINGS

GERARD REVE

'Not only a masterpiece but a cornerstone manqué of modern European literature' Tim Parks, *Guardian*